"*First Wife*, both a fascinating novel and an important historical document, reflects Elsie Chamberlain Carroll's life as a child of polygamy but also as a twentieth-century educated woman whose Mormon culture had moved beyond its polygamous passage. It is a significant addition to our understanding of that bygone culture."

Kathryn M. Daynes, PhD, professor of history and author of *More Wives Than One: Transformation of the Mormon Marriage System, 1840–1910*

"*First Wife* is a courageous book. In the 1930s when author Elsie Carroll Chamberlain began writing it, she claimed Mormonism's 'peculiar institutions' of plural marriage and communal living as her own family history from Orderville. As a member of the Young Women's Mutual Improvement Association general board, Elsie was under considerable social and familial pressure to leave that history in the past, but she wrestled with the twin questions that have continued to fascinate both novelists and historians: Why did women and men live these two challenging laws? And how could they?

"When Elsie's daughter, Helen Carroll Lloyd, first let me read the manuscript, I was associate editor of the LDS Church's adult magazine, *Ensign*, and we were not allowed to even acknowledge the existence of polygamy in print. Showing an interest, even historically, in polygamy could and did result in sanctions. Helen's son Jon and grandson Weston, Elsie's third- and fourth-generation descendants, have outlived repressive fears to let Elsie tell the story of her parents in fictionalized form. Courage didn't end in the 1950s."

Lavina Fielding Anderson, PhD, editor of *Lucy's Book: A Critical Edition of Lucy Mack Smith's Family Memoir*

"*First Wife* is an insider's nuanced look at the everyday struggles early Mormon Americans faced as human beings trying to live meaningful lives. This delightfully relatable story will make you laugh, cry, curse, and stand up and cheer. On the surface it is about polygamy, but at the core it is about the depths and complexity of relationships, with polygamy magnifying the struggle for open, intimate, and genuine ways of relating.

"In addition to preserving a significant slice of history, this work invites us to explore the archetypal human experiences of the main characters as they search their own souls for guidance about what is right. Is there ever a point at which one must abandon allegiance to the powerful truths of one's own integrity in favor of those of another? Elsie wisely offers us no definitive answers. Instead she implies an invitation: be forever open to the stirring voice within, listen carefully, and lovingly nurture the insights found there.

"I offer my deepest gratitude to Elsie Chamberlain Carroll for artfully preserving the stories of this honorable family."

> **Jeff Beyer, PhD**, Psychotherapist and Ecopsychologist, practicing psychotherapy in community settings, private practice, and at Carnegie Mellon University

"*First Wife* is a remarkable contribution to Latter-day Saint historiography. Lightly fictionalized, it creates a window through which readers may peer back in time to face Orderville, Utah, Mormon polygamy, the U. S. Government 'Raids,' and real people struggling within themselves, with loved ones, and with their God. *First Wife* is a polished narrative that includes a glossary, character profiles, and historical photographs. It is unique among polygamy histories in that its author was an eyewitness who later recounted her experiences after becoming a professor of college English. Written in lively prose, it is sure to entertain, educate, and inspire."

> **Brian C. Hales**, author of the three-volume *Joseph Smith's Polygamy: History and Theology* and webmaster of josephsmithspolygamy.org

First WIFE

A Historical Novel
by Elsie Chamberlain Carroll

Introduction by Helen Carroll Lloyd

Compiled by Jon Carroll Lloyd and Weston Lloyd

Published by Jon C. Lloyd
100 Denniston St. Apt. 204
Pittsburgh, PA 15206
412-512-3974
jlloyd@gmail.com

Designed by Melissa Neely

Printed in the United States of America.

Publisher's Cataloging-in-Publication data

Names: Carroll, Elsie Chamberlain, author. | Lloyd, Helen Carroll,
introduction author. | Lloyd, Jon Carroll, compiler. | Lloyd, Weston, compiler.

Title: First wife : a historical novel / by Elsie Chamberlain Carroll; introduction by
Helen Carroll Lloyd; compiled by Jon Carroll Lloyd and Weston Lloyd.

Description: Pittsburgh, PA: Jon Lloyd, 2023.

Identifiers: LCCN: 2022923263 | ISBN: 979-8-218-17744-7

Subjects: LCSH Mormon women—Fiction. | Polygamy—Fiction. | Utah—Fiction. |
Historical fiction. | Autobiographical fiction. | BISAC FICTION / Biographical |
FICTION / Christian / Historical | FICTION / Cultural Heritage |
FICTION / Historical / 20th Century / General

Classification: LCC PS3603 .A77 F57 2023 | DDC 813.6--dc23

This novel is a work of historical fiction. The characters, places, events,
and incidents in this book are a blended product of the author's imagination
and her lived experience.

Cover photo: Thomas Chamberlain with some of his wives, children, and
grandchildren. **Thomas Chamberlain** is the white-haired man in the middle,
back row (front cover, near spine). Author of this novel, **Elsie Chamberlain
Carroll**, is on the far left in the middle row (back cover), standing next to her
mother, **Elinor Hoyt Chamberlain**, first wife of Thomas. Author of the
Introduction, **Helen Carroll Lloyd**, is the young girl standing in front of her
grandmother, Elinor. Photo courtesy of Jon Carroll Lloyd.

In Memory

Elsie Chamberlain Carroll
(1882 - 1967)

Helen Carroll Lloyd
(1908 - 2002)

William Hardy Lloyd
(1941 - 2009)

Frances Yvonne Bonnie Vernon Lloyd
(1943 - 2018)

Contents

First Wife: A Historical Novel
by Elsie Chamberlain Carroll

Poetry by Elsie Chamberlain Carroll*

* These poems are selected from Elsie Chamberlain Carroll, *Sunshine and Shadows* (Provo, UT: Brigham Young University Press, 1967). This book of poetry is out of print, but it is available through select university libraries, or a used copy may be acquired online.

Winding Roads

By Elsie Chamberlain Carroll

*I love the lure of a winding road
That leads through country lanes
Past painted houses with potted plants
And shining window panes.*

*I love the lure of a winding road
That follows a canyon's turns
When the smell of spring is in the air,
Or when autumn's splendor burns.*

*I love the lure of a winding road
That climbs to a mountain crest,
Away from the city's shuffle and strife
To a place where the soul can rest.*

*I love the lure of a winding road
That leads through life's strange maze.
Its ups and downs and sudden turns,
Give zest to the dullest days.*

Preface

by Jon Carroll Lloyd
b. 1939

My maternal grandmother, Elsie Chamberlain Carroll (1882 - 1967), was born in and spent her early childhood years in Orderville, Utah—a small Mormon polygamist commune in Southern Utah. Elsie believed that her parents and grandparents lived lives that were rich in character-building conditions and experiences, and she saw fit, as an English professor at Brigham Young University (BYU), to record them for posterity. She began writing her story while on sabbatical leave from BYU at Columbia University in 1935. Her mentor at Columbia, the novelist Dorothy Scarborough, advised and encouraged Elsie to fictionalize her reminiscences in the form of a historical novel. When Elsie finished her sabbatical leave at Columbia, she was well into the novel. Miss Scarborough asked her to send installments until her "Mormon novel" was completed and said that she would help her find a publisher.

Elsie traveled in Europe for two months before returning to BYU. When she returned, she learned that Miss Scarborough had died. The unfinished manuscript sat on the shelf for the next twenty-two years while Elsie continued her teaching and other academic responsibilities. In 1957, she finished the manuscript in preparation for a Utah Fine Arts competition. She entered it with the title *First Wife* and won first prize. Encouraged by this success, Elsie entered *First Wife* in the annual American Pen Women's competition the following year. This garnered her first prize, a $1,000 cash award, and much encouragement to seek a publisher for her "story of the Mormons."

Elsie's award-winning, still unpublished, novel lay hidden among her papers until her daughter and my mother, Helen Carroll Lloyd, discovered the finished manuscript after Elsie's death in 1967. Helen retyped it and did some initial editing with her granddaughter, Carol Ann Lloyd-Stanger.

She then engaged Lavina Fielding Anderson to proofread and edit the entire manuscript. In 1995 Helen shared the manuscript with her children and grandchildren at a family reunion in Jackson Hole, Wyoming, with the hope that one of us would make additional refinements and find a publisher. Too much time has passed. My mother has passed away, and I am now 84. With the help of my nephew, Weston Lloyd, I have taken up the charge to publish my grandmother's award-winning novel, *First Wife*.

First Wife is Elsie's somewhat but thoughtfully fictionalized story of her early childhood in Orderville at the turn of the twentieth century. Elsie was the first surviving child of her mother's twelve children, and one of her polygamist father's fifty-five children from six wives. Believing that she and her family had lived an important piece of Mormon, American, and human history, she dealt with heavy cultural forces both in life and in writing. In her novel, Elsie recreates and explores her family members' trials, as well as their sacrifices and compromises as they adjusted to living in a plural marriage family. Now, over 125 years since the peak of Mormon polygamy, few new eyewitness accounts are emerging, yet here is one.

I was very close with my Grandma Elsie. I fondly remember her influence throughout my years as a young boy and her wise guidance as I made career decisions in college. I witnessed her great love for her family, and her family's love for her. On more than one occasion, she told me that in our rendering of life it is always best to tell what actually happens, tell it in detail, tell it with courage, and always with the grace of accuracy. In *First Wife*, she does just that.

Introduction[1]

by Helen Carroll Lloyd

1908 (Orderville, Utah) - 2002 (Salt Lake City, Utah)

My mother, Elsie Chamberlain Carroll, was a born writer and is known for her steady contribution of short stories in LDS Church periodicals during the 1940s and 1950s. In the late 1960s, a short story contest bearing her name was established in the English Department at Brigham Young University to honor her.

I believe she chose polygamy for her first and only novel because it was an interesting subject and also, I believe, she wanted to think through some of the psychological problems that living this principle would impose upon both men and women. She won a thousand dollars for *First Wife* in 1957 as the first prize in the National League of American Pen Women but chose not to publish her work. The protagonist of "First Wife," Nellie Hagen Chandler, was based on her own mother, Elinor Angeline Hoyt Chamberlain, the first of Thomas Chamberlain's six wives. Elinor was known in the family as "Ella," and my mother's use of the nickname "Nellie" is obviously drawn from the first syllable of this first wife's name. My mother knew that some family members would be distressed by this novel of family life, so although she may have wished that her work could be published, she never seriously considered it while most of her siblings were alive. When she died, the manuscript came to me.

---

1 Editor's note: Helen would have composed this Introduction sometime in the 1990s, when genealogical resources were far fewer than those accessible today. We have corrected some name spellings, and other discrepancies are noted in footnotes. We don't recommend that readers consider this Introduction to be an official source of genealogical data, as its information is secondhand and some is outdated. Changes and comments are mostly based on Jonathan and Beverly Chamberlain's book, *Happy is the Man: A Social Biography of Thomas Chamberlain* (Provo, UT: BYU Printing Services, 2010).

In the novel, Nellie (Elinor) seems preternaturally sweet and self-sacrificing, but both traits apparently characterized the historical woman. My mother felt that Elinor was truly a saint, unselfish and endlessly compassionate. Perhaps she was tempered by suffering. Her husband, Thomas Chamberlain, was born in July 1854 in Tooele, Utah, to Thomas Chamberlain, Sr., and Hannah Whale Chamberlain. Young Thomas moved south with his family to farm in Orderville and Mount Carmel where he developed a prosperous farming and ranching business. He died in March 1918 in Kanab. He was nineteen when he and Elinor were endowed and sealed in the Endowment House in Salt Lake City.

Elinor was born in October 1856 in Nephi, Utah, to Israel Hoyt and Clarissa Amanda Miller Hoyt (Isaac and Clara Hagen in the novel). She was not the fragile, marginally fertile woman that the fictional Nellie was. She gave birth to twelve children between 1874 and 1897. Her first four children, all daughters, died before my mother, Elsie, a healthy child, was born in 1882. Eva, the first child, died at age two; Harriet, the second, died at nine months. Emily died at fourteen months, and Clarissa at twenty-one months. Elsie, however, was the oldest of eight children who all survived to adulthood: Israel Hoyt (1884), Eustace Josiah (1886), Amanda (Pugh) (1888), Ella (Richards) (1891), Lillian (McAllister) (1893), Justin (1894), and Lloyd Utah (1897). Lloyd's middle name commemorates his conception near the gala festivities celebrating Utah's statehood in 1896. Elinor passed away in 1927.

The second wife, Luanna Fischer in my mother's novel, was Laura Fackrell, born in March 1856 in Bountiful, Utah, and thus seven months older than Elinor. Her eleven children were Amy Fackrell Chamberlain (1874), followed by Thomas III (1876), Susannah (1878), David (1880), Ellis Fernando (1882), Hannah Isabel (1884), Marcus Grant (1887), Mary (1888), Bertha (1890), Ira Lagrand (1893), and Karl Steven (1896). All but two, Amy and Marcus, survived to adulthood.

I believe that my mother took more liberties with the third wife, the young, emotionally unstable artist-rebel Jane in the novel. Thomas Chamberlain's third wife, Ann Carling, was born in April 1859 in Fillmore, Utah, and was thus within three years of the ages of his first two wives. Nor was there a great delay between his first two marriages and his third. Ann's first child, a son named Howard, was born in 1877, followed by Henry (1879), Lucy (1881), Edgar (1883), Isaac (1885), John (1886),[2] Sarah Asenath (1888),

---

2   *Happy is the Man* (2010) and FamilySearch.org make no mention of this John. Both list
     Ann Carling as having 8 children; Edgar is the child who didn't live to adulthood.

Joseph (1891), and Edward Leo (1893). Eight of these nine children survived to marry spouses of their own.

With the fourth wife of the novel, partially blind and much younger Minnie, I believe my mother took a final departure from biographical fact. Thomas Chamberlain's fourth wife, Ellen Alvira Carling, was born in December 1863 in Fillmore, and was only nine years his junior. Her marriage followed about three years after that of the third wife, and she bore twelve children: twin sons John G and William (1881), Edna May (1883), Flora Viola (1884), Miriam Elizabeth (1887), Edwin (1890), Guy (1892), Leslie (1894), Ann Amelia (1896), Genevieve (1899), Lyle Moroni (1901), and Verna Maurine (1903). Six of these children did not marry, although the records available to me do not say whether they died in infancy or simply chose not to marry as adults.[3]

Thomas Chamberlain's fifth wife was Chastie Ellen Covington, born in 1867 in St. George. She was the mother of eighteen children born between 1886, when she was nineteen, and 1898.[4] John, Hans C., Arthur, Hugh, Mark, Rita Ellen, Chastie Vilate, Heber Lamar, Leola, Robert Covington, Wilford Zemira, Emma, Amelia, Phebe, Inez, Esther Chloe, and two other children whose names do not appear in the records available to me. All of these children may not have been Thomas's. She was married first to Justin Chamberlain, whose relationship to Thomas I do not know, and her last six children are surnamed Heaton.[5]

Thomas took a sixth wife after the Manifesto: Mary Elizabeth (Mame) Woolley, born in 1870 in St. George to Edwin Dilworth Woolley, Jr., and Emma Geneva Bentley Woolley. She and Thomas interacted frequently because Thomas was a counselor to the stake president and Mame's father, Edwin Woolley, and Mame was their private secretary; also, Thomas was stake tithing clerk and she copied the reports he filed; furthermore, Thomas was county treasurer and Mame was the state's first female county clerk. He first proposed to her in 1897 when she was twenty-seven; she was surprised at the proposal. She later recorded, "He already had several wives and a large family, of which any man might well be proud, and I thought he should be satisfied. I was not aware that he had declared when a very young man that he was going to have six wives and sixty children. And he

---

3   *Happy is the Man* (2010) indicates that 5 of the unmarried children died as infants or young children; 1 (Edwin) did not marry.

4   Helen's information for Chastie's children does not match our sources. *Happy is the Man* indicates that Chastie gave birth to 10 children between 1886 and 1910. They are listed here, beginning with John and ending with Robert Covington.

5   Our sources do not show evidence of Chastie having children beyond Robert Covington or of her having another marriage.

had not reached the quota yet."[6] Initially she refused the proposal, but later she agreed to the marriage after extensive prayer and after she required him to get the consent of the other five wives. They were married in 1900 when she was thirty. She had two sons, Royal and Edwin Dillworth "Dee", both born while she was in hiding. She went by the last name of Howard for many years to protect Thomas from being prosecuted for polygamy. In 1911 Mame was elected president of Kanab's town board, the first woman mayor in the United States to hold that office; remarkably, the entire board was composed of women, which was also a first.

Mame described Thomas Chamberlain as "a handsome man, large and portly, about five feet ten inches in height and weighing two hundred thirty pounds, with dark brown, wavy hair, and brown eyes with a merry twinkle. He had a rather heavy brown mustache which curled slightly at the ends and always gave him the appearance of smiling, though it covered thin firmly set lips and a very determined mouth. His skin was very light and clear with just a touch of color on the cheeks. He was very attractive and his presence would command attention anywhere."[7]

I AM SORRY TO say that my genealogical interests have never been very keen. No doubt other relatives could supply a great deal more background than the sketchy information in my possession. But a point-by-point comparison between the lives of my grandparents' family and the narrative of this novel was not my purpose.

Polygamy brought both suffering and saintliness to the Chamberlain family, and Mother was keenly aware of both its positive and its negative side. Her husband's side of the family, the Carrolls, had never entered into polygamy, and when Mother once ventured to ask her father-in-law about it, he said, "When I brought it up to your mother-in-law, she didn't say anything but I looked into those brown eyes with tears welling up and I decided that was the end of the discussion." I always got the impression that they just didn't believe in it.

---

6   Mary Elizabeth Woolley Chamberlain, *Mary E. Woolley Chamberlain: Handmaiden of the Lord* (personal journal typescript compiled by Farel Chamberlain Kimball, in possession of Jon Lloyd), 172.
7   Chamberlain, 171-172.

In my own family, I do not recall that plural marriage was discussed openly at all, despite the family heritage. My parents had a most compatible marriage and both were believing Latter-day Saints, though not always active by today's standard of attending meetings every Sunday. They frequently sent me and my siblings to church but often did not go themselves. My father was not orthodox in his beliefs by today's standards, but my mother, though more orthodox, was also more open to freewheeling discussions, and religion was always a lively topic of conversation in our home.

Father died when he was forty-five years old and Mother died at age eighty-five, so she spent most of her adult life as a widow. Because we children were often her companions, we were quite close. She also greatly enjoyed the stimulation and collegiality of her teaching in BYU's English Department, although I remember her coming home and exclaiming in exasperation, "I just hate faculty meetings where you discuss things for hours and hours and then find out that the decision had already been made!"

I was aware that Mother was working on this novel during a summer away from Utah when I accompanied her to New York where she was taking classes at Columbia. I'm not aware that she ever submitted it to a press or that she ever tried to write another novel, but I think it was significant to her personally to write the novel, both for the literary experience of trying her hand at a full-length work as a means for coming to terms personally with her own conflicted heritage, and in an attempt to work out the psychological and spiritual complexities created not only by the practice of plural marriage but also by its cessation. The national honor that she won for the novel was intensely gratifying; she felt that it meant she had been able to make a difficult part of Mormonism intelligible to a wider audience.

I think the novel's greatest contribution lies in its portrait of Ted Chandler as a sensitive, honorable, and loving man confronting the social, personal, and spiritual challenges of polygamy. This contribution is, as far as I am aware, unique in Mormon fiction about plural marriage where the protagonist is almost invariably a suffering woman struggling with jealousy of sister wives and/or the unfairness of a husband who is only too willing to benefit from the sexual diversity of polygamy.

I honestly do not know how much of "Ted Chandler's" tortured doubts about his own spirituality, his reluctant obedience to authority, his distaste for the practice of plural marriage, and his ultimate disillusionment with the inspiration of Church leaders reflect anything like my grandfather's real feelings. Thomas's energetic post-Manifesto courtship of Mame Woolley, a sixth wife, including three years of fasting and prayer before George Q. Cannon authorized their marriage, bears little resemblance to Ted's feelings of being trapped into plural marriage and his dutiful but very reluctant third and fourth marriages.

I would not be surprised if much of this was my mother's attempt to create a psychologically realistic character in the environment of passionate monogamous romance of the 1940s and 1950s in which she lived her own life. The post-World War II shattering of social conventions, including monogamy as a monolith, has made one-man-one-woman lifetime monogamous marriages, even in Mormonism, much less common than they were once assumed to be, and perhaps readers in this decade [the 1990s] are much better prepared than those of the 1950s to deal with the psychological and emotional subtleties of complex marital and family relationships.

I would also not be surprised to discover that the bifurcation she makes between Nellie's sensitive spirituality (and her consequent valuing of the emotional intimacy shared with Ted) and Luanna's robust and healthy sensuality (and her consequent valuing of erotic intimacy with Ted) also bears little relationship to the real personalities and values of Elinor and Laura Chamberlain.

However, I have no doubt that Elinor Chamberlain clearly communicated to my mother the romantic ardor with which nineteen-year-old Thomas and his two seventeen-year-old brides, Elinor and Laura, began their married lives. My mother stated flatly that Thomas Chamberlain, as a teenager, "hated his stepfather and polygamy." Therefore, I would not be surprised if his feelings changed over time. It seems possible to me that a young first wife may have cherished secrets in silence all her life that a young and anguished bridegroom confided in the last months of courtship and the first months of triadic marriage—secrets that may have provided moments of private tenderness and sharing. We have all had the experience of becoming reconciled to the unacceptable, of learning to live with and even deal competently with situations that at first seemed taxing, even unendurable. Perhaps my mother's fictional triumph was in creating a man who had the strength to live his life with a divided heart, unlike the more realistic situation of letting life—the demands of family life and making a living, the pressures of time, the hurried press of events—rub away the sharp corners that first hurt so much. But these are only conjectures on my part.

IN PREPARING THIS MANUSCRIPT for publication, I was guided by the comments and reactions of my own children and grandchildren, who found the story slow moving and over-written in some aspects. While keeping my mother's distinctive voice and without changing the plot or characters, I felt it was important to reduce some of the most discursive characteristics of her 1950s prose. I appreciate the editorial assistance of Lavina Fielding Anderson in tightening the prose unobtrusively. I also eliminated the original structure into parts with a further breakdown into chapters, modernized the punctuation and the spelling, and silently corrected typographical errors.

A second area in which I took the liberty of making changes is in names and relationships. For example, Mother assigned the name "Clarabelle" to Nellie's first living daughter (herself). Raised for a generation on Disney cartoons of Clarabelle Cow, I felt that this effect was unfortunate and gave her the name of Emily Claire instead. I also assigned names to a number of characters who were not given names in the original version, including Ted's mother, who was identified only as "Sister Granger," and some of the ward members and children. Although making no attempt to duplicate the historical dimensions of Thomas Chamberlain's more than fifty children, I have tried to smooth out such discrepancies where they occur. I have not changed the names of any fictional children that coincide with the names of actual children of Thomas Chamberlain, but when I have had to create a name, I have chosen one that is not, as far as I know, that of an aunt or uncle.

A third area where I have taken liberties is with internal anachronisms. Although Mother herself would have found and solved these problems if she had been preparing the manuscript for publication, she never took the time to go back to it, knowing she would not seek publication soon. As an example, Ted marries his fourth wife only days after the public announcement of the Manifesto (October 1890) and she becomes pregnant before he leaves Salt Lake City, leading to a delivery date of July 1891. Yet in the original manuscript, this child is not born until sometime between September 1891, when Nellie and the four older children come to Provo so the children can attend Brigham Young Academy, and March 1892, which is when the story picks up. I have also tried to tidy such loose ends as an inconsistent number of children per wife at different points in the manuscripts and confusion in the names for some children.

My mother, however, would probably have devoted no concern at all to a fourth area where I have imposed my own editorial concerns, and that is historical anachronisms. Although the larger sequences of the Muddy Mission, the founding of Orderville, and its eventual demise as a United Order community are generally accurate, Mother did no research to determine details, sequence, or chronology. That was not her purpose. In her sequence, Nellie is about twelve when she comes to the Muddy Mission and about fifteen when the mission is closed. The establishment of the United Order at Orderville occurs the next year, and Ted's elevation to the counselorship delays their marriage for a year—until 1873. Mother also has the Order dissolving about a year after Brigham Young's 1877 death. The actual sequence is that the Muddy Mission was founded in 1865-67 and abandoned in 1871, but Orderville's United Order was not formed until 1874 and not dissolved until 1885. I have not changed the manuscript to correspond to these historic facts, but I think the reader should be aware of them. Furthermore, although the Orderville settlers separated themselves from the Mount Carmel settlers to practice the United Order, the Mormons in Mount Carmel were not "apostates," as she portrays them for the sake of the plot.

There are less significant examples. She had Ted serving as president of the Young Men's Mutual Improvement Association in the Muddy Mission. Since that was about five years before the organization existed, I have changed his title to the less prestigious position of Sunday School teacher, still an unusual calling in the nineteenth century for a teenager. In the original manuscript, Apostle Parley P. Pratt performed the sealings of Ted to Nellie and Luanna. Since Mother apparently used her own parents' wedding date (1873) as a rough guideline, she overlooked the historical fact that Pratt had been killed in 1857 by the undivorced husband of his final plural wife. I have quietly substituted another name, in this and similar cases.

Plural marriage is not a system I feel personal attraction to, but I am fiercely proud of my ancestors who sacrificed much, including their personal preferences, to enter it. I am grateful for their faith in dealing with its day-to-day challenges. And I am honored to belong to a family that respects and holds in honorable remembrance those faith-motivated and faith-sustained achievements. Writing *First Wife* was my mother's way of understanding plural marriage from the inside out. I hope that reading it may have the same consequence for a later generation.

Helen Carroll Lloyd with her mother,
Elsie Chamberlain Carroll

Photo courtesy of Jon Carroll Lloyd.

An excerpt from

Helen

By Elsie Chamberlain Carroll

She was my baby—
Cuddled, loved and marveled over.
I caught the first sweet smile,
The first dear word
That only mother-ears
Distinguish from the prattle.

She was my little girl,
Her sunny curls, her bright quick ways
Filled every hour with joy.
I answered endless questions
From her childish lips,
And kissed away her hurts,
And soothed her tired little body
Into dreams. Happy years!

Swift the passing years.
She is a mother now.
Her eyes look into
Upturned faces of her babies.

New happiness they bring
To my declining years;
And now my Helen cares for me,
As once I cared for her.
Life's cycles turn.

Notable Characters

Hagen Family

- **Brother Isaac Hagen**: Nellie's polygamous father, a spiritual leader in the Muddy River Mission and the United Order
- **Clara Hagen**: First wife of Isaac Hagen, Nellie's mother
    Children: Brig (Brigham), Nellie Hagen (later Nellie Chandler), Fred (Frederick), Katie
- **Auntie** (**Hannah**): Second wife of Brother Hagen
    Children: Lucy, Nick, Hyrum
- **Minnie Draper Hagen** ("blind Minnie"): Third wife of Brother Hagen
    Child: Minnie ("little Minnie")
- **Grandmother and Grandfather Miller**: Nellie's grandparents who left England for the United States and pulled handcarts across the plains to Utah

Granger Family

- **Brother Granger**: Ted Chandler's polygamous stepfather, part of the Muddy River Mission
- **Emily Chandler Granger**: Ted Chandler's mother who married Brother Granger after her husband (Ted's father) died
    Child: Ted Chandler

Key Members of the Muddy Mission (Overton, NV)

- **Cropper family**: A key polygamous family in the Muddy Mission, including **Jim Cropper** (husband), **Nora** (wife), **Jed** (son), and **Bill** (son)
- **Deborah Williams**: Nellie's friend
- **Molly Woodruff**: Nellie's friend

Chandler Family

- **Ted Chandler**: New move-in to the Muddy Mission, future leader in the Church and polygamous husband/father
- **Nellie Hagen Chandler**: First wife of Ted Chandler
    Children: Emily Claire, Ernest, Jerry

Chandler Family, continued

- **Luanna Fischer Chandler**: Second wife of Ted Chandler
     Children: Louie, Teddy, David, Martha, Jeannie, Kay
- **Jane Cameron Chandler**: Third wife of Ted Chandler
     Children: Mark and Matt (twins), Edna, Johnny
- **Minnie Hagen Chandler**: Nellie's half-sister, fourth wife of Ted Chandler
     Children: Darrel, Minnie Rose

Key People of Orderville, Utah

- **Elias Cameron** ("Brother Cameron"): One of Ted Chandler's counselors in the bishopric, Jane Cameron's father
- **Christensen family**: Polygamous family including **Gilbert** (husband who has some hostility toward Ted Chandler), **Martha** (first wife), **Maria** (wife), **Nora** (wife), and **Lizzie** (wife)
- **Parker family**: Polygamous family including Brother Parker (husband) and **Nancy** (wife)
- **Jenkins family**: Prominent family in the community, including **Nate** (later "Bishop Jenkins") and **Mary Ellen** (formerly Mary Ellen Thompson), and **Howard** (son)
- **Brother and Sister Draper**: Minnie Draper Hagen's parents
- **Jimmy Fergeson**: Son of Jim Fergeson (polygamous father) who courts Louie Chandler

Key People of Provo, Utah

- **Richard ("Dick") Langdon**: Neighbor who courts Louie Chandler
- **Betty Kimball**: Schoolmate courted by Teddy Chandler

Church Leaders

- **Joseph Smith, Jr.** (1805 – 1844): Founder of The Church of Jesus Christ of Latter-day Saints, revered by Latter-day Saints as a prophet
- **Brigham Young** (1801 – 1877): Church's second president and prophet who, among other things, advises the settlement of the West
- **Erastus Snow**: An apostle in the Church
- **John Taylor** (1838 – 1887): Church's third president and prophet, who shows little interest in the United Order
- **Wilford Woodruff** (1807 – 1898): Church's fourth president and prophet; issues a Manifesto abolishing plural marriage in the Church
- **Apostle Cook**: An apostle in the Church

First WIFE

A Historical Novel
by Elsie Chamberlain Carroll

PART 1

The Call

Overton, Nevada, and Orderville, Utah

In which:

- Nellie Hagen strives to come to terms with plural marriage

- Nellie meets Ted Chandler

- Ted makes a promise with God

- The Muddy Mission is abandoned and the United Order is established in Orderville

- Ted serves in the Church

- Nellie gets a new sister

- A group travels to Salt Lake City

- Nellie becomes Ted's first wife

one

Nellie Hagen picked up the china flower girl from the goods-box stand near the bed. She held it caressingly before placing it on the rawhide-bottomed chair beside the small mirror, the blue pincushion, and the cluster of wax cherries. Now the stand was bare except for its cross-stitched runner made from a bleached flour sack. That would not do. She put back the pincushion, then the cherries. Minnie was blind. The mirror would be of no use to her. But Father …

She shivered, slowly put the mirror back on the stand, and then, reluctantly, picked up the flower girl. She started to return it to the stand, then suddenly clasped it in both hands against her breast.

No! She would not leave it in this room. It was hers, her most treasured possession for years. Mother had given it to her when Prince broke her leg and she was so brave while Father and Brother Curtice set the bone. Grandmother Miller had brought it from England, a gift from the grand lady to whom she had been a maid. Minnie wouldn't know about that. Yet Minnie loved pretty things, even if she could not see. She seemed almost to see them through her fingers. Nellie herself loved to touch the smooth curves of the tiny figure almost as much as she loved the bright blues, pinks, and lavenders of the minute flowers in the girl's basket. This treasured ornament was the most beautiful thing she owned, the most beautiful thing she could imagine. Having the flower girl made it easier for her to do hard things.

And this was so hard. Minnie Draper was coming here to live. No, Minnie Hagen—Father's wife. Nellie felt queer whenever she thought of it, almost ill. Minnie was only seventeen, just two years older than Nellie. How could she be Father's wife? Father and Mother were more than forty years old. Even Auntie was almost thirty.

Here was Auntie now, coming to help arrange the room and move Nellie's things up to the loft where she and Lucy would sleep now along with the little girls.

"Are you almost through, Nellie? We'll have to hurry."

"I just have to take our aprons and nightgowns from behind the curtain ... and these things." She pointed to the objects on the chair. She hesitated, but Auntie was easy to talk to—easier than Mother, who was always busy and didn't talk much to anyone. "Do you think I ought to leave my flower girl, Auntie? The stand looks bare without her, but— Minnie couldn't see her anyway."

Auntie straightened up from smoothing the sheets at the foot of the bed and looked thoughtfully at Nellie. "No, dear, Minnie can't see it, but your father can. It's for him as well as for Minnie that we're preparing this room. You know that he loves pretty things."

Nellie caught her breath. That queer feeling had come back, a salty taste in her mouth and a burning around her eyes. "Will Father sleep in here—with Minnie?"

She realized at once that it was a foolish question. Minnie would be his wife, just the same as Mother and Auntie.

"Why, of course, part of the time."

Auntie stooped again over the bed, her hands working fast. Nellie stared at her for a moment, then blurted out the words she hadn't intended to say. "Don't you and Mother care? Do you think he ought to?"

Auntie flushed. She continued tucking in the quilt, the sunlight from the small window glinting on her auburn hair. If she'd been Auntie's daughter, then she might have curls like Lucy's and delicate rose skin that didn't freckle. Even auburn hair. She *could* have been Auntie's daughter. Or Minnie's! Same father, different mothers. What if Mother—good, patient Mother, who worked so hard for all of them—was one of her Father's other wives? Misery overwhelmed her.

Auntie came around from the opposite side of the bed and drew Nellie down beside her to perch on the bright quilt. Gently she brushed the hair back from Nellie's forehead. "Nellie, dear, you are old enough to know what plural marriage means in our church. It wouldn't be right for your mother or me to care. Polygamy is part of our religion. We accept it. You were just a baby when I came into the family, but your mother didn't object, and she has been like a sister to me ever since. Today, while I've been helping to get ready for Minnie, I've learned to love your mother more than ever and to realize what a noble woman she is. I'm trying to be noble, too, Nellie— worthy of your father and the gospel."

Nellie leaned against Auntie's shoulder and let the stifled tears fall on the flower girl. Auntie's arm circled her shoulders soothingly.

"You see, dear, we must learn to look at this principle in the right way. The Church leaders have taught us that marriage and children prepare us for the highest salvation in the next life. An unmarried woman must be a ministering angel to the married women in the next world. Minnie hasn't had many chances to marry, because she's blind, so the Church leaders counseled your father to marry her, to give her a chance at the highest salvation. So you see, we must feel that it's right to have her as a member of the family."

Nellie groped for words. It wasn't that she didn't want Minnie in the family. She'd always been fond of Minnie, with her dark, shining hair and her sweet, patient smile and gentle ways. But to give up her room, her bed—she didn't mind so much giving it to Minnie, but for Minnie and *Father*! That was the part she couldn't explain.

Auntie kissed her wet cheek. "You'd better take the rest of your things out now. Then maybe you can help your mother in the kitchen. Jim Healy said he passed your father and Brother Cropper's wagons on just the other side of St. Joseph, so they ought to be here soon."

Nellie wiped her eyes on the back of her hand. "I'll leave the flower girl," she said.

THE EXCITEMENT OF FATHER'S arrival made Nellie forget her confusion and unhappiness. The boxes and packages from Salt Lake City included calico and delaine for new dresses for her and Lucy. She listened eagerly to Father's stories about Salt Lake City, the theater where they'd seen a real play, the Endowment House where he and Minnie were sealed at the same time as Brother Cropper and Nora Daniels. Nora was lame. That's why the authorities had advised Brother Cropper to marry her, too. Mother had made a special supper and, in the bustle of serving it, hardly sat down at all. She was quiet, but then she always was.

Nellie was just helping to dry the last dish when Father stretched and yawned. "Well, I suppose it's about time we all went to bed," he sighed. "We've had a long, hard day."

"Hooray," shouted Nick. He and Frederick were to sleep in the wagon box beside the tent of the older boys, Brigham and Hyrum. The little fellows had been delighted to give up their loft to Lucy and Nellie.

Mother stepped forward, handing them a lantern. "Now mind you hang it on the hook as soon as you get in the wagon," she admonished. "If you drop it, the wagon will be on fire in a second."

Nellie dropped the dishtowel, suddenly swept by a wave of feelings she couldn't put a name to. Was she going to be sick? She ran outside. She didn't want to see Father go to her room with Minnie. The air was soft and fresh. She scrubbed her hands over her face and took a deep breath. Should she cross over to the next street and call Molly Woodruff? No, she couldn't let Molly know how she felt. She didn't know how she felt. It must be wicked to feel as she did.

Irresolutely, she walked toward the grove in the center of the village, the water in the irrigation ditches gurgling softly on either side. Beyond the grove, a light was shining from the Granger tent. They'd come from the Salt Lake Valley only a few weeks earlier to join the Muddy Mission. The Hagens, the Croppers, the Woodruffs, and most of the others in Overton and St. Joseph had come four years ago when President Young called them to come raise cotton.

She didn't know the family well. Ted, the one who was Brigham's age, was named Chandler, not Granger, and Brig said that when some boys teased him by saying "Hello, Ted Granger," Ted swore at them and wanted to fight.

"Why?" Nellie had wondered.

"He hates his stepfather," Brig had explained from the lofty height of his eighteen years.

Maybe Ted just didn't like it here. When Father's call came, all of the children thought it was a thrilling adventure to come to Nevada. Only now, Nellie was realizing how hard it must have been for Mother and Auntie to leave their comfortable home in Springville. But of course, there was no question that they'd do what the prophet said. Several of their neighbors had left one family in Utah and brought the other to the Muddy, but Father had insisted they were always to be one family. "Nothing halfway in this family," he had told Brig after he had said something about his "half-brother," the way the other kids did. Father was making a joke but did it in a way that Brig knew he was serious. Auntie was almost like a mother to Brig, Fred, little Katie, and her. Lucy, Nick, and Hyrum called Nellie's mother Auntie, but she took the same care of them that she did of Nellie and her other children.

What would they call Minnie? And if Minnie had children? But Nellie refused to think about it. Minnie was just a girl like herself. She couldn't think of her as a mother, especially ...

Nellie hurried into the grove and sat in one of the swings. She swayed gently, listening to the crickets. A snatch of song came from the Granger tent. It must be Ted's mother. She was a pretty woman, and Ted was such a nice-looking boy—really handsome. She had thought so the first time she'd seen him, when he came to borrow a shovel. He had dark, curly hair, big brown eyes, and a firm chin. He seemed so nice—sort of friendly and bashful at the same time. She'd half-planned to talk to him at Sunday School or sacrament meeting, but two Sundays had gone by and he hadn't come. And swearing? Maybe he was a bad boy.

She sighed and kicked her toes into the ground to push the swing higher. She hadn't realized that she'd been counting on having this nice stranger part of the small group of young people who played games at the swings and sometimes had molasses candy pulls.

"I'll give you a push," said a voice behind her. Even as she whirled to look behind her, Ted Chandler pulled the swing back, then sent her sailing high into the air. She uttered a little shriek, and he laughed, caught the swing again and pushed her higher yet. She had never swung so high before. How strong he must be! Exhilarated, she began to sing:

> *Swing, swing low and high;*
> *Up to the treetops, up to the sky.*
> *Swing, swing when it's June,*
> *Up in the starlight, up to the moon.*

"Tell me when you're tired," he called.

"I love it!" she exclaimed. "But *you* must be tired."

"You're nothing but a feather," he said. "Hang on! This time, you're going to the moon."

"I'll break off a piece and bring it back for you," she half-sang.

After a while, he slowed the swing, then brought it to a stop. He was breathing hard from the exercise, and his breath stirred her hair against her cheek. "Is there room for two?" he asked.

"Of course." She moved over for him.

He shifted onto the seat. "Where's my piece of the moon?"

She laughed and spread her hands. "Oh dear, I must have dropped it."

"No, there it is." He placed his palm over hers.

Nellie felt herself blush. He pulled her hand through the crook of his arm. The swing swayed gently.

"How is your house coming?" she asked, almost primly, to conceal the sudden acceleration of her heart.

"We finished rocking the last wall of the cellar today. Tomorrow I'm going to start making adobes."

"Do you know how?"

"Sure. I built the house Mother and I lived in in Tooele, and I was only fourteen then."

"*You* did? Was your father—?"

She stopped as she felt him stiffen. "My father was dead," he said quietly.

"Why don't you like Brother Granger?" Nellie was shocked to hear the words coming so easily from her lips. It must be the shadows, changing in the moonlight, that made nothing seem quite real. Ted answered in the same way, as if from the same dream.

"Oh, I suppose Mother married him because the authorities told her to and because she thought I was getting too much for her. And I know why he married *her*." There was a sudden note of venom in his voice. "He wanted my father's property and to have someone to bring to this godforsaken place so he wouldn't have to bring his own family."

"B-but wasn't he called by Brigham Young?" Nellie asked weakly.

"Of course. But it was all right if he left his wife and children home to take care of the farm there and Mother's property, too. *My* property. I could see through it all the time. Polygamy! Rot. None of it for me."

Nellie was aghast. Agitated, she pulled her hand away and clutched at the ropes. "But … why … it's revelation. It's part of the gospel. The Prophet Joseph Smith …"

Ted cut in curtly, "*Maybe* he had a revelation and maybe he thought he just wanted another wife."

"Oh, aren't you afraid to talk like that? I should think you'd be afraid of being struck down."

Ted gave a short laugh. "Honestly, Nellie, do *you* think it's all right?"

"Why, yes," she faltered. "Of course I do."

"Well, your father seems to be a decent man. Maybe that makes a difference. But this last marriage, to that blind girl. Do you feel all right about that?"

"Why, if Minnie didn't marry and have children—" She couldn't give Auntie's explanations. That terrible feeling was back. "I've always loved Minnie," she changed tack desperately. "She's as sweet as can be."

"But does it seem right for her to be your father's wife?" Ted insisted. "Honestly, *does* it?"

Nellie burst into tears. Quickly he put an arm around her shoulders. "I didn't mean to make you cry, but you *do* feel that it's wrong. Other things in the Church may be all right, but I can never swallow that."

Nellie struggled to control her tears. "I have to go now."

"Will you let me give you another swing sometime?"

She nodded and stood up. He took her hand and they walked toward her home. "You always go to Sunday School, don't you?" he asked unexpectedly.

"Yes."

"May I come with you next Sunday? Mother is worried because I haven't been yet, and she has enough problems being married to old Granger."

Nellie felt she should say something to defend plural marriage but was afraid she'd only start to cry again. She liked walking beside him, the warmth of his hand, the shifting patterns that the moonlight made through the poplars lining the street. The sand seemed to gleam as it stretched before them, and the unexpected chirp of a sleepy robin rose above the frog concert coming from the reservoir beyond the cotton fields.

There was no light in the window of what had been her room. She thought of the flower girl on the stand beside the bed, of Minnie and Father together in her bed. And suddenly a vague gladness stole over her—gladness that Ted Chandler did not believe in polygamy, even for salvation.

two

The horse stumbled again. This time he remained quivering on his knees until Ted got out of the saddle and coaxed him to his feet. But he continued to tremble and, in a moment, sank back upon the sand with an almost human gasp. Ted's own throat burned like fire, and he could hardly close his lips over his swollen tongue.

Ten days earlier, his stepfather had sent him to bring back the team which had broken out of the Overton pasture. Some of the Saints on the cotton farm at Washington, Utah, had seen the horses and had told his stepfather when they came to inspect the fields at the Muddy Mission.

Ted had accompanied these visitors when they returned home. His mother had protested against his going alone across the desert—Indians had recently killed a white man traveling alone—yet Brother Granger had agreed. Ted had waited for a few days in Washington, then realized that they had to have the team for the harvest and to break new land for planting in the spring. He rode one horse and led the other, on which was packed blankets, food, a keg of water, and grain.

The first day was very hot. Both he and the animals needed so much water that he began to worry almost at once. He'd heard of water-pockets on the desert but realized that he had almost no way of finding them. That night he hardly slept, clammy with fear at the thought of Indians.

The second morning, he poured water into the basin and let each horse drink, drank sparingly himself, and then began rolling up his blankets. One of the horses nipped at the other, there was a quick flurry of hooves, and one of them kicked over the water keg. Ted, calming the animals and then separating them, did not notice that they had loosened the wooden peg in the bung hole until most of the water had trickled out through the burlap wrapped around the keg. Grimly, he wrapped the keg with his blankets, hoping to save even a few drops from the relentless evaporation in such terrific heat.

In the middle of the day, he watered the horses sparingly and took a drink himself, savoring each swallow. Most of the water was gone. By nightfall, all of them were suffering from thirst. He decided to push on, trying to reach home before thirst and exhaustion overcame them. It seemed to Ted that he had traveled for hours before his horse stumbled the first time. Now it was hours later. He knew both horses were completely spent. Even the pack animal was sagging under the equipment.

He had lost all sense of location and distance. It seemed that he had traveled far enough to circle the earth. There seemed but one thing to do. He must leave the team and struggle on as far as he was able on foot. His one dim hope was that he might get near enough home that someone would find him the next day.

With difficulty, he dragged off the saddle and pack, then forced himself forward, feeling that each step would be his last. The sun had been down for hours, yet the sand was still hot.

Strangely, for a time, his physical discomfort seemed to clarify his mental processes. He went over again, as he had repeatedly done on this lone journey, all his happy associations with Nellie Hagen since that night nearly three months before, when she had wept against his shoulder in the swing under the poplar trees.

He had gone to Sunday School with her and to her home afterwards with a group of young people for molasses cake and lemonade. Her father, one of Bishop Woodruff's counselors, had invited him to come to priesthood meeting the next evening, and he had gone—not because he wanted to but because Nellie's father had asked him.

He had found it more pleasant to be with people than to be by himself or with his stepfather, so he continued to attend these meetings. He realized that his satisfaction was entirely social. He felt sure there was nothing of a religious nature in him. His mother's happiness over his new activity made him realize the deep anxiety he had caused her. He argued that making her feel better was certainly a worthwhile reason to attend church; the Church was not, in the main, bad, and he could be with Nellie. But as for polygamy, he still felt just as he had that night under the poplars. He still loathed his stepfather.

He had not talked with Nellie any more about these feelings, for he knew it worried her that he felt so. In his heart, however, he was sure that she regarded plural marriage with almost the same aversion he did—that to her, as to him, real love could grow only between one man and one woman, that anything else was a desecration. As weeks went by, Ted had come to feel more and more that for him the one woman was blue-eyed Nellie Hagen.

It had been thrilling to hold her for those few moments in the swing. He didn't even feel sorry that his blunt questions had made her cry. They had become friends quickly, talking about the homes they had left in Utah to come to the Muddy Mission, the moon, the water, the frogs croaking in the distance. She had laughed when he imitated the old bass frog that seemed to be answering the treble notes, they said, of a lady frog. He had even sung her some Scotch ballads his father had taught him when he was little more than a baby.

When she said she must go, he asked to kiss her. She had drawn back and shaken her head, but even as he wished he hadn't asked, he had taken a kiss as spontaneously as he had put his arm around her when she began to cry. After that, they had seen each other often, sometimes alone—and he liked that best—sometimes with the other young people.

One day when he was looking for a button to replace one lost from his shirt, he had found in his mother's patchwork basket a blue gutta-percha button that had come from his father's uniform before he joined the Church and left Scotland. In Ted's spare moments, he carved it into a ring with his pocket knife, taking great pains to make it smooth. On the outside, he carefully carved Nellie's initials; his own were on the inside. Even now as he stumbled along the desert road, he could almost forget the ache in his weary limbs, the torture of his bursting throat, and the black fear of approaching death when he recalled the exquisite moment of giving the ring to Nellie.

After supper he had gone to the swing. While he was waiting, Molly Woodruff and Deborah Williams had come. They had asked him to push them in the swing, trying to amuse him with silly jokes and loud compliments. Irritated at the giggles, he wondered how Nellie could care for such friends. Molly was fat and frowsy. Her round, florid face and rough hands made him more aware of Nellie's slightness and the delicate sensitiveness of her face—her high forehead, her serious blue eyes, and her tender mouth. He even liked the sprinkle of freckles across her nose and thought her brown, slightly wavy hair prettier than Lucy's dark curls that Nellie admired so much. Nellie had become beautiful to him, though he had not even considered her pretty the first time he saw her. Strangely, he had thought Deborah Williams—tall, rosy-cheeked, full-lipped, always laughing—much more attractive. But now her manner seemed bold beside Nellie's modesty and her coloring too vivid compared to Nellie's delicate pink.

All the time he had swung the girls, he was watching and listening for Nellie; and when he saw her coming, he had told them he had to go.

"Sure, we know," Molly had taunted. "You're going to meet Nellie. We know she's your girl and the rest of us haven't a chance." They ran past him and reached Nellie first. "Ted's been swinging us," they called out. "For a long time. Aren't you jealous? You'd better watch out or someone else will get him." Still giggling, they passed on down the street.

"Do you want to swing?" he asked as he and Nellie walked back toward the grove.

"I guess you're tired," she answered with an edge in her voice. Maybe she was a little bit jealous—and that meant she cared.

"I ought to be," he admitted. "Those girls are so fat and heavy. But it would be fun to swing you, even if I was tired."

He had sent her sailing into the air. They bantered about trivial things that somehow seemed sweet and significant. Then they sat side by side and he told her he was going after the team.

"But it's dangerous, crossing the desert alone. Why doesn't your fath— Brother Granger go with you?"

"I'm not afraid," he had boasted. "Anyway, I'd rather go alone than with that old—" he checked himself. "He says I'm to wait a few days with these men I'm going with, and maybe someone will be coming back this way. I'll be all right."

Her concern for him was sweet. He leaned closer so he could feel the light touch of her hair against his cheek.

"Oh, I hope so." There had been a little choke in her voice. "You'll be awfully careful, won't you? I'll pray for you."

He was touched and reached for her hand and laughed, "Will you? That will be fine. I'm afraid I've forgotten how to pray, myself."

"Oh, don't say that," she had protested. "Why, we all must pray every night and morning. I'd be afraid not to."

"I'm sure if you will pray for me it will do a lot more good than if I bothered the Lord."

"But you must pray, too," she had persisted.

"If I need to, I'll see if I can remember how."

He had changed the subject by slipping the button ring on her finger.

"It's a little trinket I made from a famous button," he explained. "Maybe it will help you to remember me while I'm gone."

"Oh, thanks. I know it's pretty just by the feel. But I wouldn't need it for that."

Her hand was small and warm in his and the tendril of her hair against his cheek smelled sweet. He turned her face up and kissed her lips.

As on the other night, she drew back, a little frightened, and cried, "Oh, you mustn't do that."

"But I did. And I want to do it again. May I?"

She slipped from the swing and started toward home, but she had let her hand remain in his and he felt sweet content. They had barely reached the well under the cedar tree when her mother opened the door and said it was time for Nellie to come in.

"Let me kiss you just once more," he pleaded, holding both her hands.

She hesitated for an instant, then lifted her face. "Because you're going away—and for the ring."

For a moment he held her close, then she ran into the house. He walked home on air, his heart racing ahead to the time when he could break from his stepfather and work for himself—and Nellie.

BUT THE THIRST BECAME more unbearable. It and the weariness blotted out all other sensations, the present misery overwhelming even the sweetness of his memories. He struggled along, despairing of ever seeing her again. The distant howls seemed to be closer. Were they just coyotes, or was he hearing wolves? The illusion of hulking Indians in the shadows became more terrifying. He tried to swallow, but the muscles of his throat refused. His limbs became heavier, weaker. He stood swaying, unable to take another step. He faced the nightmarish truth: in a few moments, he would fall and be unable to stagger to his feet. He would lie there in the dark. The howling creatures would skulk closer, then spring, or one of those menacing shadows would raise a knife and he would not be able to resist. Wavering, he sank to his knees. He must try to pray. Nellie was praying for him.

But the comfort of that thought vanished in a terrible conviction. God was punishing him for his sins. For the years since his father's death when he had refused to pray because God had taken his father in spite of all his pleas and the certainty that God knew how much he and his mother needed him. For refusing to go to church. For swearing. For hating the man his mother married. For his very doubt that there was a God. But he must try.

He raised his hands and opened his swollen lips, but only an unintelligible croak emerged. He abandoned the effort to pray aloud and formulated a covenant in his mind, a vow to his own soul that if God would forgive and save him, he would spend the rest of his life atoning for his sins by serving God through working in his church.

A strange calm overcame him. He knew there was only one explanation. There *was* a God and he had decided to give him another chance. The calm was a comforting spirit, sent to hover over him. In peace, he closed his eyes and sank upon the sand.

"NELLIE! NELLIE!" BRIG HAGEN ran into the house, calling excitedly.

His sister left her dishpan and went to the middle door. "What's the matter, Brig?"

"Ted Chandler—he's almost dead."

Nellie grasped the back of a chair. The blood drained from her face.

"When Bill and Jed Cropper took the cows to the lower pasture this morning, they saw something in the road farther on. It was Ted. He was unconscious—nearly choked to death on the desert."

"Where?—Brig, where is he now?"

Nellie jerked her apron off.

"They brought him home and Brother Granger got them to go back and help him look for the horses Ted went after."

"Auntie," Nellie called into the kitchen. "I'm going over to see—if I can help Ted's mother."

She was cold with fear as she ran toward the Grangers' new cabin. The fingers of her right hand clutched the little blue ring on the other hand. Under her breath, she was sobbing, "Please, dear Father in Heaven, let him live. Please! Please!—or let me die, too!"

three

The Overton church was packed. Bishop Woodruff had sent the deacons throughout the ward Saturday afternoon to urge every member to be at sacrament meeting the next day to hear an important message from President Brigham Young. When the bishop called the meeting to order, there was no empty space on any of the wooden benches in the hall that served for church as well as school. As Ted and Nellie had walked to church together, they had speculated like everyone else, what the message could be.

"Hasn't your father said anything about it?" Ted asked. "Being Bishop Woodruff's first counselor, he must know."

"He hasn't told us anything. But I wouldn't be surprised if it's about taxes. I know the bishopric sent a letter to the Church authorities right after those horrifying tax notices were received. They reported that there is no possible way to pay those back taxes the Nevada officials are demanding. They also reported that the harvest was no better this year than last year and that we're all destitute."

"I can't understand why the Church ever sent us out here anyway," Ted told her. "Especially without knowing that this location is in Nevada, not Utah. And when they found it out, they should have known that officials of another state would do all they could to get rid of a bunch of Mormons. Surely they haven't forgotten the days of Nauvoo and Carthage already."

"It does seem strange," Nellie conceded. Yet she felt she must uphold the Church leaders whenever Ted questioned their wisdom or judgement. "But I've heard Father say that President Young hopes to establish Latter-day Saint colonies all through the western states. They're already in Idaho, Colorado, Mexico, and Canada.

"Sure. Everyone knows that President Young is a born empire builder."

There was no bitterness in the remark. Ted's experience on the desert had made a difference in his attitude, though it had not eliminated recurring moods of doubt and questioning.

"One of Auntie's brothers was called to Mexico about the same time we were called here," she said. "I don't know just what industry the Church is planning to build up there, but it must be something like the plan to raise cotton here."

"Well, it's to be hoped other Church projects turn out better than this one."

Ted had not forgotten his promise to devote his life to God's service, but it was not easy. For weeks it seemed his life had been spared by a miracle, and he had found pleasure in doing everything his religion seemed to expect of him. He had taken active part in the auxiliary organizations, had been advanced in the priesthood, and was now a teacher in the Sunday School. But of late he was fighting against his old questionings.

"The prophet of the Lord ought to know what he's doing," he said, as they drew nearer the meetinghouse. "But it's hard for people to give up their homes and move to new places and pioneer all over again. I mean folks like your family—and Mother. Think of all they went through crossing the plains to get to Utah—and then the call to come here."

"Mother came in a handcart company," Nellie responded. "I've heard her tell the most pitiful stories—babies dying and being left only half buried—I can't bear to think of them. And my Grandfather Miller was in the Mormon Battalion and marched all the way to California. He died of fever on his way back to Independence to get his family. They were very poor but Grandmother was determined to bring the children to Utah to be with the Saints. Mother and the other children had to take turns pushing the handcart. One of her little brothers was frozen to death, buried by the side of the road. That's what I meant—it's hard to think about. Mother has told us how they would cry at night thinking of little Benny there alone on the frozen plains—maybe wolves—"

Her voice broke. Ted reached for her hand. "When Mother looked into a mirror the first time after they got to Utah, she looked like an old woman," he said. "And it was the hardships of that journey that hastened Father's death. That's why I couldn't be reconciled and was so bitter."

"Maybe sacrificing for the Church makes people love it all the more," Nellie said. "That's what Father claims. I often wonder if I would be strong enough to give up as much. Father's folks disowned him, and all his friends ridiculed him. Once, he was tarred and feathered, just like Joseph Smith, when he was trying to hold a meeting. But despite all that, he remained steadfast in his faith."

"I suppose we ought to be very thankful that the days of such persecutions are over," Ted said solemnly. "I find it hard enough just to keep from wondering if this or that is right, just to pay an honest tithing after working hard for what I earn ... little things like that. I don't know what I'd do if a real test came."

"I know," Nellie said, looking at him trustingly. "You'd do what was right, no matter how hard it was."

"You mean *you* would," he said gently, "and I *hope* I would. But I'd need a lot of help."

They had reached the meetinghouse.

"Let's go for a walk after church," Ted said as they entered.

Nellie smiled and nodded as she left him to go to the choir seats near the speaker's platform. Ted took his place at the rear of the stand with other auxiliary officers. His stepfather was sitting next to the bishop. That must mean he would be one of the speakers. Ted wished he didn't have to listen to him. Brother Granger's eloquent, oily sermons always intensified his dislike. Brother Granger, who had just returned from a trip to Farmington, was spending most of his time away from the Muddy. Ted was all the more certain Granger had married his mother for their property and to keep from moving his first family from Farmington. He was sorry for his mother's sake that he felt as he did; he *had* tried, without success, to change his attitude. He tried to be civil to his stepfather, but he hoped the man would soon find business calling him north again.

When the choir stood up for the first hymn, Ted forgot everything else as he turned his eyes to Nellie. She was beautiful in her delaine dress the color of her eyes, with its white crocheted collar. He could see the little blue gutta-percha ring as she held the hymn book. He thought happily of the time when he would put a real ring on that finger. It was sweet to be in love with Nellie Hagen.

Brother Cropper opened the meeting with prayer, and the choir sang again. Ted looked over the audience, waiting expectant and excited. He caught his mother's eye and returned her smile. He knew she was proud to see him with the other ward leaders, knew she idolized him, and felt unworthy of the sacrifices she had made for him—even her marriage to Granger. If she had not been worried about him and felt that he needed a father, perhaps she wouldn't have been such an easy mark. They had been happy together in their new little home during Granger's absence, but now she would be torn again between her love for her son and what she thought was her wifely duty. He resolved anew to try to live up to her hopes for him.

His glance shifted to the bench where Nellie's mother, Auntie, and blind Minnie sat. Nellie's mother was small and delicate, like Nellie. Quiet and hardworking, she was a skilled midwife whom everyone counted on. She must have been pretty when she was young, but now she was worn and faded, and the sad resignation in her eyes always hurt Ted. That was what polygamy had done to Sister Hagen. He grew warm with his old resentment. Well, of one thing he was certain: Nellie would not have to share his love with other women.

Auntie was more alive, with none of that apathetic look—yet. Maybe she never would have it. She was different, jolly, had a sense of humor; but it was to the older woman that his sympathy turned with a sort of reverence. He didn't think it was just because she was Nellie's mother. What was going on behind that half-veiled look in her faded blue eyes?

He respected and admired Brother Hagen. If polygamy could be lived right, Brother Hagen and his family were doing it, but Ted felt sure he did not know the inner feelings of Nellie's mother. Could it be that they were ever as close to each other as he and Nellie? As much in love, as sure of future happiness? He shifted uneasily at the vague realization of the ironic tricks life sometimes plays.

Minnie, he could see, was going to have a baby. How did Nellie feel about this? They seldom talked of polygamy, but he knew she felt much as he did—that such marriages desecrated something fundamentally sacred.

The sacrament was over. Bishop Woodruff arose. "Brothers and sisters, I am aware that you are eager to hear the message from our leader, President Brigham Young. We, your bishopric, as many of you know, wrote to President Young before Christmas about our serious tax problem and asked him to advise us what to do. This is his answer:

> *Dear Brethren:*
>
> *I was sorry to receive your discouraging report concerning the unreasonable tax assessment from Nevada officials and the poor results from your labor in trying to raise cotton. I had hoped that this Muddy Mission might prove the means of further spreading the gospel in this western hemisphere.*
>
> *But evidently our enemies are not yet willing to grant us the rights of ordinary American citizens. I have carefully considered your situation and have counseled with the Quorum of the Twelve Apostles. After due deliberation and prayers for guidance, we have reached the conclusion that the Muddy Mission will have to be abandoned for the time being.*

There was a general gasp from the audience. Most had put everything they had into their new homes, with confidence that the Church would help them overcome any difficulties that might arise. Still, none of them would presume to question the wisdom of the prophet of the Lord.

After the surprised hum subsided, the bishop finished the letter. It thanked them for their loyalty and their earnest efforts in trying to accomplish the purpose of the assignments and left them free to go wherever they chose. But it suggested that if some were willing, the Church leaders would be pleased if they would go to Long Valley in southern Utah, where a unit of the United Order was to be put into operation. Since this was part of the Church's hope to see the entire membership ultimately living, working, and holding property in common, the listeners felt it was more than a mere suggestion. Some decided immediately to take this advice. Other couples began whispered consultations, reluctantly breaking off as the bishop announced that Brother Granger, who had recently returned from Utah, would address them.

Granger got pompously to his feet. Ted's thoughts whirled. What would he do? Granger would return to his family in Farmington and his mother, of course, would be expected to go with him. Should he assert his rights and refuse to go? What would Brother Hagen do? No doubt go to Long Valley. Well, that was what he would do rather than continue living with his stepfather.

After the meeting, he and Nellie walked for a time in silence. Nellie's face was grave and she kept glancing at Ted anxiously, but he seemed scarcely conscious of her presence.

"Are we going for that walk?" she finally questioned.

"Not now," he answered grimly. "I've got to talk with Mother and Granger. I'll come over to your house later." He caught her hand and seemed to emerge for the instance from his inner retreat.

"I forgot to tell you how pretty you are in that blue dress," he said, with an effort at lightness. She smiled and pressed his fingers.

"Goodbye, now. I'll run on and catch the folks."

TED FOUND HIS MOTHER and Granger talking about moving back to Farmington.

"I wish I could have sold that team you almost ruined on the desert last summer," was Granger's greeting to Ted. "Those horses will never be the same. They certainly won't stand this move very well—may not last it out."

Ted silently hung his hat on a peg behind the door and sat on a bench under the window. Now that the time had come for him to make his declaration of independence, he felt timid and immature. And he dreaded hurting his mother. But she seemed to read something of new decision in Ted's face, for her hands began to flutter as they always did when he and Granger were at odds.

"We're going back to Farmington as soon as we can get ready," she stated, looking anxiously from one to the other.

Ted walked to the mantelpiece. "I'm not going," he said with a firmness that surprised himself. He did not look at them but took out his pocketknife and began to clean his nails.

"Why, Teddy, what in the world are you saying? Of course you're going."

He knew the worried, pleading look that would be in her eyes and kept his head bent.

"What nonsense is this you're talking?" Granger demanded.

Ted knew that neither of them took him seriously. They still considered him a child, though he had been doing a man's work since fourteen. Granger didn't object to that. He'd left him with the full responsibility of finishing the home, cultivating their allotment, and the care of his mother.

"I'm going to Long Valley, as President Young advised," he said evenly.

"You're going where we go, young man. And that's back to Farmington. You've got to thinking yourself pretty important since I've been away. Being a Sunday School teacher in a little town like this has gone to your head, hasn't it?"

Ted thrust his hands into his pockets and clenched his fists. "I'm big enough to take care of myself, and that's what I intend to do from now on, without any advice from you."

His mother started to weep. He must not let her tears weaken him. He turned back to the window, his courage rising. On many occasions when he had clashed with Granger, the latter had kicked him when he turned to leave the room. He wished the bully would try it now. He snapped his pocketknife shut, laid it on the window sill, and strode back to the fireplace, deliberately giving Granger every chance to attempt the indignity. Then he looked the older man squarely in the eye, a thing he had never dared to do before.

"You're not my father, and you can't boss me anymore," he announced. "I'm as much a man as you are. You know I've been doing a man's work and taking a man's responsibility for years. From now on, I'm going to do what I think is best for me." He turned to his weeping mother. "I'm sorry to hurt you, but I can't help it. All I hope is that, when I'm not around, he'll treat you decent."

He stopped abruptly, fearing he would say too much, and quickly left the room.

For a few moments he leaned against the corner of the house, trying to adjust to his new sense of freedom. Then he hurried to Nellie.

"I'm glad, Ted," she told him. "You shouldn't stay with them when he treats you as he does, but I'm sorry for your mother. She worships you."

"She shouldn't. I've caused her a lot of unhappiness, and I wish I could make it up to her. He's treated me like dirt, but I've always thought he was a little afraid of me and wouldn't dare mistreat Mother when I was around. He pretends to be so—so religious—the pious old hypocrite. That's what I can't stand."

Nellie tried to divert him. "We're going to Long Valley, too."

"I guess I figured you would, and that helped me have courage to make my decision."

"It won't be so bad starting over in a new place—if friends are there, too." The look in her eyes said more than her words implied.

"Father asked Mother and Auntie and Minnie where they wanted to go. Auntie said she'd like to go back to Springville because her folks are there. I think Mother would have liked that, too. One of her sisters lives close by. And all of us children clamored to go back home."

"What made you decide to go to Long Valley then?" Ted asked.

"Mother said she thought we ought to follow the advice of our president and that we should consider that Minnie's folks are going to this new place. I'm sure that's what Father wanted. Mother always seems to read his mind, but he always asks the others in the family to help decide important things."

"I think your father's a wonderful man."

"So do I," she laughed. "I wish you had one like him."

"Don't I, though!" Then he added, "All the men in a church like ours ought to be like him, but look at the way Brother Cropper treats that lame girl he married the same time your father married Minnie. I saw her out irrigating the other morning, carrying a heavy shovel and trying to put in a dam, so I stopped and did it for her. It's a disgrace when she's going to have—"

"Yes, I know," Nellie blushed. Ted talked more freely than the other boys she knew. She couldn't get used to it. Yet it seemed all right, though even her brothers would not mention the fact that Minnie was going to have a baby.

"I heard Mother saying to Father the other day that either he or the bishop ought to talk to Brother Cropper about the way he treats Nora."

"It's things like that," Ted said bitterly, "and knowing what kind of a man Granger is when he pretends be a saint, that make me sure polygamy can't be right, and make me wonder about a church that holds to such a practice."

"Of course there are things that are not just as they ought to be. But, Ted, that isn't the fault of the Church—it's the weaknesses of individuals. I can't just exactly understand about plural marriage, either, but it must be all right—the principle I mean, or why would God have revealed it to Joseph Smith? We need to do everything we can to keep the Spirit of the Lord. Then we'll feel all right, even if we can't understand everything. We must fight against doubts."

"There's one doubt I never have," Ted said, wanting to change the subject. "It's that I love you," and he drew her into his arms.

When Ted went home that evening, he carried with him something from Nellie's assurance. At least he was happy, and he thought his happiness might be the result of his promise to try to follow her suggestion that it was better not to keep questioning everything but to accept the gospel as God's eternal plan for the salvation of mankind. And he would try to think of the failures and evils as individuals' problems, and not condemn the Church. He was finding it easy to try to believe what Nellie wanted him to believe.

THE NEXT MORNING HE was awakened by his mother coming quietly into his room. It was hardly light, but he could see that her face was swollen from weeping. She sat on the edge of his bed and smoothed his hair.

"Mother, what's the matter?"

Her caress took his mind to his childhood when he had seen her running her fingers through his father's hair. If only his father could have lived!

"Teddy, I came to tell you that I'm going to Long Valley with you. I told him that I couldn't go back to Farmington without you, and he consented for me to go with you—at least for a while, until we see how things are going to work out. He says we can take one team and outfit, and he'll take the other. He's going to leave today."

Ted raised himself on his elbow and looked searchingly at his mother's averted face. He knew there was more than she was admitting to this plan of Granger's. Of course the "ruined team" would be left for them, but he was free and his mother would be with him. He was a happy man.

four

The journey from the Muddy Mission to Long Valley was not easy for any of the Saints, but for Ted and his mother, it seemed almost impossible. The horses that had suffered with him on the desert had to travel slowly with frequent rests. Naturally, Granger had also taken the best wagon, and Ted had to make repairs nearly every day to keep his wagon from falling to pieces. He had anticipated Nellie's company but had become so embarrassed at holding the Hagens back that he insisted they go on ahead, yielding only to Nellie's pleading that her brother Brig remain with them.

In Long Valley, the Muddy people found Mount Carmel. Its first settlers had been driven out by Indians, but their crude cabins were already occupied by families from various parts of Utah who had responded to Brigham Young's call for a unit of the United Order. The Muddy Mission contingent immediately started building log cabins, all of the men working on one house until it was completed, then starting on another. Several were already finished when Ted arrived. The way the men banded together helped him feel a tie of brotherhood he had not experienced before. Within a few days, he and his mother were settled with their few household belongings in a three-room cabin not far from the larger Hagen home.

Ted was absorbed at once in the unremitting labor required to clear land, dig irrigation ditches and canals, and plant spring crops. He worked with all his might, but he lived for the few moments each day that he spent with Nellie, both of them filled with hope and bright dreams for the future.

At the beginning of summer, Brigham Young arrived to organize both the ward and also the United Order. He called all the married priesthood holders together to hear details of the plan and help him select officers. Because of his experience in the Overton Ward, Isaac Hagen was selected to be president of the board that would govern the Order, and he would also serve as bishop of the ward. Elias Cameron, a volunteer from Fillmore, was chosen as first counselor. These appointments represented both contingents in the valley quite satisfactorily. Then President Young commented, "We need in this organization the enthusiasm and energy of youth, quite as much as the wisdom and experience of older men. Is a young man among you fitted to take the responsibility of second counselor?"

"What about that young Brother Chandler, who came with your company, Bishop Hagen?" asked Brother Cameron. "The way he pitched right in with the men, helping with the other cabins until it came time to build the one for him and his mother, and the way he's worked on the canal strike me as showing real character and ability in a man so young—a mere boy, you might say."

"You know the young man?" President Young asked Bishop Hagen.

"Oh, yes. Ted is a fine boy. He was somewhat—indifferent—when he first came to Overton, but before we left, he was teaching in our Sunday School and was doing a good job. He's young, though, for such a position as this—not quite nineteen, I believe."

"Years don't matter," stated Brigham Young. "It's enthusiasm, the Spirit of the Lord that counts. Such a responsibility would be the making of him if he's the right sort."

So it was settled, with the names of the officers presented the next day to the entire congregation in a quickly constructed bowery. Nellie and Ted were both stunned when his name was read from the pulpit as second counselor to her father. From his pallor and the frightened, almost defiant, look which succeeded it, she knew he was hearing the news for the first time. She smiled, trying to send him a message of courage and reassurance. As President Young continued reading the list of other officers, she kept her eyes on him and saw the color gradually return to his face, along with a new expression she had never seen before. She sighed contentedly. For an awful moment, she had wondered if he would refuse the calling. Sitting beside Ted, Emily Chandler Granger was quietly weeping tears of pride and gratitude, and Ted put a comforting arm around her.

After the meeting, the families of the newly chosen officers gathered for the ceremony of setting apart and blessing by the laying on of hands to strengthen them for their new callings. Nellie barely heard the blessing pronounced on her father, so eager was she for Ted's turn to come. Brigham Young himself pronounced this blessing, and tears sprang to her eyes as she thrilled to its wonderful words. She felt as though she was sharing in it; in her heart, she promised God that she would do all in her power to sustain

Ted and help in this and future callings. Though they were not formally engaged, she knew that he loved her and that her love for him was the most precious thing in her life. It was something to cling to throughout eternity. As the blessing ended, Ted lifted his head and looked at her. Her answering look of trust and love brought a calmness his questioning mind rarely enjoyed.

At the close of the meeting, they walked together from the small village down a shady lane which led past the recently planted fields on both sides of the creek. They sat on a flat boulder under a tree and, for the first time, talked of marriage.

"You know, Nellie," said Ted gently, "I have felt we should not plan to be married until I have something. I intended to go north and get a job for the winter as soon as I got Mother settled and our crops in. I also wanted to try to get some of our property back from Granger. I think Mother is beginning to see now that he wanted our land, teams, and farm implements, along with the convenience of a family to send to the Muddy. She wants me to try to get something that we can turn into the Order."

"Are you still planning to go?" Nellie asked.

"I don't know," he mused. "What happened today makes everything seem different. I must still see about our property, but I can't stay away for the winter. More than anything else, I want to be married. I need you to help me. I'm afraid. Why did they choose *me*? I'm not always sure of my own beliefs. You know that sometimes I've doubted everything."

"I know, but I believe that's past. You are surer than you used to be—ever since that night on the desert. It will help you to have this important office. The trust of others in you, the responsibility—"

"It's you, your trust," Ted said, looking at her soberly. "You've always done more for me than you can ever know." He took her hand and turned the little ring on her finger. "When President Young said my name, I thought I hadn't heard right. Then when everybody looked at me, I felt like yelling, 'No! I can't do it! I won't do it! I don't believe.' Then you smiled and I thought of that night on the desert and what I'd promised God, and all at once it seemed that with your help I could—I had to do it."

"Of course you can do it." She leaned against him and looked up trustingly into his eyes. "The Lord will help you. Couldn't you feel the Spirit in that wonderful blessing the president gave you? It seemed to fall around me, too—warm and holy. I—I can't even explain to you how—it was wonderful!"

He drew her close, within his arms, and she raised her face trustingly for his kiss. They sat a long time, talking of the future. As soon as possible, they would go to Salt Lake and be married in the Endowment House.

"I'd hoped the temple would be finished before I was married," Nellie said wistfully. "Father and Mother were married in the Nauvoo Temple, and I've had a strange feeling that it would seem more like being married for time and all eternity if it could be in a temple."

"That's the kind of marriage ours is going to be, no matter where we're married," Ted said with assurance. "But of course, the Endowment House, they say, has exactly the same ceremony as the Nauvoo Temple. We can't wait for them to finish the Salt Lake Temple." He smiled. "I must have you now." He bent and kissed her, and she snuggled closer in his arms.

Shadows were falling across the valley. The leaves of the tree began to whisper in the growing coolness. From a little distance came the twilight call of a meadowlark. A peaceful calm pervaded the scene.

"I wish I had a decent team," Ted sighed. "Old Sol and Pinto couldn't possibly make a long trip now."

"Maybe Father could spare one of his. I think other couples will be making the same trip by the time we're ready." Nellie refused to let anything mar the happiness of this moment.

THERE WAS MUCH WORK to be done in setting up the new United Order. Ted's new land required much of his time. Now rooms must be added to the log house. Unbroken land must be put under cultivation. New members of the Order arrived almost daily. The bishopric and board of directors were kept busy receiving the property these newcomers brought to turn into the commonwealth, and apportioning land and work to each family. New homes had to be built and various industries started.

Because Ted had had more schooling than most of the men on the board, he was asked to be clerk of the Order, requiring long hours of keeping records and accounts and following up on meeting assignments. Bishop Hagen told him that after harvest would be the time to most easily spare him. He and Nellie set their wedding date for September 20.

Nellie was busy and happy, devoting every spare moment to piecing quilts, tatting lace for chemises and nightgowns, and renovating the few dresses in her wardrobe. Each moment she and Ted spent together had to be snatched from their unremitting work, but she was content in her love, her work, and her dreams of the future. She was proud of Ted and thrilled with his amazing development. His old doubts and questionings seemed to trouble him less and less. He worked tirelessly, and she knew that her father and the other men admired his mental alertness and respected his ideas and suggestions as equal to their own.

The hours they had together were precious. She sometimes feared that she was too happy for reality and that she would awaken and find that she had been dreaming. Ted was a perfect lover. He told her in so many ways that he loved her—by the tender light in his eyes when he looked at her, by the slight trembling of his strong hands when he touched her cheek or hair, and by the sweet gentleness of his words and caresses. However, once or twice he had almost frightened her by a sudden fierce embrace or a shower of impassioned kisses. That hadn't seemed like Ted, and she had drawn impulsively away. Each time he had apologized and seemed a little ashamed—and afterwards very tender. It was only at such moments that she felt even vaguely that they did not understand each other perfectly.

IN EARLY SEPTEMBER, APOSTLE Erastus Snow arrived in Mount Carmel on his way to St. George, where he had long supervised the Church in that locality. He had been instructed to consider any problems with the Mount Carmel United Order and give any needed counsel. The Hagen family was proud to entertain him. Mother and Auntie exerted all their skill in preparing the most delicious meals possible, with their limited resources, to do him honor. There was the rare luxury of molasses cake and rice pudding, besides fried chicken and fresh vegetables. The excited children tried to be on their best behavior.

On the evening of his arrival was a meeting of the bishopric and Board of Control, with a priesthood meeting the next morning and a congregational meeting in the afternoon. At the breakfast table the second day, Nellie noticed that her father regarded her in a strange, solicitous manner. When the meal was over, he told Apostle Snow: "I'll join you at the meetinghouse in a few moments," then beckoned Nellie to follow him. Wondering if she had displeased him, she obeyed. He stopped near the rock cellar behind the house, cleared his throat, and began to speak without looking at her.

"Nellie, you know that Apostle Snow has been sent to help us with our problems and bring us advice from President Young." He cleared his throat again and nervously broke into bits a twig from the lilac bush. Why was he telling *her* this? "At our board meeting, Brother Snow was very surprised to find a man as young as Ted in such a responsible position and particularly surprised to learn that he is not married."

"But we're going to be married in three weeks," she reminded him.

"Yes, I explained that your wedding has been postponed until we get things going here." Bishop Hagen dropped the last fragment of the stick, then took his knife from his pocket and began opening and closing the blade mechanically. Nellie could not remember having seen him so disturbed.

"You see, my girl," he finally continued, "the prophet of the Lord is advising a more general acceptance of the principle of celestial marriage by members of the Church and particularly that the priesthood men who hold important positions in the Church organization accept—"

"NO! NO!" Nellie cried out, clutching the stone wall of the cellar. For a moment, she could not see her father. She felt as if she were going to faint. She felt hollow inside, as if all vitality had been drained from her being. When her mind cleared, she looked desperately at her father. Surely she had misunderstood him. His face was still averted.

Huskily he said, "I know it is sometimes difficult to understand the ways of the Lord and to accept at first some of the things his gospel requires, but I am sure you and Ted will come to understand and find strength to do what may be required. It should not be difficult for you to feel all right about the principle. We are practicing it in our own family—with peace and I hope happiness. But Ted's experience has been unfortunate. It will be a severe ordeal for him. That is why I wanted to tell you about it now. He will need your strength and help."

He reached out and patted her bent head. "You're a good girl, Nellie, and will be a wonderful helpmate to your husband as your mother has been to me."

He cleared his throat again as if he wanted to say something more but only stroked her hair with his rough hand, very gently, then turned quickly and walked away.

Nellie pressed her clenched hands and forehead against the hard wall. Her heart was shrieking in protest but her lips were tight. She finally moved them in an effort to pray, but the sobbing words flew back to her. She didn't know whether minutes or hours had passed when she heard her mother calling. She was numb and desolate. Only one thing burned like fire in her tortured mind. Ted—another wife! Finally, she tried to assure herself that it could not be. Ted had sworn to her that the practice was abhorrent to him.

And yet—

He was a bishop's counselor. The president of the Church, the prophet of God was asking this. Counsel was more potent than commands would be.

In the flash of an eye, her whole world had changed. She had planned to wash her hair, sew a new collar on her blue dress, and wear it to the afternoon meeting where she could look at Ted, but now her plans fell dead about her. She had been so happy. Ted would come after the meeting. They would walk together, dream of the future together. She would feel his arms around her, his kisses on her lips and hair. But now, her whole world had changed. The sun was eclipsed. She felt alien to all she had ever known—alone in the universe.

Her mother called again, standing in the kitchen door. "Nellie, Nellie. What in the world are you doing out here?"

Nellie pulled herself together, dragging herself toward the house. Her mother looked at her sharply. "You're white as a ghost. Go lie down. The little girls can help Lucy with the dishes."

Tears burned in her eyes. She longed to rush to her mother's arms and unburden herself of this awful truth that she felt was killing her, but Martha Christensen came running around the house.

"Sister Hagen, can you come now? Mary's pains are only a few minutes apart, and she's carrying on dreadful."

Clara Hagen whipped off her apron and reached for her sunbonnet in the same gesture. "It's too bad she couldn't have waited until Apostle Snow had gone," she said. "Lucy, tell your mother I've had to go to Mary Kelly. Maybe she can get Melissa Kennedy or Harriet Losee to make a rice pudding or some dried apple pies for dinner. They both offered to do something to help and would feel it was an honor. Nellie, you'd better take a dose of soda and go lie down."

She reached to the top of a cupboard for a worn black bag and a rolled blanket, gave one worried look about the untidied room, then hurried to follow Martha down the street. Auntie came in from the front room she had been dusting. Minnie, who had been shelling new peas from the second planting out under a wild juniper tree, made her cautious way inside.

"She'll be the next one to need Mother," Nellie thought. As she observed the blind girl's figure, her mind flashed back to that late afternoon in Overton when she had stood holding a little china ornament in her hands and felt a strange, sickening sensation all over—as she felt now. That was the night Ted came into her life.

"What's the matter, Nellie?" Auntie asked kindly, turning her around to the light of the window. "You've been working too hard at your quilts. You must let the rest of us help you more. Now, you go in and lie down, as your mother told you. We'll get along. They won't be here for dinner before twelve-thirty anyway, and we'll leave the dishes until after the general meeting."

Nellie clung to Auntie's hand for a moment. If things were not in such a hubbub, she could tell Auntie what was the matter. But she turned and said, "I'll go for a walk until I feel better."

She put on her pink gingham bonnet and hurried outside, away from the questioning glances of her sisters. She hoped none of the children would follow her. She had to be alone, and that was impossible when she was in the house.

SHE WALKED TOWARD THE foothills. Soon she reached the edge of the village and began to climb. When she stopped to rest, she looked back at the rows of garden plots behind each house on both sides of the single street that ran through their small town. She gazed at the fields farther away with the creek running through. To the south was the pasture where a group of boys played as they watched the cows. The peaceful scene contrasted with the tumult in Nellie's mind and heart. She was scarcely conscious of anything except that one unbelievable fact—Ted was expected to marry another woman besides herself.

At last she forced herself to analyze her feelings, this sickening revulsion that smothered her. Why did she feel as she did? Why should she rebel against polygamy? There had been Father, Mother, and Auntie as long as she could remember. And it seemed perfectly natural and right. As a child, she had even suffered from secret guilt because she loved Auntie, at times, more than Mother.

Reconciling herself to Father's marriage to Minnie had been hard at first, but gradually that, too, had come to seem normal. At least, it was no longer revolting to her.

Father was invariably kind but seldom demonstrative. She could not recall ever having seen him kiss either Mother or Auntie, except when he was going away or returning from an absence of a few days. He was very affectionate with the children, particularly when they were young. He cuddled and caressed the babies, gave the older ones an occasional pat on the shoulders or a playful pinch of the cheek. He treated Minnie much as he did her and Lucy—as an older daughter. But the blind girl was so affectionate herself that the children and even Mother and Auntie were always tenderly demonstrative with her.

Nellie compelled her mind to go over what her father had said. It was true that plural marriage had been practiced with harmony and happiness in their family, and she knew other families where such was likewise true. But there were some cases ... She cringed to think of them. Yet it was a divine ordinance of the Church. *That* she had always accepted. But to accept it in her life—to know that Ted would love someone else as he did her, that he would hold another girl in his arms and look at her with that adoring light in his eyes, that he would touch another with a kind of reverence and kiss her lips and call her loving names— Oh, she could not bear it!

She threw herself on the ground and wept until only dry sobs shook her body. She remained huddled there for a long time, wishing she could have died that morning while the sun was shining and while there was joy in the world.

Then her father's words came back to her: "I'm sure you will feel all right about it." How could he think that? Could it be that he knew something of what she would suffer? Was that why he had kept clearing his throat and could not look at her? Why he had made such a point of her need to help Ted? Was that his way of trying to help her? "It's going to be an ordeal for him, and you are the one who can help him."

Ordeal! The word was too weak. Suddenly, she realized what Ted must be going through, feeling as he did about his mother's marriage, his denunciation of Brother Cropper's treatment of Nora, his vow that first night they met. It had given her great comfort that night, but he had been ready to denounce the entire Church. Things were different now. He was earnest and devout. He had great leadership potential. Sometimes she felt he had outstripped her in spiritual development. Certainly, he would be a power in the Church.

She told herself that plural marriage was just as much a principle of the gospel as baptism, as belief in the Godhead and the resurrection, as the continuation of family relationships after this life. It was as much a part of the gospel as belief in the divine mission of Joseph Smith and the Book of Mormon. Joseph Smith had received a revelation from God about this principle. It was divine. Why was it so hard to accept?

Sermons had explained the duty of members of the only true Church to give bodies to as many of the spirits waiting in heaven as possible. Earthly experience was a necessary part of eternal salvation. The sermons had sounded logical and convincing, but she had not thought what accepting the principle would mean. The Saints had always been persecuted, forced to do the seemingly impossible. It was so when Christ was on the earth and was true again in her own time. Christ had given his life for the truth. Joseph Smith had been a martyr for it, too. Her own forebears had suffered and sacrificed. Now it was her turn. This was her test.

She must accept polygamy as right, though it seemed so wrong. She kept saying that over and over, trying to make it seem true. God moves in a mysterious way. How true. God, President Young, and even Father wanted Ted to marry another woman besides her. It came down to that hard fact. She must give him the courage to do what would bring him spiritual growth now and salvation and glory in the world to come. In the next world, righteous men would be gods, who would people worlds of their own. That was the glory she must help Ted to attain. How many wives had helped God create the countless spirits on this earth and those waiting to come. Of course he had many wives. Didn't she sing often in church:

> *In the heavens are parents single?*
> *No! the thought makes reason stare.*
> *Truth is reason. Truth eternal*
> *Tells me I've a mother there.*

A strange thought came to Nellie. Had God's first wife suffered as she was suffering?

When she had left the house, Nellie had felt she must find some place where she could be alone and pray for strength. That feeling came again. She must pray. Suddenly she knew that she would pray not to her Father in Heaven, but to her Mother in Heaven who alone could know and understand.

She shifted to her knees and lifted her face, letting her sunbonnet fall back on her shoulders. She whispered: "Dear Mother in Heaven, I don't know how to tell you, but I know you will understand. Maybe you know how I love Ted and want him to be good and great, and exalted in this life and in the life to come. Help me not to care—about the other wife, you know. Show me how to help him to see that it must be right. But, oh, it seems ... so wrong ... so wrong. Mother in Heaven, please understand—and help. Amen."

The prayer made her feel that she had relinquished part of herself to something not of herself, and she wept again. With exhaustion came calm. She got to her feet. She was trembling, her face was swollen, and her throat was tight. But her course was clear. Renunciation was not sweet, but it was endurable. The soft twitter of a bird in the tree above her almost seemed an assurance that her prayer had been heard. She did not know how it could be answered. But if the sacrifice were for Ted's good ... She had always thought she could do anything for Ted.

She looked down into the valley. It still lay there in silence and peace. She sighed, brokenly but with a sort of resignation. She felt strangely old and desolate as she drew her bonnet back upon her head and started slowly down.

five

When Apostle Snow had given his counsel about plural marriage for the ward and board leaders of Mount Carmel, Ted, who was taking minutes, went on writing for a few seconds before the full meaning of what he had heard struck him, almost like a physical blow. Apostle Snow was saying that all men holding leadership offices were asked to accept plural marriage on the same basis as other principles and ordinances of the gospel. It was as binding as any of them. Ted wrote the closing words mechanically: "This solemn advice comes to you from our prophet, seer, and revelator, our inspired leader, President Brigham Young. Both your temporal and spiritual salvation are dependent upon heeding this counsel and, in so doing, magnifying your important service to our Lord."

He fought against the feeling that these words were meant particularly for him, but nearly every other member of the board already had more than one wife. So Apostle Snow hadn't been satisfied by Bishop Hagen's explanation of his forthcoming marriage? He looked appealingly at his future father-in-law. Surely he could not want that for Nellie! But Bishop Hagen avoided his eyes and, in concluding the leadership meeting, thanked the apostle and said he was sure all present were willing and eager to live the gospel to its fullest.

Baffled and wretched, Ted had hurried out the door, pretending not to hear Brother Cameron call him. He almost ran along the dark street, whispering, "I can't! I won't! It's wrong!"

He was relieved that his mother had not waited up for him. Standing by his window, he could see lights in a few other houses along the single street. One of them was the Hagen home. The bishop and Apostle Snow had doubtless arrived. Nellie would be in bed, never dreaming of what had happened. No! It couldn't happen to them. He would give up the Church, as much as it had come to mean to him, before he would practice polygamy. What did love mean if not the cherishing of the one and only person in the world that filled one's need for happiness and contentment, as Nellie filled that need for him? How could he hold another girl in his arms, caressing her, wanting her to be the mother of his children? He would go to Bishop Hagen in the morning, resign from the board, and tell him frankly how he felt—how Nellie felt—about plural marriage for them.

He knew he would be censured, perhaps even excommunicated. His mother would suffer even more than she had during his conflicts with Granger. Nellie would suffer, too, particularly from displeasing her parents and being condemned by the Church. They would probably have to move away, but even that—anything—would be better than desecrating their love.

The moon rose over the eastern hills, flooding the little valley with soft radiance. The houses, barns, and sheds seemed peaceful and calm. Ted longed to feel that magical peace in his own soul, but the serenity outside only intensified his unhappiness. Whatever course he took would bring conflict and misery, but he must stand by his convictions of what was right. Anything else was unthinkable.

HE WENT TO BED but did not sleep. He kept wondering how good men—godly men like President Young, Bishop Hagen, and scores of others he knew, could harmonize polygamy with the other principles of the gospel. The Word of Wisdom was based on good laws of health. Tithing taught unselfishness and sacrifice. Hallowing the Sabbath, chastity, care of the unfortunate—in fact, all the other principles seemed reasonable and good. Chastity was given particular emphasis. Infidelity brought excommunication. Only one other sin, denying the Holy Ghost, was a greater sin. Yet polygamy was accepted as a divine command.

Ted rose early the next morning, hoping to get the conference with Bishop Hagen over but also longing for a few words with Nellie before he saw her father. He made a bare pretense of eating breakfast and hurried away. To his surprise, Bishop Hagen was already walking quickly down the street toward the meetinghouse. It must be later than he thought. He quickened his steps, then Bishop Hagen joined Apostle Snow and Brother Cameron, who were waiting for him outside the Cameron cabin, and the three men moved on together. Ted hesitated, irresolute.

"Good morning, Brother Chandler," came a cheerful voice from behind. It was Brother Parker, a newcomer to the Order. "I thought I was going to be late. One of the children was ill last night, and we didn't get around as early as usual this morning. That'll be one advantage of the Order. We won't have to wait for our breakfasts until our wives are ready to prepare it." He laughed heartily.

Brother Yates came out from his house and fell into step with them. "Good morning, Brother Parker. Good morning, Ted. I suppose I should call you Brother Chandler, now you're a member of the bishopric, but you seem such a boy, it's hard to change."

"'Ted' sounds better to me," he replied, borne along between the two men. It seemed as if some power outside himself was pushing him on to his fate.

Brother Yates was a member of the board and eyed Ted quizzically. "You got it pretty straight from Apostle Snow last night, didn't you, boy?"

Ted clenched his hands but said nothing.

"I could see it worried you, what he said about plural marriage. I knew how you felt—that marrying someone else besides that pretty little bishop's daughter seemed impossible. I felt that way once myself. But when you look at it in a common sense way, even leaving religion out of it, it's a wise plan. Don't you think so, Brother Parker? I know one woman could get awfully tired of me, if she had to have me around all the time." The two older men chuckled knowingly.

"And maybe you don't know it yet, being so young," Brother Yates went on in a lower tone, "but you'll find out as you grow older and have experience, that men are really polygamous. You think now, of course, that it will be impossible for you to love anyone but Nellie. I'm not saying you'll find anyone that you'll love in quite the same way—your first love and a wonderful girl like her. She'll be the kind of wife every man should have, if he has one or twenty—to keep him at his best, if you know what I mean. But you'll find there are elements in your nature that a girl like Nellie can't understand—maybe can't satisfy. You'll realize that it may be better for her, even, as well as for you, to have another wife—another kind of wife."

Ted's face burned with resentment and disgust. Yet even in his angry indignation, he recalled Nellie's startled fright, almost aversion, when his caresses had been over-ardent. Still, putting marriage merely on a physical basis, as these men were doing, made him all the firmer in his resolve to be free.

He hesitated at the door of the meetinghouse. Obviously he could not see Bishop Hagen until later. Reluctantly, he followed the other men inside and tried to slip into a seat at the rear of the room. Bishop Hagen beckoned him to the stand, and mechanically he obeyed. He felt as if he were caught in a horrible net from which he could not extricate himself.

Apostle Snow addressed the group briefly, then the men were organized into committees to carry out various parts of the work of the new organization. When Ted's name was mentioned for a committee, he had a wild impulse to stand up and shout the things that were raging within him. But the eyes of the apostle and the bishop were regarding him with kindly expectancy. He swallowed and nodded. He felt the threads of the web tightening.

The group meeting broke up early so there would be time for committee meetings. Almost in a dream, Ted started toward his committee in one corner. Bishop Hagen intercepted him and said, "We'd like you to come to the house for dinner when your committee has finished. Brother Cameron is coming. It will give us a little time as a bishopric to speak further with Apostle Snow. Besides, Nellie will be glad to see you, of course."

Ted nodded without speaking. His mind seemed divided in two for the next hour: carrying on the committee work competently and struggling with his problem. When the committee meeting ended, he found the bishop standing outside with a group of strangers.

"Ted," he called, "come meet these folks. This is Brother Fischer and his family, come from Farmington to join the Order. This is Brother Chandler, one of my counselors. Sister Fischer, and their oldest daughter, Luanna. The other children have gone to find a drink."

The daughter stepped forward, smiling provocatively, and held out her hand.

"You look terribly young and handsome to be in a bishopric," she said. Her full red lips revealed white, even teeth. Dark curls showed under her red bonnet, tipped slightly to one side. Bishop Hagen was conversing with the parents.

"I'm at least too young and not considered handsome," Ted answered, taken aback by her boldness.

"Didn't you used to live in Farmington?" she queried.

"Yes, my mother remarried and her husband moved us down to the Muddy Mission almost two years ago."

"That was right after we moved to Farmington," Luanna confided, moving closer. "I wanted to go play run-sheep-run with you and some other boys, but the girls I was with said you were the roughest boy in town and wouldn't go." She laughed up at him, and he couldn't help smiling. "And to think that now you're a bishop—almost."

Bishop Hagen called to Ted. "Could you and your mother take care of part of Brother Fischer's family for a few days? He'll draw a lot and some farm land tomorrow, and we can fix up some tents and wagons for them while we're building a house. Brother Cameron will take the others."

"It'll be all right," Ted answered. "I'm sure Mother will be glad to have them."

"Come meet my other wife and some of the children," Brother Fischer invited. Ted followed him to the two covered wagons and shook hands with a faded, middle-aged woman nursing a baby. Two other children poked their heads out from under the wagon cover. A half-grown boy shared the seat with the woman.

Luanna was close behind Ted. "I hope your wife's as nice as you are and won't object to uninvited guests," she murmured.

"My mother is much nicer than I am," he responded, "and will be glad to have you."

Luanna took off her bonnet and shook her hair. A red ribbon among her curls matched the color of her cheeks. Before she could speak, Bishop Hagen bustled up and they quickly divided the families. Ted got Luanna, her mother, and three of the children. He got into the wagon to show them the way, introduced them to his mother, helped the boys attend to the team, and then stepped back into the house. "Mother, the bishop wants Brother Cameron and me to join him and go over some matters with Apostle Snow before the meeting this afternoon."

"But you haven't had your dinner, Teddy, and you scarcely touched your breakfast. I've been worried that you'll get sick."

"Bishop Hagen has invited us to eat over there."

"Oh, I see," Emily Chandler Granger smiled at her guests and confided, "Teddy and Bishop Hagen's Nellie are going to be married very soon, and he feels about as much at home over there as here."

Luanna, who had started setting other places at the table, looked up quickly. "You might have told me you as good as had a wife." She pretended to pout.

Ted didn't answer, but as he went out, Luanna called after him, "See you later, Bishop!"

She reminded him of Deborah Williams, but she was much prettier and her forwardness was not so offensive. But Nellie! His thoughts rushed to her. Did she know? What would become of them and their dreams for the future?

Six

The table was set and Nellie was filling glasses when Ted entered. She looked at him and smiled, but her hands trembled and she spilled water on the checkered tablecloth. The bishop was coming toward him, and Nellie slipped into the kitchen, but not before Ted noticed her pale cheeks and the circles under her eyes. She'd been crying. "She knows," he thought. He couldn't bear to have her hurt.

He took a step toward her, but the bishop announced, "The womenfolk have arranged for us to eat by ourselves so we can talk about necessary matters before the meeting." He pressed Ted into a chair and sat down opposite Apostle Snow.

Through the open kitchen door, Ted could see Nellie serving the children. Auntie brought in the platter of chicken and vegetables, then stood quietly by for the blessing. Where was Clara Hagen? How would she feel about this situation? Though she never complained, he had always felt pained by the thoughts and feelings that he guessed lay behind her patient, faded eyes. No matter how crowded the house was, Sister Hagen was somehow alone. Ted wished she were here today. Her presence would somehow give him more courage.

Apostle Snow, at the bishop's invitation, was pronouncing the blessing on the food, but it was not the customary short grace. "Help us, our Father, to accept thy will in all things. Help us to remember our covenants with thee—"

A chill ran down Ted's spine. Covenants! That night on the desert! He'd promised God—

"—and willingly sacrifice that our hearts may be pure before thee and dedicated to the building of thy kingdom ..."

Surely God had not spared his life only to subject him and Nellie to a lifetime of living torment!

"Have some potatoes, Ted, and pass them to Brother Cameron." Bishop Hagen was looking at him quizzically. Mechanically he picked up the bowl. Why had he begged God to save him that night? Death would be easier—better for him and Nellie, too!

"Will you pass the peas, Ted? These and the radishes are from our garden—a second crop. One thing that is going to help the Order, Brother Snow, is the fertility of the soil. I've never seen things grow as they do here. And compared to our troubles on the Muddy ..."

Ted felt as if each mouthful was choking him.

"One of the matters we need your counsel about, Brother Snow," Bishop Hagen continued, "is the return of some former settlers. They moved away because of Indian trouble, and some of the new Order members moved into houses they left and planted land they had partially cultivated. Now, many are coming back and demanding their property."

"Why is that a problem?" queried the apostle. "Won't they fit into the Order?"

"Some of them will, but some are apostates or at best indifferent Mormons. A few days ago, the Peters and Kraus families arrived. They're bent on trouble. They're demanding their houses. Both of them have been repaired and enlarged. They'd hardly worked their land at all and now we have cultivated those fields and have good stands of wheat on them. We're refusing to let them have the homes back without remuneration for the improvements and will hold the land until after harvest, but they're acting very ugly and warn that we can expect plenty of trouble."

"That certainly does make a serious situation," the apostle agreed. "Apostates are a terrible menace. Once a member of the Church allows the spirit of evil to take possession of him and put doubt into his mind, he is tempted from his duty to the Church and to God. He becomes a lost soul."

The words seemed directed at Ted. His stomach lurched.

"Even our enemies," Brother Snow continued, "our bitterest enemies out in the world are not to be feared and shunned as much as these sons of perdition who have once been of us and have enjoyed the Holy Ghost and then denied it. According to the word of the Lord, they are condemned to eternal damnation."

Ted's mouth was dry. There was a painful knot in the pit of his stomach. Could this Church leader read what was in his heart? Had he discerned what Ted had resolved to do? What *was* he to do? He felt utterly confused and desperate.

"It may be necessary," the apostle continued, "if these people continue with their antagonistic spirit, for you to move farther up the valley where there can be no question concerning property rights."

"That will be hard after all we've done here," sighed Brother Cameron. "Months of hard work. And most of us were just feeling there was a chance to get our feet under us after those years of sacrifice on the Muddy."

"I hope such a move will not be necessary," Brother Snow answered. "But harmony is absolutely essential within the United Order. So unless these people can be converted to the movement and brought back into the spirit of cooperation, going away will be the only option for you. It may mean further sacrifices, but remember, 'Whom the Lord loveth he chasteneth.' Isn't there a suitable site a few miles north of here?" Bishop Hagen nodded slowly. "You could probably move many of your houses that short distance and continue to farm the land that hadn't been claimed here before."

Little of the conversation registered with Ted. He had come here determined to extricate himself from this snare only to find escape impossible. He was desperate to see Nellie for a moment, but the bishop rose from the table and called, "Leave everything as it is so you won't be late to the meeting," and ushered his guests out the door. Nellie had disappeared from Ted's view during the meal; and though he lingered on the steps for a moment, hoping she would appear, she did not come. Was she avoiding him?

He felt he was in a nightmare as he walked down the street after the men. Services had already begun when Nellie slipped into the bench beside Auntie. He knew she was suffering as much as he. Her face was drawn and very pale. A look of dread was in her eyes. His mother also came late, accompanied by Brother Fischer, the two wives, and some of the children. Luanna was not with them. He thought distractedly of her and the red ribbon fluttering in her curls.

He heard nothing of the meeting. His eyes were fixed on Nellie, but she never looked up. When the meeting ended, she waited for him and they silently moved away, as quickly as possible, from the knots of people visiting outside the meetinghouse. He slipped her arm through his and covered her hand with his own as they walked. It was cold.

When they reached the flat boulder where they had first talked of marriage, he drew her into his arms. "Darling, what are we going to do?" His voice was husky with emotion.

She leaned against him, her body quivering. He took off her hat and laid it on the rock beside them. When he bent to kiss her, Nellie felt his tears falling upon her hair and face. They clung together like children, helpless and afraid.

"I thought about it all night," Ted said.

"I dreamed about our happiness all night. But then I woke up, and—" She tried to check the sob that rose in her throat. He held her close, showering kisses on her cheeks and lips.

"Nellie, I made up my mind last night to tell them I couldn't do it. I felt it wouldn't matter what happened. I thought I didn't care. Even if they cut us off from the Church, we would have each other and that would be everything. I tried to tell your father this morning but didn't get a chance. And then Apostle Snow asked the blessing on the food—though it wasn't that kind of prayer. Something he said—but Nellie, I'll forget what it did to me. I don't care what I promised, that night I thought I was dying on the desert. I don't care if I do have to suffer eternal damnation. I—"

"Ted! Ted! No! No! Don't say such things." Her hand was on his lips. "Oh, darling, don't you see? This is our test. Maybe God can help us to bear it. We must beg him to."

She slid to her knees by the rock. He knelt beside her. Neither spoke aloud. Minutes passed. After a while, she lifted her face from her wet palms. He raised her into his arms. Prayer had deadened their pain. For the moment, at least, they were resigned.

After a time, Ted said, "I want you to know one thing, darling, and I want you to remember it always. No matter what happens, you are the only one I will ever love like this. You will always be my first love, my *first*—oh, God, why can't I say it—my *only* wife!"

seven

Ted and Nellie sat on the rock beside the creek while the afternoon slipped by, and day turned into night as the moon came up over the mountain behind them. A strange peace gradually calmed their troubled souls. They felt a kind of exaltation, a lifting of the spirit, a sort of divine benediction on their sacrifice.

In Ted's mind was an undefined wish that they could die, here, now, in each other's arms with the moonlight sifting through the willows and the sound of the water softly lapping against the pebbles. They said little. The spell was too fragile for words.

At last, Nellie said with a deep sigh, "It's getting late. I think we ought to go." But still they sat on, dreading to end this hour of tranquility after the storm had racked their beings to the depths. When they stood, they still clung to each other, half aware that when they left this spot, which their hours together had made sacred, they would be leaving behind a part of their lives ineffably sweet, to which they could never return.

"Don't ever forget what I told you," Ted whispered.

"And don't you ever forget that I love you so much that I can bear whatever has to come—even if it breaks my heart."

"Darling, how can we accept it?"

They clung together once more before starting toward the village. When they reached the edge of town, they could hear music coming from the bowery; Pap Sorenson's fiddle and Lew Simon's accordion were sending strains of a reel out on the evening air. Soon they could hear dancing feet.

They had both forgotten the weekly Friday-night dance. Nellie could hardly believe that only this morning she had thought so happily of the dance, the new collar and cuffs for her dress, and washing her hair. How far away the morning seemed. She felt years older and sadder.

"Do you want to go to the dance?" Ted asked.

"How could I?"

The sound of laughing voices mingled with the music and feet shuffling on the crude floor. The music changed. Jim Cropper's voice rose in calling the figures of a square dance: "Circle all! Sashay out and swing on the corner! Balance your partners and all promenade."

"I wonder if we ought to go over for a few minutes," Ted said as they drew nearer.

"It must be almost time to close," Nellie responded. "But if you'd like to go—"

A little feeling of dread came over her. She'd always loved the dances. But it would be different now. When the other girls told her what a good dancer Ted was, she'd only been proud and happy, never jealous. He was hers alone. But now— Oh, no, she must not let her mind go in that direction. Hadn't Ted sworn that always she would be … But that promise did not bring back her old content.

They turned toward the bowery.

"Well, where have you two been all evening?" "Did you come to dismiss the dance?" greeted them as they joined the crowd.

"Come on, here's a place for another couple," someone called as the dancers formed squares. Ted and Nellie stepped to the place and the music began.

As Nellie advanced to the center of the set, her hand out to make the turn with the girl from the opposite corner of the square, she found herself looking into a pair of flashing black eyes she had never seen before and heard the girl laugh past her shoulder, "Well, good evening, Bishop Chandler. I don't think you're very polite to invite people to your home and then run off and not see them again."

These must be the new arrivals, come to join the Order. Her heart sank. Why hadn't Ted mentioned that this pretty girl was staying at his home? She was so striking. Her dress was silk, red silk, the color of her lips and the ribbons in her hair. Nellie suddenly felt shabby and dull.

When the dance ended, Ted introduced them. Luanna held out her hand, smiling and friendly.

"I've been wanting to meet you. Do you know that this young bishop of yours had the reputation of being the worst boy in town? I was warned not to play with him and can hardly believe he's all saint yet. He's too good looking."

"I suppose no one is all saint." Nellie tried to make her voice sound light and bantering to match, but her mouth felt dry. She felt common and colorless beside the vivacious stranger. Ted stood smiling at them both.

"Choose partners for a polka," Brother Cropper called.

"You'll let me dance with him this time, won't you?" Luanna begged Nellie. "I've been hearing what a fine dancer the bad boy has turned out to be."

"Of course. He dances with whomever he wants to."

Nellie could see that Ted's face had flushed from mingled pleasure and embarrassment. She turned to accept Nate Jenkins's invitation to dance. With a glance asking her to understand, Ted drew Luanna's arm through his and joined the couples promenading around the hall. Nate and Nellie followed as Pap's bow squeaked across the fiddle strings in his preliminary flourish.

The evening was almost over. When the call came, "Take partners for the last dance," Nellie noted a general rush of the young men in Luanna's direction. Ted's eyes followed hers, but he came directly to her.

"No wonder she's so popular," Nellie said. "I've never seen such a pretty girl before."

"She makes me think of Deb Williams," he answered. Nellie knew he had never liked Deborah's boldness. They danced in silence. Whenever they circled into one of the corners where a lantern had burned out, he held her closer. Once he bent his cheek close to hers and whispered, "I love you! I love you!" Her body thrilled to his nearness and dearness.

THE LAST OF THE wheat was harvested the second week in September. Nellie and Ted were poised to leave for Salt Lake. Mother had remodeled her grandmother's wedding dress, one of their few heirlooms (along with the china flower girl) brought across the plains from another life in faraway England before the gospel had been restored. She had a simple white dress to wear with her temple clothes in the Endowment House, where the marriage ceremony would be performed, but she would wear the wedding gown at the supper and dance in their honor when they returned home.

Mother and Auntie had also made her a warm dress from wool they had washed, carded, spun, and woven themselves—dark gray trimmed with blue velvet that Auntie had taken from a hat which had been her mother's before she crossed the plains.

Nate Jenkins and Mary Ellen Thompson were going with them to be married at the same time.

"Brother Christensen wants to go with us, too," Ted told Nellie one evening after she had been showing him her dresses and the log-cabin quilt the neighbors had finished at a quilting bee that afternoon.

"What for?" Nellie asked.

"He's going to marry Maria Dougall."

"Oh!" Though this was news, she was not much surprised. Since Apostle Snow's visit, several of the brethren with one wife had been devoting their attentions to young girls. Nellie had seen Brother Christensen talking and laughing with Luanna several times. She was conscious of a vague disappointment that Luanna was not the new wife-to-be.

The Fischers were still living with the Camerons and Grangers. Because of the complications with the old settlers, no more new houses were being built until the problem could be settled. The board of directors agreed that the site in the northern end of the valley was desirable in every way—wider than the present location, nearer some fine springs and a waterfall, and even a small lake which would be valuable assets as the community grew.

"I thought Brother Christensen was shining up to Luanna," Nellie ventured. For no reason at all, she felt a queer, sick sensation sweep over her.

"He has been."

Ted got up from the sofa where they had been sitting and walked to the window. "He's been pestering her ever since she got here, but she doesn't want him."

Something in his voice intensified the sick feeling that had come over Nellie. She moistened her lips, her hands aimlessly folding the dress and quilt.

Sister Fischer had accompanied Ted's mother to the quilting that afternoon. Later Luanna had come and helped with the refreshments. She had been pretty and gay as usual, keeping everyone laughing with her light chatter. She had admired the quilt and told about one in her hope chest of pink sateen filled with down. It had belonged to an aunt who had died just before her marriage and had been given to Luanna, her namesake. Luanna had laughed at everything, sometimes almost hysterically. She had sung snatches of happy little songs Nellie had never heard before and had wanted to caress everyone she came near.

Nellie realized now that all afternoon she had been pushing back a dreaded something that hovered on the edge of her mind. Now she knew she could no longer crowd it back. Ted stood very still looking out into the darkness. The lamp on the table beside the sofa made a pool of light around her. The rest of the room was in comparative shadow. She had a frightening sensation that the shadow was a deep gulf lying between them, a gulf she could not cross.

That dark patch in the rag carpet—Nellie's mind procrastinated. That was from a pair of Father's trousers. She had woven that strip herself and Mother had scolded her for not breaking the dark ball and inserting some color. That little strip of red had been Lucy's ... But why go on with this mental evasion? She had to face it. She stirred ever so slightly.

Ted wheeled about and came to her quickly. His face was white. It seemed he had grown older as he had stood by the window looking into the darkness. He knelt beside her and took her hands.

"Nellie, we know it—has to come. Would you mind very much—if—if it were Luanna?"

He clung to her like a child, begging for understanding. A second ago she had thought he looked old. Now she felt old enough to be his mother. He seemed very young and pleading, in need of sympathetic understanding.

"It's all right, dear," she whispered, kissing the lock of dark hair that had fallen over his damp forehead. He pressed her cold hands to his lips.

"You're an angel!" he breathed.

She was one dull pain, but the worst was over—almost the worst. There was one torturing question to which she must have an answer.

"Would you like—do you want her to go with us?"

He sprang up, startled. She would always be glad for that look. He had not asked Luanna before asking her. It was a tiny touch of balm to her spirit.

"Good Lord, no! I didn't mean that. I don't even know if she cares enough. But so many are after her, I—I thought if I might say something—before we go—"

After a little pause, she said gropingly, "I wonder—if it might be—easier—maybe better for us all to go together."

NELLIE WAS GLAD WHEN her mother called her soon after she had gone to bed, for she felt as if she would never be able to sleep again, or even to feel again, after what had happened and Ted had told her good night. They had talked quietly for a little while after her suggestion but had come to no decision. With a leaden heart, she had sent him to take part of his love to another woman.

"It's Minnie," Mother said. "You'll have to help me. She'll probably have a long, hard time, poor girl. She's been in labor since early this morning but didn't want to tell anyone."

Nellie dressed quickly, thankful for something to clear her mind of its brooding unhappiness. Bringing hot towels and blankets and keeping the kitchen fire going for hot water gave her blessed release. Auntie had gone to stay the night with sick old Granny Watson, otherwise she would have been Mother's assistant.

Father went alternatively to Minnie's room and outside for more wood or water. Once when he was filling the kettles, Mother came into the kitchen. "I think we should get Minnie's parents."

He nodded agreement and went to fetch Brother and Sister Draper.

Anxious hours passed. Sister Draper kept asking Mother, "When will it be over? Poor girl! If only I could suffer for her!"

Once or twice, Nellie saw Father sitting beside Minnie's bed, holding her hands. His face was drawn with deep concern.

Once Mother had put her hand on Nellie's shoulder and said, "This is hard for you. Maybe you should have such an experience since you are about to be married, but I wish it were a more natural, an easier birth."

It was a terrible strain for them all to see the blind girl writhing in pain and to hear her tortured moans. Her father paced the floor, praying silently, going back and forth from the bedroom to the kitchen. Her mother wept and wrung her hands each time after she stood for a moment beside the bed.

Nellie had never dreamed birth was like this. Her own body seemed to suffer with the other girl's.

"I'm sorry it's like this, Nellie," Mother said solicitously. "If I'd known, I wouldn't have called you."

"If I could only do something to help," Nellie answered. "It wouldn't seem so terrible. And to think, Mother, you went through this for me—for each one of us. We could never know." She wanted to put her arms around her mother and kiss her over and over for what she had suffered for her and for her quiet calmness now as she worked to try to help Minnie.

As time went on and the baby did not come, Nellie saw the lines deepening on her mother's face. All the simple methods she had ever used had failed her now.

"Ask your father and Brother Draper to come and administer to her again," she said anxiously to Nellie when she had come to the room with hot towels.

Nellie hurried with the summons and brought them the consecrated olive oil from the cupboard. The father and the husband, both men of nearly the same age, anointed Minnie's tossing head and prayed that if it was the will of the Father that her suffering might cease and her child be safely born. She seemed a little easier for a while and then as dawn came, the baby was born, a little girl with dark hair.

With tears of relief and thanksgiving, Nellie held the little form, wrapped in a blanket that had been warmed in the oven. Just then, Auntie came from her vigil with Granny Watson.

"I'm glad you're here, Hannah," Mother said. "You'll have to wash and dress the baby. Nellie can help you. I can't leave Minnie." She hurried back into the bedroom.

Auntie began pouring warm water into the basin. "I can tell it's been bad from your mother's face."

"Oh, Auntie! It's been terrible. She's suffered so all night long."

The baby wailed thinly as Auntie bathed her, then dressed her in a tiny gown Nellie had helped make.

"Go see how she is while I finish here," Auntie said. "I feel dreadfully worried."

Minnie was lying quiet, sightless eyes closed, her face as white as wax. Her breathing was slow, irregular. Sometimes she moaned faintly. It was Mother's face that frightened Nellie. She was leaning over, kneading Minnie's abdomen, and looking around with a kind of desperation in her eyes that Nellie had never seen before.

"Isaac—it doesn't contract—the womb. She's bleeding to death. Nellie, bring me more cloths, quickly!"

Sister Draper left the room sobbing. Minnie stirred. "The baby—" she whispered. "Is it all right?"

"Yes, Minnie, a beautiful little girl. She looks like you," Clara Hagen answered steadily. As Nellie hurried in with the cloths, Sister Hagen said, "Tell Auntie to bring the baby."

Nellie knew by her mother's face that Minnie was dying. They laid her little daughter in her arms. Gently, the blind girl's sensitive fingers went over the tiny face and the curled little hands.

"Her eyes?" she questioned.

"Perfect," Auntie told her.

"She's sweet. I'm so thankful she's here and is all right. The pain doesn't matter."

A tired sigh passed her lips. Her hands fluttered down. There was a strange gasp in her throat and her blind eyes flew open. Nellie saw her mother collapse beside the bed. Father lifted her in his arms and carried her to the couch in the other room.

"Isaac, I tried so hard to save her," Mother sobbed.

"I know you did, darling."

Darling! Nellie had never heard him use that endearing word before. Tears filled her eyes.

Auntie took the baby from Minnie's side and handed her to Nellie.

"Put her in the cradle there by the stove. Then go see if Sister Croft and Sister Jenkins can come help lay her out."

Nellie looked at her motherless little sister. How strange it seemed. The sun was shining brightly in the windows with the freshness of early morning, but the house was strangely silent with only broken sobs from shadowy corners. Nellie threw her shawl around her shoulders and ran toward the homes of the sisters she was to summon. The night had been like years: love and sacrifice, birth and death. Was that life's repeated pattern?

eight

Ted's mind was confused as he walked home after Nellie had told him it was all right for him to court Luanna Fischer. His heart kept telling him it was not right, and he felt that it had broken Nellie's heart to say those words. But he tried to be practical, unemotional. There seemed no way out. He must accept this principle he had abhorred.

But why had he settled on Luanna? He forced himself to face his feelings. It had been pleasant having her around. She was always laughing, joking that if he was old and fat and married like Brother Christensen, then maybe he'd notice her. He'd noticed her, even against his will, and she knew it. No one could be around Luanna and not notice her. It was not just her pretty, glowing face and laughing disposition, but a certain look in her eyes. He couldn't be mistaken—her eyes reached out hungrily for love.

He was ashamed of the quickening of his pulse as he recalled the incident which had impelled him to ask Nellie if it could be Luanna. It happened as he opened the door to leave for Nellie's that evening.

"Wait a minute, Ted—I mean, Bishop Chandler." She liked to tease him with a drawled, "Biiiishop Chandler," though she sometimes called him "Teddy," like his mother. "Your collar's crooked. Let me fix it."

He had been sure his collar was perfectly straight, but he stopped and she stood in front of him, the top of her dark head coming to his chin, a little taller than Nellie, he had thought, with fuller breasts and wider hips. The warmth of her body as she reached up and tweaked and patted his collar seemed suddenly to enfold him. Her hair had a different fragrance from Nellie's. When her fingers brushed his chin, his body tingled. He'd lifted his eyes to the ceiling to avoid the expression in her eyes.

"There, that looks very nice," she'd said. "I only wish you were old and already married and were coming to see me instead of Nellie." She stepped back and he glanced down at her. She moistened her full, red lips.

"Thanks," he had said quickly, and his voice sounded gruff. Then he hurried away, refusing to let his mind analyze the sensations his body was feeling. He had walked the long way around to Bishop Hagen's house, trying to throw off his mingled feelings of pleasure and guilt. Finally the impossible thought came: Why not both?

And so he had asked for Luanna, and Nellie said it was all right. But he knew it was not all right. The pain in Nellie's sensitive face tortured him. He had felt like a brute and had wished he had not spoken. The old conflict had torn him again until he left her. But now, as he neared his own home and saw Luanna sitting on the doorstep in the moonlight, the strange thrill returned. Why should he feel that it was beastly? Brigham Young, Apostle Snow, Nellie's own father—all were urging him to accept the practice. And hadn't he promised God he would do what the Church asked of him?

Luanna was huddled against the door casing and did not move as he stood before her. She gave a low sob.

"Why, Luanna, what's the matter?" Ted sat down beside her.

"I—I feel just awful! That big fat Brother Christensen has been here again, coaxing me to marry him. He's got someone else to promise to be his second wife, but he says he hasn't given up hope of marrying me, too." She sobbed again.

"Don't you believe in polygamy?" he asked.

"Of course I do, but I don't believe it means marrying just anybody—whether you care for them or not. Do you?"

"Most certainly not." He paused, then added, "Sometimes I'm not sure I believe in it at all, but—"

"Well, we know it was a revelation. And it seems natural for folks to want to get married, and there are a lot more women than men in the Church—and more of them joining all the time."

"I suppose you're right. But it seems strange that a girl like you could believe in it and be willing to share her husband with someone else." He could see Nellie's face as she had looked that afternoon by the creek, and even more touchingly when she had tried to smile and tell him it was all right.

Luanna wiped her cheeks on her sleeve. "Of course having the right kind of man all to yourself would be the ideal way. Every honest woman would have to admit that. But I'd rather share the right kind of man than have a whole one like—you-know-who. I'd rather never marry at all than have that."

They were silent for a few moments without words. Finally Luanna said, "I don't blame you for being crazy about Nellie. She's so grand. I think she's the sweetest girl I've ever known."

"I think that, too."

Even with the way cleared for him, with Luanna's nearness, even with the advice, almost the command of the authorities of the church he'd pledged to serve, Ted couldn't feel that what he'd decided to do was right, was decent.

Luanna stood up and stretched herself, the moonlight sliding over her soft young curves.

"If you want to know what I think, Nellie's the luckiest girl in the whole world. Well, good night. I didn't want Mother to know I'd been crying. That's why I was sitting out here." She looked at him and ran the tip of her tongue over her lips. Slowly she reached for the doorknob.

Ted stood up and caught her hand. "Luanna, would you like to go to Salt Lake with Nellie and me—and be married, too?"

"To—do you mean to you?"

"Yes."

"Teddy! Oh, Teddy!" She threw herself into his arms and drew his face down to her warm, moist lips. "You know I'd like that more than anything else in the world."

For a moment Ted held himself rigid. Then he gave himself to the thrill of holding her, feeling her feverish lips answer his own, flinging into the face of his tortured conscience the Church maxim, "Man is that he might have joy." He had always thought it meant spiritual joy, from prayer and sacrifice and duty. Could it mean this, too? Why should he feel guilty? It was what God, at least God's prophet, said he should do.

Gradually, mingled with the strange confusion of his emotions, came a new feeling of self-importance he had never known before. It was really *something* to be loved by two such girls as Nellie and Luanna!

MINNIE'S FUNERAL WOULD BE in the late afternoon. Nellie felt stunned, unreal, as she moved about the kitchen, mechanically helping with breakfast. Nellie had never before been in the actual presence of either birth or death, and scenes from the long night and the dawn death kept replaying themselves. Minnie had given her life to bring her child into the world. The baby, living and moving, was part of Minnie, part of her life still flowing on in that little body.

As Nellie stood by the cradle, trying to comprehend the mysteries she had witnessed, her heart still bleeding from her last agonizing hour with Ted, it seemed suddenly that the world crumbled. Her head seemed to be whirling like a great wheel, with Minnie, the baby, Ted, Luanna, herself spinning dizzily, about to fly off into space. She felt her knees giving way and saw the floor coming up toward her face.

She vaguely knew that someone lifted her and put her to bed. Mercifully, the wheel stopped spinning.

When Nellie awoke, she couldn't remember what had happened. Something terrible. Someone was dead. Was it Ted? No. It was Minnie, and Ted—

With a rush, memory returned. She closed her eyes. After all, would it be so terrible to die?

She dressed and went to the kitchen where neighbors clustered, talking in hushed tones, urging the family to eat. Nellie drank a glass of milk someone pressed into her hand.

Outside she could see Brother Cameron and Ted talking solemnly with Father, arranging for the funeral, of course. Ted saw her, came in, and kissed her, though the room was full of people. She was glad he said nothing. Confused in her mind were Minnie, lying in the next room with saltpetre cloths on her face, and last night's terrible question, "Has he talked to Luanna yet?"

After a moment, Ted said, "Your father wants me to go with Brother Cameron to see about the coffin and the grave. I'll come back later."

In the doorway, he passed his mother and Luanna. Nellie saw Luanna reach out and touch his hand, saw their eyes meet. She felt faint and made her way into the next room, but Luanna followed her. She put her arms around Nellie's unresisting form and kissed her. "I'm so sorry about Minnie. What can I do to help?"

"I don't know," Nellie murmured, "I'll find Mother."

Luanna put her hand on her arm, stopping her. "Nellie, maybe I shouldn't speak of it now, but I'm so happy. Teddy—Oh, Nellie, I think you're grand!" Her embrace was stifling.

Nellie, unable to speak, searched for her mother, finding her at last in her own room, sitting in the rocker by the window and embroidering fig leaves on a square of green silk. It was part of the ritual clothing in which Minnie would be buried.

"I was making this apron for your temple clothes, Nellie, but there will be time to make another for you. Minnie's was cotton, so I wanted her to have this."

She looked haggard. Nellie bent and kissed her cheek.

"You're so good, Mother. But you should be resting. You look ill. Couldn't someone else finish that? The house is full of people wanting to help."

Nellie felt that she had never really known her mother before the terrible events of the previous night. She felt closer to her than she ever had.

The baby stirred in her cradle across the room. Nellie took her up and, still holding the little form, knelt beside her mother.

"Mother, all last night, I was thinking how wonderful you are, the way you worked with Minnie—your husband's wife. I wondered how you could do it. How you could be so big."

Clara Hagen looked closely at her daughter and put down her sewing. "I love your father, Nellie. I have loved him longer than you have lived. I couldn't save Minnie for him, but I—can be a mother to her baby for him." She sighed, then said briskly, "It's a mercy that Mary Kelly had her baby. She's agreed to nurse Minnie's for a few months."

Could it be, Nellie wondered, that it was not the gospel but the love her father and mother had for each other that made it possible for them to live the kind of life that was theirs?

I love your father!

Could her own love for Ted be as big, as lasting, as self-sacrificing as that?

nine

There were eight in the wedding party that left Monday morning, a week after Minnie's funeral. Nate Jenkins and Mary Ellen Thompson rode in the wagon with Brother Christensen and Maria Dougall. Brother Fischer was with Ted, Nellie, and Luanna. He was returning to Farmington for the remainder of his household goods and farming implements. He had the same carefree disposition as Luanna. In fact, Nellie observed, none of the Fischers were as serious—almost grim—as most of the people she knew. Was it because they had joined the Church more recently, after the tragedies endured by those who crossed the plains? They were well-to-do, too, converted in a colony of German emigrants in Minnesota. Luanna had silk dresses, a down quilt, and many other beautiful things.

Nellie was fond of Brother Fischer and grateful for his inexhaustible store of anecdotes and German folksongs, which kept her from thinking too much about the life ahead.

They made twenty or thirty miles a day, even over the rough roads, cooked their meals over a campfire, and sang, told stories, and played games in the evening. At night, the girls slept in the wagons while the men made their beds on pine or cedar boughs.

They hoped to reach Salt Lake in about ten days, rest for a day, then be married in the Endowment House. Then Ted and Brother Fischer would go to Farmington while Nellie and Luanna shopped frugally in the city and saw the sights. They were looking forward to seeing the progress on the great Salt Lake Temple. They would visit the famed Salt Lake Tabernacle, the huge egg-domed structure with unusual acoustical features that had been built without nails. And there was a new railroad station they had never seen.

They camped on the outskirts of Springville, Nellie's old home town, admiring the steep slopes of the mountains, brilliant with fall colors. Mount Timpanogos and Kolob Peak brought back memories of Nellie's childhood, but the memories seemed to belong to someone else. The mountains looked strange, as if she had dreamed she were looking at them—as if she had dreamed all that had happened since she last saw them. She had been a child then, making hollyhock dolls with Lucy and hunting for bright pebbles in the dry creek bed. There had been no Ted, no longings, doubts, and sacrifices. How could one slip through the doorway between childhood and womanhood without realizing how or when the transition came?

Nellie had suggested they stay with Auntie's sister, but Brother Fischer pointed out that their company was too large to impose on anyone's hospitality. After supper, however, Ted, Luanna, and Nellie walked into town to visit these relatives.

"Why ever didn't you come and stay with us?" Aunt Kate scolded between hugs. "We could have managed."

"Nellie has to stay anyway," declared eleven-year-old Amy. She had always been a welcome tagalong in the girls' games and now was fascinated that Nellie was going to be married and that Luanna was going to be another bride.

Shushing her, Aunt Kate showed them the new wing built on the house, new sheds and barn-lofts, and the thriving orchard, now bearing apples, peaches, and grapes which she urged on the visitors. Afterward they sat in the parlor, exchanging family news, with Aunt Kate frequently chiding them for camping out as if they were strangers.

When they prepared to leave, she loaded her largest bucket with fruit for the rest of the party. Again Amy insisted Nellie stay with them. "I've got lots of things to show you and even a wedding present," she whispered, clinging to Nellie possessively.

"Land sakes, yes," urged Aunt Kate. "We haven't had nearly long enough of a visit."

"If Nellie wants to stay," said Luanna sweetly, "we could call for her in the morning, couldn't we, Teddy?"

Nellie didn't want to stay and had been trying to disentangle Amy. She froze at Luanna's words.

"Why, of course we could—if you want to, Nellie," Ted said slowly, not looking at either girl.

"We'll have to bring the bucket back anyway," Luanna reminded.

"There now. You haven't any excuse at all," Amy challenged triumphantly.

"All right, I'll stay," Nellie said. Her voice sounded far away in her own ears.

"Good night, Nellie," said Luanna promptly. "I'll be lonesome without you. Guess I'll let Pop and Teddy have our bed, and I'll sleep with Mary Ellen and Maria."

"Why don't you stay, too?" Aunt Kate invited.

"Oh, it's almost dark," she laughed. "Teddy would be afraid to walk back alone." She gave Nellie a quick kiss and walked toward the door, Ted following her with the bucket of fruit. As he passed Nellie, his free hand pressed one of hers.

"Good night." His voice sounded strained. He looked into her eyes, and she knew he was trying to reassure her of his love. But that long walk alone with Luanna!

"Come on, Amy," said Nellie abruptly and turned to leave the room. "Let's see your things."

THE WEDDING PARTY REACHED Salt Lake in the middle of the afternoon two days later. Brother Christensen and his party stayed with relatives. Brother Fischer knew a friend who had a boarding house, and they engaged two rooms, divided by a hall. One room, the parlor, contained a folding bed, an organ, a bookcase, a center-table, and a chair. They felt fortunate to find such comfortable quarters for a reasonable price and to be in the center of the city.

From a window, they could see the gray wall around the temple block and the top of the ZCMI store. Several large buildings were under construction, and men were laying track for a street-car system to take the place of horse-drawn carts. To Nellie the city seemed immense and "worldly," though she hardly knew what the word, so commonly used in sermons, actually meant. She had heard about the *Salt Lake Tribune,* a newspaper run by Gentiles bent on persecuting the Saints. Silver and copper mines in the nearby canyons were drawing more Gentiles into Zion. Even though life on the Muddy and in Mount Carmel seemed hard and uneventful, perhaps, after all, it had its blessings.

Ted left the girls to settle into the lodging house and walked down Main Street. The last time he had been to the city had been as a child when his father was still alive. Then it was a large town of low, scattered buildings with straggling gardens in the rear. Now there were rows of fine dwellings with painted fences, flowers, and lawns. He liked the air of enterprise, the sense of bustle and progress.

He eyed the prosperously dressed men, conversing in twos and threes. Had any of them been compelled to choose a way of life other than they might have wished? Had some of them even married two wives simultaneously? The situation seemed grotesque, but at least everything had gone well so far—Nellie in her sweet quietness and Luanna with her sparkling gaiety. It had helped having the others along, too, defusing the intensity that would have surrounded the three of them alone.

He made his way to a jewelry store Brother Fischer had told him about and bought two rings, feeling keenly the unusualness of his errand. As he put the two small boxes in his pocket, he had a strange feeling that he was divided in two. One part was the old Ted, doubting, questioning, loving only Nellie. The second was a new being, determined to fill an obligation he felt binding and finding in that course satisfactions he had not believed could ever be. He wondered if all his life he would feel within him two spirits struggling against each other.

He felt no urge to hurry back to the boarding house. In fact, he dreaded—well, he scarcely knew what. He had made his decision. Why did he have so many qualms? Then a sentence from a cluster of men in intent conversation caught his attention. "Our troubles with polygamy have not even begun."

Ted stopped. It was almost as if he had been challenged.

"What do you mean?" asked a tall man with a long gray beard.

"I mean that the Church is in for persecution as bad as it's ever known. Our enemies are determined to wipe us out, and they'll use plural marriage as their weapon."

"But, Brother Fielding," protested a third, "how can you say that when the Church is growing so fast? Don't you know there were three thousand converts from England alone last year?"

The first speaker retorted promptly, "And don't you know, Brother Kimball, the stories being circulated about those conversions? Lies about our missionaries kidnapping young girls and forcing them into plural marriage. Stories like that are being published right along, not only in foreign papers, but right here in this country. I venture to prophesy that there'll soon be stories in the *Tribune*, that new organ of the devil that's being published right here in our own midst, as bad as any of them."

A fourth man interposed, "Looks to me as if the government's beginning to see the light. There was no challenge when the legislature granted suffrage to our women. What states have that?—let alone territories."

"You're blind not to see through that," Brother Fielding counterattacked.

"They granted suffrage because they thought our women would vote for the anti-polygamy bill. Now they're finding out that Mormon wives accept plural marriage like their husbands. So they'll find something else."

"How do you account for the strong stand of the women against that bill," asked an anemic-looking little man on the edge of the circle. "I've always felt that if Mormon women really had much of a chance they'd be against polygamy."

"Why, they know it's a revelation," Fielding explained, shooting the questioner a sharp glance. "And I imagine if any of them felt like voting against it, the debates between our apostles and those ministers showed them where the finger of the Lord was pointing."

"You're right, brother," the gray-bearded man nodded. "The Lord surely spoke through our brethren in that debate, but the ministers didn't know they were licked. And some of the women didn't know it either, I've heard, until their husbands added a few words." Most of the group chuckled.

"I can see how a lot of the things we believe in would look darned odd to an outsider," ventured a young man who, like Ted, had stopped to listen. He looked at Ted and said in an undertone, "One of the apostles married my best friend's girl last week, for instance." He turned to the group, "Did you read that article in the *Tribune* yesterday about the Deseret coinage and the Deseret alphabet in the fifties? That article made us look like a bunch of half-baked idiots."

"You'd better be careful, young man," exclaimed Brother Fielding, bouncing on his toes. "Don't get off on the wrong foot because your friend lost his girl to a better man. A wrong attitude is the first step toward apostasy."

The young man shrugged and walked away. Ted looked after him, then turned back as the men scoffed at the rumor that the Gentiles planned to arrest President Young for polygamy. He fingered the two boxes in his pocket, his old doubts returning. If only he knew! If only there were some way to be sure he was doing what was right. Perhaps he should not have taken up with Luanna so quickly. He'd known her such a short time. Had it been her pretty face and her obvious liking for him that drew him? If he felt only physical attraction, what would the future bring? But he mustn't think of that now. He had gone too far.

He returned slowly to the boarding house. Luanna met him at the door and threw her arms around him.

"Teddy, we were beginning to worry. You were gone so long. Did you get our rings?"

He felt constrained. He liked Luanna's impulsive caresses, but in the presence of others, particularly Nellie, they embarrassed him. Nellie, sitting by the window, looked up from her book and quickly dropped her eyes again.

Silently, he took a box from his pocket and opened it. Luanna took it eagerly and removed the ring.

"Let me put it on and imagine how it will seem to be married!" She slipped the ring on her third finger and pressed it against her cheek. "It's beautiful—and it makes me feel ... Oh, Teddy, I'm so happy!" She rushed toward Nellie. "See, Nellie—my wedding ring. Where's hers, Teddy?"

Ted felt awkward and confused. He was sure Nellie would rather wait until the wedding ceremony, receiving it from him in association with that sacred rite.

"I'm going to show mine to Mrs. Kreuger," Luanna exclaimed and rushed out the door.

Ted sat on the arm of Nellie's chair. "Do you want to try it on?"

She shook her head. "Maybe I should. Luanna may think it's strange if I don't. But I— It seems that I already have *my* ring." She held up her hand with the little blue ring.

"Nellie, you're sweet." He lifted her face to look into her eyes. He wished he could see into her soul. "Nellie, are you sure—do you think—that we're going to be happy?"

"Of course, dear. You mustn't worry. Everything is—going to be all right."

"God, I hope so!"

They heard Luanna's laugh in the hall. Nellie quickly took the gold band and put it on her finger. Luanna hesitated in the doorway, but Nellie held out her hand toward her.

"They're beautiful, aren't they?"

ten

It was a strange wedding ceremony the next day in the Endowment House. To Nellie everything about it was very impressive. The building itself was beautiful. A spirit of sacredness prevailed everywhere. She thought that Luanna and Mary Ellen, even Maria, looked lovely in their long white temple robes and filmy veils; but Ted and the other grooms did not look natural in the clothes they wore. Luanna had giggled when she caught her first glimpse of them. "Halloween ghosts," she had whispered.

Nellie thought it was an apt comparison, even while she was shocked at the sacrilege. She stifled such thoughts. This was the most wonderful experience of her life. She wanted to make a memory she could cherish forever. She was sure the Spirit of the Lord was hovering near them in this holy place.

As they passed through the different rooms, taking vows and receiving accompanying blessings and promises, she felt such a spiritual uplift that she knew she could bear even the cross of plural marriage. The new spiritual strength reminded her of Christian martyrs through the ages, who had borne torture and death unflinchingly. She could understand how Grandmother Miller could keep on pulling her handcart after Grandfather was gone and how she could leave a dead baby in a shallow grave on the lonely plains. Now she knew she could make any sacrifice that might face her—for the gospel, for Ted.

When they reached the altar room where the sealing ceremony or marriage was performed, Apostle Cannon was waiting to officiate. Brother Christensen and Maria were married first. Nellie thought the blessing, uniting them for time and all eternity, was the most beautiful thing she had ever heard. In this room, the spiritual atmosphere which had pervaded all the rooms seemed to be intensified. She felt close to tears.

Eternity! They were to be joined for time and all eternity. Eternity without Ted would be unthinkable, just as life here and now without him was unthinkable.

The everlasting promise this marriage gave was that if they remained true to the vows they made, true to each other, they would be companions through endless time in a world free from the trials of this life. Everything would be more perfect than it could be here. It was more pleasant, she thought, to contemplate eternity than life on this earth. There would be no more heartaches...

The apostle's voice broke Nellie's train of thought.

"Brother Theodore Chandler, Sister Nellie Hagen, and Sister Luanna Fischer, please take your places at the altar."

Apostle Cannon held out his hand to Ted, beaming approval. He beckoned for the girls to kneel on one side of the low altar, Ted on the other. He was looking at them, wondering, she knew, which was to be first wife. Had Ted thought about it—that even if they were married in the same ceremony, one had to be first? Luanna was older than she, although in most ways she seemed more youthful.

Nellie felt herself growing slightly dizzy with an unexplainable anxiety. Why should it suddenly seem to matter so much which would be named first? They would both be Ted's wives for time and all eternity! The exalted feeling of bravery and self-sacrifice suddenly ebbed. She was all human—all woman desiring her mate. She felt she would die if—

The apostle was speaking. "Who is to be first, Brother Chandler?"

Nellie's heart began to formulate a prayer: "Mother in Heaven—"

But there was not a second of hesitation. "Nellie will be first." Ted's voice was firm and clear.

The apostle placed her hands in Ted's across the altar. She knew tears were falling on the corner of her veil.

THE ROGERS FAMILY, WITH whom Brother Christensen and his party were staying, invited Ted and his brides to spend the wedding evening at their home with a number of other relatives, neighbors, and friends. There were games, music, and refreshments. The women were kind to Nellie and Luanna, but Tom and Jim Rogers and two or three of their young friends about Ted's age almost immediately launched into a series of jokes about wedding nights. Nellie wished they had not come. Luanna laughed and joked back, but Nellie shrank into herself with discomfort. Finally, feeling she could endure no more, she suggested that it was time to go.

"Wait a minute! Wait a minute!" Tom objected. "To prevent a first family quarrel from taking place in a boarding house, let's help this trio make an important decision. Jim, get some straws. The brides draw for the groom's company."

Some of the crowd laughed, but Ted's face flushed. He clenched his fists and took a step toward Tom, but Luanna laughed, "I speak to draw first. Long straw wins!"

She danced to Jim and plucked out a straw.

"She wins," Jim Rogers said, holding up the shorter straw toward Nellie.

"That evens things up," said Luanna. "Nellie is first wife."

Ted whisked them out the door. All three were quiet on their way to the rooming-house. Nellie was sorry that Brother Fischer had already left for Farmington. They needed something to help them break the restraint.

Nellie waited for Ted to speak, but he said nothing. Luanna broke the silence. "We'd better draw cuts to see who *doesn't* sleep in that cupboard!" she exclaimed, pointing to the folding bed.

"It isn't bad," said Ted. "Brother Fischer and I managed very well."

Nellie heard herself saying, "I speak for it. I've wanted to try one ever since I knew there was such a thing. Luanna, you and Ted take the other room." She tried to make her voice light, but it hardly sounded natural.

"Oh, Nellie, I didn't mean anything by what I said down there. But I *am* afraid to sleep alone in a strange place like this." She looked at Ted, a slow smile curving her lips.

Nellie turned away abruptly. "Well, I'm not afraid, and I do want to try this contraption." She began opening the catches to let the bed down. Ted stood silent a moment, then came to help her.

"It's really quite comfortable," he said awkwardly.

Luanna picked up a candle and started for the other room. "I'll bring your suitcase, Nellie, if you really want to sleep here."

Ted walked to the window and stared out miserably. Nellie knew he was unhappy and struggled to find words to make this strange situation as easy as possible. Nothing came to her mind. She concentrated on smoothing the pillows and sheets.

"Here are your things," said Luanna brightly. She came around to Nellie and gave her an impulsive little hug. "Good night, Nellie. You're awfully sweet—and brave."

As she left, Ted crossed the room and took Nellie in his arms, his eyes pleading for understanding.

"It's all right, dear," she whispered. "I know—"

He cut off her words with kisses.

"You know that you are and always will be first!" His voice shook.

He held her close and whispered over and over. "I love you, darling. I love you. You are an angel!"

Another lingering kiss, then he was gone. For a moment, Nellie stood looking down at the bed, then she blew out the lights and groped to the window. She couldn't guess how long she stood there with her burning forehead pressed against the cool glass, unable to think, to feel.

At last she began to weep.

It was not jealousy, she told herself. She was not burning for Ted's physical nearness as she knew Luanna was. Sometimes she even recoiled from the thought of the physical part of marriage. It was the soul of her loved one that she wanted to feel merging into hers. She'd often felt, as they sat together, that their souls went out of their bodies to meet each other and to merge—like two flames, burning brighter and more beautiful than either burned alone.

Would she ever feel like that again? Part of Ted belonged to Luanna now. He already seemed more remote. There were things he couldn't share with her any more. Now, at this very moment, he was in Luanna's arms. Perhaps their souls, too, intertwined ... How could she bear it?

She sank down on the window seat and buried her face in her arms. She felt that she must weep forever.

NELLIE DID NOT KNOW she had been asleep. She had not seen the moon when it rose and flooded the room with light. She had not heard the door open. But Ted was standing over her, looking at her huddled on the window-seat in the moonlight. She was cold. He lifted her in his arms and sat in a rocking chair, holding her as if she were a child. She vaguely remembered the night he asked her about Luanna, when she had wanted to comfort him, as if she were his mother. Now she clung to him as if he were her father and she a forlorn child.

He did not speak, but he kissed her hair, her cheeks, her eyelids. She felt warm tears on her forehead. Their spirits were one once more.

Somehow, it was morning. She heard Luanna's voice and opened her eyes. She was still in Ted's arms.

"Why didn't you wake me up, Teddy? You folks must have been up for hours. Shall I fold the cupboard up? Let's hurry and get some breakfast. I'm starved."

PART 2

Building

Orderville (Long Valley), Utah

In which:

- Luanna and Nellie build a life
- Brigham Young visits Orderville
- Ted leads in the Church and takes another wife
- Nellie struggles to bear children, yet mothers all
- "The Raid" begins
- The United Order is dissolved
- Ted prospers economically
- The family dines with unexpected guests
- Ted serves time
- The family reunites, missing one

eleven

Three years had passed since that strange wedding night. Today, Nellie sat wrapped in blankets, propped with pillows near a window, looking out across the square. Beyond the long frame structure containing the bakery, kitchen, and dining hall stood the section of connected buildings where her mother lived. They were called the shanties, since they had been intended to be only temporary sleeping quarters after the Saints moved from Mount Carmel and established the Order. Above them rose the roof of the tannery, the shoe shop, the bucket factory, the tailoring and cabinet shops, the commissary, and the blacksmith shop. Why hadn't she asked Ted to close the window? The unpleasant smell from the mixture of blue dye and grease scraps boiling in the huge soap kettles near the tailoring shop burned her nostrils.

Girls and women in calico dresses and sunbonnets passed back and forth between the shanties and the kitchen. The breakfast shift was over, and preparations for dinner were about to begin.

It would be good to help again—to stand with the other women peeling potatoes or washing dishes in the huge kitchen, or placing the serving platters, heavy with good food, on the long tables in the dining hall. Her last day, a few weeks earlier, had been hideous with nausea. Then, just as she'd started outside in hopes that the fresher air would keep her from throwing up, she'd heard Libby Backman whisper to Olive Tanner, "Isn't Nellie just pretending that the smell of food makes her sick?"

She had forced herself to come back later, in spite of her weakness, and finish her shift. But she fainted as she was leaving the kitchen, and Mother and Ted had not permitted her to work again.

A wagon had just driven up to the baker's, and men were unloading flour brought from the gristmill up the canyon. Inside, Brother Bigler would be sponging or mixing the salt-rising bread in the great vats, using a hundred and fifty pounds of flour to a mixing. Sometimes he had to bake twice a day. She liked working in the bakery, forming the dough into loaves for the long pans, then tipping the brown, sweet-smelling loaves out to cool.

There were shifts she liked better, such as helping Brother Pulsifer in the tailoring shop, sewing buttons on the calico mother hubbard or linsey-wolsey dresses or the suits made from cloth manufactured in the woolen factory in the canyon north of town. She also liked to help color some of the homemade fabrics, mixing the interesting dyes from copperas, logwood, wild sagebrush, and walnut shells. But best of all was the millinery shop—bleaching, splitting, or braiding long wheat straws, or making flowers to trim the finished hats, using horsehair, feathers, and wool.

She hoped it would not be long until she could be back at work again, doing her share just as before. Before the weeks of patient waiting for her baby to be born. Before the terrible moment, exhausted from the long delivery, when she looked into her mother's weeping but steadfast eyes. Before she took in her arms for the only time, the body of her tiny daughter, born too soon to live.

She looked again toward her mother's door. Father must be worse, or Mother would have come earlier. How serious was the blood poisoning in his injured leg? Would Father die?

The tears gathering in her eyes fell down her cheeks, and she did not try to stop them. She knew she must pull herself together—not go on weeping, weeping. It made Ted so sad when he looked at her. He'd even been afraid, she felt, to make a fuss over Luanna's little one. When Louie had followed him into Nellie's room this morning, he had picked her up with loving gentleness but took her back to Luanna, not wanting—Nellie felt—to make her think of her own loss.

And now Luanna was going to have another baby—and didn't want it, not so soon. It was strange that God let things become so mixed up. She had wanted her little stillborn baby more than any of them could know. She must stop crying or Luanna would hear her.

"Nellie, did you call?" Luanna came to the door, Louie not quite steady on her feet, clinging to her skirts. "Oh, Nellie," Luanna exclaimed, "you mustn't keep grieving like this or you'll never get well and strong. I know it was awful to lose your baby, but—"

Awful. Luanna couldn't know. If it had been her baby— No, she must not let herself think such wicked thoughts. She tried desperately to keep from becoming hysterical.

Luanna came in. "Shall I help you back to bed? Your mother said you mustn't sit up long the first time or two, and you've been here since Ted left, haven't you?"

Nellie choked back her tears. "I'm all right. I'm sorry. You're all so good to me. I wonder if Father is worse. Mother's so late coming over."

"Ted thought he was better last night, but several babies are sick. Maybe your mother is seeing to some of them."

Luanna straightened, a hand on her bulging abdomen. Would it be a boy? That would please Ted.

"Could you eat something now, Nellie?"

"No, but thank you, Luanna. I'll be all right until Mother comes."

"Well, if you need anything, call me. I'm putting Louie down for her nap. She's driving me crazy, underfoot every step I take."

Luanna left and Nellie forced herself to think about Father. What if he should die after working so hard to get the Order going? Brother Cameron and Ted had helped, of course, but Brother Cameron was not a leader, and Ted was inexperienced. Yet he had worked untiringly, overseeing the foremen for the various departments, settling newcomers, visiting the ranches, the dairies, and mills, and keeping the records and accounts. Even Father had been no busier than Ted. Six hundred was a large group to live and work as one family.

The responsibility had been good for Ted. He seemed to thrive on it, with no time for his old questioning, brooding moods. But he also didn't have much time for her and Luanna. She leaned her head back on the pillow, fighting off a wave of loneliness and self-pity. Wasn't Ted's happiness in the Church what she wanted more than anything else? The weeks immediately after their wedding had been so tense. He was so upset. She lived in daily fear that he would say they must leave. What would she have done? She couldn't live without Ted, but how could she have given up the Church and left her parents?

Louie began crying, and Luanna cried, "Oh, I can't stand your everlasting howling! What is it you want? Go to sleep, or I'll—"

Nellie heard the door open and close sharply. Ted's mother crooned, "Oh, you poor baby. Come to Grandma, darling. Your mother doesn't—"

Nellie put her hands over her ears. Emily was interfering again, and Luanna was fighting back. Why had Ted moved his mother into their own building? He should have seen that it was better for her not to be so close to them. His mother spoiled Ted, but she knew how to get her own way. At first, she had chided Nellie for not showing Ted enough affection and praised Luanna. Nellie had felt so jealous, even though she was sure Ted knew it was not her nature to be demonstrative when others were around. And now Emily nagged at Luanna for not taking better care of the baby. Both Nellie and Luanna disliked having Emily around, yet felt guilty for their feelings.

How different married life had been from her old dreams. Was life always like this—a mixture of broken dreams and buried hopes?

The door across the hall slammed as Luanna snatched back Louie and glared at Emily from the other side of the room. Nellie glanced around her own room, pleasant with June sunshine coming through the cheesecloth curtains and falling in bright pools on her log-cabin quilt and rag carpet. The china flower-girl was poised, shining and gay, on her homemade dressing table. The small bookcase contained her greatest treasure, the works of Shakespeare. Grandmother Miller had patiently pulled her handcart, giving precious space to the hand-carved chest containing the books, the wedding dress, and the flower girl. Mother had often told how Grandmother had refused to sell them, even for the food and clothes her children needed, disregarding the insistence of the authorities to use the space for necessities. Nellie could understand that these things *were* necessities, remnants of a past life she had sacrificed for her new beliefs. The books and wedding dress had been Clara's gift to Nellie, understanding how she loved them. Even Ted thought that reading books was a waste of time when there was so much work to be done.

He hadn't said anything recently about the apostates in Mount Carmel—he was probably trying not to worry her. Most of them had refused to join the Order and were constantly annoying the residents of Orderville. A group of the boys tantalized the herd boys, taunted the young people, and rode through the town late at night, swearing and yelling to disturb the old people.

Bishop Hagen hoped to bring these families into the Church and insisted on further patience and tolerance, but Ted was completely disgusted. He felt they needed a sharp lesson. He'd been furious when Brother Cameron confessed that one of these renegade boys had coaxed his seventeen-year-old daughter Jane to go horseback riding. Nellie thought she might be encouraging the boys, just to worry her father.

A step sounded in the hall. "Oh, Mother, I've been watching for you. How's Father?"

Her mother heard the worry in her voice and answered comfortably. "I've been around to see Maria Christensen's baby. Your father's really better today. I'm sure he's going to get well, though he may be a little lame."

"Lame? You mean his leg is permanently injured?"

"I'm afraid so. Blood-poisoning frequently settles in the joints, you know. But with all he's gone through, we must be thankful he's with us." Clara took her daughter's hand. "We didn't let you know how bad he's been."

"And you've had me to take care of, too."

"Auntie's taken all of the responsibility of the house and helps with your father. But he seems to want me there most of the time. That's why I haven't been able to spend more time with you."

Nellie squeezed her mother's hand. She wanted to say, "You're so quiet and calm, Mother. I wish I could be just like you!" But she knew if she spoke, the tears would come again. Would she ever get over being on the verge of tears all the time?

"You look tired. Have you been sitting up long?"

"Ted carried me over here before he went to work. I *am* tired."

Clara helped her back to bed, and Nellie sank into her pillow, closing her eyes for a moment. It felt good—her bed, her worry about Father abated, and her awareness of Mother's quiet movements as she put things in order.

THE DINNER BELL ACROSS the square rang for the first table. The men ate first, the children second, and the women last. Would Ted come in for a moment before dinner? She mustn't expect it. He was too busy. It would be good when she could go to the dining hall and not have her meals brought to her. Good to work again. Then it wouldn't be so hard to keep from brooding about the baby.

"I suppose some of the women who thought I was putting on about being sick think I should be back to work," she murmured.

Her mother answered calmly. "Don't let things like that worry you. There can't help being friction with so many people living together. I'm surprised there isn't more. Oh, I forgot to tell you. Your father got a letter from President Young in the mail this morning. He'll be down next month to hold a conference with us. I remember how exciting it was in Springville when the Church authorities would visit us. And when President Young came, it was like Christmas or Pioneer Day."

She paused, then continued, her voice steady. "I think he should release your father. It's been a terrible responsibility getting things going here. I believe it was because he was rundown that he had this awful infection. He'll never be really back to his full strength, and he shouldn't have so much to worry about."

"But however would we get along? Brother Cameron would never do. Ted says he can't make a decision to save him."

"No, Brother Cameron wouldn't do for bishop, but perhaps ... There are others. No one is indispensable. How's Luanna?"

Nellie had a strange feeling that her mother had broken off because Ted's name was on her lips. The thought excited her.

"She doesn't feel well, not as she did before Louie was born. I wish Ted's mother wouldn't keep at her so. It gets her down."

"Sister Granger shouldn't have moved over here with you folks. Ted should have seen that it wouldn't work. But of course he was so young and she was so insistent." Clara glanced sharply at Nellie. "If he can't see what's happening between his mother and Luanna, maybe you should tell him."

"Me! Oh, I couldn't!"

"Sometimes little things become serious. Like Jane Cameron fooling around with that Kraus boy. Brother Cameron wanted your father to talk to Jane, but I wouldn't stand for it. I told him to talk with Ted. But who can do anything if her parents can't?"

"And she's such a pretty little thing," said Nellie. "Does she love this boy?"

"Brother Cameron thinks she's just defying him. He'd like her to get married, but she's such a harum-scarum, I don't know who would want her." Clara smoothed down her apron and stood up. "He's afraid those Mount Carmel boys'll just get her into trouble to annoy us." She sighed, then added briskly, "Shall I have Lucy bring your dinner? Or will Ted?"

"I'm not hungry," Nellie said. "If Ted can't come, there are things here for Luanna to fix me something."

"Well, you must try to eat, and don't sit up too long at a time for a few more days. Try to sleep now."

Nellie nodded obediently, but her mind flitted from one thing to another. What could she say to Ted about the situation with his mother? Would he think she was just meddling? What if her father were going to be crippled all his life ... How could Mother take it so calmly?

If only she could learn to be calm like that! Think of how Mother was with Auntie. If only she could love Luanna that way. It was disgraceful the way some wives quarreled and gossiped about each other. It made you wonder what the Lord must think about this divine practice of his. Nellie remembered the way both mother and Auntie had been with Minnie, and how sweetly both of them were taking care of baby Minnie. If Luanna should die, could Nellie be a real mother to Louie? She loved her, but, oh, it was her own baby she wanted. She was so little, so dead.

There was Louie crying again. She must have just wakened from her nap. Where was Luanna? Only last week, Louie'd fallen from the bed, and Sister Granger had said terrible things to Luanna. Didn't Ted see?

Ted—if Father resigned, would they make Ted bishop? How could she bear it? New people coming to join the Order all the time, more work, more responsibilities, more problems. So little time for her, for things that made life sweet and happy. But it would give him greater opportunities for development, and he had such boundless energy.

Oh, no! Louie *had* fallen. Should she try to go? No, there was Luanna coming—no, Sister Granger.

"That mother of yours doesn't deserve a baby, does she, darling? There, there, Grandma has you. You're not hurt." She came to Nellie's door holding Louie. "Do you know where she is, Nellie?"

"I'm sure she was there just a minute ago."

"It's a wicked shame the way she neglects this child. Look at that apron. Why doesn't she keep her clean?"

"I'm sure Luanna doesn't feel well," said Nellie defensively. Her head was starting to hurt.

"She feels well enough to gallivant across the square and gossip with Mary Ellen a couple of times a day. If I didn't have this rheumatism, I'd do the washing myself. It's a disgrace not to keep a baby clean." Louie had stopped crying. "How do you feel, Nellie? I was coming in, but Lizzie Cameron came to tell me how worried she was about Jane and stayed on and on. She wants some steady brother to marry Jane, see if that will settle her down."

Nellie turned her head restlessly on her pillow but asked politely, "How is your rheumatism today?"

"It's worse when I have my hands in water. I washed Ted's clothes yesterday." She chirruped to Louie. "Shall we go see if we can find your mother? If I could find a clean apron for her, I'd take her when I go to dinner. Where can Luanna be so long?"

"Maybe I could tend her here on the bed," offered Nellie.

"Well, just for a few minutes while I look for something to put on her. You can never find anything in there, though." She put Louie down beside Nellie.

Louie reached for Nellie's braids, gurgling cheerfully. Her eyes and forehead looked more like Ted's than she had noticed before. She wondered what kind of eyes her own little girl would have had.

There was Luanna, coming back now. She hoped Sister Granger wouldn't scold. Luanna seldom said anything back, but Nellie was always afraid she was going to—or did she secretly wish she would?

"Well!" began Emily Granger harshly. "If you come home some time and find that baby killed, you'll wish you'd taken care of her. Why didn't you tell me you were going out?"

"She was sound asleep," said Luanna carelessly. "I just went to make some milk toast for Nellie. She's hardly eaten at all today. I guess Ted was too busy to bring her something when he went to dinner."

Nellie decided she *must* talk to Ted. Luanna wasn't at all like her old self—making milk toast for her. She used to be gay. But she shouldn't have left the baby alone.

Ted came in before afternoon work began. "Are you feeling better?" he asked, stopping to kiss her. "I just came from your father. He's a hundred percent better than he was a few days ago."

"I'm so glad. You look tired, darling. Can't you sit and rest a little while?"

"Just for a few minutes. I *am* tired. I've been going like a thrashing machine since daylight. Two loads of supplies from the city and we had to check everything, then set up some new equipment at the gristmill. After that I had to make some changes in the work schedules—always someone dissatisfied with his assignment. Then I had to look over the commissary to get ready for the next order."

"You have too much to do, Ted. Can't you give someone else some of the responsibilities?"

Ted barely paid attention. "And that's not the half. What takes most of the time is going over some changes we want to make with the hard-heads who will be sure to object if I don't sell them on it first. For instance, we want to give everyone a clothing allowance—so much homemade, so much imported. A lot of folks are wasteful because they think they can get what they need whenever they want it. And we'd like to even accounts at the end of each year. We're going to ask that those who may have a larger credit than others for their property and work to let us apply it to those who haven't enough credit to cover their necessities. If we're really interested in living like a united family, it will make for the spirit of unselfishness and unity we need."

"Can't some of the other board members take some of this responsibility?" Nellie persisted.

Ted glanced at her. "They do, but someone still has to see to it all. Brother Cameron's never been one to go ahead, and he's so upset about Jane right now he can't think of anything else." Ted's face sobered. "I'm afraid that the Mount Carmel riffraff are putting their boys up to devilry just to irritate us."

"But don't you think Jane would have the sense and decency to keep away if she's made to understand what it's doing to the whole community?"

"I wasn't thinking about that, but there are other things. We found a strip of fence around our alfalfa field torn out this morning and a bunch of bloated calves in the lucern. We moved up here to be rid of that element, but that hasn't seemed to solve the problem. I'm going down there this afternoon. We can't let them run over us this way. Your father's been too patient and optimistic."

"And here I lie, doing nothing," Nellie sighed.

"Here you lie getting well," Ted squeezed her hand. "That's the most important thing you could be doing and all we want you to be doing now. But the busier the better for me. I like the challenge when there's a little more to do than is possible."

Nellie smiled. "Well, you ought to be very happy right now!"

Ted continued, "And some new families are coming. Men with big families and not much property, probably, or men too lazy to get out and dig for a living. I suppose I shouldn't talk this way, but it's that kind of thing that's likely to do us in."

"It's a shame that Brother Cameron isn't more help to you. You've had too much responsibility," said Nellie with a flash of indignation. "And now with President Young's visit … Mother thinks Father should resign."

"What? That's nonsense. He mustn't even think of such a thing. We'd collapse if Brother Cameron were the bishop. He's a good man but no executive."

He doesn't even think of himself as ever being bishop, Nellie thought contently. It consoled her to observe how obsessed with work he seemed to be. She wrapped both hands around his. Should she try to talk with him about his mother and Luanna? She didn't want to spoil these precious few moments of companionship, yet if she could prevent real trouble …

"It's wonderful to see the color coming back into your cheeks," he said.

"I do wish I were stronger. I'd like to help Luanna with the baby. She doesn't feel well, and … and it worries your mother so that sometimes she says things …

Ted's eyes clouded. "I know Mother seems awfully fussy, but she's getting old. And Luanna *should* be more careful. About a lot of things!"

"But at a time like this, we should all make allowances for her. Maybe if … if you could remind your mother …"

Ted got up frowning. Nellie wished she hadn't spoken. He was worried, perhaps angry. "Luanna's dreadfully careless with Louie. That's what Mother can't stand."

"But if *you* talked to her about it," coaxed Nellie, "she wouldn't mind as much. And if your mother could only see that nagging makes things worse."

Ted reached impatiently for his hat and gave her a brusque kiss. "They ought to have sense enough to understand each other. It seems so petty, the things women make mountains of."

She had never heard him speak like that. It surprised and hurt her. She turned her head toward the window and closed her eyes on a film of tears. She shouldn't have spoken. Or at least she should have waited for a better time. She wanted to be a good wife, and now he thought she was meddling.

There was a swift step on the threshold, and he was bending over her again, whispering, "Darling, forgive me. You're right. I must help Mother and Luanna understand each other. It was sweet of you to show me. You're my guardian angel." He brushed the tears from her cheeks and gave her the kind of kiss she longed for.

She heard Louie toddling in the hall.

"Bring the baby here, Ted. I'd like to amuse her while Luanna lies down for a while."

twelve

The prophet of the Lord was coming! For days they'd been preparing. The meetinghouse was cleaned and decorated, the shops and factories were put in order with exhibits of the work done in each. Now a feast was waiting—delicacies not often provided even for holiday occasions. Wildflowers gave the dining hall a festive look. Nothing had been spared to add to the honor and loyalty the community felt for their great leader.

A delegation, with Ted Chandler at their head and the band playing, had gone up the canyon to meet the president's party. The people were gathered in the square, anxiously waiting.

Ted would be exhausted. He had organized and directed all of the preparations, then spent hours every evening over the reports. The night prior, he had worked until he had fallen asleep over his papers, sitting at Nellie's table so the baby would not disturb him. It was almost three when she woke and saw him with his head on the table. She had called to him and he started to undress without being fully awake. When she gently reminded him that Luanna would be expecting him, he answered that he didn't want to disturb the baby. Had he told Luanna this morning? She was almost sure he hadn't. He had left in such a hurry.

She hoped Luanna would understand. A few months earlier, Ted had stayed with Nellie out of turn, just after Luanna discovered she was pregnant. Even through the closed door, Nellie had heard her shouting that she didn't want another howling baby before the last one was out of diapers, that she never wanted to see him again. Nellie had hard work to persuade Ted that Luanna was only upset because she was sick from the pregnancy.

But now those things were forgotten in the excitement of the day. From her window, where she watched alongside her mother, Nellie could see Mary Ellen sitting with Luanna, who was looking heavy and miserable. Nellie had felt that way too, waiting for the birth of her own baby. But she had wanted that baby so much.

Father was still on crutches and looked ill. How he'd aged!

The Primary children were becoming restless. They were lined up, the girls in white aprons and the boys in light blouses, on both sides of the entrance, carrying flowers gathered the previous evening to throw into the carriage while they sang, "Hail to the prophet."

Nellie wondered who would be with President Young—Amelia, his favorite young wife? Zina, who had spiritual gifts and helped Eliza R. Snow organize the Relief Societies? Which of the other General Authorities?

The square was crowded. It was a holiday from all but absolutely essential work. Behind the children stood the Relief Society women in their best basques and skirts. The men, arranged in priesthood quorums, wore frock coats. Their boots shone from vinegar and soot. The Pioneer Day banners had been refurbished: "Zion's Best Crop," "One for All and All for One."

Outside the entrance to the square, Nellie could see a group of the young apostates from Mount Carmel. They sat on their horses, looking curiously at the waiting crowd. Planning special mischief? Since Ted had threatened to call in the law after the calves had bloated, there had been no further depredations.

Jane Cameron was standing with the Mutual girls, her eyes alternately shifting from the boys to her father, who was talking to Bishop Hagen. Jane could be so attractive with her small brown face and long dark lashes, but when she was mischievous, her pointed face looked impudent. And today, with her furtive eyes, she looked like a little imp. Nellie felt a sudden dislike. It was disgusting that this child should have the power to worry a whole community. Poor Brother Cameron, having to ask Bishop Hagen and even Ted for advice! She resented Ted's time being taken with such trifles.

One of the boys, looking directly at Jane, took off his hat, banged it twice on his thigh, and put it back on again. Jane immediately put her right hand on her left shoulder. It was a conspicuous gesture. Taken together, it looked like a signal, and Brother Cameron started toward her. Nellie felt that Jane had wanted him to see it.

Wouldn't the problem go away if Brother Cameron ignored her? She could remember deliberately making a fuss over Auntie, hoping that Mother would be worried when she was feeling resentful and misunderstood as a young girl. Nellie felt a momentary sympathy. Maybe someday Jane would appreciate her parents and regret her own foolishness.

Suddenly, the sound of fifes and drums became audible. The crowd stirred with expectancy. At last they were coming! Brother Cameron stopped short, then scurried back to stand by Bishop Hagen. Nellie did hope everything would go off well. They had all worked so hard. Ted hoped to take the prophet over the whole operation, even to the dairies and mills up the canyon. He was very proud of the accomplishments of the Order, and Bishop Hagen had been outspoken in his praise of Ted's enormous role in that success. If her father resigned, Ted would surely be asked to take his place, and everyone would bring their problems to him. That would be a hard part of the work, but he would make a fine bishop, better in some ways than Father.

The band was playing "In Our Lovely Deseret." Sister Granger had Louie with her. She adored the little girl almost as much as she did Ted. Would she have loved *Nellie's* baby as much? She knew Ted hoped Luanna's coming baby would be a boy. Oh, she must not permit those jealous, brooding thoughts, but she had so hoped to give him his first son. Surely God might grant her that!

Now Sister Jenkins was standing in front of the Primary children. "Everybody join in the chorus," she called up the line. "We'll begin as soon as the band stops."

Nellie caught a glimpse of Ted, erect on a horse ahead of the wagon. He looked strong and handsome. The band tootled a final flourish, the children's voices rose in "Hail to the Prophet," and her eyes followed Ted as he led the procession to the dining hall. She could see Ted's excitement.

She squeezed her mother's arm. "Doesn't he look wonderful!"

"He's aging."

Nellie started, then realized her mother had been looking at President Young. Chagrined at her lack of respect, she fastened her eyes on the dignified, white-haired man in the long duster, getting out of the black-topped carriage.

The plan was to feed the visitors the carefully prepared dinner, then take them on an inspection trip to show them how this experiment in community living was progressing. Then President Young and the two apostles would meet with the board of directors of the Order, while the visiting sisters met with the women. Then supper, then an evening meeting for the whole community.

At the meal's conclusion, Bishop Hagen announced to the prophet, "Brother Cameron and Brother Chandler will show you about. I've been laid up for some weeks and am not of much use yet. These brethren have been able to carry on very well without me."

Ted hastened to protest. "Not without you, bishop. We only tried to be of a little more help than before your illness."

Brother Cameron deferred completely to Ted in explaining the operations of each part. The older members of the board followed, here or there loyally adding a fuller explanation or unselfishly pointing out Ted's part in planning and managing some specific unit.

President Young listened carefully, asking astute questions, as Ted explained how the work shifts were organized, how supplies were purchased and distributed, how records were maintained of the property each family brought into the Order, how work was credited for each member with allowances for age, illness, refusal to accept certain assignments, and other special situations, and how they handled requests to withdraw from the Order.

President Young was easy to talk to and not intimidating, but something about the great leader thrilled Ted. His mother had known people present at the meeting soon after the martyrdom of the prophet Joseph Smith when the people had beheld the mantle of Joseph fall upon Brigham Young. Ted had always wondered if the people, bereft, frightened, and desperately in need of a leader, had not imagined seeing a change come over Brigham Young. But now he was convinced that there was some strange power in this man, something he had never felt in the presence of others. Ted had gone through periods when he would have given the world for a testimony of such strength. There were still moments when he had to fight against doubt and disbelief. But now, with this uplift of spirit in the presence of President Young, Ted had a half-defined hope that today he might receive the burning, lasting testimony he needed if he was to go on in his promised service.

Ted and Brother Cameron asked many questions and asked for advice on numerous points. At one point, President Young surprised Ted by asking, "Don't you brethren find that this system is, in a way, against the very idea for which it is established? It is to be a way of life in which all the members are equal. They come into the Order giving all their earthly goods. They share equal credit for their work. But at the end of the year, if Brother Cameron has been more careful with the supplies he has drawn than you, he will have a larger credit than you. So there you have the very inequality creeping in that we are hoping to eliminate in the Church. We want to live as brothers, sharing all of God's blessings alike."

Ted was glad that the president had brought this up himself and explained the concept of starting over at the beginning of each year as equals, those with excess credit returning it to the organization.

President Young looked at him gravely. "Are you following that plan now?"

"We have agreed to follow it for a time. I don't see any other way to show that we are unselfish enough to live as we are trying to live. Some have larger families. Some are not physically able to work hard or work every day. We've got to be big enough to be willing and glad to help each other—to be really brothers in the gospel."

"Splendid, my boy, splendid!" exclaimed President Young. "That is just why we are experimenting with this United Order system—to see if we really are big enough to call ourselves 'saints.' Who suggested this last change?"

"Why, we have suggested it in our board meetings several times, and we haven't been—"

Brother Cameron interrupted. "It was Brother Chandler who thought of it, just as he has thought of so many other successful proceedings. If we could all think as clearly and work as hard, and get along with people as well as he does, we might hope to have a successful organization someday."

Ted flushed. He often felt guilty for going ahead, especially as he had done since Bishop Hagen's illness. He sometimes felt almost a contempt for the inefficiency of other members of the board and their willingness to follow instead of lead. Now he felt ashamed that Brother Cameron, instead of resenting his taking the lead, was praising him for it.

"That's a generous, brotherly tribute to you, Brother Chandler," the prophet said. "If you have such unusual abilities, be grateful for them as a gift from God and keep the Spirit of the Lord to guide you that your power for good may increase." He placed his hand on Ted's shoulder in an affectionate, fatherly way that filled Ted with humble gratitude. He felt almost as he had that night in the desert, willing to dedicate his life to something greater than himself and far more important. Perhaps if he rededicated himself now, he could be free of his tormenting doubts.

This sense of almost exaltation stayed with him all afternoon and intensified during the board meeting as he heard apostles pray for their success. For the first time, he felt that perhaps he could obtain a real testimony, one that would carry him through his duties to the sense of dedication and joy he ought to feel.

After the reports were over, the president spoke of the importance of the Order to the whole Church. "It will help us find out if our members are strong and valiant, capable of living the golden rule. Many are, to be sure. You people here are among them. The time has come when the strong must help the weak or our entire system will collapse. I shall have more to say on this topic at our meeting this evening. I am pleased with what you have been able to accomplish and pray that our Heavenly Father will continue to bless you."

Ted hung on every word of his beloved leader. He didn't want to lose the new spirit of zeal and harmony he felt.

AFTER THE VISITORS' TALKS, Bishop Hagen addressed the board, expressing gratitude for their visit and appreciation for the loyal work of each board member. Then he said heavily, "I hope to continue to be of some small service to the Church. But since I am still unable to carry on my duties as bishop of this ward and president of the board of the United Order, I desire to offer my resignation so that someone else may carry the work forward with more vigor."

Although Ted had half-expected this announcement, still it came as a shock. Without letting the truth form fully in his mind, he also realized that he was the logical successor. Confusedly, through his consciousness ran several themes: He was the youngest member of the board. Some of the men, particularly Brother Christensen, would be antagonistic—he had not been friendly since Ted married Luanna. There would be so many problems. And Brother Cameron was thinking of course that Ted would take Bishop Hagen's place. Someone else would have to take minutes—minutes Ted should be writing now.

As he settled to his work again, he could feel many pairs of eyes on him. President Young was speaking again: "You are sure, Brother Hagen, that it will be best for you to resign?"

"Yes, President Young, best for me and for our organization."

Bishop Hagen looked tired, Ted thought. He needed to be relieved of so much responsibility. Perhaps he had been too tolerant in some matters. The situation in Mount Carmel was getting out of hand. The previous day, Ted had been requested to do an interview with Jane Cameron to try and quell her rebelliousness. "Those Mount Carmel boys are just as good as the goodie-goodie Orderville boys who think they're little gods," Jane had flashed at him, her face stubborn and resentful, "and they're a darn lot more fun to be with." And then that tirade against her father: "It's him that's bad—always thinking things about people that he shouldn't." When she had finally collapsed in tears, Ted did not sense contrition, only humiliation that he had had to leave his work. When he'd tried to comfort her for crying, she had been sweet and apologetic, but she wouldn't tell him anything about the boys and she wouldn't promise to stop worrying her parents. Yes, the new bishop would have plenty of problems.

President Young was speaking again. "You, of course, should know best about your own situation, Bishop Hagen, but it seems too bad to change leaders before the system becomes a little better established. What you've done is so promising, and the Church will need the combined strength of all its members to hold the ground it has gained. However, if you feel that this is the proper action, we will release you at the meeting tonight with gratitude and our blessing for the splendid work you have done."

Bishop Hagen nodded firmly, then closed his eyes.

President Young looked over the members of the board. "The problem now is to select someone to take your place. You brethren are better acquainted with your individual qualifications than I am. I should like the board itself to suggest a leader."

There was a short hush, then Brother Christensen cleared his throat. "Brother Cameron has served as first counselor to Bishop Hagen ever since we were organized. He is the logical one to take Bishop Hagen's place."

Brother Cameron immediately protested. "I shall go on helping in every way I can, of course, but I realize better than any of you that I am not fitted to be your bishop. I'm sure that Bishop Hagen's other counselor, Brother Chandler is the right man for this office. The rest of you can't know as well as Bishop Hagen and I know how well Brother Chandler has proved his leadership during our bishop's illness. President Young, I nominate Brother Chandler."

Brother Christensen cleared his throat again. "Of course, I haven't anything against Brother Chandler, but he is extremely young in a situation like this where wisdom and experience are so necessary. If Brother Cameron doesn't feel that he wishes to be considered, I will nominate—"

"Just a minute, please," President Young interrupted, "let us not become too involved here. If Brother Cameron is asking not to be considered, we still have another nomination. We must avoid a situation which might create future friction or unpleasant relationships. Brother Hagen, what is your opinion about the qualifications of Brother Chandler?"

Bishop Hagen smiled. "Perhaps, President Young, I should disqualify myself since Brother Chandler is my son-in-law, but since you have asked,

I must say that he has unusual wisdom for his age. With Brother Cameron he has carried on the work during my illness better, I could say, than it was carried on before my accident. I think you brethren will remember that Ted's youth was called into question when he was made a counselor to the bishop, but Apostle Snow told us that youth was an asset, particularly when accompanied by judgment and enthusiasm. I am sure you all agree that Brother Chandler has both of those qualities. Much of our success, I feel, is largely due to his initiative and energy."

President Young asked if there were any more comments. There was a long pause. Ted glanced up. President Young was looking deliberately around the table. Brother Christensen was staring down at the table without moving. Ted dropped his eyes to the minute book again and recorded in a steady hand as President Young began to speak again, "Then all those in favor of Brother Chandler becoming bishop of Orderville and president of the Board of Directors of the United Order will please manifest it."

Ted wished he could have seen whether Brother Christensen and Brother Jenkins raised their hands, but he kept his eyes on the pen moving over the line.

"At the evening meeting, I shall present Brother Chandler's name before the ward," announced President Young, and the meeting continued.

THE MEETING LASTED UNTIL just before supper, so Ted did not see Nellie until his name was presented at the meeting. He felt the warmth of her love and pride in her smile. His mother, turning to grip Nellie's arm in disbelief and joy, dabbed at her eyes throughout the meeting. Was she thinking of the years of youthful rebellion after his father's death? Though he already felt the weight of his new responsibility, he was glad for his mother's pleasure.

Luanna was not there. What would her reaction be? She already felt he neglected them for the Church and called herself and Nellie "church widows" with a spiteful little laugh.

His own feelings were far from calm. The spiritual uplift he had felt during the day was still with him, but he realized that the new burden would be heavy and often disheartening. That burden intensified during the last part of the meeting.

"The Gentiles are not willing to let us live our lives in peace," President Young said, "even out here. You doubtless know that they are agitating themselves over our revelation on celestial marriage. I myself was arrested some time ago for practicing this principle. Nothing serious came of it because of legal complications, and the plan to defeat us by granting suffrage to our women has failed; but our enemies have not given up. I predict that days of trial and persecution are ahead of us."

A ripple ran over the audience, but he continued: "The subject I wish to stress bears upon it indirectly. I wish to sound a warning against the weakness and lack of zeal within the Church itself. Some of our members lack a living, burning testimony that this is God's Church, restored by Joseph Smith for the salvation of mankind. They lack a testimony strong enough to make them willing to give up all else—even life itself, if need be.

"Because of this laxity, we are encouraging a retrenchment activity throughout the entire Church, a reformation, as it were. We want the weak to face their weakness, to confess it and to repent. Many have done so. We have heard confessions and disclosures that have amazed and alarmed us.

"You are aware of our doctrine of blood atonement—that he who has once received a knowledge of God and the gift of the Holy Ghost but denies it has committed the unpardonable sin, which only his blood can wash away. Otherwise he will be consigned to eternal damnation. A few of our members have confessed to that horrifying sin and are taking steps to assure their salvation in the life to come.

"Others are guilty of less serious sins and are making restitution. I proclaim to you that a great wave of reform must sweep over us and cleanse this chosen people so that the work of the Lord may go forth. To us is given the redemption of the world. Therefore, I say to any of you who are not living your religion fully—Repent! Repudiate your sins, for you are on the road to destruction."

The congregation sat in hushed silence. President Young uttered his concluding words in a tense tone just above a whisper that vibrated through the room. "If any of you under the sound of my voice has a great weakness or is hiding a secret sin, I call upon you to confess, to ask God's forgiveness before it is too late." He paused, then concluded in his normal voice: "I now turn the time over to you for the bearing of testimonies. May the Spirit of the Lord open your hearts and your mouths. Amen."

As expectancy throbbed through the room, Ted felt an urge to stand and confess his lack of that living, burning testimony President Young had said was necessary. Perhaps if he did, this new spiritual consciousness would remain with him, making it possible to do the work expected of him. Perhaps the burning testimony he so desperately needed would come. He couldn't allow these people to think he was something he was not. He had often borne testimonies of gratitude for his family, for the opportunities for growth and advancement that activity in the Church offers, and once had told of his terrifying experience on the desert. But a living, burning testimony? He *must* speak.

He forced himself to his feet. All eyes were on him. He went hot, then cold. His mind was blank. A sense of unworthiness possessed him. Then he heard his voice saying, "My brothers and sisters, you have sustained me as your bishop. But I am one of the weak. I'm not worthy of this high calling. Much of the time I—" He struggled vainly for words. He stood there a moment with bowed head, then sank into his seat. The audience sat breathless. He was ashamed, humiliated, frightened. What was to become of him?

One of the two wives who had accompanied President Young to Orderville arose. "I feel impressed to speak in tongues to your young bishop," she said, her voice calm and sweet.

There was a sudden intake of breath throughout the room. Most of those present had heard of the gift of tongues, but few had seen it exercised.

Sister Young moved to stand beside Ted. She closed her eyes and began to speak in a high-pitched voice, very different from her usual speaking voice. It sounded very strange. Tenseness filled the room. She reached out and touched Ted's forehead with her fingers. A strange sensation ran through him. Was it from weakness or from his sense of shame? Sister Young withdrew her hand, said a few more words, and then stopped. She opened her eyes and moved quietly to her seat. A waiting silence filled the room.

President Young rose. "Does anyone have the interpretation to that blessing?" His voice was calm, assured.

There was a brief pause, then Brother Cameron arose. "I believe I have the interpretation," he said, his voice choked with emotion. He reached toward Ted, palms down.

"Brother Chandler, the Spirit of the Lord is hovering around you. You feel weak because so much is depending on you. But you are endowed with rare gifts, and if you will open your heart, the Holy Ghost will enter and make you strong and valiant. You have a marvelous mission before you. To you will be given the power to touch the souls of the wavering and the wayward and bring them back to repentance and righteousness. Where others fail, you shall have the power to succeed, and your name shall become more and more blessed. During the years ahead, your influence will be a lamp in the darkness, guiding the weak and sinful to the feet of God. Amen."

Brother Cameron sat down. The breathless silence was broken by a sudden hysterical cry. All eyes turned toward the rear as Jane, her face white with terror, struggled from her seat and stumbled to the door.

thirteen

Nearly a month had passed since President Young had ordained Ted bishop of the little community. Nellie had known for days that he was troubled about something. What could it be? The responsibilities of his new office were heavy, but she knew that he was enjoying his work. He liked the feeling of importance and respect, the ability to initiate decisions directly, and the additional weight his requests now had. She wished he would confide in her what this new worry was about.

He was trying to complete the accounts so he could turn them over to the new clerk, and each evening by lamplight Nellie helped him, entering items in a huge ledger as Ted, on the other side of table, dictated items, picking up time-slips for work done, debit memoranda, and miscellaneous records.

His voice paused. She glanced up. Ted sat staring past her at the wall, the almost forgotten brooding look shadowing his eyes. She touched his hand. "What is it, Ted? Why can't you tell me?"

He gripped her fingers almost painfully and dragged his eyes unwillingly to meet hers. "Brother Cameron wants me to marry Jane."

"Oh, no!"

Her pen fell from her fingers, making an ugly splotch on the record book. She had surmised many things, but not this. Dumbly she wrenched her eyes away. Her glance fell on the dresser, the china flower girl in its center. Instantly she recognized her sick, smothering sensation as the queer feeling she had felt when helping Auntie prepare her room for Father and blind Minnie.

Ted came around the table to her, pressing his cheek against hers. "Don't look like that, darling. I've been saying *no* inside myself ever since he talked to me. That's what I told him, but he begged me to think it over." He paused, then went on hurriedly, "It comes from what President Young said about the reformation, the duty of the strong to save the weak. That's what put it into his head."

Nellie tried to speak, but her tongue would not move.

"They haven't told anyone, but when Jane screamed and ran out, her mother caught her on the edge of the mill-race. She was going to drown herself. President Young's warning, the tongues, her father's interpretation—all of it together frightened her. She declared that she was too wicked to live."

"Wicked? Has she …" Nellie avoided Ted's eyes.

"No, not that. She swears to her folks that she doesn't really care for those Mount Carmel scoundrels. Brother Cameron's sure she's kept herself straight but was just trying to worry them and the rest of us. Jane thinks she was possessed of the devil. She started to laugh when Sister Young began to talk in tongues, then something happened inside her and she panicked with guilt and fear. She was sure God was going to strike her dead. It was Jane herself who suggested—the marriage. She says if I'll marry her she can be saved."

"But you—you don't—you can't love her!"

"Of course I can't. That's what I told her father. And she doesn't love me. I told him such a marriage would be a sin. But he kept on about what the prophet said and mentioned many cases where there was not real love—your father's marriage to Minnie, for instance. Such marriages can be good ones. Good can result."

Silence fell between them. Nellie felt empty and sick inside. She knew Ted was as miserable as she. Surely she must be dreaming. The flame flared in the lamp, then subsided as a breeze stirred the papers on the table. Her eyes stared at the rim of soot the gust of wind had left on the lamp chimney she had so carefully cleaned that morning.

"I hate it! It can't be right!" Ted said vehemently.

It made her think of his declaring a similar feeling that moonlit night of their discovery of each other. Even then, when new happiness was awakening within her, she had realized it was born largely of the feeling that his denunciation of polygamy was a way of saying he would never love anyone else. His avowal had seemed a guarantee of future happiness. What had become of those early dreams? First Luanna—but—oh, please God, not this.

Her cheeks were wet. Were the tears hers or his? He swept her up in his arms and took her to the rocking chair where she clung to him and sobbed.

"I had made up my mind not to mention it," Ted's low voice came again. "Not even to you. I would just tell Brother Cameron that it could not be. I should have said 'nothing' when you asked me what was troubling me. I had no right to hurt you with something so absurd."

"But it was my right to know, to try to help," Nellie whispered, wiping her eyes. She went on more resolutely. "You must never think there are things you must keep from me because they would hurt. If we are one, your hurts are mine, too."

Nellie knew how much it meant to Ted to be chosen bishop. President Young's blessings had awed her. Ted would be a leader among leaders, a light unto salvation to many. Could that mean he was to be the light to guide Jane unto salvation? To save a foolish young girl from herself?

She tried to close her mind to the sickening thought. She tried to think only of the joy of being there in Ted's arms, a joy she experienced too seldom now, the satisfaction of knowing that he loved her—loved her so much he had to share this tormenting worry with her because they were *one.*

If he refused to marry Jane, would that be going against President Young? Against God? What a strange pattern of life they were weaving. It must be God's design for them, even the parts she couldn't understand—like Sister Granger, always fretting about such trivial things, like Luanna, indifferent to Louie and resenting her pregnancy, like herself feeling sorry for Luanna and for Ted's inability to understand Luanna's moods. Could it be in God's design that Jane be with Ted? She couldn't bear to think of it—of Ted, every third night, going to that strange, wild little creature, a mere child.

She had been able to understand about Ted and Luanna. Luanna attracted him. She adored him. In some ways, she was a fitter mate for him than herself. But Jane! It was hard enough having Luanna giving him the children *she* seemed unable to bear. And a man's eternal glory depended upon his posterity.

Ted's gentle voice interrupted her jumbled thoughts. "You must stop crying, darling. You'll make yourself sick. I should never have told you. I'll tell him it's impossible. It wouldn't be right for any of us."

"But now that you're bishop," she protested, "I can understand how Brother and Sister Cameron must think that it's your duty, after that meeting. And Jane, too, if she really has repented and wants someone to help her go straight. Of course she could love you—probably does already, or she never would have thought of such a thing. But—oh, Ted, I love you so much. I'm not big enough to be a bishop's wife."

"Nellie, you know I don't want to marry her, and I don't feel I should, in spite of what President Young said—and without thinking of you and Luanna. I've been going through torment for days."

She knew that was true. Her love must stand aside and help her help Ted do whatever his duty was. He must find peace of soul again. She suggested they say no more about it until the next night, until they had fasted and prayed.

THE NEXT NIGHT, NELLIE spoke first. "Ted, it seems unthinkable, but if it means saving a soul … What would happen if you refused to obey the authorities? Would it mean going against God? We wouldn't dare to do that. But why does he give us such hard things to do?"

"Nellie," sighed Ted, "I've fasted, but I couldn't pray. I think I'm afraid. I'm afraid I'll see what I have to do and I can't do it."

At that moment a summons came. Luanna was in labor. Nellie helped her mother, determinedly holding back her own terrible unhappiness at the premature birth of her baby. In a few hours, Ted's son was born.

Nellie held the baby while her mother cared for Luanna. She tried to crowd back the bitterness, the feeling that God was not fair. She longed to be holding her own baby. Why couldn't she have given Ted his first son?

Ted came into the room, beaming with the exultant pride all fathers feel at the birth of their first male child.

"He's a husky little fellow, isn't he?" he said, bending over to look more closely. He saw Nellie's tears and gently caressed the hand circling the baby's head. "You know that I wish he could have been yours, darling," he whispered.

WHEN LUANNA'S LITTLE SON was a few weeks old, Ted went to Salt Lake City to marry Jane. The decision had not been easy for him, even after days of fasting and praying, even after Nellie's acceptance. Fasting nearly always brought Ted peace and a renewal of religious fervor. He sometimes wondered if this resulted from reaching the point where he could bend his own will or the effects of physical weakness; but it didn't matter. It was then that he enjoyed his work most and had the assurance that he *was* one of God's chosen. In this case, though, his feelings had not changed. It still felt wrong to marry Jane.

Finally, he talked to Nellie's father. Brother Hagen was sure he should marry the girl. "We are here to carry out the plans of our Father in Heaven, Ted," he counseled. "We must consider his wishes, not our own. When we perform difficult tasks, we grow in strength to perform greater work. Jane's soul is worth saving. If you can save it by marrying her and making her a mother in Israel, it is your duty to do so. Our prophet made it clear that the strong must be willing to help the weak."

"But I'm not strong," Ted protested. "Sometimes I'm not sure of my own feelings of my own faith. Plural marriage sometimes seems … You know how I felt before I married Luanna."

"That is because you were—and still are—young. You have ideas about romantic love. As you sacrifice more for the Church, it will become easier for you to accept the Lord's will when it seems to conflict with your own."

Troubled, Ted had talked again with Nellie and then, for the first time, talked with Luanna. Luanna's immediate reaction was resentment. "Think of Jane, of all girls, being a bishop's wife!" she exclaimed. "You'll have to spend all your time keeping her from running around with those apostates."

"That's hardly fair, Luanna," Ted had reprimanded. "Jane has repented of her foolishness and needs help."

"There's no doubt she'll need plenty of it, and goodness knows you've little time for me and Nellie as it is."

"I know I'm busy, but I try to feel it's work for the Lord. And if—I marry Jane, it will be part of that work."

"Is that the only reason you married me?" Luanna demanded.

Nellie noted Ted's quick flush. Since the baby's birth, Luanna's old lure was back, her eyes flashing, her lips red and full. No longer irritable, she had tried in every way she could to make Ted know that she loved him as much as ever, and their physical bond was working its old magic.

"You know that isn't the only reason I married you. I loved you; and if I marry Jane I shall try to love her. If I do, all of us have a duty to live this principle righteously."

"I don't see how anyone, even the Lord, can be sure that Jane's repentance will last," Luanna said sulkily. "But of course, if you want to marry her, I'll fall in line with Nellie. If she thinks it's all right, we'll try to welcome this child-wife—"

"She isn't a child," Ted remonstrated. "Jane's as old as Nellie was when we were married."

"In years, maybe," muttered Luanna. "But what about sense?"

Ted was miserable as he went to see Jane for the first time, his decision made, but still hoping that somehow it would become impossible. He dreaded going. It seemed unnatural, almost against decency. He had struggled with himself until he could marry her as a religious duty. His talk with Jane as a counselor in the bishopric almost two months earlier had set a definite relationship between them—he was giving her counsel. She was a disobedient child, worrying her parents and her community. She made this second meeting easier than he had dared hope. Evidently her father had given her the impression that the marriage was not in doubt.

"Well, Bishop, you didn't know what you were letting yourself in for, that day you came to scold me, did you?" Her voice was half-jocular and there was still a suggestion of willfulness in the lift of her chin, although the old audacity was gone. Her face looked thinner, her hair pulled back neatly.

"I didn't come to scold you that day. I came to help you, and that's why I'm here today."

How absurd! A bishop coming to woo a wayward child. He was determined there would be no false pretense on his part. He continued very seriously, "Jane, are you sure it would be easier for you to do the things you know are right if—"

"If you married me?" She nodded solemnly. "I'm sure, Bishop. It was awful cheeky for me to even think of it—me marrying a bishop. But I just can't keep the devil out of me without someone to help me. The way you talked to me made me know you can help. Pa and Ma make me worse when they talk to me. They think such horrid things of me. I've been afraid sometimes that I'd get to be as bad as they think I am."

"They don't think you're bad, Jane. They know you're—well, foolish—but they love you and want to help you."

"No," she insisted. "They maybe love me, just because they borned me, but they think I'm bad. Right now they're not sure I haven't done wrong with those boys. That's why they're so anxious for me to get married." She looked at Ted steadily. "Maybe you're not sure either. But it's the truth. I'm as good—that way—as any girl in town."

Ted hadn't admitted even to himself that he had any doubt about her chastity, yet the look in her clear gray eyes gave him a sense of relief that surprised him and made him all the more willing to help her. She seemed such a pathetic little creature, haunted by her own mad impulses and the constant censure of her anxious parents.

"If I hadn't been good that way, I wouldn't want you to marry me. I'm not *that* bad." Her pointed chin quivered and tears filled her eyes.

Ted was all sympathy. She *was* worth saving. She was a lonely, misunderstood child. Now, willingly, he accepted this part of his work for the Lord.

TED'S MOTHER ACCOMPANIED HIM and Jane to Salt Lake City for the marriage. She had received several letters from Brother Granger asking her to come to Farmington, keep house for him, and care for the children of his dead first wife. Ted resented this characteristic selfishness of his stepfather and had tried to persuade her not to go. He had tried before this to persuade her to divorce Granger, but Emily had strong regard for her marriage vows, even though she had admitted the failure of this marriage by coming with Ted from the Muddy Mission, instead of going with Granger. Now she felt it was her duty to go to him.

Ted had finally given up, suggesting that she try it a while and then, if it didn't work out, come back to Orderville. He was genuinely fond of his mother. Her devotion to him and pride in what he was doing buoyed him up.

Luanna was openly glad when her mother-in-law decided to go. Nellie, though fond of Sister Granger, knew her going would lessen some of the complications of their family life.

fourteen

When Ted returned with Jane after their marriage, he went at his Church work with renewed vigor. Because many new members had joined the Order, more dwellings had to be provided, additional acreage put under cultivation, and larger shops and storerooms constructed.

The Order started a school for the children, with adult instruction provided at night. Reading circles studied Church works, history, and politics. Nellie led a group in reading Shakespeare's plays. Occasionally lecturers came from the north—Salt Lake City or from the Church academy at Provo. As the Order ran more smoothly, social activities like dances, concerts, home dramatics, and holiday celebrations added interest to life.

The manner of living brought people close. They all shared common interests, common goals. Their assurance that they were working out a plan of their Father in Heaven, to be adopted later by the entire Church, gave them zest for their labors and a sense of great satisfaction.

Ted realized that their zeal lessened the natural difficulties of communal life. Their earnestness and sense of dedication kept up his spirits. Yet despite the best efforts of the majority, discouragements also came and problems also arose. Periodically Ted suffered from the old tormenting feelings of doubt in the divinity of some principles of the gospel. He longed for an *abiding* assurance that he was living his life in accordance with God's will.

As he had foreseen, more and more families with small means and little ambition joined the community, gradually reducing the standard of living. What, for instance, was he to do with a man like Brother Kinnair? He had arrived with two wives, eleven children, and nothing else. No matter what job he was assigned to do, he began to suffer various aches and pains and had to stop working for days, in spite of the fact that there was nothing physically wrong with him that Ted could see. Then others had to support his large family.

Additionally, the General Authorities had encouraged a large number of widows with families to "go and help build up the Order." Ted wondered why they couldn't see how such members would weaken the organization.

Then there were the inevitable frictions of living and working together. Brother Black and Brother Jensen decided to marry each others' daughters as plural wives, but young Howard Firth was in love with Nancy Black and asked Ted to intervene. Ted felt that the plan of these older men was outrageous and had great sympathy for Howard. Yet when he told the brethren they were abusing the principle of plural marriage, they asked Ted if he had been thinking only of the spiritual aspects of celestial marriage when he had taken his wives. The interview had ended in bitter recriminations.

Brother Jensen withdrew from the Order, demanding payment for flour and other commodities he had turned in to the Order at the price they were worth when he came, though it had dropped on most items during the time he had been there. He also demanded another horse to replace one that had died soon after he came.

Ted did have one satisfaction over this unpleasant affair: Howard's gratitude, and his and Nancy's happiness.

Another disturbing experience, yet one which made him feel that perhaps God was directing him, was the episode of young George Dangerfield. George had never fit in well with the community. Ted felt sorry for him, remembering how it felt to be an outcast at the Muddy Mission. He tried to help George adjust. Then he learned that the boy was sneaking off to play cards with the Mount Carmel renegades.

One day when Ted was inspecting the building where the wool was stored, he discovered a loosened board at the rear of the storehouse. Investigation showed that a large number of fleeces had been removed. Like a flash, Ted thought of George. He felt that it had been revealed to him. He went directly to George.

"I've come to talk with you about the wool," he said calmly.

George's face whitened. He started to deny it, but his lips were dry and he couldn't look Ted in the face. He stammered, "Who told you?"

"The Lord," Ted answered, and felt that it was true. "Did you take it to pay your gambling debts in Mount Carmel?"

George looked up startled, then nodded his head and drew his sleeve across his face. In a few moments, he begged to know what he could do.

"Come to my office for what money you need," said Ted gently. "You can buy back the wool and replace it tonight. Then you can pay the money back a little at a time from your credit allowance. Nail the board in place." He paused. "George, you can't afford to let anything like this happen again."

The boy's gratitude and a change in his attitude made Ted feel that he had been inspired. But why, he wondered, if God helped him detect a thief, did he leave him to muddle through other problems with such uncertainty? What about the problems in his own household? Above all, he wanted to live the principle of plural marriage as it should be lived.

He recognized that his mother's presence would have made life more difficult for all of them, yet he missed her. He missed her trust in his judgement, her pride, and her love. He knew that Nellie's love, trust, and loyalty were as deep, but she was more restrained. His mother's lavish praise and foolish little attentions to his personal comfort that no one else thought of were indulgences, yet he missed them every day.

Jane had his mother's room and took a child's pleasure in fixing it up. She crocheted tidies for the backs of chairs, made artificial flowers to pin on the curtains, and embroidered covers for the pillows. Yet, like a child, she complained that Nellie and Luanna didn't like her.

Luanna had tried to be friendly with Jane and make her feel like part of the family, but she did it by letting her share the care of the children as she always had with Nellie. Jane resented this attitude and flatly refused to tend the baby one day when Luanna wanted to gather wild currants in the canyon with Mary Ellen Jenkins.

Nellie had heard them fussing and came to smooth things over. "I'll take the children with me," she offered. "I'm going across the square to Mother's. She's helping me sew a dress I'm making over. I know you're busy, Jane, working on your quilt." Nellie had spoken gently, but she was irritated with both women. They were saying such foolish things. What would Ted think if he could hear them?

"Bishop didn't marry me to tend your babies," Jane had said, so loudly Nellie feared those in other parts of the building could hear them. Jane always called Ted "Bishop." Nellie rather liked it. It showed respect.

"No," Luanna had flashed back. "He married you to keep you from going to the devil."

Nellie wished Luanna were not so quick to speak. Often she was sorry afterwards, and she could be so sweet when she wanted to. How terrible it would be if Ted's wives should get the reputation of quarreling. It would hurt and humiliate him almost more than anything she could think of. She must try to prevent it—and try to prevent his finding out. She hoped neither of them would tell him, but she guessed Jane probably would, with the way she had slammed out of the room.

Luanna stood for a moment, looking irritably at the children who were playing on the floor.

"Did you ever see anyone so selfish?" she asked.

"She'll be different when she has children of her own." Then Nellie wished she hadn't said the words. They hurt. Of course Jane would have children, but saying the words had made them real.

"I don't have to go with Mary Ellen," Luanna said. "We just thought it would be nice to make some currant jelly to have in case of sickness."

"It would be nice. Go right along. I love to tend the children."

"You're so good, Nellie. Thanks!" Luanna gave her a little hug and went for her things.

Ted was a devoted father. It sometimes seemed to Nellie that he gave most of his time at home to the children, romping with them before they went to bed. She was ashamed that sometimes, after she'd waited eagerly for his homecoming, the children would swarm over him, leaving her feeling excluded and jealous. Later when they were together, he would wonder why she was serious or sad. But of course, she could never tell him. On one occasion he had surmised something of her feelings and had said reproachfully, "Nellie, you *can't* be jealous of the children?"

He seemed to think that, because they were his, they were also hers. How could he know the depth of her hunger for children of her own? Luanna loved her children but envied Nellie's freedom, her carefree disposition chafing under the responsibilities.

"It's just one endless round of feeding, changing, and washing," she complained.

Nellie said nothing but thought privately that she neglected both the feeding and the washing. Teddy had had stomach upsets several times of late, and Nellie feared it was because Luanna was careless about what he ate. Though he was only ten months old, she often gave him what the others had.

Now, face alight, Luanna paused at the door with her things. "You won't need to bother about feeding the baby till supper time, and I'll be back by then," she said. "Some of the other children were playing with Louie and fed him while they were having play dinner."

"And he eated nearly all the gooseberries and bread and 'lasses," Louie volunteered.

Luanna looked at Nellie guiltily.

"You didn't feed him gooseberries, did you, Louie?" asked Nellie gently.

"Jackie did. He liked to see him pull funny faces."

"I can't think he'd eat many. They're so sour," Luanna said.

"They didn't have more than half a cup for all of them."

But, before Luanna was back, little Teddy was desperately ill. Nellie longed for her mother, but she was delivering a baby in Mount Carmel. Some of the Saints criticized her for going among the apostates, but she declared that she would help any woman, no matter what anybody thought or said.

Auntie came to help. Teddy was in great pain, his stomach distended. He screamed when the warm towels were put on and taken off. Auntie suggested giving him an emetic of lobelia, but he went into convulsions.

Nellie was terrified. She thought he was dying. She sent Jane for Ted and dispatched several boys to the canyon for Luanna. When Ted came, he and some of the brethren encircled Teddy, anointing the baby's head with the consecrated olive oil used in this ordinance. Exercising the power of their priesthood, they petitioned their Father in Heaven to relieve his suffering and restore him to health. Yet, for hours Teddy lay between life and death. At times he would barely relax from one convulsion before stiffening into another. Then he would lie white and exhausted.

Luanna was hysterical. She sobbed and prayed, begging Ted and God to forgive her for her carelessness.

"Don't look like that!" she pleaded with Ted. "You think I've killed him."

Nellie, too, felt she could not bear the tragic look on Ted's face, though it was not a look of accusation. Nellie had not realized fully how much this little son meant to him. She forgot that she had ever felt jealous of the children. She forgot the void in her heart left by her own lost baby. She only prayed that little Teddy would be spared.

Hour after hour, they watched anxiously, putting him into hot, then cold, baths when the convulsions came. He was growing weaker all the time. When morning came, the convulsions were over, but he seemed to be barely alive. When Clara Hagen returned, she hurried to them, made a careful examination and asked many questions, but assured them that the crisis was past. Teddy was exhausted and would require great care for many days, but he would live.

Luanna was so relieved that she completely collapsed. Jane helped Nellie put her to bed, while Ted, glad for something to do, went across the square to the kitchen to get fresh eggs for the albumen water Clara prescribed for the baby. Nellie felt as if she had awakened from a terrible nightmare.

She went to her own room and, light-headed from anxiety and sleepless-ness, stood looking out at the approaching dawn. The drab buildings were softened into the peaceful beauty of first light. Within them were sleepers, their toil, strife, struggles, and moments of happiness forgotten. It seemed as if she were part of the dream world. She wished that the morning would not come to sharpen the buildings into ugliness, to waken the sleepers into reality with its struggles and pain.

She heard her door open, then felt Ted's arms about her. "You were mar-velous, darling," he whispered. "You're going to be a better nurse than your mother. Nellie, do you know—you must know—that you saved our baby's life." He held her close. Nellie's heart was pounding with a strange new joy. He had said "*our* baby." Those words and the experience of struggling with death for a precious life made her feel that Ted's little son was hers, almost as much as he was Luanna's.

fifteen

A few months after little Teddy's recovery, in the full heat of August, word reached Orderville of the death of President Young. Ted received a letter from the General Authorities with the announcement, followed in a few days by the *Deseret News* with a full account of the death and the impressive funeral services. As suggested in the letter, Ted and his counselors made arrangements for a memorial service at which Brigham Young's life was reviewed and honored.

Ted felt that no other community in the entire Church would feel the loss of Brigham Young as much as Orderville, and that few individuals would feel a greater personal bereavement than he.

Although Joseph Smith had been given the revelation about the United Order, it was Brigham Young who had carried it out. When Ted was discouraged, he had always found solace in the thought that he and his brothers and sisters were co-partners with this great man of God in a plan for man's temporal and spiritual salvation. He had never forgotten the inspiration of his direct contact with the prophet when he had been called as bishop. Something in the man's personality had given him an assurance he had lacked, but for which he had longed and striven. He wondered now, in the stark realization of this great loss, how much of his testimony of the divinity of the gospel plan was dependent upon his feeling of reverence for President Young.

He knew that by nature he was lacking in religious zeal. It was his habit to analyze things in their logical relations. He constantly tried to use his testimony as a check to his natural skepticism. In times of perplexity, the prophet had been the anchor to which he had held. Many times he had concluded a mental and spiritual conflict by saying to himself, "Even though I cannot understand this, it must be right, for the prophet of the Lord stands for it, and I stand for and believe in the prophet."

That feeling had made it possible for him to marry Jane Cameron against his own instincts. And it had sustained him in other difficult situations. It had not been easy for him to excommunicate George Dangerfield, particularly because of his sympathy for the boy and his hope for the lad's reform. It had been harder, too, because some of his associates did not know of all the circumstances and felt Jane's association with the Mount Carmel boys, who had drawn George into their circle, had influenced Ted against them. But when he had discovered, a few months after the wool-stealing escapade, that George had killed a steer and sold the meat to pay gambling debts and that he was joining his undesirable companions in drinking and ridiculing the Church, he knew that if he were true to the trust President Young had placed in him, he must act. In consideration of the boy's parents, he had told no one of the graver offenses—only that there were other things besides drinking and gambling which made the action necessary.

This assurance in President Young's divine insight had also helped him in his stand on various questioned regulations he had adopted in his operation of the Order. More and more, those who worked faithfully and tried in every way to make it a success resisted including those who lowered their standard of living. But Ted felt that he was powerless to prevent this, since they had been instructed to accept all members who wished to join. He didn't wonder at the complaints. The entire group suffered from the condition. The food supply was insufficient and the living quarters greatly overcrowded. He had continued to assure himself that President Young had their welfare at heart and wanted the institution to succeed, that he would soon reward their efforts and sacrifices by sending relief from Church funds, or would encourage more prosperous members to join them. It would not be out of keeping with his policies to call members to the United Order as he had called people to go on the Muddy Mission or out on proselyting missions.

But help had not come, and now the president was gone. What would happen? Would the new president have the same views as Brigham Young? Ted pondered these questions as he sat in the board room after the memorial services. He reread the *Deseret News* and regretted that he could not have been present at the services in the great Tabernacle. He himself had spoken at the services they had just held, and he felt proud of the tribute he had given.

Then he picked up the *Salt Lake Tribune*, which had come in the mail that morning. Knowing that it was antagonistic to the Church, he seldom read it. Now he wanted to see its report of the president's funeral.

To his surprise he found it very fair. The man's outstanding leadership was eulogized. He was referred to as a great empire builder, a great colonizer, a man with a magnetic personality and an indomitable will. As Ted's eyes traveled down the page, he suddenly halted and looked to see if he had read aright. "It is estimated that the Mormon leader's personal property amounts to something like a million dollars in value."

He stared at the words and reread them. It must be a mistake. A vicious lie. It was well-known that the *Tribune* had been unscrupulous in its attacks on the Church. But why would it lie about such a point as that? The article as a whole was fair and generous, and this information was given matter-of-factly, without commentary.

What if that were true? While he and his family, and the other Saints here were spending every ounce of their strength and courage to obey President Young, living on meager rations of potatoes and gravy and bread and molasses...

He got up and paced the floor. *If that were true—but it couldn't be.* With a mighty effort he pushed away the ugly thoughts that were forming in his mind. He would not let himself believe it. If he permitted himself to doubt Brigham Young, he would have no foundation to stand on. He crumpled the paper and left the room.

WHEN TED SENT IN the tithing and ward reports at the end of the year, he wrote a long letter to President John Taylor explaining the serious conditions in the community, emphasizing their desperate need for help. Weeks passed. Then a receipt for the tithing came with a note that a letter would follow.

The physical condition of the ward was not the young bishop's only concern. Even though they were so remote, they were constantly aware that the agitation against polygamy was increasing. The indictments against Brigham Young and other Church leaders earlier had not led to general prosecution, yet no one believed that the nation had grown more accepting of the new practice.

It seemed that each year some new bill was introduced in Congress striking at polygamy. Sensational circulars and books were constantly being published, branding Mormons as lawbreakers, as immoral, a menace to society. Most of the Saints took these signs of impending new persecutions as a matter of course. The early Christians, their own pioneer fathers and mothers—such people had always suffered for their beliefs. If God wanted to test the worthiness of his Latter-day Saints to be given the divine principle of celestial marriage by allowing their enemies to misjudge and abuse them, they, too, could suffer for "conscience's sake."

Ted sometimes felt that some of the brethren took an egotistical pride in their being God's chosen people, different from the rest of the world and possessing the only keys to salvation and eternal life, with the mission of calling the rest of mankind to repent and bring them into the fold. This attitude troubled him. He wished the Church did not have to be so peculiar, so hated.

He dreaded to think what might come of this national determination to stamp out polygamy. What if the Latter-day Saints should be disfranchised, barred from citizenship in their own country, a country to which the pilgrims had come in search of religious freedom? How disturbing it was to be regarded as a criminal, an adulterer, the father of illegitimate children. And the children—

It was more difficult for him to shut such misgivings from his mind now that President Young was gone. He wished he could forget that disturbing statement in the *Tribune* about the president's million-dollar estate. He kept telling himself that it was not true. But—could it be true?

He tried to convince himself that, if it were true, the prophet had some purpose not known to the newspaper man. Perhaps he was preparing to start another unit of the Order, or had some plan to help this one, which would be easier to put in operation if he had personal control of funds. There surely must be some explanation. He would not permit himself to think otherwise.

AS ALWAYS WHEN TROUBLED in his mind or spirit, Ted found his greatest release in hard work. He was now trying desperately to get the organization back on the sound basis it had once had. He tried to inspire, by example as well as by precept, a desire in his associates to follow the golden rule, which was of course the very cornerstone of their community way of living. But results were far from satisfactory.

His family, too, brought him increasing responsibilities. A little over a year after they had come so near to losing his little son, Jane gave birth to twin boys. Nellie attended the birth, cared for the babies, and tried to spare Jane in every possible way. She still prayed for the blessing of motherhood, although she now felt that she shared these children who were Ted's. Was it to be her lot, she wondered, to go through life experiencing only vicariously the joys of motherhood? It would be a heavy cross, for the Church taught that a woman's glory rested in her children. The more children a woman brought into this world, the greater would be her glory in the next, the nearer she would be to God, and the more she would contribute to the godhood of her husband, who might, as reward for his services on this earth, be privileged to create and people a world of his own.

Nellie was troubled, too, about the recurring rumors of coming persecutions against polygamists. How terrible it would be to have Ted arrested and sent to prison. He was so sensitive and proud. His citizenship in a free country meant so much to him.

That she was his first wife had always been a deep, secret satisfaction to her. It was always she who signed legal papers with Ted when such was necessary. If trouble should come, she would be considered by law his only wife. She had a sense of guilt that this meant so much to her; the Church held all wives to be equal in their relationship with their husbands. Yet, she could not deny the spark of joy that burned deep within her. Sometimes she wondered if her childlessness was a punishment for that feeling.

This brewing trouble made her wonder how Ted must feel not to have any child that would be considered a legal heir—to have all his children regarded by law as out of wedlock. She couldn't bring herself to talk to him about it, but sometimes she had a vague, painful feeling that perhaps she should step aside and let him make Luanna his legal wife.

She finally decided to ask her father. Brother Hagen had never fully recovered from his sickness following his accident. Since that time he had walked with a cane and sometimes even went back to his crutches. He had aged pitifully. Mother was almost as old but looked much younger now, something unusual, for most of the first wives she knew looked much older than their husbands. Auntie might almost be taken for Father's daughter. Nellie thought how wonderful her father had been in his own family—so wise, so kind and understanding. If only Ted's family could live as harmoniously! There was much bickering between Luanna and Jane. She herself was often morose and brooding. Ted was frequently quick and impatient. She knew that her father was an unusual man and her mother and Auntie were exceptional women. She always felt that her father had an unseen power that kept them all at their best through their long years together. They lived in a home built upon mutual love and respect. She couldn't remember any serious friction in their relations with each other.

When she put her question about her personal worry, her father disappointed and humbled her. Very quietly he said, "I am surprised, Nellie, that you are concerned about who is Ted's legal wife. Here in Zion we are trying to live by God's laws. They are higher than the laws made by man. This is one thing we must always keep in mind. God's laws do not recognize the distinction that seems to be worrying you. You are Ted's wife. So are the other women he has married. We must remember that plural marriage is our way of life. We must live worthily if it is to be sanctified in the eyes of our Father in Heaven, and it must not be abused and degraded, as I am grieved to say that it is by some individuals who call themselves Saints."

He seemed like a saint of old, Nellie, thought, with his long, white beard and calm, blue eyes and quiet voice. Serenity had always marked his face, but now there seemed something more. Could he even now be seeing beyond the veil separating this life from the life to come? His peace and certainty were reassuring, but she left him with an ache in her heart which made her fear he would not be with them long.

She returned home determined to forget her perplexities and her concern about his health by helping more with the children and trying to establish greater family harmony. She knew this pleased Ted. She knew he depended on her to help keep up his spirits. She liked his assumption that she was as interested in the children as he and their mothers were. He often asked for help with problems concerning them.

"I wish you could see if you can do something about Louie's ugly little fits of temper," he said one day. "She's getting worse all the time, and if we don't correct the habit, it will spoil her personality."

Always he made such requests when they were alone. It helped to keep a precious bond between them. It let her know that he needed her—depended on her—even though she had not been able to give him children. Once he had said, "Jane handles the babies too much, doesn't she? Maybe you can make her realize that they are not playthings."

More and more she accepted these pleas for help and Ted's dependence upon her to keep the wheels of the family relationships running smoothly. Sometimes Luanna and Jane resented her suggestions, but usually they recognized that she was trying to help them and trusted her better judgment. Their children adored her. Louie's baby name for her was "Nennie" and later Ted taught her to say "Aunt Nennie," and that was what all the children came to call her—first Teddy, then the twins, Mark and Matt.

THE SPRING AFTER PRESIDENT Young's death, Ted sent a long report to President Taylor. By now he was utterly discouraged. If they were to continue, something must be done to help them. In part, his message said:

> *Many families are becoming discontented and are*
> *withdrawing from the organization. It is difficult to effect*
> *a satisfactory settlement with them—that is, satisfactory to*
> *them and fair to us. When we return to them the equivalent*
> *of what they turned in to the Order, it leaves us more*
> *destitute, since only those who contributed liberally when*
> *they joined seem to be leaving, while those who brought*
> *little are anxious to stay. New families of the second class*
> *are continuing to join us. We are losing the spirit for which*
> *this community was organized because of the differences of*
> *opinion constantly arising and because of the unsatisfactory*
> *conditions. My counselors and I, and the entire Board of*
> *Directors, feel that some changes, or some help, are absolutely*
> *necessary if we are to go on.*

Ted was shocked at the reply which came almost immediately to this report. It advised the dissolution of the Order. This came as a blow to his faith. It was inconceivable that this inspired plan introduced by President Young should be set aside with no apparent effort on the part of the Church to see it through. Of course what President Taylor wrote might be a valid reason: "Apparently the Saints are not yet ready for such an altruistic way of living." But Ted knew that many had proved themselves ready. The failure was due to those who had come with the wrong spirit, the desire for receiving personal benefits instead of demonstrating that it is possible to live unselfishly for the good of others as well as for self. He felt that, with sympathetic cooperation and financial help from the Church, the project could still succeed.

When he read the president's letter in the sacrament meeting, there were varied reactions. Some were glad. They had come from a sense of duty, of willingness to assist in a plan they believed was inspired. Now they could return to their former homes, duty done. Others were even more disappointed than Ted. They felt that after all their sacrifices and hard work they had not been given a fair deal and that if President Young had lived, this breakup would have been averted.

Most of the board felt the latter and wrote President Taylor, asking if the Church would not give them some financial aid and permit them to try operating on a somewhat different basis, which they felt would avoid the pitfalls that had caused the failure.

The president answered that the Order was officially dissolved as of the date of his former communication. However, he said, if some of them wanted to form a private company, pooling the property they received when the division had been completed, there would be no objection, but that such a project would not be considered in any way a continuation of the United Order or an adjunct to the Church.

DURING THE NEXT SIX months Ted and his association officers, went through the process of dissolving the complicated organization and "settling up" with the various members.

The first change was to discontinue cooking and eating together. Many temporary adjustments had to be made, while stoves and other pieces of household equipment were brought from Salt Lake City. The division of property was made on the basis of what the members had brought into the Order and the amount of credit for work on the ledgers. The land and cattle and sheep were divided as fairly as possible, though there was an inevitable amount of dissatisfaction.

Ted realized that the poor and the shiftless could not be left utterly destitute, as perhaps some of them deserved. This meant that the more deserving received less than they should have had. But in the main there was a spirit of unselfishness and willingness to share—a carry-over from the early idealism the community had enjoyed.

Ted learned much about human nature during this period and received good training in diplomacy. He was grateful to come through with few enemies and with many staunch friends and supporters who wanted him to head a new organization such as President Taylor had mentioned. But he was tired of such responsibilities and declined to join. He felt that his increasing family needed his full time and energy.

When the division was completed, he owned three of the small joined-dwellings of the square, a city lot, ten acres of farming land a short distance up the valley, a few farming implements and a small flock of sheep.

Thus, equipped and with three wives and four children, he was ready to begin a new era.

sixteen

Congress's passage of the Edmunds Act in 1882 made Ted feel that his community and family had survived one blow only to be sent reeling from another. Now plural marriage was a crime for the guilty male, subject not only to fine and imprisonment, but also depriving him of the right to vote or hold office. Since the passage of anti-bigamy laws more than twenty years before, there had been repeated efforts to stop the practice of Mormon polygamy. But clumsy legal machinery and the Civil War had delayed vigorous enforcement. Now this new law indicated that persecution was imminent for offenders.

It was the blow Ted had long dreaded. Fine and imprisonment were not so humiliating as to lose one's citizenship privileges, his right to vote, and the right to hold office. After the discontinuance of the Order, the Church organization had given way to civil law. Most of the civil offices were held by men with more than one wife. Now it was necessary for them to relinquish these offices to others who, in the main, had inferior qualifications. Ted, president of the town council, had been humiliated to be supplanted by Ben Long, who had one wife but who was lacking in business integrity, as the community was well aware. He had been involved in several questionable transactions since the breakup of the Order and had taken advantage of persons who had trusted him.

Though Ted said little, Nellie knew he was going through a severe ordeal. She knew he was still disappointed and puzzled over the manner in which the United Order had been abandoned. Once he had said bitterly, "President Taylor seems to think that the Order was a private little scheme we thought up ourselves—that the Church had nothing to do with it."

She wished she knew how to make it easier for him. She feared his old misgivings about the very fundamentals of the gospel. With his life so involved with the doctrines, especially the doctrine of plural marriage, there could be no peace for him anywhere if he lost his faith. In his earlier periods of doubt and depression, Ted had argued that if the Church were not divine, polygamy was all their enemies said it was. Once he had exclaimed, "If this principle is not of God, we have destroyed the very foundation of moral decency."

Nellie wished, and she knew Ted wished, that he could have the unchanging assurance of her father and of other good men in the community. Some of them had gone through bitter trials in the early days of the Church, but they had kept the faith. Sacrifices and persecutions had made it shine brighter. They could have easily given their lives for the gospel, even as the Prophet Joseph had done.

Ted tried to think of such men more frequently and less of men like his stepfather, Brother Christensen, and Brother Harper, who professed to be a saint but who ... well, if Senator Edmunds judged the Church by such men as Dick Harper, no wonder he had fought so tenaciously for the passage of his bill. If they were all like that, the Republican Party was right in calling polygamy "a cancer" in the body of the United States.

One day while Nellie sat with her father, now bedfast, she said, "I wish you would talk to Ted, Father. He's so terribly upset over this new law. He doesn't say much, but he isn't himself at all. Last night he was walking back and forth under the trees long after midnight."

Her father responded, his voice a reedy whisper, "He shouldn't be so concerned with the laws of men. They change with the years. Only the laws of God are eternal."

But that very night he became worse and died the next day. His death was beautiful, Nellie thought, even though she knew how they would all miss him. He died as serenely as he had lived, slipping away quietly with Mother holding his hand and Auntie on the other side, her arm around little Minnie, who was quietly weeping. It was beautiful how Mother and Auntie comforted each other afterwards, and their tenderness for Minnie was sweet. Nellie wished that the Gentiles persecuting the Mormons, especially that Senator Edmunds, could have known her father. Would they want to send *him* to prison, to brand him as a sinner?

A FEW WEEKS LATER, Nellie discovered that she was pregnant. Her happiness made it easy for her to forget the shadows of approaching persecutions and Ted's dark moods. He tried for her sake to hide his foreboding and was tenderer toward her than he had been during the early period of their marriage when they were expecting their first child.

Nellie resolved to be very careful, to conserve her strength for the child, yet she wondered how the others would get along without her help. Luanna depended on her for so many things, and Jane was expecting another baby within a few months. It was strange how much of the responsibility for these other wives she had assumed.

Louie and Teddy were old enough now to do many things for themselves and to help with little David, Luanna's third child. But they still ran to "Aunt Nennie" for many little services they never thought of expecting from their mother. How could Luanna help being jealous? But if she was, she never revealed it. That was what Nellie admired most in Luanna. She wished she could be as free from jealousy.

Luanna sometimes disagreed with Nellie, often quarreled with Jane, and sometimes sulked at Ted, but she never resented Nellie's closeness to the children and seemed to appreciate her help. After Teddy's serious illness with the gooseberries, she had been more careful about food for the children, but she was careless of many other things. Nellie knew how this irritated Ted. In consequence, she had taken on more and more of the children's personal care. She tried to be tactful and not offend Luanna. She would say, "I'm going to wash out a few things this morning. Haven't you something of the children's I could do?"

At first Luanna would say, "Oh, don't bother. I'll be washing in a few days." She never had regular days for doing things. Nellie would gather up what soiled clothes she found while they talked, then quietly bring them back laundered. Later Luanna would protest, "You shouldn't have done that, Nellie," but Nellie knew she had counted on it. It was not long until Luanna would tell the children, "Go see if Aunt Nennie knows where there's a clean apron or blouse for you to put on." Nellie's reward was seeing the children fresh and clean and feeling Ted's silent understanding and gratitude.

With Jane it was different. Jane had always depended on her as if she were an older sister and seemed so helpless that Nellie naturally took on her responsibilities. Jane loved to make fancy things for her room, but she despised dishwashing and dusting, couldn't make a bed properly, and simply "cobbled up," as she said herself, the holes in any stocking she tried to darn. How could Jane take care of one baby, let alone two? Naturally, when the twins came, Nellie supervised their care.

At first the little fellows had been so much alike they had to tie a string around the wrist of one to tell them apart, but Matt soon outgrew Mark and they were completely unlike in disposition. Because she had given them so much of her time, Nellie almost felt they were hers, but Jane was passionately fond of her babies and very possessive. It grieved her when they would turn to Nellie, so Nellie, as they grew older, had to be more distant to avoid Jane's jealousy.

In her joy of expecting a baby, Nellie thought how wonderful it would be to have a warm little body beside her when she woke in the night, as she often did, lonely with knowing that Ted was holding Luanna or Jane in his arms. Sometimes she wondered if Ted would love her baby a little more than the others because she had waited so long for it—and because it was hers. She was ashamed of the thought, but it gave her a glow to think it might be so. It was the same kind of feeling that she cherished from being the first wife, a feeling she knew was not just right but was very sweet.

Ted was devoted to all the children, but Nellie sometimes thought he was partial to Teddy. That perhaps was natural. Teddy was his first son. Once they had almost lost him. At times she wondered if he would love her own baby as much. Ted's simple words, "our son," had somehow melted her jealousy and she felt that Teddy, more than the others, belonged to her. She had saved him for Ted. That had given her a share.

She worried that Ted would think her shallow and foolish to care so much about being the first wife and wishing Teddy could have been hers. Being first wife meant nothing in most polygamous families. Many were pitied. There was Martha Christensen, the first wife, old and neglected. Brother Christensen had taken two more young wives after Maria, whom he had married on the same trip to the Endowment House as when Ted married Nellie and Luanna, and gave all his attention to the last wife, sluttish young Lizzie. No wonder Martha Christensen had grown old and querulous. And Auntie had written about a terrible case in Springville last winter. A Brother Brixler had found his first wife, the mother of eight children, frozen to death on the roof of the lean-to bedroom where he'd slept with the young wife he'd brought home the day before. Had she not given her permission to marry another wife? Or maybe Sister Brixler had been afraid to let him know how she felt.

It took a lot of courage to say no. She would never forget the night Ted had asked her about marrying Luanna. At first she had felt she was dying. Then she had wished she *could* die. Then his face had told her it was as hard for him as it was for her. She had measured her love and found it deep enough even for that. And when Jane …

But all men were not like Ted. Some had accepted the principle eagerly, lustfully. Their wives needed the pity. There was Sister Parks. Surely she could not have consented willingly to Brother Parks marrying Evie, the little girl they'd befriended when her parents died crossing the plains. She'd not quite been fourteen when Brother Parks married her. He had said it was to give her a home, that they wouldn't live together until she was older. But she had a baby in nine months, and Sister Parks had treated her terribly when it should have been Brother Parks who was punished.

She was thankful that their household was as pleasant as it was. It wasn't ideal, of course, like Father's and Mother's and Auntie's home had been, but at least there was respect and decency. She didn't love Luanna and Jane as Mother and Auntie loved each other, nor as Brother Seeger's wives loved each other. People said his wives thought more of each other than of Brother Seeger and always joined ranks against him in a disagreement. At Father's funeral, Mother and Auntie had sat with little Minnie between them, their hands clasped on the little girl's lap, with the rest of children on either side. No one could have told by the seating arrangements which woman was the mother of any child. She and Lucy had sat together, whispering their gratitude for such a father.

She regretted that her father had been taken before he'd talked with Ted. But everyone missed him. He'd been a friend to everyone in the community, a wise counselor, a stabilizing and needed influence.

Now that the Order was dissolved, each of Father's wives could have had a home by herself, but their chief interest was to make a happy home for little Minnie. Nellie's mother spent much time gone, since she was on call constantly as a midwife and nurse. Auntie took the chief responsibility for keeping their home clean, comfortable, and cheerful, a welcoming place to which the children and grandchildren loved to make frequent visits. She was appointed postmistress, an easy task in that small town, and one she could carry out from the room attached to the living room, but the small, assured income gave all three of them security.

Ted came in one morning to talk with Nellie about the farm. He was building a home on the ten-acre piece of land a short distance up the valley. His plan was to buy more land as he could afford it and build up the place for his family. One of the wives would move to the farm so he would not have to go back and forth each day. Nellie wished she might be the one, but there would be hired men to cook for and all the work of farm chores. She could risk losing her baby. Jane was well and strong, even in her pregnancy, but she wouldn't know how to make butter and tend chickens. Luanna was a careless housekeeper, but she was competent and worked quickly. And, Nellie had to admit it, she would be good company for Ted. He needed her cheerfulness, her lightness, and her never-failing sense of humor. Luanna was just as pretty as when she had married. Nellie wished she could be as pretty—and as spontaneous in showing her love. She was sure Ted knew how deep and self-sacrificing her love was, but he liked Luanna's impulsive caresses.

Ted looked tired. He was still harassed by disgruntled members who felt the final property settlement had not been fair. Criticism hurt him, and he worried about others' discontent. He spent hours trying to make satisfactory adjustments, advising on exchanges of land and property, and writing letters to dispose of machinery and shop equipment to shops and mills throughout the territory. Most of the people still looked upon him as their leader and brought him their troubles.

"The house is almost finished," he told Nellie. "I think we can live in it quite comfortably while the finishing is going on. Luanna hates living out of town, but I suppose she'd better go."

"I wish I could go, Ted."

"We mustn't even consider it. And when we get part of the children up there, you'll have a better chance to rest more. You must stop letting those rascally twins expect so much from you. You'll have to be stern if they get too rough. Jane spoils them."

"We all do," she said. "They won't know how to get along without Teddy, and neither will I."

Ted smiled and patted her hand. "You're a real mother to all of them, Nellie. I hope you know how much that means to me. You are wonderful, and I can't tell you how much I love you."

Her eyes filled. It was sweet to have him tell her. "I wonder if I will love my own baby as much as I do the ones we have now," she murmured.

seventeen

Nellie's little daughter was born in September, when Jane's new daughter was three months old. She felt that she had never known perfect happiness before. Sometimes, immediately after the birth, she would wake up weeping from dreams that this baby was dead, too; then she would look at the cradle beside her bed with her child sleeping sweetly, or hear a soft baby sound, and her heart would stretch almost to bursting with gratitude and peace.

"And I wondered," she would whisper, "if I could love my baby as much as I love the others."

The other children were as dear as ever—Teddy with his serious brown eyes so much like Ted's, Louie with her fiery temper which she was gradually learning to control, the twins with Jane's pointed little chin and whimsical ways, lovable little David, and Jane's beautiful Edna. She loved them all but this baby—her baby—was a part of her very self and part of Ted. To think that she and Ted would go on living after they were dead in this little daughter—living on and on in her children and theirs to the end of time. It was a kind of immortality. Not the kind of immortality the Church describes—a state of perfection in another world where each inhabitant would keep his or her earthly identity, where all imperfections would be erased, and where only love and harmony would prevail as people did pleasant work and progressed forever. She could comprehend the hereditary kind of immortality better; in fact, it had fewer complications. How could even God bring harmony, love, and perfection in a family like Brother Christensen's? It would be wonderful if she could send a little prayer down through the waiting years that only the best of her and Ted would be perpetuated in the procession of their posterity. But why let her mind wander into inexplicables when she could take into her arms the most precious being in all the world? How wonderful to be a mother—a co-partner with God in creating a human being.

One morning a few days after her baby came, Nellie lay dreamily philosophizing, then turned her head at a sound and saw Ted tiptoe in. "I thought you might still be asleep," he said, bending to kiss her. He sat on the side of her bed, eyes shining as they had the night Teddy was born.

"I'm too happy to sleep," she told him.

He turned back the blanket and touched the baby's tiny curled fingers. She loved the tenderness of his mouth when he talked to or about his children.

"What beautiful hair she has—so long and curly."

"It's like Lucy's. I remember how I used to grieve secretly that I wasn't Auntie's child so I could have hair like Lucy's, and now our baby has it."

"Do you remember telling me once about that secret wish, and I told you your hair was prettier, and that I liked the sprinkle of freckles across your nose?"

Their quiet laughter was happy with memories of those first thrilling days.

"Of course I remember. We were in the swing at Overton under the poplars, and the moon was dropping little pieces of silver all over us. I remember all the foolish words you ever said to me."

"Then promise to remember this—which isn't foolish." He bent close, looking deep into her eyes. "If I could give this little girl of ours the most priceless gift in all the world, I would make her just like you."

Nellie knew that was the sweetest compliment a mother ever heard. For a moment, she buried her face against his shoulder, too happy to speak or look at him.

Ted wanted to name the baby Nellie, but she told him she had secretly cherished a name for years for this daughter—Emily Claire, for both their mothers. "It will please them, Ted," she urged, "and it's a pretty name."

"I would still like it to be Nellie, but we won't quarrel."

So the baby was taken to church when she was a month old, given her name, and endowed with a father's blessing.

TED'S CROPS WERE GOOD that fall. He sold part of his wheat for cash and traded his small flock of sheep, drawn from the Order, for more land. From selling the shop and factory equipment, Ted received enough in his share to make their homes comfortable.

Many of the old joined-dwellings had been taken apart and rebuilt on the city lots, laid out and apportioned when the Order was dissolved. Ted had left his section intact. "We'll wait until we can build something really like a home before we make any changes."

Now the problem was whether to build one comfortable home in town for all of them or work toward building three houses. He talked it over with Nellie. "We could build one fairly good house with not too much additional material and could fix it up to be very comfortable. Are we to go on living in one household as your father's folks did or should we have separate homes?"

There was something wistful in his reference to her father, Nellie thought. She knew he had hoped his own family might live as harmoniously as her father's. She also knew that he keenly felt he lacked her father's qualities which had made such harmony possible. He lacked Bishop Hagen's serenity, his unquestioning trust in God, and his never-wavering assurance that Church leaders were inspired men. Besides, Ted often lost his temper, sometimes over trifling matters, and spoke sharply even to those he loved. He was glum when things displeased him. He recognized these weaknesses and constantly tried to overcome them, particularly his tendency to brood over his doubts.

"If Luanna and Jane and I were like Mother and Auntie—and you were more like Father—of course we could go on living together no matter how large the family becomes. But we're not." She hesitated, quite sure that what she would say was against Ted's hopes. "I think, darling, that it will be better for us to have separate homes as soon as we can afford it." She knew there was something selfish in her choice. It had always been hard for her to see Luanna caressing Ted, hard to go to her room alone at night, knowing that Ted was so near with Jane or Luanna. She had hoped to get over these feelings but doubted she ever would. Yet how could she explain this to Ted? She added, "I think it would be easier as the children grow older if each of us had our own home. Too many mothers might be the ruination of the children. I know that it will be more expensive for us to live that way. We must consider that, of course."

"Yes, it will cost a great deal more to keep up three homes than one," Ted said slowly. He looked thoughtfully out of the window. She felt she had let him down.

"I do hope," Ted continued after a pause, "that we will always feel like *one* family. If separating means that the children would feel that they are *half* brothers and sisters—I would hate that." Then he added almost vehemently:

"Nellie, the one thing I want more than anything else, now that we're in this peculiar way of life, is to live it right. If it's not right, it's damnable!"

She had seldom seen him so disturbed, but she understood. It seemed that his faith in the gospel was connected with how his family lived plural marriage.

"We're living it more nearly right than most families," she said reassuringly. "Don't worry too much over little things. In all families, there's bound to be friction. It's human nature for people to look at things differently."

"Of course, but if this is a divinely—" he broke off suddenly, then resumed in a different tone, "You really think it will be better to plan on three homes?"

She nodded. "Yes, when we can afford it. Why not build one home now, making it one of the permanent homes? We can take turns staying on the farm. Then later we can build another; and in time, maybe two other homes here in town."

Later, Ted brought up the question when they were all together. Luanna thought they should live together. This surprised both Ted and Nellie because she and Jane clashed so often.

"It makes the work easier," explained Luanna. "One of us can tend all the children as easily as just our own and we're not so tied down. Besides, the children like being together."

Nellie could feel Ted's eyes upon her. What Luanna said appealed to him. The children did like being together. He hoped they always would. But she kept her face averted. It was hard to go against him, but Luanna was thinking of her own convenience as much as of the children. She liked to be free to visit and attend all the community's socials. Perhaps her own reasons for wanting separate homes was as selfish as Luanna's for wanting to live together. But Ted ought to see that Luanna always shirked her own responsibilities if someone was there to do her tasks, and the only way Jane would ever grow up would be if she had to depend on herself. Now, she only did what she liked.

"If we could each have two or three rooms of our own and fix them up as we like," Jane said, "but still do the cooking and washing together, I think that would be best." Then she added quickly, "But I think we should each take care of our own children."

This little thrust at Luanna was obvious. Nellie noticed Ted's flush. Jane had never liked tending Luanna's children, although she was passionately fond of her own. Nellie wondered why it was so hard for Ted to be decisive in his own family when he could make business decisions quickly and well. He seemed to be waiting for her to speak.

"I think we should help each other all we can and certainly give the children every opportunity to enjoy each other," she began. "But I believe it would be better for each mother to have a home of her own where she can train her children more easily than where there are so many different people giving the children so many different instructions. It's the good of the children that we're all concerned about after all."

"Teddy's always worrying for fear they won't feel like real brothers and sisters," Luanna said. "They surely won't feel that way if they don't live together."

"They'll be more likely to than if they live together and quarrel and fight like ours yesterday." Jane looked belligerently at Luanna. "You know, while you went off with Mary Ellen and left me to look after them all."

Nellie winced. She knew there had been some fuss about the children, but she had not tried to intervene as she usually did. Ted hated these scenes between his wives. Nellie thought this should convince him that they ought not to go on living together, but it was hard for him to give up a pet idea.

Luanna flared up. "The children would be all right if you—"

There was a commotion in the hall. Matt and Mark both wanted the kitten Louie had brought from the farm and she was shrieking that they were pulling it in two. Both mothers rushed from the room. When the twins were pacified, Ted got his hat.

"I suppose that's a clinching argument for separate homes," he smiled. "By the time each of you has a houseful of youngsters, we'd certainly have bedlam if we were always together."

Luanna saw Mary Ellen Jenkins through the window and went out to talk with her. Jane, still petting the twins, turned to Nellie: "I'd like to live with you all right, but I won't be nursemaid for her while she gads around."

Nellie sighed, "Remember, Jane, I have a baby now that I'll want to leave for someone to tend at times."

She looked at the cradle and felt that she would never want to be out of sight of her child.

Jane was still glowering. "I hate the way she acts over Bishop, too, when folks are around. Don't you?"

"But haven't you noticed, Jane, that he likes it? All men like to have a fuss made over them, I suppose."

"But you don't do it," protested Jane. "Strangers would think *she* was his last wife." Jane, still pouting, left the room.

Nellie sat still. Doubtless to many, "last wife" did have the particular connotation of "favorite wife," and probably many considered Luanna to be Ted's favorite wife. But what did it matter to her as long as she had that secret feeling within her, that although Luanna gave him something she herself was incapable of giving, even aside from the fact that her name had been spoken first in their marriage ceremony, she was and always would be, Ted's *first* wife.

She smiled, recalling a story one of the sisters had told in a Relief Society work meeting, about a Brother Somebody up north who prided himself on always treating his two wives just alike. Both wives died before him with a place between their graves for his. At the end of his will, his heirs found a short postscript: "When you bury me, tip me a little toward Tillie."

eighteen

It was a hot afternoon in August 1886, the year when persecutions against the Mormons for the practice of polygamy was reaching its height. Many of the more than one thousand who were found guilty of the offense were still serving terms in the penitentiary in Salt Lake City. Most of the General Authorities of the Church were either there or in hiding—"on the underground" as such living was termed. The United States had determined to stamp out the practice of plural marriage at any cost. All Church property except buildings used for religious purposes had been confiscated by the government. Immigration of converts had been stopped by law. President John Taylor was a fugitive, separated from his families and suffering from the illness that would carry him away the next summer, but still staunch in his belief that plural marriage was a law from God and should be continued in the Church of the Lord. What was to be done regarding this divine law given to Joseph Smith?

"The Raid" as the Mormons called this movement against them, was in full swing. All the polygamists in Orderville who had not been apprehended were in momentary dread that they would be next. Ted Chandler and one of his farmer neighbors were discussing their precarious situation at the very moment that Brig Harper was riding down the valley to warn that the "deps" were coming.

Jim Fergeson, who had come from his farm a few miles south of Ted's, wanted to see him about exchanging harvest help. He said, "I saw by the paper when I was in town this morning that more than a hundred cohabs, as they call us, were arrested in the north last week, and that there will be a push down here right away. It looks like what we've been hearing rumors about for so long is actually happening. As President Young used to say, 'We'll have to suffer for conscience's sake.'"

Nellie watched Ted's face anxiously. It was true they had been expecting something like this for a long time, so long in fact, that the terror they once had was now, in a sense, deadened. Yet, she knew that Ted, even after living in polygamy for fifteen years, still had times when he wondered about its sanctity. She wished he could settle once and for all his tormenting doubts. If only he could feel as most of the other brethren did—absolutely sure that they were living as God wanted them to live! Not that he expressed his doubts as he used to; she sometimes wished that he would talk to relieve himself and give her a better chance to try to reassure him. Often his troubled expression and manner told her plainer than words that he was suffering from his old misgivings.

At Fergeson's words, Ted's eyes swept around his family group scattered on the porch and lawn in front of the farmhouse. They were all present except Luanna and little Kay. Jane had come to the farm a few days before to help cook for the threshers. "At least she thinks she helps," Nellie thought, as she glanced at Jane swaying back and forth in a low rocker near the morning-glory vines screening the end of the porch. She's pregnant again, Nellie had decided that morning—Jane had been craving pickles and complaining that the boys' shoes smelled of manure when they hadn't yet been near the corral. It would have been easier to do for the harvesters and threshers without Jane around. Her children seldom caused trouble at the farm if Jane was not there. But as soon as Jane arrived, three-year-old Johnny commenced to whine and six-year-old Edna to tease. Even the twins, who were usually no trouble at all, behaved badly when their mother was around.

Ted was plainly concerned over what Jim Fergeson was telling him. He was devoted to the children and hated what this new persecution would do to them. As he looked around at them now, his glance seemed to caress each one as it lingered before passing on to the next.

He must be aware, Nellie mused, that Louie was going to be prettier even than Luanna had been. She sat now under the maple tree near the gate, smiling up at Jimmy Fergeson, who had come with his father. Although she was only a little past thirteen, she seemed almost as mature as Luanna had been when she came to Mount Carmel with her family to join the Order. Louie had the same rosy cheeks and full, moist red lips and flashing black eyes. In many ways she was years older than Teddy, instead of barely eleven months. Yet, he, too, was mature for his age—such a serious, manly fellow! Nellie still loved him in a special sort of way. Her eyes followed Ted's to the group playing marbles in the driveway—her young boys (Jerry and Ernest) and Jane's older twins (Mark and Matt).

They were unconscious of the serious conversation between their father and Brother Fergeson and how it concerned their own future. When Ted looked at Emily Claire sitting with a book on the porch steps reading to Luanna's David and little Martha and Jeannie, there seemed to be a special tenderness in his eyes. Nellie smiled to observe that David was as interested as the little girls. He was Emily Claire's slave; and though he was almost eleven now, he preferred listening to her read to playing with his brothers.

She wished she could know what was in Ted's mind as he looked from one to another of those twelve children, most of whom, according to the officers who were searching for him, he had no right to claim.

Jim was elaborating on what he had read in the paper. "It said that Apostle Moore had been taken and that even his young wife, who refused to testify against him, had been imprisoned—and she's about to have a baby. There were others of the leading authorities, too, but I can't think of their names. They'll be in for six months to a year and will have to pay a fine."

Nellie tried to comprehend the seriousness of what she was hearing, but they lived so far away from the rest of the world—even the northern part of the territory—that what was happening in Salt Lake City seemed remote and hardly real. A worried line creased Ted's forehead, but he did not seem particularly excited. She thought he did not fear any immediate danger of arrest. No doubt he was concerned more about how he would be able to provide the kind of life for his family that he hoped to give them. He had done remarkably well in his various business ventures during the seven years since the abandonment of the United Order, but when his family were together, their support did suggest a tremendous job for one man.

Nellie considered Ted a genius to provide so well for them and wished he did not feel that he should do more. No one in the community was better situated than they. The two homes in town were more convenient and comfortable than those of most of their neighbors, for they had planned carefully from the beginning and had not added one makeshift after another as some of the residents had. Luanna's home, the one they had all lived in for a time, was a two-story frame structure with eight rooms and two porches. A rock cellar and a store room were between it and other outbuildings and the barnyard in the middle of the lot. At the rear of the house were a garden and small orchard; in front, flowers and shrubs.

On the other side of the lot, with a lane joining both houses to the outbuildings, was Jane's rambling one-story home. Jane's wild-flower garden was her pride. She loved to go into the hills and bring back plants and unusual rocks for her garden.

The farmhouse was considered Nellie's home, but it was large enough for them all and usually housed others besides her and her own children. She sometimes recalled her arguments for separate homes. She had thought then that there would be times when she and Ted and her children would be in a home such as she had dreamed of years ago when she was very young and the thought of plural marriage in her life was inconceivable. Now they were seldom by themselves—she and her children and their father. And when they were, the children were not contented. Emily Claire missed Luanna's little girls and David, and her boys idolized Jane's twins who were heroes to them because of the things they, being years older, could accomplish. And Nellie discovered that she, too, missed the other children and was happier when the house was full. She was glad they felt as much at home with her as with their mothers.

Often they had talked of what they would do if Ted should be sent to prison, since that dreaded possibility was always hanging over them. Today it seemed less remote than usual. Nellie wondered just what it would mean. Would it break up the family? What would be the effect on the children? Would they have a sense of shame and disgrace? They must try and avoid such a thing. That would be the hardest thing for Ted to bear.

To crowd such thoughts from her mind, Nellie turned her full attention to what Jim was saying.

"Of course it may be months before the officers get down here, but there's no doubt but what they'll be after us. What I've been thinking is that if we can keep out of their way until we get our crops up, it might pay us to give ourselves up this fall—serve our terms, you see, and get it over with during the winter when there isn't much work to do."

"Get it over with?" Ted questioned. "How can it ever be over with? What they mean to do is to break up our families, change our whole lives."

Jim stopped whittling and stared at Ted. "What do you mean?"

Ted did not answer for a moment, then he said, "I wish I knew what anything means. It's all such a muddle. It makes me sick."

"I don't think it will be as serious as you seem to think, Ted. Last week I was talking with Brother Harper, who just got back from Salt Lake, you know. He said he talked with some of the brethren up there. He didn't say anything about it breaking up families like you suggest. He got the idea that all we'll have to do is to pay a fine and spend a little time in jail, then we won't have to worry; we'll be let alone. We'll be done with it."

"Done with it?" Ted repeated.

"He thinks they won't bother us anymore—especially us away down here. What have they done about seeing that us cohabs don't hold civil offices? The town would have gone to the dogs if they'd really enforced that law. If the rest of us had held out like you did and refused to step back into our old responsibilities, where would we be? You should have stayed on the council—though I guess you do still about run it, with everybody coming to you for advice."

Ted said nothing. He didn't like to think of the struggle he had with himself when most of the other elders had decided to go on doing their civic work unofficially, as if there had been no change in the law. He and Melvin Jackman were the only ones who had resigned. He knew that it was true what Jim said about his still running the board. Brother Cameron, who took his place, never made a move without consulting him.

But he hated evasion. He couldn't do as so many of the others did, feel perfectly at peace with themselves, even when they knew they were breaking the law of the land. He tried to get that feeling that the laws of God the Church was obeying were higher than the laws of man. Was he a coward in God's sight?

The suggestion of Fergeson's that they get their harvesting done and then give themselves up appealed to Ted. He began thinking how it might work out with him. The wheat was ready now. Jim and other helpers were coming in the morning to start on the harvesting. The men would cut the grain with their scythes and the boys would bind and shock it. It would not be many years that he would have to exchange help with his neighbors. He and his boys could do it alone. Seven sons! But none of them was old enough to manage the farm if he had to go. Perhaps with Nellie to guide them, and a hired man—but why cross that bridge before he had to?

"Well, Jimmy, if we're to be here by daylight in the morning we'd better go home," Fergeson said throwing down the stick he'd been whittling and putting his knife in his pocket.

"Can't I stay a little longer, Pa?" replied Jimmy. "Louie and I were just going down to the orchard for some apples."

At that moment the sound of hoof beats turned all eyes to the road. A rider came at full speed around the bend near the dugway a few hundred yards north of the house.

"It's Brig Harper," Teddy cried. "I wonder what's the matter. Look at the foam on the horse's bit."

"He's turning in here," Louie exclaimed, looking anxiously at her father.

They had all risen and some of them were moving toward the driveway. The little boys left their marbles and Emily Claire laid down her book. She came to stand by Nellie.

Brig drew in his reins as he neared the gate. His face was grimy with sweat and dirt, but his eyes were wide with excitement.

"Brother Chandler, Pa said to tell you to get out of the way quick. The deps are coming!"

There was general excitement.

"Where?" several voices demanded at once. The younger children gathered close around Nellie and Jane, regarding Brig with startled faces.

"They were at the sawmill. They've arrested Brother Christensen and Brother Lawson."

"How did your father find out?" Ted asked.

"We were there getting a load of lumber. As soon as we saw what was happening, Pa gave me a sign and we slipped behind the mill where our horses were feeding while we were loading. Pa told me to hurry down the valley and warn everybody. He got out of sight in the brush and struck out for the hills. I don't think anybody saw him. I better hurry and warn the other farmers and the men in town."

As Brig turned his horse back to the road he called over his shoulder, "Pa said the women better scatter, too. He'll send Ma to the dairy."

Ted and Jim Fergeson stared at each other for a moment, scarcely realizing that what they had been talking about but a moment ago was actually happening. Ted's eyes swept over the frightened group around him. There was a clamor among the children.

"What's the matter?" "Who's coming?" "What are they going to do?"

"Well, it looks like this is it," Jim said. "It's come sooner than we thought." He looked down the road toward his own home. "What will we do?"

Ted jerked himself into action. "I don't think they'll hurt the women," he said with forced assurance. "Maybe subpoena some of them for witnesses if they can find them. Teddy, you boys hitch the team to the buggy and take Aunt Jane to town. You'd better stay with your folks a few days, Jane. Send word to Luanna to go to her folks, too. Jim, you know Sile's Cave in the hills here. We'd better hit for that. I saw it once when I was hunting a calf and I thought then if—Jane, you mustn't let yourself get so upset. No, they won't hurt the children."

Nellie forced back the feeling of panic that had seized her. Ted's calmness helped. This was a critical moment. She must not lose her head. She must help, not make the situation more difficult.

She put her arm around Jane and turned her toward the door.

"Louie, will you help Aunt Jane get her things ready?" she called. "Ted, I'll get some blankets and food for you to take to the cave. The children had better all stay here, hadn't they?"

Jane was weeping hysterically. She had tried to gather her four children into her arms. But the twins had pulled away to go to help Teddy with the team.

"Yes, by all means keep the children here," Ted answered Nellie as he looked at the hills, then the house.

The children were still clamoring to know what was happening. Nellie tried to reassure them.

"Emily Claire, take the children inside and tell them stories, won't you dear?" Emily Claire started to ask questions, but Nellie said, "In a little while I'll come and explain everything." A look from Ted when she made that statement made her wish that he, too, could accept the explanation she would try to give the children.

Jim Fergeson had sent Jimmy with instructions to his family. He would go with Ted to the cave. "Take your mother to Grandma Kirk's," he had instructed him. "Tell her not to answer any questions if the officers find her. Have her leave the children with Aunt Kate. You come back to the farm and see to things until—I can come."

Soon the buggy stopped in the driveway for Jane. She was still hysterical. She was determined to take the children. Nellie had to be firm.

"Don't you see, Jane, if they should find you and want to take you for a witness, it would be better for Ted if the children were not with you. If they were all here with me—the officers wouldn't know—they might think—they are all mine. We must all help to make it as easy as we can for Ted."

Finally they got Jane into the vehicle. As it disappeared around a bend in the road, Nellie turned back to the house. She was trembling. How could she face the officers of the law—perhaps lie to them? Would she have to lie? Instruct the children to lie? How terrible! She knew how Ted detested dishonesty in any form. She did, too. But if she had to, she could lie for Ted. It wouldn't seem quite the same as lying if she told them she didn't know where he was. Or would it? Well, they were only doing what the Church—what God—wanted them to do. That was the bulwark to which she could always return and regain strength.

She prayed that the officers would not question the children. They were too young to understand. They must not lose their pride in their father—in their certainty that he was the best man in the world. She feared that the officers might come at any moment so decided not to say more than was necessary to the children until she had more time.

She went to her bedroom where Emily Claire had taken them. They gathered close around her, eager for the explanation she had promised.

"I can't talk to you now," she said as calmly as she could, "but I want you to do something for me and for Papa. It is very important. Some strange men may be here any time. They have a lot of wrong ideas about us, especially about Papa. If they ask you where he is, we will just have to tell them that we don't know. And about other things they may ask, too.

Louie came downstairs from where she had been helping Jane with her things. She burst into the room where Nellie was talking to the children. "Isn't it awful—those horrid deps! One thing is sure, I'm never going to marry into polygamy." She burst into angry tears.

Nellie's heart went out to her. She had observed the look in Louie's dark eyes when she had been talking with Jimmy Fergeson. There was something more in this outburst than dread of the present situation. Poor Louie! Was she beginning to have dreams like those she and Ted had once had in the swing under the poplar trees where they had first met?

The children were demanding answers to questions. "Why did Papa and Brother Fergeson go running up the hill?" "Why did Aunt Jane have to go home so quick when she just came?" "Why must we say we don't know about things?" "Where is Sile's Cave?" "Can we go there sometime?"

Nellie was in despair. "Some other time we can answer your questions," she promised frantically, straining her ears for the sound of their dreaded adversaries. She felt that anything she might try to tell the children at this time would only bewilder them more. What could she do to save them from being more upset when the officers arrived?

"Wouldn't you all like to go upstairs and have a party? A quiet party on the sleeping porch? Emily Claire, you know some good guessing games, and you could tell one of the stories—you know the kind you make up—each telling a part in turn. Louie can bring your suppers up there to you. You can play that your bread and milk are party refreshments."

She was urging them toward the stairway as she talked. Louie was still wiping her eyes.

"Wait," Nellie said. "Before you go, let us go back in the bedroom and have our night prayer. Since we won't be having regular supper, we can kneel around my bed instead of the table."

Why hadn't she thought of praying before? Her prayer was short, only a few words, asking for protection, wisdom, and guidance. But it made her feel less alone, a little more calm.

While the children were going upstairs, she looked out of the window toward the road. No one was in sight yet. She strove for her childhood faith that she would have an immediate answer to her prayer. If God had heard it, maybe he would send the officers back.

The children were talking as they went up the stairs. She heard Johnny asking Emily Claire, "What does protect mean?" And Jerry's puzzled, "Why was Mama crying when she was saying the prayer?"

She went into the kitchen where Louie was pouring milk from a pan into a pitcher. She had mugs on a tray and a large plate of homemade bread.

"I can't see why Heavenly Father wants men to have a lot of wives," she said. "Why *do* we have polygamy in our church, Aunt Nennie? I can't understand it."

"There will always be things we can't understand, Louie. We just have to accept what Heavenly Father has revealed and trust him. Will you go to the cellar and get some honey and cheese for the party, dear?" While Louie was gone, Nellie tried to think of something comforting she could say to her. But she couldn't.

The food was ready and Louie was just going to take it up to the children when the sound of wheels was heard in the graveled driveway.

"Oh, Aunt Nennie, it's … it's a black-topped buggy. It's the deps. Aren't you afraid?"

"You go on upstairs, Louie. Try to keep the children quiet and from coming down."

"But … aren't you afraid?"

"Of course not." Nellie found the lie easier than walking to the door to answer an insistent knock.

nineteen

Nellie's emotions were in a tumult. What would the officers say? Of one thing she was sure. She would lie, if necessary, to save Ted—and she hoped God would forgive her.

The imperative knocking was repeated. Her heart pounded, and fear smothered her. Could that story they'd heard when the Raid first started be true—an officer insulting the young daughter of the man he was seeking? She was glad Louie was upstairs.

A third time came the bang of a heavy fist on the door, and she could hear a voice cursing outside. As she reached for the knob, it turned and the door was flung open.

Sudden anger washed away her fear and confusion. What right had anyone to do that? Eyes burning with indignation, she faced the two men confronting her. Why were these men after Ted anyway? What had he ever done to hurt anyone? They wanted to send him to prison for being a good husband, a good father. They wanted to punish him for obeying a law when his obedience had already tortured him almost beyond endurance.

"So you wouldn't answer the door until he got under the bed," the younger, stocky, red-faced man sneered. He pushed past her into the room, his eyes darting quickly about.

The other man, some years older, tall and pale, with kindly eyes and a weary expression, lifted his hat. "We're here to see Mr. Chandler. Is he home?" His voice was polite.

"No, he isn't." Nellie's eyes followed the first speaker who had walked to the middle door and was looking into the living room.

"So you say," he jeered. He pushed open the door to her bedroom. "That doesn't mean anything."

"Sir!" she choked, enraged at his tone and impudent manner. "He is not here!"

"Oh, you don't need to be so indignant," he called back from the bedroom. "I've a hunch that somebody warned you. We've had nothing but lies all down this valley. You can't tell us there wouldn't be a single man on all these farms this time of year. We did get two at the sawmill, but that's not the catch we expected. Liars and adulterers! That's what your religion teaches, isn't it?"

Nellie felt the blood leave her face. For a moment, she thought she was going to faint. The older man stepped quickly forward and pushed a chair toward her.

"That will do, Burrell!" he called out sharply to his companion.

The other man, who had returned to the kitchen, wheeled on him. "You know damn well it's the truth. What did we find at that ranch the other night? A woman standing there in the door, lying like this one, until one of the kids gave us the clue to the potato cellar where the cohab was hiding with one of his concubines. I'm getting damn sick of your attitude, Geary. Where does all your soft politeness get us? It just gives these philandering lawbreakers more time to get away. Come on. Let's begin the search."

He started back across the room.

Nellie couldn't bear to have the children questioned by this insufferable human being. She sprang to her feet, no longer afraid. "What right have you to come into my home and insult me? There should be a law demanding common decency from officers who—"

The young deputy laughed as he strode about, opening closet doors, looking into chests and behind curtains. "So you're stalling to give hubby and his latest mistress a little more time? Are you the latest? What number are you? Two or three—maybe four? You don't look very old. If you're number one, they're the ones we usually meet. I'm surprised that you defend him. He has more than a dozen kids, we're told. How the devil do they support such litters, Geary? Keeps me hustling to take care of one wife and no kids." He opened the cellar door and ran down the steps.

"I'm sorry, madam," Geary apologized. "His recent appointment has gone to his head."

But Nellie scarcely heard. She was outraged at the other man's behavior. There were many things she would like to say, but she was afraid she would cry if she talked.

"What's the matter, Geary?" called the man in the cellar. "Why don't you get busy? What do you think Uncle Sam sent us on this jaunt for? Not to feel sorry for these law-breaking cohabs and their lying wives ..."

Nellie had her anger under sufficient control to ask icily when the man emerged: "Did Uncle Sam send you to break into the homes of decent citizens of this country and insult them?"

Burrell laughed sneeringly. "Decent? Do you hear that, Geary? *Brother* Chandler's concubine thinks I'm insulting her. But you don't think the man you're married to insults you when he sleeps with half a dozen other women."

He started toward the stairway door, but Nellie stepped in front of him, her back to the door. She felt strangely detached from herself, as if she were the very embodiment of hate.

"You! You! You're not fit to touch my husband's shoes. Get out of this house!"

The young deputy was taken aback for a moment by this outburst. Then he laughed again. "Pretty good dramatics. No doubt Geary here would like to applaud. You really look quite pretty when you get on your high horse like that. But we're wasting time. Get away from that door."

Nellie did not move. He glared down at her, then seized her arm and jerked her aside.

"You're using poor tactics, Burrell," Geary objected. "There's no need antagonizing them more than necessary. That doesn't get us anywhere."

"Well, did the polite scheme you used yesterday at that first farm work? It lost our man. You local deps don't have any spirit. Remember, you're only my assistant. I have to make the report." He opened the door.

Rubbing her arm, Nellie looked appealing at Geary.

"You must understand that we do have the legal right to search," he told her.

The children were huddled together at the top of the stairs.

"Come down, children," Nellie said weakly, and they came with a rush, eyeing the strangers with distrust and fear. The smaller ones clung to Nellie's skirts. Edna began to whimper and Jerry hid his face in his arms. David stepped fearlessly between the officers and Nellie, his little clenched fists raised in front of him as if seriously thinking about taking a swing at them. Ted and Luanna worried about him because he liked to play with his sisters and wasn't like the other boys. If they could see him now!

"One, two, three, … six, nine— Lord, how many more?" sneered Burrell. "They said he had more than a dozen."

Louie came down last, her black eyes flashing and cheeks scarlet.

"Hello, Beautiful!" exclaimed Burrell. "You must be the latest Mrs. Chandler. We'll want to ask you some special questions. How old are you? How many of these kids are yours?"

She threw back her head defiantly. "I'll soon be fourteen, and they're all mine," she snapped insolently. "I have three grown sons who will be here soon with their shotguns. It's their job to keep the house clear of filthy rats." Head high, she marched into the kitchen.

Burrell laughed at her spirit, realizing she was only a child.

"You go look through the outbuildings, Geary. I'll search upstairs."

Geary apologized. "I'm sorry, Mrs. Chandler, about how this is being done. Some of us non-Mormons who have lived in the territory for years have been drafted as deputies, but we don't enjoy it. These young officers, sent out fresh from the East, judge you folks from a lot of prejudiced propaganda. Some of them make asses of themselves, as you see."

Nellie looked at him gratefully. "I told you the truth. My husband is not here, so can't you go?"

He hesitated. She knew he was not fully convinced. From the rooms above came the sounds of opening doors and moving furniture.

He lowered his voice. "A good many of your people in the north are giving themselves up, not trying to resist the law. They'll probably get lighter sentences than those who try to evade us."

She felt he was trying to help, yet she, too, was suspicious. Perhaps he was being friendly in an effort to get her to reveal Ted's hiding place. He stepped outside and walked around the house.

The children began a chorus of questions. She tried to calm them. "They'd better not try to hurt you, Aunt Nennie!" David exclaimed. He reminded her of a young rooster, looking for a fight. She smiled at him. Louie stood by the kitchen window, chin lifted, eyes still burning with indignation. Nellie sighed. This experience certainly wouldn't help her feel differently about plural marriage. How could she help Louie understand the spiritual side to living the principle of plural marriage?

They heard Burrell coming down the stairs. Would he question the children? Should she have told them exactly what to say? To deliberately lie? The situation was intolerable from every angle.

Burrell's face was flushed with anger and frustration. "Now look here, woman," he shouted. "We've been sent here in the name of the law for Theodore Chandler. Where is he? In the name of the law, I command you to tell me where he's hiding."

Before she could answer, David flew at the man like a young wildcat, his small fists striking the officer's stomach and sides. "You leave my Aunt Nennie alone, you mean man. You leave her alone!" he shrieked.

Geary appeared at the door. Burrell seized David by the collar and shook him angrily. "You little badger, what do you mean? I ought to choke you."

The children began to scream. Louie ran to the defense of her little brother. Nellie grabbed the man's arm. "Oh, please don't hurt him. He's only a child."

"For God's sake, let the kid go," Geary demanded, striding across the room. "You can't blame him if you look at yourself through his eyes. I say we'd better be moving on before the ones farther down the valley get away. I've looked through all the outbuildings."

"Well, you haven't seen the last of us," Burrell fumed, giving David a shove which sent him sprawling. "And you'd better tell that skunk of a husband, when he comes crawling out of his hole, that the longer he resists, the harder it will go with him when we do catch him." He stalked from the house and in a few moments the black-topped buggy drove away.

THAT WAS THE BEGINNING of a period of constant dread in Orderville. Some of the polygamists moved their families to Mexico where they were freer to live their way of life. Others went to Canada. Most went on the underground. The plural wives took assumed names and went to other communities to live. The men spent much time in hiding and often wore disguises while doing necessary business where they would be known. They were ready at any moment to slip into a hiding place. The Church urged those who could afford it to go on missions to foreign countries.

Ted found the strain terrible. No martyr's exaltation sustained him as it did some of his associates. A letter from the General Authorities asking him to undertake a mission only added to his confusion. To refuse a mission call was evidence of lack of faith—a step toward apostasy. Many accepted calls at great sacrifice to themselves and their families, trusting that the Lord would provide. They regarded being called on a mission as a great honor, a stepping-stone to promotion in the Church. Ted's letter was not a call, yet many members would regard it as such.

Ted brooded over the letter. He felt too disturbed about many things in the Church, and strongly felt that he could not leave his family to care for themselves. To be sure, they wouldn't be as bad off as Brother Draper's wives who had gone into the fields to work. Myra had never been strong and was pregnant when he left. She and the baby both died during the premature birth. Brother Draper looked upon it as an added test; Ted felt it was little short of murder. Brother Draper hadn't even come back.

If he went, Ted meditated, Nellie would have to assume the burden of responsibility. She would accept it willingly—in fact, probably urge him to do it, hoping it would make him more zealous as a Church member.

Ted still slept in Sile's Cave back in the hills. Each evening, his boys would go up the road and brush out the wheel tracks along a narrow place on a dugway. Each morning as soon as it was light, they would examine that part of the road. If no vehicle had passed during the night, one of them would climb a cliff opposite the farm, which also commanded a view of the road in both directions for about a mile. A blast from a horn would tell Ted that the coast was clear and he could come out of hiding to begin his day's work. The sentinel on the cliff would watch all day, signaling with the horn and a red flag if anyone approached.

If wheel tracks showed on the swept roadway, his son would not sound a blast and Ted would remain in the hills until the all-clear sounded. On two occasions, the deps had lain in wait for him during the night, only to give up in exasperation after several hours. On other occasions, the lookout had warned him in time for him to hide in the brush along the creek bed which skirted his land. But he had chafed under the constant strain, determined to give himself up as soon as the crops were harvested.

One afternoon a short time before the letter about a mission came, he had a very narrow escape. The twins, who were on guard that day, became so interested in some squirrels that they did not see the dreaded black-topped buggy until it rounded the bend overlooking the field in which Ted was working. At the signal, Ted looked up, saw the buggy whirling toward him, dropped his scythe, and dashed toward the willows. Shouting at him to stop, the deputies fired at him.

Nellie, watching from the front porch, was petrified with fear. Ted disappeared into the willows with his pursuers only a few steps behind. She waited for what seemed like hours. Her sole comfort was that the shots had stopped. Then the officers emerged from the willows. Ted was not with them. Was he lying wounded or dead in the willows?

She watched the men go into the field and talk to Teddy and to the neighbor boys who were binding and shocking the oats. What would Teddy say? They had always taught him to tell the truth. Now his honesty was in conflict with his need to protect his father. What were these experiences doing to the children? Would their minds and souls be warped?

After a few moments, the men returned to the willows. What had Teddy told them? The suspense was agonizing. At last the two deps emerged from the creek bed upstream. They were wet and bedraggled. They looked toward the house and talked for a few minutes but got into their buggy and drove slowly down the road, glancing frequently over their shoulders.

As soon as they were out of sight, Teddy hurried from the field, his eyes wide with fear. The other children who had watched with Nellie were asking questions.

"Aunt Nennie, did you know they shot at Papa?" Teddy choked. Nellie put her arms around him. He went on brokenly. "They said if they didn't get him this time, they surely would the next time."

She determined to beg Ted to give himself up, if … if … but what if he were dead!

Mark crept down from the cliff, leaving Matt to watch. He was heart-broken. "Aunt Nennie, those men shot at Papa. If—if they killed him, it's our fault. We didn't watch good. They were almost here when we saw them. What … what can we do?"

"We'll go down to that place under the bank where he hides and tell him the officers have gone."

She wondered if she should take the children with her to look for Ted. No, she must not think of it. What if … Oh, no, not that …

The second time she called, Ted answered. Nellie clutched the willows for support, relief overwhelming her. His voice had come from almost under her. In a moment, his face appeared, relieved and smiling, from an overhanging bank where the water had washed out a sort of cave. He was wet and chilled but unhurt.

"They almost stepped on my fingers," he said as he pulled himself up. "When I saw them so close, I knew they'd get me if I couldn't beat them to this place. I hadn't thought of their shooting, or I wouldn't have taken the chance. They were almost up with me when I swung under here. If they hadn't been so excited, they could have heard me breathe as they scrambled back and forth, swearing and cursing."

They were still recovering from this fear when the letter had come, inquiring about a mission. Nellie saw it as a means of escape. And perhaps it was the way Ted could have an experience that would settle his doubts once and for all.

She had been surprised when he tossed the letter aside and commented bitterly, "It's a strange time to be sending out missionaries. Especially us polygamists. Naturally it sets all our enemies the more against us."

"But to a foreign country!" Nellie had protested. "People there wouldn't know, and you'd be safe."

"It isn't safety I need," retorted Ted. "It's peace of mind. How could I go on a mission and leave all of you to look after yourselves? What kind of missionary work could I do when I was worrying all the time and wondering? Nellie, you know how all my old doubts have come upon me. It's hell. Worse than the kind of punishment the law wants to give me. What's this life doing to us? And to these innocent children? They didn't ask to be brought into this kind of life. Sometimes I feel that it's driving me mad."

"Oh, Ted, don't!" begged Nellie. "Don't torture yourself like this. You do know—most of the time anyway."

"I know only one thing right now. I'm not going to evade the officers any longer. I hope I can get things in shape for the winter before they come again. But I can't endure this hiding, lying, letting the children—oh God! It's horrible!"

She did not try to argue. She was so confused and unhappy that she did not know how to help him. If only her father were alive, perhaps he could help them understand better. But no, she was thankful he had escaped the current persecution. He had already suffered for the Church most of his life. Why should God want his chosen people to go through such experiences, every moment filled with dread, and that unbearable sense that they were violating their own integrity and that of their children by these deceptions?

Thank heaven, even the Raid brought a few experiences they could laugh at. The week after Ted's narrow escape, Howard Jenkins stopped at the Chandler farm on his way to town from his father's shearing corrals. "Uncle Lem sure got away with a slick one," he began. "The deps have been after him since the beginning of the Raid. The other day he was right there at the table with the other shearers when the old black-top drove up. Aunt Carrie was there, too, waiting on the table. The deps were standing in the door before any of us knew they were around. One of them asked, 'Is Lemuel Jenkins here?' and before anyone could answer, Uncle Lem said, 'Why, no. He left about a half hour ago. He took a bunch of stray lambs over to Jack Hunter's place. That's where Lem went, wasn't it, boys?' The fellows caught on, and two or three said, 'Yes, that was where Lem went.' Then if Uncle Lem didn't up and ask the deps to sit up and have dinner. I think they guessed from something in the air that they were being fooled. They sat up to the places Ma and Aunt Carrie fixed for them, but their eyes kept searching the faces of the men on both sides of the table. Uncle Lem kept talking and joking as if nothing was the matter, but the rest of us were mighty nervous.

"About in the middle of the meal, if Jake Laws didn't forget himself and say, 'Pass the sorghum, Lem,' and for a minute there was dead silence, the deps waiting for a move they thought would give Uncle Lem away. But I'll be darned—Uncle Lem didn't bat an eye and about a half dozen hands reached for the sorghum jug." Howard was convulsed with his story and the memory of the deps riding toward Hunter's place. But Nellie noticed that Ted listened grim-faced, disturbed at the children's laughter.

But the tragedies outnumbered the comedies. Brother Mariner slipped on a loose rock when he was running along a ravine, fell over a ledge, and was dead when help reached him. Lily Peterson became so frightened when the officers subpoenaed her that she miscarried. The *Deseret News* reported that Martha Harris Moore had her baby in jail because she refused to testify against her husband.

Ted wrote the First Presidency that he could not leave his family then for a mission. He labored over his letter for hours, but in his final version, he gave no reason. Nellie wondered what the Brethren would think. They could not know that his real reason was his lack of faith.

Many of those taken by the officers felt that they were martyrs; their families looked upon them as heroes, suffering for a divine principle. They felt no shame in going to prison. They were given farewell testimonials like departing missionaries, and their wards turned out to see them off and shipped along boxes of delicacies to offset prison fare. Their letters from "the pen" were read in church.

Ted understood this response and was glad that his children would not regard him in the light he often regarded himself. But when they were no longer children—what would they think of him then? Yes, he could pay the fine and spend a year in the territorial penitentiary, but what would be his course after he had served his term? His problems would still remain.

twenty

Ted slapped the reins on the backs of the team and tilted the plow into the curve at the end of the row. He was plowing along the row of potatoes, spilling them out on ground where Teddy, David, and Ernest could pick them up in the buckets they were dragging along. It had been a long day. A faint rustle caught his ear and he glanced toward the bushes lining the creek. Most of the leaves were gone, but even through the bare stems, he could see nothing.

He gripped the plow handles again and felt the horses settle into their stride. He heard the crackle from the bushes again, then a quick thudding sound. Even as he whirled around, a hand was on his shoulder.

"Hold it right there, Chandler," growled a rough voice. The young deputy who was gripping him held a revolver pointed at his heart. Two steps behind him was another deputy also holding a gun. In one hand was a folded paper.

Ted said quietly, "You've got me. I won't resist." Behind him he could hear Teddy drop his bucket and prayed that the boys would do nothing foolish.

The first deputy backed up a couple of steps, still holding the gun on him. "Where's that warrant, Geary?" he growled.

"Right here, Burrell," the other answered, and put it in Burrell's outstretched hand.

"This is a warrant for your arrest for the offense of unlawful cohabitation," the officer began, holding it where Ted could see it. He ran his eye over it quickly. The date jumped out at him. The fifteenth. That was almost a month away.

"All right," he said quietly. "I'll be in Beaver on the fifteenth. Do I have to go to jail, or can I finish this potato harvest?"

Geary reholstered his pistol. "Well, that's up to you, Mr. Chandler," he said. "If you'll give us your word of honor that you won't run and will come to court, we're authorized to release you on your own recognizance."

"You have my word," said Ted. "Shake on it?"

"Not so fast," muttered Burrell. "It's a long way back to Mount Carmel and we're about tuckered in, getting here before sunrise and crawling through the bushes. It's a deal if you'll put us up for the night."

Ted cocked his head on one side and looked at them. They both looked tired. They were dusty, and their pants and boots were muddy from crawling near the creek. Burrell had a long scratch across one cheek, and his shirt was ripped near the shoulder. Geary's hands were crosshatched with scratches and one eye was swollen from an insect bite. They hadn't lurked in the bushes all day because they were filled with malice but because they were obligated—because it was their duty. He'd been doing uncongenial things all his life because of duty. A feeling of brotherhood stirred faintly within him.

"Where's your outfit?" he asked. "You must have hidden it someplace up the canyon or my watchers would have spotted you."

"You're right," sighed the older man. "We left it behind some trees a mile or so on the other side of that narrow place on the dugway you've been sweeping for tracks every night. That was a clever stunt, Chandler. If I wasn't so beastly tired, I'd take my hat off to you."

"If I wasn't so sure it would do no good," pursued Ted, "I'd ask who told you."

"Oh," interjected Burrell, "there are a few people in the territory who have a sense of loyalty to their country."

"I wouldn't hold up that guy who told us about Chandler as a shining example of citizenship," Geary said dryly.

"Could my boys find your outfit and bring it down to save your walking back?" Ted enquired.

The officers looked at each other questioningly. Teddy, David, and Ernest approached, clutching their half-filled buckets.

"Yes, I believe they could," Geary said, regarding the children. "The kids could find it all right, couldn't they, Burrell?" The younger man nodded. "It would be a favor," he continued, his voice more affable.

Ted nodded and said quietly, "Teddy, we won't do any more work today. All of you put your buckets in the wagon. Unhitch the team from the plow and drive the wagon to the yard. Then you and David ride Prince up the road to the place these gentlemen will tell you and Teddy can drive the buckboard down. Put their horses in the east stalls and feed them. These men will stay with us tonight."

Teddy nodded slowly.

"It's a queer business, isn't it, boys?" Geary said, putting the warrant into his pocket. As the officers moved past the boys with Ted, Geary tried to pat David on the shoulder, but the boy drew back, fire smoldering in his eyes. Geary laughed uncomfortably. "Guess we can't blame you. We won't hurt your daddy, and we haven't enjoyed crawling around all day in the brush and rocks looking for him and your neighbors up the valley."

Before they crossed the field, Ted could see Nellie going into the kitchen from the storehouse. At the driveway, Ted said, "If you'll sit here on the porch for a few minutes, I'll explain the situation to my wife."

"No monkey business," warned Burrell. "We've taken your word on this, and it'll go damned hard on you if you try to run out now."

Ted flushed angrily. "Then come in with me," he said coldly.

"Good Lord, no," Geary remonstrated. "A Mormon's word should be as good as yours or mine, Burrell." He sat down heavily on the rocker.

Nellie was just inside the living room, pale and trembling. Jerry was clinging to her.

"Ted, is ..."

"Yes, it's over and I'm glad. I'm going to court on the fifteenth of next month. I'm released on my own bond until then."

Nellie put her arms around him, her breath coming in a long sigh. Then she raised her head questioningly, "But how did it happen? Didn't the twins warn you?"

"Someone told them the system. They left their outfit hidden up the road and crawled down the creek bed through the brush. Nellie, they need to stay here tonight."

"Oh, Ted, no!"

"I know it seems hard, but that's their condition for leaving me free until court. It gives me nearly a month to get things in shape."

She sensed Ted's relief, but her mind reeled at the thought of extending hospitality to their persecutors, especially to that insulting Burrell.

"They're pretty tired and hungry, Nellie. Could you fix supper right away? Make something special, will you? Which room shall I take them to?"

Nellie's mind was working again. "They can have my room. I'll get some water and towels, so they won't have to come out back to wash. I'll sleep upstairs with the children. Oh, Ted, are our children supposed to sit at the table with these—"

"What can we do? Geary seems pretty human. The other ... I don't know."

"Well, I do. He's a brute."

She was bringing her night things from the bedroom when Ted ushered them in and introduced them. She forced herself to smile politely but made no effort to shake hands.

Geary remarked gallantly, "We've met Mrs. Chandler before, but we little thought she'd be our hostess."

"I don't suppose you'll give us the honor of meeting the other wives?" Burrell queried facetiously.

"They're not here; but after that little ceremony in the field, I doubt if they would feel very cordial toward you." Ted was surprised that he could speak with such ease.

"You'll find water and towels on the washstand," Nellie said stiffly. "Supper will be ready in about half an hour."

The younger children were hovering wonderingly near the doorway. As soon as the bedroom door closed, Martha ran to Nellie crying, "Will they kill us? They have guns in their belts."

"Are they going to take Papa to prison?" Jerry whimpered.

"Why, they looked just like any men," Emily Claire remarked, puzzled.

Ted wondered if the Gentiles had ideas more grotesque about the Mormons than his children had about the deputies. Mark and Matt burst into the kitchen.

"Were those men really the deps?" Mark asked. "We were watching real good, but we didn't see them until they came up out of the brush right by you, Papa."

Ted put his arms around both boys. "I know. You weren't to blame."

"Did those old devils arrest you?" demanded Matt in a tone Nellie was sure—and glad—that the men could hear.

"Yes, they served a warrant for my arrest. I'll be away from you for most of the winter in prison. They're going to stay with us tonight, but they won't hurt anyone."

"Stay with us? Right here in this house?" Mark almost shouted.

"Yes, they'll have supper and sleep here, but it's all right. Now all of you get washed for supper and see what you can do to help."

A little later when Nellie returned from the cellar with a large pitcher of creamy milk to go with the cornmeal mush bubbling on the stove, she heard the deputies talking with Ted in the living room. Louie and Emily Claire were setting the table.

"They don't look a bit mean, do they, Aunt Nennie? Not even the one who was so horrid that other time," Louie said in an undertone.

"Mama," said Emily Claire, coming from the dining room, "One of those deps is trying to get Jerry to sit on his knee."

Nellie bit her lip in vexation. How could she interfere? And why had Ted agreed to shelter them in exchange for being free until the trial? It seemed too much, especially when they would eat better than the family. The children would eat mush and milk and bottled fruit; but for them she had stirred up buttermilk biscuits to eat with peach preserves and honey. She was brown-hashing potatoes left from dinner and had sent Emily Claire to the cellar for cheese.

She went to the living room door and beckoned to Ted. "Don't you think we'd better have them eat first, alone?" she asked low-voiced.

"No, we'll let them see a real Mormon supper table. It may do them good. And the children have ideas about them that shall be corrected."

He went back to the living room. How could he sit there, joking and laughing with those men?

Teddy and David came in just as Nellie was putting the food on the table.

"Did you take care of the horses?" Ted asked.

"Yes," answered Teddy. "We left the buggy in the driveway."

The boys were mystified at the welcome the deps were receiving and shot hostile glances at them sideways.

Ted said mildly, "You can wait to do your chores until after supper. Let's sit up."

When Nellie indicated a place by David for one of the men, David slipped down to the foot of the table. She squeezed in a chair on the corner between her and Edna. The deputies stood where Nellie had indicated, curiously looking at the chairs with their backs turned to the table.

Ted said, "Let us pray." The children knelt readily, the deputies awkwardly, folding their arms on the seats of their chairs like the children. How could Ted pray with them intruding in their family circle!

Ted's voice was husky. He thanked God for the blessings of life, health, shelter, and food. He stumbled over the customary plea for protection from their enemies and the request for wisdom and strength to bear whatever trials would come. But his voice grew firm and fervent as he prayed for guidance in caring for his family, in training his children in the paths of rectitude and honor. He prayed for the leaders of our great nation and for the leaders of the Father's divinely established Church and for the time when all mankind would recognize the fatherhood of God and the brotherhood of man.

The faces of both officers were grave when they rose from their knees. Ted called on Ernest to say grace. The strangers watched everything with curious interest. As the meal began, Ted made a special effort to put the officers at ease and to overcome the children's restraint. The visitors, too, seemed to make an effort, telling jokes and interesting experiences. The shyness of the children melted and they were soon chattering with their ordinary spontaneity.

Before the meal was over, Mark confided, "You wouldn't have got Papa if we'd had a signal to tell him someone was in the brush. At first we thought you were Brother Webb's calves, trying to get into our lucerne."

The deps both laughed. "Well, it wasn't much fun wiggling through the bushes," said Burrell. "Look at all these scratches." Nellie was surprised that even Burrell could be human.

When she went into the living room after the dishes were done, the deputies were grouped around the fireplace with the children. Jerry was sitting on Burrell's knee, playing with his silver watch chain. Martha was showing Geary her collection of beetles. But Louie, Teddy, and the twins were on the sofa, watching the others with puzzled expressions. She knew how they felt.

She didn't join either group, though both guests arose when she entered and offered her their chairs. She excused herself, saying she must get the children to bed.

Later, when the deps had gone to their room and the house was quiet, Ted and Nellie sat before the dying fire, trying to plan the future. The trial would be a mere formality, for Ted would plead guilty. Nellie would stay on the farm and supervise the winter work. But she couldn't manage without help. And would Jane and Luanna be all right in town? Many problems were still unresolved when they rose wearily for bed.

"Look, Ted," said Nellie. Lying on the mantlepiece were the officers' pistols. They could not have paid the family a higher compliment.

THE NEXT MORNING, NELLIE served their guests breakfast while the boys harnessed the team and buggy. Ted refused their offer of pay for their accommodations. "No, no," he said. "We never accept pay for sharing food and shelter."

"It's a damned queer world," Burrell muttered, "you taking us in under circumstances like this."

"It's a queer world under any circumstances," Ted sighed.

"You do understand we're only doing what we have to do, Chandler," Geary said awkwardly.

"Of course. And I appreciate the reprieve you've given me. It will help a lot. I'm glad my children had a chance to learn that you're not the monsters they'd pictured you."

Geary held out his hand and said warmly, "Mrs. Chandler, I know this is all very hard for you. Thanks for letting us stay in your home."

To her surprise, Burrell also held out his hand, smiling sheepishly. "I don't think I'll ever behave again as I did the time of our first meeting," he apologized awkwardly. "I wish I might hope you can forget it."

"I can try," she said and tried to smile.

twenty-one

Nellie walked with Ted and Luanna toward the meetinghouse for the farewell party the ward was giving Ted as he left to serve his term in the penitentiary. She was thinking how strange this would be to their enemies: public honors for a convicted criminal. In the morning, Ted would leave for Beaver, two hundred miles away, where he would be tried and sentenced to fine and imprisonment. But tonight he was the hero of the community, praised for the very course of life he was to be punished for.

He had asked to be released as bishop soon after the breakup of the United Order and declined an invitation to serve on the stake high council, saying it would not be possible for him to attend the necessary meetings. He was relieved to have this excuse accepted but, to his dismay, was then given what was actually a more difficult assignment, that of being a patriarch. It was unusual for one so young to be ordained a patriarch, since the calling was a revelatory one, requiring the patriarch to give blessings declaring the Israelite lineage of individual Saints and pronouncing upon their heads individualized blessings that God had in store. Despite his misgivings, Ted had accepted the calling. Dutifully and doggedly he fulfilled his responsibilities, struggling with his frequent feelings that he was unworthy of the absolute respect and confidence of most of his associations, afflicted by dark moods and times of questioning. Only Nellie knew of his mental and spiritual suffering.

When they arrived, the hall was filled with well-wishers. Jane hurried in late, holding Johnny by the hand just as Bishop Blackmore was announcing the opening hymn, "God Moves in a Mysterious Way." He beckoned Jane to sit on the stand with the rest of the family. Awkward from her pregnancy, Jane came up the aisle.

This baby would be born before Ted returned. Nellie dreaded the responsibility. Jane had been depressed before Johnny's birth and listless for a long time afterwards. The birth had been hard. Clara Hagen was getting too old to deal with difficult cases of childbirth, but there was no one more proficient. Susan Larsen often accompanied Nellie's mother and sometimes went alone; but few had the confidence in her that they did in Clara.

Ever since Ted's arrest, Nellie had felt the heaviness of her responsibilities. Harvest was over, but to stay on the farm during the winter without him was something she dreaded. Henry Burke would help with the heavy work, but there were so many other things.

How would Luanna and Jane manage? Luanna was so extravagant and careless. Could she manage the supplies? And Jane had seemed so restless of late. Even Ted had commented about how Jane's old wild impulses seemed to take possession of her. Once, after she had quarreled with Luanna, she hid in the potato bin. They had searched for her nearly all night. When she learned that this baby was coming, she had gone off into the hills, not returning until dawn. Nellie couldn't understand it. Jane had wanted her other babies and doted on them when they came. Could there be anything to the rumor that Fritz Kraus was trying to be friendly with Jane again? What if …

Nellie forced her mind back to the service. The choir was singing its second song. She'd had to give up the choir, now that she lived on the farm—too far away to come for practices. With gusto, Miles Larsen was leading out in the chorus of "Praise to the Man":

> *Hail to the prophet, ascended to heaven,*
> *Traitors and tyrants now fight him in vain;*
> *Mingling with Gods he can plan for his brethren …*

If that were true, Nellie thought, why couldn't the martyred Joseph Smith do something about the persecution of those practicing the polygamy he had begun? Was he mingling with gods? Was God too busy to know what was happening?

The bishop announced Bishop Butler as the first speaker. Nellie knew what he would say. He was considered the town orator. He usually gave the formal speeches on the Fourth of July and on Pioneer Day. He had talked at the farewells for Brother Christensen and Brother Kirk before they went off to serve their sentences. He would stress the nobility of suffering for the principles of the gospel and the rewards in store for the faithful—especially the mansions of glory in the life to come. She winced as she remembered his praise of the harmony in Brother Christensen's home. Everyone knew that Martha Christensen and Maria didn't get along at all and that Maria had made a terrible fuss when Gilbert Christensen had begun courting Lizzie Adamson.

What if Luanna had married Gilbert Christensen? He had always wanted her and always held it against Ted that he got her. How far away seemed that night in her father's home in Mount Carmel, when she had been showing Ted her grandmother's wedding dress and her new quilts. She still remembered how her heart stood still for a moment as she realized something was troubling him. He was standing by the window, looking out. The room was shadowy between them. He had wheeled about and come to her swiftly, his face pale and pleading. "Nellie, we know it—has to come. Would you mind very much if—if it were to be Luanna?"

She must listen to Brother Butler. That wouldn't be as painful as these memories. He was saying, with deep emotion, "The world looks upon Brother Chandler as a lawbreaker, a criminal. But we know he is a man of God. Look at his splendid family, sitting here before you. Three noble women and thirteen fine children. It is for them he is going to the penitentiary—because he has lived according to the laws of God, according to the dictates of his own conscience ..."

Ted shifted uneasily. The audience was rapt, intent on Brother Butler's sonorous cadences, but Ted mistrusted such effusions. He looked tired and worn. She knew the grinding struggle he had with his own conscience. *Was he living the laws of God? How she loved him!* If they had met somewhere else, outside Utah, there would have been no Luanna or Jane, no—

She checked herself sharply. What was she thinking? Without Luanna and Jane there would not have been manly little Teddy or the twins— She looked at the children, scrubbed to shining, happy with the attention they were receiving. Her heart swelled with pride. They idolized Ted. And each one was almost as dear to her as her own three.

The Meyer sisters sang a duet. Sister Harker gave a comic reading. Brother O'Conner, a member of Ted's high priests' quorum, paid a tribute. Then Ted was called on for a response. Nellie thrilled as he stood, straight and handsome. She saw his hands clutch the pulpit nervously, closed her eyes, and breathed a silent prayer for him. It seemed that a prayer on his behalf was always ready. She had only to close her eyes for that special prayer to rise from her heart to her mind.

"I appreciate this demonstration of your friendship and good will," he began. "And I hope I shall always be worthy of it. I do feel like a criminal being sent to prison. I have always done the best I knew how, and I hope the Lord will give me and my family strength to live right during this coming ordeal." His voice wavered. He coughed, then went on with a conscious attempt at lightness. "I shall try to remember all of the interesting things that happen while I'm a guest at Uncle Sam's hotel so I can tell you about them when I come home."

After the program came a social hour with dancing, games, and refreshments. Ted received several books, stockings, and handkerchiefs, and the ward members had written an autograph book full of advice, some items serious, and some humorous.

The next morning, the family gathered around the buckboard in which he would travel to Beaver. Henry Burke would drive him up and bring back the outfit. No witnesses were going; Ted would confess to the warrant as stated.

The children were very excited and Nellie was relieved that they understood so little of what Ted's departure meant. Luanna was crying. Where was that dratted Jane? She hadn't been around all morning. She'd barely escaped being subpoenaed in the raid after Ted's arrest—she had hidden in a closet when the deps came to her mother's house and had hardly been herself since then.

Ted was making the rounds of the children, giving each a kiss and a word of advice. "Teddy, you're the oldest son. You need to be responsible and help your mother and Aunt Nennie as much as possible. Louie, try not to worry your mother and Aunt Nennie but help them instead. Emily Claire, keep on being a teacher to the children. They love you." And so on to Luanna's baby, Jeannie.

When he kissed Luanna, she clung to him as if she could not bear to let him go. Nellie wished again that she could show her need so openly.

"Where's your mama, Johnny?" Ted was asking Jane's youngest son.

"She went for a walk, and she wouldn't let me go," said the little fellow.

A shadow crossed Ted's face. Nellie said reassuringly, "I'm sure she's all right. I think she was just afraid that she'd be so upset at saying goodbye that it would be hard for you."

Swiftly Ted turned to Nellie, taking her in his arms. "It's going to be hard, Nellie, having the responsibility of them all." His voice broke. Her chin quivered, but she determined she would not break down. That would only make it harder for Ted. She couldn't keep from trembling. He held her close, his cheek warm against hers. It made her think of their first baby's birth. She had come out of an unconscious stupor to find him kneeling beside her bed, his tears falling on her face. She felt just as weak and dependent as she had that day, but she lifted her head and stepped back.

"We'll get along all right, darling. It won't be long. You mustn't worry."

He smiled gratefully and swung up to the buckboard's seat. The children shouted goodbyes until he was out of sight.

"Why do you suppose Jane went off like that?" Luanna asked Nellie, still sniffing, as they turned toward the house.

"I think she didn't want to be upset. You know how nervous she's been after last month."

Luanna was exasperated. "You know very well saying good-bye is nothing like having the deps after her. I think she just wanted to annoy Ted."

"Well, he'll overlook it. He knows none of us are ourselves when we're in her condition. Good-natured as you are, don't you remember how you were before Teddy was born?"

"I was horrid," Luanna cheerfully agreed. "I wonder sometimes if that's why Teddy likes you better than he does me."

"Luanna, don't be foolish. Of course he doesn't. But I love him almost as much as I do my own children." She put her arm through Luanna's and they went into the house.

Ted had told Nellie and the older children to finish husking the corn and topping the carrots that would be used for feeding the animals. Nellie called them together quickly to prepare for the drive back to the farm. Just then, she saw Jane going up the walk to her own house. "Oh, Jane's back," she exclaimed to Luanna. "I'm glad she's all right. When the baby comes, I think I'd better come down and take care of her. With Louie I could manage things here, if you wouldn't mind going to the farm."

Luanna grimaced but said, "Of course. I couldn't take care of her even if she'd let me. But I'll die on the farm." She paused, then added slowly, "Nellie, have you heard those rumors—that Jane has been talking to that awful Kraus man from Mount Carmel?"

Nellie didn't want even Luanna to know that she was worried. "Oh, the way some people gossip makes me tired, doesn't it you? Jane wouldn't do anything to hurt Ted."

Luanna looked at her squarely. "I wish I could see as much good in her as you ... pretend to."

twenty-two

Ted's letters from the pen were cheerful but did not breathe an ardent martyrdom like those of others. One of Brother Christensen's was read in stake quarterly conference. The Spirit was with his fellow Mormon convicts, he testified. He felt sure the Gentiles could feel it emanating from these men, who were living heavenly laws. It was a rare blessing to be housed in a cell near that of the apostles. At the meetings they were allowed to hold, the Holy Spirit was poured out in rich abundance. This was one of the greatest events of his life. "We know the Lord is with us," his letter concluded, "for he is turning our so-called trial and sacrifice into a lasting blessing."

Nellie wished Ted could feel as certain as Brother Christensen that he was being punished for righteousness' sake. At least he was not the only Orderville prisoner who failed to share Brother Christensen's enthusiasm. They complained of the food, the discipline, and the unpleasantness of mingling with criminals. Brother Bollanger, who had a humorous outlook on life, amused them with wry anecdotes. "Today Brother Covington didn't get out of his cell quickly enough when the doors were unlocked at supper time. The door automatically locked itself, and he thought he would go supperless to bed, but he played 'The Old Man's Prayer' on his fiddle so pitifully that a guard came to release him—and he got an extra dessert." In another letter, he quipped, "If Brother Chandler had a blue cap with white stars, you could almost take him for the American flag in his striped suit. He is so tall and dignified that I wouldn't be surprised if the inmates salute him." He added, "My new striped suit came near to getting me into trouble when I first put it on. We cohabs are permitted to go over the deadline when we're exercising, but for some reason, the guard on the tower took me for Larry Sullivan, a burly Irish tough in here for lynching. He was about to shoot me when I looked up. He started to laugh and yelled, 'Don't be so proud of your new duds that you strut like Sullivan.'"

Ted said little about himself or prison. He wrote personal messages to the children, encouraged his wives, and gave instructions about the farm work. Nellie wished she knew what his thoughts and feelings were. It would be so much easier if he could feel like a crusader or see the funny side of things. He had never denied the deep assurance he felt when in Brigham Young's presence, when he had seen the sick healed after his administrations, or when he had pronounced patriarchal blessings on the faithful. But she was certain he also still suffered from his old doubts, now perhaps more than ever. At such times, he needed her most. Her own faith was simple, but she could do what he could not. She could close her mind to troubling questions and be satisfied that if such good people as Father and Mother and Auntie and scores of other upright people had unwavering testimonies, then their faith could anchor hers.

LATE ONE AFTERNOON WHEN Ted had been gone about three months, Mark came for Nellie. Jane had gone into labor. Nellie's mother was already there. Luanna gathered the younger children and prepared to leave for the farm. She drew Nellie aside and whispered, "She's been acting awfully strange. She hardly treats the children decent. They've been eating with us for days because she won't fix meals. I don't know what to make of it. She's always been crazy about her kids, though she doesn't care for yours or mine."

Jane hardly stirred when Nellie entered. "It will be good to have it over," Nellie said reassuringly. Jane made no reply.

When Clara came in with a hot pack, Nellie followed her to the kitchen. "What can I do, Mother? She's in a bad way, isn't she?"

Clara's face was grim. "See if you can get her to help herself a little. She doesn't seem to care about anything—not even the contractions."

"Isn't her mother coming?"

"Jane sent her away. She's behaving just like she did before she was married."

"I wish Ted were here," Nellie said helplessly.

Next morning, the baby was born. Jane simply stared blankly when they told her it was a little boy, not very strong, and turned her face away when Nellie tried to put it in her arms. A few hours later, the baby died, and Jane burst into hysterical laughter. "God did answer my prayer. The first time ever. I told him I didn't want it. I told him I would hate it. I told him I wouldn't have it." She laughed again.

Nellie was horrified, but Clara's calmness steadied her. "She's weak and all wrought up," Clara murmured. "She's not responsible for what she's saying. You mustn't let it upset you."

After the hysterical outburst, Jane relapsed again into cold indifference. Nellie tried again, when the body was ready for burial.

"You do want to see your baby before he is buried, don't you, Jane?"

"No," said Jane. "I killed it with my prayers! I would have hated it if it had lived."

"Oh, Jane," begged Nellie. "Please don't talk like that. You don't know what you're saying. Think of Ted."

Jane flung Nellie's hand from her shoulder and moved nearer the wall. "I don't want to think of him. Of anybody. I want to die, too. I'm praying I can die. Go away."

"Jane, please," whispered Nellie. "I can't bear to see you like this." She took Jane's hand. It was limp and clammy. She rubbed it, her tears falling on it. She had to reach Jane somehow, for Ted's sake. It would hurt Ted so to know that Jane was like this.

Suddenly Jane turned over and clutched Nellie's arm. She burst into violent weeping. "I want to die, Nellie. I have to die. I'm a wicked sinner to kill my baby. Nellie, ask God to let me die, too. He isn't listening to me."

Nellie tried to soothe her, although she was terribly alarmed. What had caused such a state of mind? At last Jane sobbed herself into exhausted sleep.

AS NELLIE STOOD BETWEEN the new grave that held Jane's son and the tiny grave of her own daughter, one baby unwanted, the other so desperately wanted, she wept for them both, for Jane, and for Ted. She felt she was weeping for all of the people in the world who might be groping blindly through life, not knowing why such suffering came.

When she wrote to Ted, Nellie said nothing about Jane's behavior, trying to accept her mother's explanation that Ted's arrest, Jane's own near arrest, and the disruption to the family accounted for it. But two weeks passed, and Jane stayed almost the same. When Ted's letter came, Jane only glanced at the pages and dropped it on the bedstand without reading it.

"Would you like me to read your letter to you?" Nellie asked.

"No." Jane looked at Nellie stonily and turned her head away.

Gradually she grew stronger, in spite of herself, it seemed. In a month, she was up and moving around, though she said little and showed no interest in anything. Nellie prepared to return to the farm. She knew Luanna was impatient to get back to town, and she was desperate to be in her own home.

"Would you like me to take Johnny to the farm, Jane?" she asked. "Until you're feeling better, you know."

Jane continued to stare out of the window. "Yes, and Edna, too. The twins can take care of themselves and eat at Luanna's. I can't stand the children. Their noise drives me crazy."

"Oh, Jane," whispered Nellie, "I wish I could do something for you. I hate to leave you like this."

"I'm all right. I wish you'd all just let me alone."

"But you're not all right. You're not at all like your old self."

Jane gave a hard little laugh. "What was my old self? I haven't any self. I shift from one self to another. I despise all my selves."

"Jane, I can't leave you when you feel like this!" Nellie was frightened. Would Jane do something desperate?

Jane looked up and laughed again. "You don't need be afraid. I know what you're thinking. I won't kill myself. I'm too big a coward or I'd have done it already. I get ready and suddenly I repent and pray and imagine I'll be good again."

"But you *are* good, Jane. It's only because you've been through so much and are still weak ..."

"Didn't I hate everybody when I knew I was going to have another baby? Didn't I pray for it to die? I'm a murderer. And that's not all. Sometimes I—"

She broke off abruptly, staring at the stark branches of the wild shrubs she'd transplanted from the hills. The silence lengthened. Surely there couldn't be anything to those rumors. Jane wouldn't ...

Jane suddenly reached for her hand. "You carry too many loads, Nellie. I'm really all right physically. Maybe I can get hold of myself quicker mentally if I'm left alone. I have a wild streak that calls me to get out of doors. I haven't been able to be off by myself for a long time. I think that's all that's wrong. Leave me alone, and the next time you come to town, this devil in me may be gone."

But the next time Nellie came to town was a week later when Jane's mother sent for her. She was frantic.

"She goes off into the hills. You know, Nellie, that her father and I have never been able to do anything with her. She goes all the time. What if—"

"But she always comes back," Nellie tried to be reassuring but she felt panic in herself, too. "She has always loved the hills."

"Nellie, I hate to mention it, but have you heard rumors about her seeing one of those awful Mount Carmel boys, the one they say informs to the deps?"

"I've heard little whispers," Nellie admitted, "but you know Jane always likes to appear worse than she is. I can't think there's anything to that talk."

"I tried to feel that way," Sister Cameron confessed, "but I got so worried that I—I asked Mark and Matt to follow her and ..."

"Oh, no! You didn't! Made her own children spy on her?"

"I had to, Nellie. I couldn't go myself, my lame back, you know, and I *had* to know. They've heard all the gossip. She doesn't pay any attention to them. They have to fix their own meals or go to Luanna's or come here."

Between sobs, Sister Cameron said the boys had seen their mother meet a tall dark man in Dry Hollow and sit talking to him until it was nearly dark. "They didn't know him. He wasn't from around here. They were so cold they had to come home, leaving her there."

Nellie was stunned. What would this do to the boys? to Ted? She tried to think of something comforting to say. "He may have been hunting stray calves or sheep. They may have met by accident. Those Mount Carmel men do run cattle up Dry Hollow. Jane used to be friendly with ..."

"Why do you try to shield her?" burst out Sister Cameron. "She's Brother Chandler's wife. You must try to help us save her."

"But what can I do?"

"Talk to her. She won't listen to me. Make her see what she's doing to Brother Chandler, to the children, to all of you and all of us."

"I'll try," Nellie promised, filled with misgivings.

NO ONE ANSWERED WHEN she opened Jane's door and called. She called again and went inside. "Jane, Jane, are you home?"

As she walked through the living room, Jane came out of the bedroom, closing it behind her, but not before Nellie caught a glimpse of an open traveling case, and dresses and shoes on the bed and chairs. Jane's face was flushed and her eyes avoided Nellie's face. She dropped into the chair near the bedroom door and said sullenly, "I didn't know you were in town."

"I just got here. Henry had to bring some bran and grain down for Luanna's cow and chickens, so I decided to come along. How are you feeling? Do you need any supplies from the farm?"

"I don't know," said Jane indifferently. "The boys do the chores."

"Of course. They would have let us know if you are out of something." Nellie kept her voice light as she removed her wraps and sat on the couch near the window. "How have you been feeling anyhow?"

"All right."

"I didn't think about coming until the last minute, or I would have brought Edna and Johnny," Nellie chattered on. "They'd gone up to Websters' with Emily Claire to get old Malsy and her kittens. She'd carried her whole litter, one at a time, clear up there in the night. She's a discontented old mother cat if I ever knew one. She's tried to move two or three times since the kittens came."

Jane said nothing. Nellie was finding her task more difficult every moment. She continued, groping for a subject. "I've been having school with the children every day. You'd be surprised how quick they are. Last night after Jerry and Johnny had gone to bed, I heard them arguing about how *picture* is spelled. They wouldn't take Ernest's word and finally came downstairs to ask me. You should have seen how proud Jerry was because Johnny was right—prouder than if he'd been right, because Johnny is younger. He's a wonderful little boy, Jane, your Johnny. He sees everything in nature. I think he'll be a scientist."

Jane's hands moved nervously in her lap, but she did not look up or speak.

"The children are busy getting their Christmas box ready for Ted," Nellie continued, hoping to strike a spark of interest. "They parch corn every night or make cookies or molasses candy. Emily Claire writes the stories and poems they like to put in a book, and I wish you could see the pictures Edna draws. She's as good as Mark at her age. They get their artistry from you, Jane. You love pretty things and can make them from almost nothing."

Still Jane sat silent and nervous. Nellie went on. "They're all writing their letters. The little ones dictate to me. They're making a puzzle for their father. A scrapbook with a lock of hair on each page. Ted's to guess which lock came from which wife or child. Ted will like that." She paused, then went on. "Jane, I cut a lock of hair from your baby's head before we buried him. It was so pretty, almost the color of yours. Maybe you'd like to send it to Ted? It's with the scraps left from the burial clothes in the bottom drawer of your dresser."

Jane jumped to her feet. "What are you trying to do to me?" she demanded fiercely. "I know you didn't just come down with Henry. You came to—to try and stop me, didn't you?" Her voice shook with anger and resentment.

"Stop you? What are you talking about?"

Jane swooped toward Nellie, turned away, and then turned back. "I'm going away with Fritz Kraus. I'm going to marry him. I want a husband. I'm not really married to your husband. I was never a real wife. You know what's going to happen? The law will dissolve this whole church. All the men, not just the polygamists, will be barred from voting. All the families will be broken up. I won't have even the pretense of a husband that I've had. My children are illegitimate. I'll be no better than a streetwalker."

She paused for breath. Nellie seized Jane's arm. "Don't, Jane. How can you say such things? The laws of God are higher than the laws of men. You're Ted's wife and will be through all eternity."

Jane jerked away. "Don't talk to me about eternity. I want a life now, even if I never have one in the future. I want to be considered respectable by other people, not by this little handful of so-called Saints. I want a husband of my own. I don't care what you or Bishop or God himself thinks of me!"

Nellie was helpless before this flood of passion. But she had to do something for Ted's sake. His faith was not strong enough to bear this disgrace. "Jane," she pleaded, "think of your beautiful children. What will this do to them? Think of Ted."

"No!" Jane screamed. "I won't think of anyone but myself. Ted is your husband, not mine. He only married me because my parents begged him to, because I begged him to. Why didn't he say no? He was too softhearted, afraid of what the brethren would say. I did love my children once. It seems like ages ago. Now they don't seem like mine. They'll be better off without me when this law is passed. You're their father's first wife, his only legal wife. I'm giving them to you, Nellie, so they won't be illegitimate. Do you hear, Nellie? I'm giving my children to you so they won't be bastards!"

She wheeled around, rushed into her bedroom, and slammed the door. Stunned and disbelieving, Nellie heard the bolt slide into place.

WRITING TO TED WAS the hardest ordeal of Nellie's life. Over and over she asked herself if she could have prevented what happened. But she had done all she knew how. She had failed.

But to write quickly to Ted before he got a gossip-distorted version—what could she say? She knew that people who had been suspecting Jane, even her own family, would think more terrible things of her than were true. Nellie was sure that Jane had not been unfaithful to Ted and also felt confident that Jane would not live with Fritz until they were married. Her heart ached for Jane. No matter how different she was from most Mormon women, her conscience, trained throughout her whole life, would torment her. Nellie knew she would yearn for her children. She felt sorrier for Jane even than she felt for Ted, but it was his pain she wanted to soften.

She tore up many sheets before she finally finished her letter. Briefly she told him that Jane had never been well since the baby's death, then said she had gone away:

> When she locked the door, I begged her to let me in, but she did not answer. There was hardly a sound after she went in. I waited a long time, trying the door and talking to her constantly. Finally I saw Henry drive up and started through the kitchen to speak to him. Then I saw the secret panel to her closet was open. I went through. She was gone and hadn't taken anything although dresser drawers were open and things in the closet were disarrayed. The bed was neatly made with the suitcase on it, partially packed. It made me hope she would be back. We all know how she often goes away by herself.
>
> But it has been three days now. Fritz Kraus left Mount Carmel the same day with a team and buggy. No one knows where he is. We sent Henry and Jane's brother to search the hills and canyons, but they found no trace of her.
>
> I brought the twins home with me and tried to explain to all of the children that she doesn't realize what she is doing—that maybe she will get well and come back. But of course it will hurt them all their lives—especially Mark. He and Jane had a special bond. I can't bear to think of it.
>
> She seemed to think that this new law would make everything different. She didn't realize that it is God's laws we need to be concerned about and have faith that everything will come out all right, even though we don't understand and even though we have to suffer. I feel sorry for her, Ted. She can't have known what she was doing.
>
> Please, darling, try not to let this hurt you too much or feel that there was anything you could do. You've done your duty. She wasn't running away from you. She was running away from her fear of the future.
>
> I pray that our Father in Heaven will help you to know that it was no fault of yours and that he will bless and comfort you and poor Jane.

> Yours always,
> Nellie

TED'S WORLD WAS ALREADY in turmoil. The law had already dissolved the Church and disfranchised its twelve thousand voting men. He felt that his whole world was falling to pieces.

The next Sunday, Apostles Lyman and Cannon requested that only Mormons attend the Sunday meeting, though it was customarily open to all in the prison. Apostle Lyman said, "Many of you are thinking that this law means the breaking up of your families—that when you go home, you must give up all but your first wife, that your children will not be legitimately yours. Many brethren throughout the territory are planning to move to Mexico, but I want to tell you confidentially that I think this is not necessary. You know yourselves how splendidly we are treated here, what unusual privileges we are given. The very officers who arrested us did it by stifling their better selves. The deputy who served papers on me apologized and has frequently sent me books and magazines. Many of you have had similar experiences. It isn't the people in our own midst who are against us. They respect us, even though they do not understand and cannot accept our beliefs. It is only because of pressure from bitter enemies outside our territory that we are being persecuted. The fact that most of us who are living the law of plural marriage have served or are serving terms of imprisonment, together with the fact that the law deprives us of our legal rights, will satisfy most of our adversaries. They will turn their attention to something else and leave us alone."

One man asked, "Don't you think, then, that we should move to Mexico where we can live our religion in peace?"

"I don't intend to," Apostle Lyman said reassuringly. "President Woodruff will do what is best for the Church, and he is not advising anyone to move. I believe—and this is confidential—that he will tell us before long of a revelation suspending plural marriages for the time being. That will appease our enemies, and in the end we will be given back our rights."

This comforting explanation did not solve Ted's problem. He asked, "When we go back home, will we be able to go on living with all our families?" The men waited eagerly. Lyman meditated. "That would be against the law just as it was before, wouldn't it?" Ted continued.

"It will not be against the law of the Lord, Brother Chandler. It is living his laws that should concern you most."

Ted was baffled and unhappy. The continual compromise with his own conscience was destroying his integrity, yet the thought of breaking up his family, of regarding Luanna and Jane as other than legal wives, of seeing their children as anything but legitimate made him so wretched he could not bear to keep on thinking. He longed again for a great spiritual experience, a peace that he had seldom known and had never been able to attain. Repeatedly he fasted and prayed for it. Many had it and lived by it, but when he prayed, his words seemed to fly back into his face.

He had married Luanna and Jane against his will, on some level, because the Church expected him to. Yet now their lives were as inseparably part of his as Nellie's. He cherished his first love. Luanna had given him deep passion, gaiety, and pleasant companionship that he needed and appreciated. Jane had been a frightened child, needing his strength and protection. He often felt that he and Jane were strangers and always would be, but her impulsiveness, her love of beauty, her intense devotion to their children and her homage for him had endeared her to him. Both Luanna and Jane had borne him children. That alone united their lives to his for all eternity, but his conscience still tormented him.

Then Nellie's letter plunged him into deeper confusion and despondency. He was shocked and humiliated. He felt disgraced. What would it do to the children? He must have failed Jane somehow or she could never have done this terrible thing. She had begged him to marry her to save her from a rash act like this, and he had failed. He cursed Kraus, but he blamed himself. For Jane he felt only pity.

As he brooded over his situation in the heart-wrenching days that followed, he finally reached a decision. He could not be true to himself if he continued breaking his country's laws. He would move to Mexico where he could be true to his family, to the Church, and to himself. As soon as he returned home, he would sell his property. It would be better to leave the community where others would always remind Jane's children about their mother.

BY THE TIME TED was released, the gossip had somewhat died down. The only word had been a missionary who reportedly said he had seen her and Kraus in San Francisco. Nellie had tried to shield the children as much as possible. The fact that they loved her and had spent almost as much time at her house as in Jane's made it easier. Edna and Johnny scarcely seemed to miss her at all, but the twins were old enough to feel the shame.

That day in Jane's house, Nellie had felt numb but her mind had worked clearly. She had gone to the school, explained to the twins that she needed them on the farm and that she would teach them there with the other children.

"Isn't Teddy going to help, too?" they asked.

"He'll need to do the chores at his place and yours," Nellie said briefly.

"We'd better tell Mama goodbye," said Mark.

"Your mama isn't home," said Nellie through stiff lips. "I just came from there. But she'll know it's all right."

First there had been waiting to be sure that Jane was really gone and the letter to Ted. Then she prayed all morning and afternoon for guidance and wisdom to tell the children. She must break it to them gently. After the younger children were in bed, she asked the twins to come to her room. They were very different, and their reactions would be, too. Matt was larger than Mark, but his mother's whimsical smile and quick restlessness made him seem younger. He was affectionate and dependent, constantly in need of reassurance. Mark was small and wiry like Jane, but he had Ted's brooding eyes and questioned everything. He was tense, passionate in his feelings, and warmly devoted to his mother, even since her recent indifference to the children. When Matt complained, Mark always defended her. It would be hardest on him.

She began gently, "It's about your mama ..."

Mark flashed indignantly, "I don't believe what Granny thinks about her. Nor what some of the kids say—that she's bad. She's my mama, and I love her." Angry, loyal tears glistened in his eyes.

Nellie reached for his clenched fist and drew him beside her. "Of course, you love her, and so does Matt. We all love her. But she has been sick a long time. Sometimes when people are sick they do things they'd never do if they were well, so it really isn't their fault. Your mama has gone away."

They both clutched her, frightened. She felt that she was failing miserably, but she had to go on. "It isn't really her fault. It's that man—"

"I'll kill him if he's hurt my mama," Mark cried. "What has he done, Aunt Nennie?"

"He has taken her away."

"Where? Where?"

"We don't know, dear, but he won't hurt her. He has loved her for a long time, so I'm sure he will be good to her."

"I—I can't believe that she's gone ..." Matt seemed stunned.

"I'd like to kill him for taking her away and I'd like to kill anybody that says bad things about her." Mark was trembling, his face white and drawn, making him look much older.

Nellie put her arms around him. "You mustn't want to kill anybody. Maybe your mama wanted to go away. If she's happier, we mustn't mind too much."

"But why would she want to leave us?" Matt questioned. Both were sobbing, leaning forlornly against Nellie. She wept with them and she kept trying to explain the impossible.

"Will she come back when she gets well?" Mark asked.

"We can hope so. We can always pray for her and take care of Edna and Johnny. And while she is away, let me be your mother. I love you as much as a mother can love her children." Matt clung to her, but Mark, his eyes dark and baffled, stood away. She was glad they were so young. Time would help heal the hurt.

She went with them to their room and told stories until she thought they were asleep. But later, hearing Mark's smothered sobs, she went back. He pretended to be asleep when she bent over him, but his cheeks were hot and wet. She smoothed back his hair, kissed his forehead, then knelt by the bed and prayed for comfort to all their aching hearts.

twenty-three

In early spring, the Chandler family received word that Ted was free and would be home in a week. The ward would honor him with a homecoming reception, but it would be hard for him to mingle freely with his old acquaintances, their sympathy about Jane well-meant but cutting.

Nellie could hardly wait to see him and have some of the responsibility lifted from her shoulders. Spring had come early that year. She had tried to help Henry and the children with the planting but realized she was not strong enough to do the heavy physical work some women did and that it was foolish to exhaust her physical strength.

Luanna planted her garden in town with the help of her sons and made no complaint about Louie and Teddy going to the farm as soon as they were needed. Nellie sometimes felt Luanna enjoyed having the children gone, as it lessened her work and gave her more time to visit and help in the Church auxiliaries. She enjoyed that kind of activity much more than housework and was very proficient in it.

They had closed Jane's house, and her children stayed on the farm with Nellie. All winter she had held a few hours of school each day for all seven. They enjoyed it, and she enjoyed teaching them. She could not bear to send the twins to school to face their schoolmates, and she hoped Ted could help them catch up in arithmetic.

Her joy over Ted's homecoming was darkened by the thought of his humiliation and sadness over Jane's flight. The rest had grown accustomed to her absence, though she knew that Mark still grieved. He often sat alone, a brooding look in his eyes. Her heart ached for him, but he rebuffed her attentions, fiercely resenting what he felt was her pity. He disapproved of Matt's fondness for her, accusing his brother of disloyalty to their mother. The antagonism between the boys was a constant source of tension. Even though she understood the cause, Nellie could not bring herself to discuss it with the boys.

One day Luanna said, "Nellie, I don't see how you can take so much from someone else's children." The twins had been quarreling, and Mark had been impudent to Nellie when she interfered.

"They're my children, now," Nellie replied simply. But she realized how desperately she wanted Ted home to share the responsibility and discipline with her.

The children were excitedly planning a homecoming party for their father. Emily Claire and David were writing a comedy depicting the humorous disasters that had occurred while he was away. One scene would show Louie trying to remove her freckles with a bran pack, only to have it almost skin her face when she pulled it off. Another scene would depict Nellie trying to nurse all seven of them down simultaneously with measles, all complaining and clamoring for attention at once. Besides the play there would be songs and poems, and good things to eat.

Nellie and Luanna were puzzled over something Ted had said in his last letter. "Of course we cannot go on living as we did before in the United States. Perhaps the only thing to do is to go to Mexico."

"What does he mean?" Luanna had asked.

Haltingly, Nellie told her what she thought it meant—that the Edmunds-Tucker Act had not only dissolved the Church and taken away the franchise from the men but had made it positively illegal to go on living in polygamy.

"But aren't the men who are moving the ones who want to take more wives?" Luanna asked. "That's surely what Brother Hales and Brother Norman had up their sleeves. I don't want to go to Mexico, and I should think that Teddy wouldn't want more wives. But of course, with men you can never tell."

Nellie saw that Luanna had missed the point. In Mexico, living with *Luanna* would not be illegal. But she did not try to explain. Again she had that guilty little gladness that she was the first wife.

"I think it's horrid," Luanna went on, "that Brother Spencer and Brother Pearson are abandoning their second wives. They never should have gone into polygamy in the first place. Neither one has enough ambition to support even one wife decently. I guess they thought the United Order would take care of their families. Now they're using this new law to get out of their responsibility. I wonder what Effie and Nancy will do."

"They've been practically supporting themselves since the Order broke up, with some help from the bishop, I believe," Nellie said.

"Yes, I know. I guess it's just as well in cases like that if their husbands stop living with them—having more children for someone else to support." Nellie did not ask her about Brother Morris's solution to the problem. He had persuaded Caroline, his first wife, to give him a divorce so he could make Emmie his legal wife. Caroline had been his childhood sweetheart, borne him eight children, and helped accumulate the property which now made their lives comfortable. But she was past childbearing now. Emmie was young and pretty and could go on building up his posterity for glory in the next world.

Nellie was worried. She knew Ted's nature. She could satisfy herself by feeling that the laws of God were more important than the laws of man, even if obedience brought sacrifices and persecution. She could feel that it was right for them to go on living together as they had before. But evidently Ted could not. He was troubled, that was clear.

HENRY DROVE NORTH TO the railroad terminal to meet Ted, and the next day the children went in a body up the canyon to meet him. Nellie and Luanna stayed home to prepare a special dinner. Every few minutes, one of them would go to the window or door to look up the road. It was almost two o'clock when they heard the children singing and the rattle of wheels. Luanna rushed out with a glad cry. Nellie felt smothered with a strange dread and hurried to her room, catching her breath in quick little sobs. The future? What would it be? This was the beginning of a new period in their lives with its waiting, unrevealed experiences.

After a moment she composed herself and went to the porch. The children were piling from the rig and from the riding ponies. Nellie's eyes blurred. Indistinctly she saw Ted step from the wagon, the children clinging to him. She saw Luanna throw herself into his arms, saw the hunger of his own arms closing around her, but simultaneously, his eyes were searching her own. She went down the steps to receive his embrace.

Her first real look into his eyes confirmed her fear. He was tormented with the same conflict. She longed to comfort and reassure him.

They were soon seated around the long table. As they bowed their heads, Nellie breathed a secret prayer that she might be able to help her beloved in this time of adjustment. Ted's prayer was brief—gratefulness for being together with his family, for the blessing of health, for the unity they enjoyed, for the food before them.

During the meal there was much laughing and even shouting, as each child tried to be heard above the others. Only Mark sat silent, his eyes bitter and lonely.

When the meal was finished, the children dragged their father into the living room for the program. Nellie couldn't concentrate. After a while she slipped out, quietly closing the door after her. Ted seemed to be thoroughly enjoying the performance, but she knew he must be thinking of Jane and what he was going to do in this new situation. He was holding Edna on his lap and had been especially attentive to little Johnny.

Luanna was radiantly happy, her color high, her eyes flashing. She was even more attractive now in a richer, riper way than she had been in the first years of marriage. Nellie was aware of the old unhappiness that always ached when she realized that Luanna's love for Ted had a quality hers lacked, something that Ted, perhaps every man, needed. With all her devotion to him, with the sure knowledge that he adored her and that with him she was first, still she lacked something that Luanna gave him effortlessly. Shoulders drooping a little, Nellie went quietly into the kitchen, wondering why the brightness of life's sweetest moments was always a little shadowed.

As she quietly began to clear the table, she suddenly stopped. A child's smothered sob came to her ears. She listened a moment, then hurried to the pantry door, and pulled Mark into her arms. She had not noticed when he had left the group. At first, he stiffened and tried to pull back, but as her own tears overflowed, falling on his head, he leaned against her and they wept together.

In a few moments, Mark lifted his eyes to her face and began to pat her arm. "Aunt Nennie, what's the matter? Please don't cry. What makes you feel bad?"

She dried her tears, sat down, and drew him beside her. "Oh, Mark, it hurts me that you are so unhappy. I know you want your mama. I don't know how to be a real mother to you. That makes me want to cry."

He studied her for a moment, puzzled, then buried his face on her shoulder and said brokenly, "Oh, you do! You are so good to me, and I love you. Only, I wish … I wish things didn't have to be like they shouldn't be."

"So do I, honey," replied Nellie with all her heart. "But I suppose there will always be things to cry about. Life is like that. We just have to keep looking for the other things—the things that make us glad. Most of the time we can find them, if we look really hard."

"Mark, Mark, where are you? It's time for your part!" Emily Claire was calling from the doorway.

"He'll be there in a minute," Nellie said, shielding him from his sister's eyes. "He's just going to get a drink."

She drew him gently to the wash bench by the kitchen door and quickly bathed and dried his eyes, smoothed his hair, dipped a cup of water from the bucket, and held it out to him.

"Now you go in and do your part, dear," she murmured. "We have to pretend to others sometimes that nothing is the matter."

He searched her face, and Nellie felt the barrier between them crumble away. She turned back with a sigh to the dishes.

LATER, WHEN SHE SLIPPED back into the living room, a lively discussion was going on about moving to Mexico. Luanna's face was flushed. Ted's was grave and worried. The children were all excited.

"That's where I want to go," said David, swinging his arm. "Spaniards live there, don't they? Maybe we could learn Spanish."

"Won't it be fun to travel in covered wagons, like the pioneers crossing the plains!" cried Emily Claire.

"Can we take our rabbits and dog?" Ernest wanted to know.

"And the lambs and kittens," put in Martha. "And the calves and ponies."

"Are we really going to move? When will we start, Papa?" Louie asked earnestly.

Ted's glance traveled uneasily from Luanna to Nellie. "We're not sure about anything yet," he said. "I'll need to talk it over with your mothers before we decide."

"Well, I'm sure," Luanna said decisively. "I don't want to move to Mexico!" She sprang to her feet and left the room. She did not come back for over an hour, when Nellie was trying to persuade the excited younger children that it was their bedtime.

Ted, who had been watching the children distractedly, roused himself to give kisses all around as they filed past his chair. Nellie settled them in their beds, then returned to the living room, feeling drained. Ted and Luanna were sitting on the sofa, their hands clasped. Nellie stood in the doorway. The bond between them, which she did not share, made the air alive and tingling.

"But if we don't go to Mexico," Ted was pleading, "can't you see what it means, Luanna?" His voice was husky.

"Do you … do you mean that I … won't be your wife anymore?" Her eyes widened in alarm as, for the first time, she realized the import of the new law.

"If we go on living as we did before, I'll be laying myself liable to the penitentiary again." He got up and paced restlessly about the room. Nellie came in quietly and sank into a chair. He glanced at her abstractedly. Luanna had never taken her eyes off him.

"But everybody says," she protested, "that it's over. The officers have performed their duty. You've served your term." Her hands clasped and unclasped in her lap. Her dark eyes glittered with unshed tears.

Nellie's heart filled with pity for them. Her heart ached for Luanna, suddenly facing the possibility of separation from Ted. And her love for Ted made his suffering her own. The thought came to her that maybe she couldn't sense the depth of Luanna's feeling. Her love for Ted was so different. A sudden fear made her sick and dizzy. Could it be that after all Luanna was his *real* wife?

But her heart protested. She couldn't be the one to give him up. She was first. She'd always been first. He had said she always would be, no matter what happened. If they had not been Mormons, if plural marriage had not been their destined way of life, her love would have satisfied him. He would not have missed Luanna's passion if he'd never known it. The thought of Caroline Morris being discarded for a younger wife swept over her in a wave. She felt suffocated by fear and unhappiness. She could not make a sacrifice like that. It was too much to ask.

The clock on the mantel ticked with hideous loudness. Ted continued to pace back and forth, the knuckles of his clenched hands showing white. Luanna, breathing hard to keep back the sobs, stared out the window into blackness. Suddenly she sprang to her feet and turned on Nellie. "Don't sit there like that, so smug and sure. You're his first wife, so this doesn't hurt you. But it's killing me! I can't bear it!" She rushed outside, slamming the door behind her.

Stunned, Nellie looked at Ted. His face was a bitter mask that frightened her. He laughed unnaturally. "So this is what I get for trying to live my religion! What kind of game is God playing? What kind of God is he to torture us like this?"

She had never seen Ted like this. It terrified her. She sprang to her feet and crossed quickly to his side. She must do something to help him—anything. "Ted, please. Please don't look like this. We must talk. There must be a way."

She drew him to the sofa and coaxed him down, then held him, his head on her breast. She wanted so much to help, but what could she do? Broken bits of memory floated through her mind ... another dark night, a tragic face, an impossible sacrifice. She had felt more like a mother than a sweetheart when Ted had knelt beside her and asked, "Would you mind if it is Luanna?" No, no! Not again? Had Caroline Morris felt like this? Unbelievingly, from far away, she heard herself saying words she had been sure she could not say: "Darling, let me step aside. I could still have the children and ..."

"Nellie, what are you saying?" He straightened and looked at her incredulously.

"I mean, if you can have only one wife ... Luanna needs you and you ..."

"My God, Nellie, what are you saying!" he exclaimed. He sprang to his feet and once more she coaxed him to the sofa, sinking down beside him. "If you stepped out of my life, my life would be nothing," Ted insisted, his face stark. "It is you who holds the world together for me. Help me now. What must we do?"

He clung to her again, like Mark, when she drew him alone and desolate out of the dark pantry. She stroked his hair and whispered, "I can only say what I have said before. God's laws are higher than man's. You broke the law of the land, but you have the blessing of your wonderful children and the happiness you have given your wives, and the service you have rendered the Church. Remember that the chosen people have always suffered for their beliefs. I wish you could compromise with your conscience. Forget the conflict and let all of us find what happiness we can. But if you feel that you can no longer break the law with peace of mind, then let me be the one to make the sacrifice. I love you enough for that."

They were silent for a long time. A strange thought went through Ted's mind. Did Adam hesitate in the Garden of Eden when Eve held out the forbidden fruit? He knew he could never be rid of the conflict, but he could try. A deep sigh quivered through his body. He got to his feet and looked down at her. "Thanks, darling. You know I could not give you up, so maybe I can try to compromise. I'll try to feel that I'm doing what the Lord wants me to do. If only I had your faith and goodness and strength."

He sat down again, took her in his arms, and gave her the tender caresses she had hungered for throughout his long absence. She wished they could remain there in each other's arms, but she thought of Luanna, alone and desolate in the darkness. With one last lingering caress, she drew back, then stood up. Quite steadily she said, "You had better go and find Luanna." Then she turned and went to her room, alone, as she had been on her wedding night.

PART 3

Falling

Orderville, Utah, and Provo, Utah

In which:

- Ted works for his family and keeps a new promise
- Ted struggles with old doubts
- The family divides between Orderville and Provo
- Louie has a close call
- Mark goes on a mission
- Ted is rejected
- Nellie journeys to California

twenty-four

After Ted's release from the penitentiary, he tried to follow Nellie's suggestion as he struggled for peace of mind. He worked at suppressing his doubts, instead taking the position that he was a Latter-day Saint and that the Church had a great mission in the world. He concentrated also on his family—two devoted wives who loved and respected him, and wonderful children who were worth living and working for and, when need be, suffering for. He deliberately did not think of Jane. Luanna asked to live on the farm. She felt that she had come so near losing Ted that she wanted to be with him as much as possible. Ted sold Jane's house and enlarged Luanna's, where Nellie lived with her children and Jane's.

The best medicine for his troubled spirit was hard work, so he poured his energy into building for his family's future and giving them as many advantages as he could. He added more land to his original allotment, bought a herd of sheep, acquired range, and herded more cattle. Naturally astute, he found that his experience with the United Order stood him in good stead, and he was soon recognized as one of the outstanding businessmen in the southern territory. He retained holdings in the woollen factory and sawmill that had continued as private enterprises after the breakup of the Order, homesteaded land in the canyon to increase grazing, and found greater satisfaction in his prosperity than he had expected.

He never lost sight of the fact that he was doing all of this for his children. As soon as each child was old enough, he gave them definite responsibility. Teddy and the twins received a few acres to cultivate as their own with a few head of sheep and cattle branded as their own, from which they would receive the profit. The children and wives were given allowances which they budgeted to meet their various needs.

Although Ted spent less time on civic and religious duties, he still chaired an irrigation board and helped develop a tract for dry-farming. He served as head of his high priests' quorum and as a home missionary. In this capacity, he went from ward to ward in the stake with other brethren, urging the Saints to live their religion more zealously.

He did not find the satisfaction he wanted in his church participation and felt uneasy urging people to develop a fervor he himself lacked. It had become somewhat easier to give patriarchal blessings with the passage of time, but he never felt completely at ease in the calling. He knew that some members of the Church regarded patriarchal blessings almost as fortunes, foretelling their futures. Even though promised blessings were predicated upon faithful adherence to the commandments, they sometimes left the fulfillment up to the Lord, blaming the patriarch if the promises were not fulfilled. Ted felt that he lacked the natural spirituality needed for such a call and accepted reluctantly. Few members ever refused a call to serve; if they did, they were looked upon as backsliders, treading the road to apostasy. Refusing two calls would have been too much. He knew that people were already watching him, fearful that he had lost the Spirit of the Lord.

Shaken by spiritual doubts, Ted always tried his best, fasting and praying before giving a patriarchal blessing. Sometimes, thrillingly, he felt himself being directed by a power beyond himself. He cherished one such occasion—the blessing he gave Nellie's half-sister, Minnie Hagen.

As a young girl, Minnie had discovered an inherited weakness in her sight. Though she was not blind, her sight was limited and Clara feared that it was a progressive condition. Though she was pretty, sweet, and musically talented, the young men of the community shunned her. Ted knew that she was lonely, longing for the happiness of marriage and children.

When she asked Ted for a patriarchal blessing, he prayed with extra diligence, hoping he could say something to provide true comfort. He laid his hands on her head and moved haltingly through the preliminaries, then heard himself saying, "You shall receive the choicest blessings your heart desires. Much joy and happiness are in store for you. You will be a wife and a mother in Israel and will have joy in fulfilling God's plans for you."

He felt Minnie trembling under his hands and was stricken with consternation. How could he have made such promises? Minnie would believe every word he uttered. Ted stumbled through the customary conclusion of the blessing, his throat burning. Perspiration beaded his forehead. Even though the words had come from outside him, he could not feel that he had really been inspired. The promise was simply improbable. He must have pitied her so that he was overcome with the wish that she could have what she desired. He wished he could unsay those words.

When he took his hands from her head, she looked up at him, face aglow. "Oh, Brother Chandler, I don't know how to thank you for that wonderful blessing. Of course it wasn't you but the Lord that gave it to me. I thank you both, and I will try so hard to live worthy of its fulfillment."

Ted felt like a Judas. Worse, Minnie's words reminded him that he had omitted the customary phrase—that fulfillment depended on her obedience to the commandments. But what would be the difference? No life could be more innocent, more worthy of blessings than hers. For weeks, whenever he saw the pale, dark-haired girl with that new radiance in her face, his heart sank. Should he tell her that what he said was not a promise from God, only his own wish for her? Finally he told Nellie of his doubts.

Nellie responded calmly, "Ted, if the words came to you, why can't you believe they were from the Lord? No matter how much you want Minnie to be happy, you would not have said such things of your own volition. And is it truly so impossible? Minnie's mother was totally blind."

It was meager comfort, but Ted grasped it, hoping for Minnie's sake that it was true.

EXCEPT FOR THE UNREMITTING spiritual doubts, Ted knew he was happy. The children were healthy and hard-working, harmony prevailed between Luanna and Nellie, and with Ted's newfound prosperity the family could invest in some comforts—sketching materials for Mark, more books and magazines, and even a piano. Ted deliberately turned away from news from the outside world. It was always disturbing, and he knew that his peace of mind was fragile, vulnerable to the next challenge. Adversaries of the Church continued their accusations. Idaho required an oath that voters swear they were neither polygamists nor members of an organization that encouraged polygamy. One monogamous Mormon had been prosecuted for conspiracy and jailed. The editor of the *Deseret News* was jailed for contempt when he refused to answer, in a court hearing about a different matter, the irrelevant question: "How many wives do you have?" Several converts were denied citizenship because they had been through the Endowment House. There was talk of refusing to allow Mormon converts from abroad to enter the United States. Ted tried to keep his thoughts on the small world in which he lived, away from the larger world that was fighting against it. He knew he was compromising his own integrity, but he tried not to think about it.

One day as he was leaving the co-op, he met Nellie's mother. He had not seen her for several weeks and was shocked to notice how feeble she seemed. He shook hands warmly with her. He had always admired her calmness, even when he wondered what she was thinking behind her inscrutable eyes. She was a strength in the community, not only because of her expertise as a midwife but because of her calmness in emergencies.

"Ted," she said, after exchanging news of the family, "I need to talk to you alone and there never seems to be a chance."

"Let me give you a ride home," Ted offered. He was surprised at her seriousness. Had he done something to displease her? Maybe she thought Nellie was working too hard. It was true. He constantly tried to get her to have the children do more. She had always been frail compared to Luanna, yet she persisted in doing more than her share of the work.

He helped her into the wagon. "We can take the long way home," he smiled and turned the horses down the road away from her house.

She was not smiling. She sat with her blue-veined hands folded on the checked gingham apron. Then she looked at him steadily. "I need to ask you to do a very hard thing for me."

"What is it? You know any of us, I, especially, would be happy—"

"Wait. I wish I didn't have to ask you to do this, Teddy, but I must." Her voice trembled slightly.

She had never before used his mother's own nickname for him. He gazed at her in astonishment.

"Teddy, will you marry Minnie?"

"But—why, you—you know that's impossible!"

She continued steadily, "Don't think I don't know what you went through in deciding to marry Luanna. I know what that decision did to Nellie, but I felt even sorrier for you. Our gospel is a hard one for one of your nature. I've realized all along your constant interior fight. You're not the only one with conflicts. Some can't go on. They either leave the Church or stay in it but have to compromise their idealism and self-respect to do so. They are never at peace with themselves."

Ted had never heard her make such a long speech and was struck by her insight into his own problem. He said nothing.

"I admire you for how you've faced your trying situation. In spite of everything, you have remained a man. Even with that terrible experience with Jane, you kept yourself fine and sound. What I'm asking shouldn't be as hard. You have learned how to fight your battles and not go down. That blessing you gave Minnie—surely you've noticed the change. It gave her hope, something to live for. I'm getting old, Ted. I can't bear to think of leaving her, hoping and praying and having no one to care for her after I'm gone."

"But Sister Hagen ..."

"I'm not finished. You might say older men who are still looking for young wives would be glad to take her. I couldn't bear that for Minnie, Ted. Neither could you. She wants babies, but she would die if they were not begotten in love and decency."

Clara Hagen's soft wrinkled face flushed. She stared straight ahead.

Ted dropped his eyes to his hands. "In the blessing ... I can't understand how I could have said such things. I don't mind telling you that I'm never sure I'm saying what the Lord wants me to say. I often think I should have refused the calling. And when I saw what that promise meant to her, I wished I could unsay it. But that was impossible. I hoped some good young man would see what a wonderful wife she would make ..."

"So did I, Ted, but who is there? The young men want wives who can be real helpmates, not a girl with a handicap."

"But how could you think of me? What will this do to Nellie and Luanna? And in the face of the opposition to us ..."

"I realize all that, but plural marriage is still a principle of the gospel, and men are still taking wives. Please think about it, Ted, and let me talk with Nellie and Luanna about it. Will you do that for me, Teddy?"

Ted sat still so long that the horses shook their heads. The mechanical jingle of their bits roused him. Ted had abstractedly guided them to Clara Hagen's house and now they waited impatiently. He thought about her life, a life lived for others. And now she was asking something, not for herself, but for another. It would be harder than marrying Luanna or even Jane. He would be liable to severer legal penalties. Other men were marrying wives in Mexico, then bringing them back and having them live in other communities under assumed names. What she said about Minnie's future was true. And perhaps in making that promise, he had a responsibility to see to its fulfillment.

He sighed. He felt trapped with no way out. He was glad she had asked to talk to Nellie and Luanna. He honestly didn't feel he could face them. He put his hand over hers. "It's the first thing you have ever asked of me, Mother Hagen. And you've done so much for me and mine. We'll talk again after you've talked with Nellie and Luanna."

A FEW WEEKS LATER in the closing days of September, Ted and Minnie started for Salt Lake City. Auntie went with them to visit her sister in Springville. Ted was anxious to see if his mother, now widowed, would come back to Orderville with him. He worried that she was struggling but would not tell him because he had been so opposed to her marriage.

They saw no newspapers on their way, so Ted was unprepared for the news that President Wilford Woodruff had issued an announcement counseling members to refrain from contracting illegal marriages. Bishop Jenkins had suggested that something might be happening at general conference, but he had congratulated Ted for his willingness to take a new wife and had willingly issued the recommends. Delayed en route by problems with a horse, they reached Springville after conference was over, only to learn that President Woodruff had issued a press release a few days before conference and the general conference had voted to accept it.

Auntie's brother-in-law, Gordon Heppler, was shocked to learn that Minnie was Ted's prospective wife. He exclaimed, "Good heavens, man! You haven't heard? Read this!"

With shaking hands Ted took the copy of the *Deseret News* the man thrust at him and read, unbelievingly:

> *Inasmuch as laws have been enacted by Congress forbidding plural marriages, which laws have been pronounced constitutional by the court of last resort, I hereby declare my intention to submit to those laws, and to use my influence with the members of the Church over which I preside to have them do likewise.*
>
> *There is nothing in my teachings to the Church, or in those of my associates, during the time specified, which can be reasonably construed to inculcate or encourage polygamy, and when any Elder of the Church has used language which appeared to convey any such teachings, he has been promptly reproved. And I now publicly declare that my advice to the Latter-day Saints is to refrain from contracting any marriage forbidden by the law of the land.*

Ted looked up blankly. He had been muttering the words aloud. Now Minnie, uttering a little cry, swayed and fell to the floor in a faint. When she lay recovering on the couch, Ted read the article again. The Church had practically forced him into polygamy lest he lose his salvation. Now it was ready to condemn him for it. If plural marriage had been so urgently necessary for the Lord's work, then how could this sudden change be from God? And if the Church had repudiated polygamy, he was left without any anchor to his honor.

Brother Heppler patted Ted comfortingly on the shoulder. "I'm sorry I gave the little girl such a shock," he apologized. "I didn't stop to think what it would mean to her. But it isn't as bad as it looks. The Manifesto says *advice*, not *commandment*. President Woodruff doesn't say he's received another revelation. This isn't the word of the Lord. It's just a necessary expedient. You go on and marry that little girl. God's law is still in operation."

"But how can I?" asked Ted. "Surely they're not still performing sealings in Salt Lake City."

"Oh, I think there are ways," chuckled Brother Heppler. "A short while ago, Apostle Cook spoke at stake conference, gave a strong sermon, he did, on strict obedience to the revelations of the Prophet Joseph. He said that some outward changes—yes, he used that very word—would be necessary but he urged the people to remain faithful. 'Ways will be opened,' he said, 'whereby the Lord's will can be followed in all things pertaining to his great work.' Now, doesn't that sound as if they've thought through all this? Go to him and you'll see that all is well."

Ted couldn't feel that all was well, now or ever. How could President Woodruff make this announcement and have members of the Church vote to accept it while apostles were giving other advice?

Yet there was his promise to Minnie and to Sister Hagen. He decided to see Apostle Cook.

A few days later, Ted and Minnie embarked on a boat on the Great Salt Lake, and in a cramped cabin were married by Apostle Cook. They were thus not on the *land* whose laws they were disobeying. Ted, sickened by the childish subterfuge, swallowed hard and said nothing.

After the ritual had been completed, the officiating apostle counseled, "Because of these precarious circumstances now surrounding us, you must keep all circumstance of this marriage secret for the time being. Brother Chandler, your young wife should take another name and go to another community when her children are born." Again, Ted swallowed hard and said nothing.

Ted arranged for his mother to accompany him home. Auntie advised him to leave Minnie in Springville with her until they could work out a plan for the future. Ted drove home, trying to enter into his mother's happy conversation, yet looming ever larger at the back of his mind was a vague mistrust. Minnie's happiness was so great that it almost frightened him, yet it made him feel that some good had come of the entire business. Minnie was sure the Lord was fulfilling the promised blessing and her heart was filled with love and thanksgiving. Determinedly, Ted suppressed thinking about his situation. There was no solution to his problem, as far as he could see, unless he could somehow convince himself that the apostle was right. He knew only that he was trying to do the best he could with life as it had come to him.

twenty-five

When news of the Manifesto reached Orderville, everyone wondered whether Ted and Minnie had reached Salt Lake City before the edict had been given. Nellie, Clara Hagen, and Luanna brooded over it incessantly. When Clara had talked to Ted's wives about the marriage, Luanna had protested. "Just think of all we went through with Jane!"

"Luanna, the two cases are not to be compared in any way," Clara Hagen had replied earnestly. "You know how empty Minnie's life will be without children. You know how much her sweetness could add to any family. Jane failed to fit into plans that others made. The two are different in every way; the need for them to marry is not the same."

Luanna did not hold out long. She respected and loved Clara Hagen, and felt secure in the intensity of Ted's physical need for herself.

Nellie assented willingly out of deep love for her orphaned sister, but she realized it would add much to Ted's already heavy burdens and his ever-present conflicts. She thought of the time when Minnie's mother came into her girlhood home, and the memories were of bewilderment and pain, yet of happiness, too, for it was the evening when she and Ted had discovered each other and the beginnings of love.

Although Clara said little, she dreaded that the marriage had not been performed. What would this do to Minnie's faith? Luanna was openly relieved. "Won't you be glad, really, Nellie, if that announcement stopped the marriage?" she asked Nellie. "Teddy is such a hand to brood. He'd be sure to feel that he shouldn't have gone through with it, even if they did get there in time."

Nellie sidestepped the question. "I feel sorry for Minnie. To have a little son or daughter would mean so much to her. I shall never forget the joy on her mother's face, holding her for those few moments before she died."

Louie, who had been in the room, cried vehemently, "Well, I sure hope something happens so Papa can't marry again! It was awful when they left. Minnie's just a girl. I almost hated them both."

"Louie Chandler, whatever are you saying!" rebuked Luanna.

Louie burst into tears. Nellie got up and put her arms around her. Her eyes went to the little china flower girl on the mantel above the fireplace, oddly out of place with the cheap trinkets around it.

"Let me talk to her, Luanna. I understand exactly how she feels. Let's go sit on the porch, Louie." She breathed a prayer that she could be as wise and comforting as Auntie.

WHEN TED RETURNED WITH his mother but without Minnie, he simply explained that they had arrived after conference and that Auntie and Minnie had decided to remain for a visit. Everyone took it for granted that there had been no marriage. Only Nellie, Luanna, and Clara Hagen knew the truth.

"Too bad you didn't get there a day or two earlier," Bishop Jenkins consoled. "I imagine there are a lot of men who would have hurried if this hadn't come so suddenly. How do the people seem to feel about it? Will this satisfy our persecutors so they'll be willing to let us exist?"

"I wasn't around many people," Ted said. "I was busy getting Mother's affairs settled. The few I talked to differed greatly. Some feel President Woodrufff did the only possible thing under the circumstances. Others go so far as to say he betrayed the Church."

"Well, I hardly know how I feel myself," the bishop admitted. "I'm glad you brought your mother back with you. We'll be happy to have her in the community again. She'll stay with one of your families, I suppose?"

"No, I'll build a little home for her on that lot I own next to Nellie's folks. She wouldn't enjoy it on the farm, and there are so many of us when we're in town. I think it's probably better for old people not to have to put up with youngsters all the time."

But Ted's chief reason was to provide a place for Minnie. When she returned to Orderville with Auntie, she would be Mrs. Graham and the story would be that she had married an elderly widower in Springville and come home on a visit. She could divide her time between his mother, who was very fond of her, and Clara Hagen.

Ted hoped there would not have to be too many lies before the need for deception ceased. He had received the impression from the apostle who married them that the Church would still recognize new plural marriages and, soon, would do it openly. He went at his work with an almost vicious energy, pouring his attention into new projects to increase the family income and make their lives more comfortable.

Nellie worried about him. The old brooding look was in his eyes all the time. He was aging daily, she thought.

About two months later, Auntie wrote that Minnie was pregnant. She was happy about the baby but wanted to come home. She missed Clara Hagen and needed her particularly now. Auntie wanted Ted's advice.

Sister Hagen thought she should come. Since Nellie's brother Brig would be taking a load of wool north the next week, they could come back with him.

"Nellie, where is all this going to end?" Ted asked in despair. "It gets worse and worse. How can Minnie come back and live a lie? It isn't right to expect her to. Yet if she doesn't, what will happen to her? To me? To all of us? Is there any answer?"

"Ted, you did only what you thought was right," Nellie tried to comfort him. "Think what it will mean to Minnie to be a mother, even if she cannot have a normal life for a while. It will be a blessing to her. I know how you hate this deception, but the apostle approved. Can't you trust one so near the head?"

"He was sincere," Ted groaned. "He believed what he told me. But how can such a situation ever work out entirely right? I've always struggled against polygamy, yet I've gone into it deeper and deeper, hoping I was doing the will of God in following the leaders. But could the apostles really be representing the policy of the Church? How can the Church pretend to abolish the practice and simultaneously go on with it? Nellie, if we have to live a lie within the Church itself ..."

"Ted, please let's talk of something else and try to trust."

He heaved a deep sigh and was silent.

Nellie continued, her voice determinedly cheerful. "I've been thinking about the children and their education. Do you realize that Louie and the twins and Teddy have had about all they can get in our school? Couldn't we send them to Brigham Young Academy in Provo? Or, better still, take them? Either Luanna or I could go to take care of them. What do you think?"

As she hoped, this topic caught his interest at once. Giving his children the best advantages he could was the great aim of his life. He had a vague feeling, which he had never tried fully to define, that he had brought them into troubles for which they were not responsible and he ought to do all he could to compensate for what he feared they might have to face. He agreed and they talked about the matter for a long time.

Then Ted commented, "I'm wondering if we shouldn't have sent Louie away to school last year. She isn't herself. She's growing away from me. I passed her as she was setting the table for dinner and reached out to pat her cheek. She shrank away so I couldn't touch her."

"You know what adolescence does to children," Nellie reminded, then forced herself to go on. "I think she knows about Minnie. Luanna and I have talked about it enough and we haven't always been careful in front of her. Do you remember the swing in Overton when you found me the night my father brought Minnie's mother home as his wife? I felt I couldn't bear it."

"Oh my God, Nellie," Ted groaned. "She thinks of me as you felt that night, as I felt about Mother and Granger, about polygamy itself then!"

"Don't take it too hard, darling, even if she can't understand right now. I think I can talk to her better even than Luanna. I remember how Auntie helped me. She'll get over it as she gets older. But I think I should tell her the full truth now."

"Of course," Ted agreed wearily. Nellie hastened to bring his thoughts back to the topic of school.

"It will do Louie a lot of good to meet new people. She will enjoy it. She makes friends easily, just as Luanna always does. She's so pretty and bright. She'll be popular and make us all proud of her."

"Emily Claire's the quick one," Ted said. "She'll shine in school."

Nellie nestled close. She felt he had a special corner in his heart for her first born.

"Teddy ought to do well, too," Ted went on, growing more enthusiastic. "Don't you think he has a scientific bent? He does pretty well on the farm, but he doesn't enjoy it like Matt. Matt will be the farmer. We must give him a chance to study agriculture."

"And Mark will be good in art," Nellie said. She was thinking how much he was like Jane. There was a special bond between them and sometimes they talked of Jane. She would describe Jane's lovely wildflower garden, the ornaments from the silky pods of milkweeds, bark of trees, pressed ferns and flowers, the pretty pebbles and shells glued to old bottles and broken dishes. Mark spoke of her very seldom and only to Nellie.

Once he had said, "When I'm big, I'm going to find my mama and bring her back." Then after a brooding silence, he had asked, "But maybe the rest of you wouldn't want her back ... would you?"

Nellie had put her arm around him. "Of course we would want her back, if she wanted to come." She tried to keep him supplied with art materials and praised his efforts. She knew she was nearer to him than Ted, or even Matt. Ted knew it, too, and now he said, "What would poor little Mark ever have done without you, darling?"

"I've always felt so sorry for him," she answered. "He has never got over the longing for his mother. It used to break my heart to see him staring into space with that sad, bewildered look on his face, that hopeless yearning for a lost mother."

"But he's had a real mother," Ted praised, "the only real one he ever had. You are a real mother more than Jane could ever have been. You know what that means to me, darling."

After this long talk, Ted felt as if there was an incentive to dream. He resolved again to throw off his frustrating feeling that life was a baffling paradox. But the rumors began as soon as Minnie was back in town. There had been reports of other secret marriages, of wives using assumed names. When some of the brethren in the ward asked Ted if that was what he had done, he answered evasively but felt they understood his half answer. In a way, he was relieved. He didn't feel they were living quite so much a lie.

Minnie was radiantly happy over her coming motherhood and made no demands on Ted, who tried scrupulously to treat her as he had before, when she was a young sister-in-law. She was contented to know that she was married to a good man who would lead her to exaltation in the world to come. Minnie had a room in Emily Granger's house, where she visited often, but she preferred being with Clara Hagen.

ALL THAT SUMMER, TED, Nellie, and Luanna debated whether the four oldest children could keep house for themselves or whether Nellie or Luanna would go with them. It was beyond the family means to have all four of them board. Furthermore, food from the farm would cut down their expenses considerably. The children were eager to be on their own and felt entirely competent to run a household. Luanna was willing. "The professors who come to talk up the school seem to think it's the cheapest way and gives them good experience," she declared.

"But most of the students would not be so far away from home as ours," Nellie reminded. She was as interested in the question as Ted or Luanna, even though Emily Claire was still too young to go.

"Why not give them a chance to see what they can do by themselves?" Luanna urged. "It will make them appreciate what we do for them all the time, and it will be nice for us not to have so many to wait on."

"I'm afraid we'll miss them more than they'll miss us," Nellie said. "They will be having new experiences. We'll be wondering if they're well and worrying about them."

"It will be more expensive if they go by themselves," Ted remarked. "Naturally they won't be able to manage very efficiently." All three of them accepted that Luanna could not get along on an allowance comparable to Nellie's. This had been a matter of friction when Ted had first begun giving them a monthly allowance. Jane had been completely impossible. But Nellie had made Ted see that it was a matter of personality and had persuaded him to make Luanna's allowance larger, instead of trying to make her over. Even if Luanna couldn't make appetizing dishes out of leftovers or a new-looking dress from two old ones, she had other qualities that meant much more to all of them. But she dreaded to think of Ted angry at Louie if the girl turned out to have the same careless ways.

"I think Louie would manage much better than most girls her age," Nellie said. "But what if they should get sick, way off up there?"

"Well, Nellie, do you want to go with them?" laughed Luanna. "You're the nurse, and it's you always talking about an education for them, and of course you're a lot better manager than I am."

"I wish *I* could go," Ted said with a touch of bitterness. Government officials were beginning to investigate post-Manifesto marriages, and the Church had taken no stand or made no protest. Nellie knew Ted wished he could get away from the continual worry.

"How would it be if each of you went for part of the winter?" Ted finally asked. "But we won't have to decide that tonight."

"Nellie seems to think we must go, so I guess that settles it," said Luanna petulantly and flounced out. She did not often flare up that way anymore, but Nellie didn't worry about it either. Luanna didn't hold grudges, yet she knew it worried Ted. Luanna's reaction was somewhat justified. Ted *did* take her suggestions more often than Luanna's when they differed, and she knew that he had tried to be tactful. She also knew that very likely by morning Luanna would be sorry for her fit of temper. She would either apologize frankly or do some nice, little, unexpected thing. Through the years, Luanna and Nellie had adjusted to each other. A strange but very sincere love had grown between them and a genuine loyalty. They would even sometimes stand together against Ted. Nellie would often make excuses to him for Luanna's shortcomings, and Luanna as unselfishly stood by her. If Nellie was ill, Luanna would work untiringly to do things as she knew Nellie would want them done though her own way would be much more lax. If someone should intimate that Nellie was Ted's favorite wife, Luanna would say, "Of course she is. And why not? He was hers for years before I ever knew him. I think it was grand of her to let me have a share."

When they had to decide on the Provo arrangement, Ted said to Nellie, "I suppose I'd better tell Luanna to go with the children. I really thought she would want to go. She enjoys getting away from home more than most women do."

"But she doesn't want to go, Ted, and I'm willing."

"But why should you? None of the children are yours."

"Oh, Ted, how can you say that?" Her voice wavered with tears. "I feel that they are all mine."

He apologized. "Nellie, it's wonderful, if you really feel that way."

"I do, Ted. Have you forgotten when we thought we were going to lose Teddy and then at last knew he was going to live? I didn't know that I would ever have a baby of my own. You came into my room just at dawn and said you had been thanking God for saving *our* baby. That *our* gave me comfort. It opened a door somewhere in my heart and let out the bitterness. Ever since that morning, Ted, all your children have been mine, too."

He kissed her with the tenderness of their younger years, when his love for her was mixed with reverence. He recalled their wedding night, when he found her huddled in the windowseat of a strange boardinghouse, her face damp with tears, and the night when he returned from the penitentiary and she had given him back his self-respect yet sent him away from her rightful claim into the darkness to find Luanna. Such moments were precious compensation for the complicated life they lived.

"Nellie, what would my life be without you? How could I get along with you two hundred miles away?

"You would miss Luanna just as much, only maybe in a different way," Nellie smiled. He couldn't deny it, but he held her closer. "There are several reasons why I should go," Nellie continued. "First, Luanna would rather not. The next few years are going to be important in Mark's life. He will need a mother. He will need me, Ted, right now, more than he needs you." Ted murmured his recognition. "Then there wouldn't be so many of us to keep in the city if I went. I'm sure Edna and Johnny would stay here with Luanna and the younger children."

Ted smiled. "And you can live on less because you're a better manager. I could mention other reasons. Louie needs to be with you, to get the kind of training she cannot get from Luanna. And perhaps the most important, you can stimulate the children in their work and give them wise counsel in other things."

Nellie paused, then said, "Louie is maturing very early and is so pretty—so much like Luanna at her age. Jimmy Fergeson is crazy about her. Jimmy is a nice boy, but his folks don't seem to have much ambition or interest in education. Maybe I shouldn't say this, but I hope she can find someone a little, well, more her equal."

Ted nodded. "Yes, that's another reason to let the children get away. There's already been so much intermarriage. Nearly everybody is related some way or another."

They were silent for a time. "Do you really think you ought to go, Nellie?" Ted asked again. "I know your mother isn't well. She'll miss you almost as much as I, and so will Minnie. She'll have the baby while you're gone."

"Yes," said Nellie resolutely. I've thought of all these things, and there are more reasons to go. But if Mother gets down, you'll send for me, won't you?"

"Of course, darling. Can you imagine what this community will do when she passes on?"

"Oh, don't speak of it," Nellie said, her breath catching. "I can imagine how eagerly Father is waiting for her. They loved each other beautifully, Ted."

"Yes, I know. Their love was like ours. Your mother is his first wife, too."

Nellie wished she could keep the fragile beauty of this moment forever. The moonlight fell across the little flower girl on the mantel. It had become a reminder that even in the drabness and hardness of their lives, such moments were possible.

twenty-six

Nellie looked up from the sock she was darning as the door opened to their small rental home in Provo, then closed quickly. Mark rushed in, beaming.

"Aunt Nellie, see!" he exclaimed. "My term paper in religious education. An 'A.' And listen to what Professor Kimball wrote on it: 'Excellent work on a significant subject. You would make a good missionary. Come into my office and talk to me about it.' Aunt Nellie, do you think Pa would let me go on a mission?"

Nellie smiled up at Mark affectionately. He was usually so quiet and self-contained that one had to guess what he was thinking and feeling. She took the paper, looked at the grade, read the teacher's comment, and rejoiced, "That's wonderful, Mark! Think how proud your father will be. And won't it make Teddy and Matt and Louie feel like working harder! None of them got such high marks."

"But about the mission, Aunt Nellie. Do you think I can go?"

She looked at him attentively. He spoke with unusual urgency and earnestness. "We've always looked forward to all of you boys having that opportunity, but you are so young, Mark, and have had only one year at the academy. Don't you think you would do more good for the Church and get more out of a mission yourself if you waited a few years? And there's Teddy, nearly four years older than you. Shouldn't we think about him going first?"

Mark's face fell. "Ted doesn't want to go on a mission as bad as I do. Nobody does. Aunt Nellie, won't you talk to Pa about it?"

She pointed to a chair beside her. "Sit down, Mark. Tell me about it. Why do you want to go more than anyone else?"

He sat for several seconds, locking and unlocking his fingers. Jane's hands, that day she had run away, had locked and unlocked in her lap just that way. Mark had his mother's pointed chin and other physical characteristics besides her artistry. How could she be so fond of Mark when he reminded her so much of his mother? The other three—Matt, Edna, and Johnny, were all more like Ted. Yet Mark was nearer to her than any of the others. He needed her now. She hoped she could help him.

"It's hard to tell you," he faltered. "I hoped I wouldn't have to tell anybody. But if it will make you want to help me, Aunt Nellie, I want to go on a mission to see if I ... if I can find my mother." He sat, head bowed.

Nellie's heart went out to him. How he must have suffered through the years, lying awake at nights, dreaming of finding the mother who had abandoned him but whom he still loved and perhaps pitied. She didn't know what to say. She stared at the sock lying in her lap beside the theology paper. Finally she looked at his troubled face. "Where do you want to go, Mark?"

"I heard Granny say that someone saw her in California. She might still be there, don't you think?"

"Of course it's possible, but if all you want to go on a mission for is just to see if you can find her ..."

"I do want to preach the gospel," he interrupted eagerly. "I've thought about it as long as I can remember. But I've thought about finding her, too. I've dreamed about knocking on a strange door with missionary tracts and her coming to the door, or about preaching on street corners and seeing her in the audience and her not knowing me. But her getting interested in the gospel and then finding out who I was and ... Oh, Aunt Nellie, maybe ... maybe I could save her."

He was trembling. She had never guessed he was living with such dreams. She reached for his hands and gripped them. "I'll do all I can to see that you get a mission call, Mark. But you mustn't be too disappointed if you don't find your mother. She could be anywhere."

He gave her a grateful look. "I know, but I might." He hesitated. "Could you talk to Pa, without telling him about ... without mentioning my mother?"

Nellie hesitated. She had kept few things from Ted all their married life. She studied Mark's face a moment and tried to sense what his wild desire meant to him. "I think I can, Mark," she said slowly. "I'll try to make him see that you ought to have a chance, even before Teddy and Matt because you've done so much better in your religion class and because of what Brother Kimball said."

"Thanks, Aunt Nellie. Thanks!" He stood up, still clinging to her hands. For a moment, she thought he was going to kiss her, but he only said, "You're so good. I don't know how anybody can be as good as you are." His voice broke.

"Go along with your blarney," she laughed, breaking the emotional tension. "If you were Matt, I'd know you'd been in the cookie jar or torn your best shirt." She freed her hands and gave his arm a loving pat. Mark took his paper and left the room, whistling.

Nellie picked up the sock but sat still, wondering how to persuade Ted to send Mark on a mission. Then Louie burst through the front door, her dark curls bouncing around her rosy cheeks, her eyes flashing. She threw her books on a table and came to the chair Mark had left.

"I've had the grandest day, Aunt Nellie. When I was going back to school after lunch, what do you think? That good-looking Bill Smith ran to catch up with me and carried my books and we laughed and talked and he asked me for a date. But even more thrilling, when I was coming home just now, who do you think came out of his gate and walked clear home with me?"

Nellie's smile died. "You don't mean that young Langdon fellow who lives on the corner?"

"No one else! You should have heard the compliments about my eyes and ..."

"Louie, don't you know he's a Gentile and—"

"He won't bite, Aunt Nellie. He's just awfully nice and he talks just like a book. I like him. And he's lonesome. People treat him like poison just because he doesn't belong to the Church. Isn't that narrow? It's not Christian. We think it's awful the way the Gentiles treat us, and we're just as bad."

"But Louie, he's a stranger. You don't know anything about him."

"That's what you think," Louie gloated. "I know a lot about him, and he's handsome and interesting. Why, he's been all over the world, practically. He's going to tell me all about coral reefs for my science paper and he's promised to let me use some photographs he took himself."

"Louie," gasped Nellie, "surely you're not going to take such favors from a stranger. You don't know what danger you might be putting yourself into."

"Oh, you old darling! I want fun! Interesting things to do. Interesting people to know. I just answered when he said 'good morning' and then walked a block with him while I was on the way to school and he was going to his office. What's dangerous about that? He's our neighbor. We ought to be friendly. You don't need to worry, dear."

"But I am worried," Nellie insisted. "What would your parents say if they knew you were walking and talking with a Gentile?"

"I'll tell them. I'll write this very night and tell them how much fun I'm having and thank them for letting me come here to school and tell them about Bill Smith and Dick Langdon. Oh, it's fun to be popular! Bill's an apostle's nephew. That ought to please them." Louie danced a few steps across the room. "Shall I start supper, Aunt Nellie? I'm starved. Have the boys come yet? Where are the children?"

Nellie laughed in spite of herself. "Yes, you may start supper. Only Mark is home. Emily Claire went to the library. Ernest and Jerry haven't come home from Primary yet."

Nellie put her work basket away and went to the kitchen. From the window, she could see majestic Mount Timpanogos, bathed in the soft radiance of a March sunset. For the past six months, she had often gazed at that towering mountain. She doubted if there were more inspiring summits in the entire Rocky Mountain range. Each time she looked at Timpanogos, she seemed to catch a different mood. She had grown to regard it as a personality. It not only gave inspiration but also a sense of protection, strength, and steadfastness, like the great Eternal. Now, concerned over Mark's desire to go on a mission to find his mother and Louie's infatuation for a Gentile, she longed for the strength, the wisdom, and the steadfastness the mountain peaks seemed to stand for.

Soon the family had arrived. There was the confusion of many voices, each eager to share the day's events. Nellie liked the hubbub of these early evening hours when she shared the broadening life of the older children, and she liked the quietness of the later hours when they sat around the dinner table with their books. The winter had been filled with diversified interests and experiences for each of them but no serious worries. Nellie was glad that none of them had suffered from homesickness and that they had all kept well. Down in Orderville, Ted was driving himself to the limit, buying more land and trading sheep for cattle. She knew he was busy every waking moment, not only to provide for his family but also to crowd out disturbing thoughts.

She wished she could know how the constantly growing rumors about the secretive marriages were affecting him and hoped he did not hear the ugly things she sometimes read or heard. His letters were invariably cheerful, filled with details about his work, family news, and suggestions. He usually slipped in a separate note just for her, but usually it was only a few words: "I love you, darling, and miss you more than you can know"; or "Last night I dreamed you were in my arms." Once he wrote, "You're doing wonders with our educational contingent. You should read what the children write about you." After Minnie's son was born, he wrote: "He's a fine, healthy baby and has beautiful strong eyes. She had a hard time. For a while, we were afraid she was going to slip away. Your mother, as always, was marvelous, and insists that she is all right—feels fine. But she is not her old self. Next to me, she is the one who misses you most. Sometimes I feel that I must see you, hear you telling me the things I need to hear, to help me hold on." The letter described Minnie's happiness in her motherhood and ended, "Perhaps this is compensation for what this marriage is costing us all."

Nellie couldn't make up her mind immediately about writing to Ted. Would it be better to wait and talk to him when he came up to general conference in April? And there was her worry, too, about Louie and the stranger down the street.

She tore up several starts but finally told him about Mark's theology paper and his teacher's comments. "Mark wants very much to go on a mission as soon as school is out this spring, if you are willing and think you can afford the expense. You know the Church is now sending very young men into the mission field, and you know what a developing experience it is for any boy. I heard a young returned missionary speak in church last Sunday. His parents must be very proud of him. He expressed such deep gratitude to them and to the Church for the privilege they had given him to fill a mission. Schooling and missions have always been our dreams for our children. Mark is much more eager to go and better prepared than the other boys. It means so much to him. Think it over, Ted, and talk to Luanna. Then we can decide when you are here for conference."

twenty-seven

Ted drove up in his wagon, carrying supplies for the rest of the school year, arriving in Provo the forenoon before the conference's opening day. These semi-annual, three-day general conferences, held in the great oval Tabernacle on Temple Square, were very important to all Church members. Reports were given, officials sustained, new policies explained, and inspired sermons preached. To members away from the center of Zion, going to conference was not only a religious duty but a sort of vacation, an opportunity to do business, and a time to visit friends.

Ted brought his mother and Bishop and Sister Jenkins with him. As they would need to continue their journey that afternoon, Ted had written for Nellie to be ready to go on to the city with them.

All day Nellie had been troubled about going. As she had feared, the confusion of the arrival of the travelers and having a larger group to dinner meant that there was no chance to talk privately with Ted. She was worried about Louie and young Langdon. Twice within the last week, they had gone riding together. Louie had talked less about her friends and what she was doing and had made evasive excuses when she was late coming from school. She had canceled a date with the very Bill Smith whose attentions had flattered her until recently, and she was refusing dates from other young men.

"Couldn't Louie go to conference with us?" Nellie had asked Ted almost as soon as he arrived. "She hasn't been to the city for a long time. The trip would do her good."

"Why Louie?" Mark asked. He had hurried home between classes to see if his father had arrived. Nellie knew he could hardly wait to find out what Ted thought about his mission. Professor Kimball had told him a group of young men would be leaving on missions as soon as the school year was over. Could his name be included on the list? Nellie knew how much it would mean to him to attend this conference. She also knew Louie had no interest in going. But she was desperate, hoping that a weekend with her father would make her see what she was doing.

"Yes, why Louie?" Ted repeated Mark's question. "Why have Louie go when you're going? She should stay and keep house for the rest. Besides, there she will miss a day or two of school. I wonder if we ought to take any of the children."

Before Nellie could answer, Mark said, "Professor Kimball advised as many of his students to go as possible. He feels that the academy should be closed so all students could attend. He especially urged anyone who may be going on a mission soon to attend. He said we—they would get much more from the conference than from school."

Ted looked thoughtfully at Mark. "So you really want to go on a mission this year, son?"

"Oh, yes. Do you think I can?" His face flushed and his eyes pleaded. He looked at Nellie appealingly.

Quickly she said, "We must talk it over when we get back from conference and when your father has more time. Now we must decide who is going to Salt Lake. Isn't there room for Mark and Louie both, Ted? I'm sure that others can manage. I've baked plenty of bread and have a roast and a pan of baked beans. They'd get along all right."

"I haven't heard Louie say anything about wanting to go," Mark said. "Why can't she stay and Teddy or Matt go?"

Nellie felt defeated. "I'd especially like Louie to go, Mark."

He glanced sharply at her, then comprehension dawned. "Oh, of course," he exclaimed. "You're worried about her and that Gentile and don't want to leave her here. Well, I guess you're right. She sluffed assembly this morning to go walking with him, and he hangs around the halls every day waiting for her to come out of class."

Nellie was heartsick. He had said all of this before Bishop Jenkins and Mary Ellen, Luanna's closest friend, and before Ted's mother, too. Ted looked at her with questioning concern, but Emily Granger was already demanding, "Gentile? What in the world do you mean? Is she gallivanting around with a Gentile?"

"I don't think there's anything to get upset about," said Nellie, trying hard to stay calm. "You know how popular Louie is. This young man is a neighbor and has helped her write a science paper. Several young men walk her home and take her out." She cast Ted an urgent glance.

"I suppose we could make room for two or three more," said Ted. "Perhaps we can borrow another spring seat. That way, Mark, Louie, and either Teddy or Matt can go. Everyone will be here at noon for dinner, won't they?" he asked Nellie.

"Yes, of course."

But Mark again unwittingly undid her by saying, "Unless Dick Langdon takes Louie to the drugstore for lunch like he did Tuesday."

"Mark," Nellie said quickly, "pack a suitcase with your things and Teddy's, and I'll put Louie's in with mine so we'll be ready to go as soon as dinner is over."

Wishing with all her heart that she had written her first worries to Ted, she went into the bedroom to pack. As she hoped, Ted followed her in. "Nellie, is there really something to be alarmed over?"

"Oh, Ted," she said, leaning against him, grateful for his strength. "I'm afraid so. I should have written, but I kept hoping it wasn't anything serious and I hated to worry you and Luanna. I thought at first she was just having a good time. You know how Louie is—so full of life and fun. Everybody takes to her. But all this week, I've been dreadfully worried. There's a difference in Louie herself. She's always been so frank and confidential. I've always felt that she was telling me everything. But she isn't talking now. I think she's worried and confused. I'm afraid she thinks she's falling in love with this stranger."

"What kind of a fellow is he?" asked Ted. "Just because he isn't a member of the Church shouldn't mean she can't be friends with him. I hope we're not that narrow and smug."

"No, I suppose not," Nellie returned weakly. She knew that Ted had liberal views about mixing with outsiders. When Brother Christensen had announced loudly that he'd rather bury his children than have them marry outside the Church, Ted had been disgusted for weeks.

"I don't really know much about him, Ted," Nellie admitted. I understand that his uncle bought that house on the corner about Christmas. He has something to do with that copper mine in the west Salt Lake Valley. I've never met either the uncle or aunt, but the neighbors say they hate Mormons and gloat over our persecutions. They have servants and travel a lot. They go to Salt Lake almost every week and go to California or Denver every few months. This young fellow came only four or five weeks ago when they were on a trip; they're still not back. He's traveled a great deal, but I don't know anything about his own family or where he grew up. He's waiting to start working with his uncle, says he's lonesome. He met her just by saying hello when she was walking past."

"I see," said Ted thoughtfully. "An outsider could be mighty lonely in a Mormon community; but if she's stopped talking to you and is missing school to be with him … Of course we'll take her with us."

Nellie, feeling relieved, went to the kitchen and began serving dinner, but Louie did not come. Nellie felt almost frantic, and Ted was soon as anxious as Nellie. As soon as Matt had finished, Nellie suggested he walk toward school and find her so they would not be delayed. He was feeling pleased and important at being left in charge and had promised Nellie that he would take care of Ernest and Jerry.

Matt returned before the dishes were finished. Louie had said she couldn't go. She had too many lessons and a journal to turn in on Monday. "But I think—" Matt looked at Bishop Jenkins and didn't finish.

Emily Granger demanded, "You think what, Matthew? Was she with that Gentile?"

"Yes," Matt admitted reluctantly. "They'd been looking for botany specimens on Temple Hill."

"Doesn't she know that her father and the rest of us are here?" Sister Granger insisted.

"Yes, and she said she was sorry to miss you," Matt said apologetically. "She said she had to classify her plants now, while they were fresh, and she'll see you Monday when you get back."

"Well," said Nellie cheerfully, "I'll just take her things out of my suitcase." As soon as Ted joined her in the bedroom, she said, low-voiced, "I won't go, Ted. I'm so sorry I said anything about her going before the others. Now they'll imagine all kinds of things."

"But what will they think if you don't go? If you really feel so worried that you think you shouldn't go, I'd better stay, too. We could let the boys drive the team, and with the bishop and Mother along, they would be all right."

Nellie hesitated. That was what she would like. She felt that the situation was too grave for her to handle alone. But she had also been hoping that Ted would hear something at this conference to give him peace that he had done the right thing by marrying Minnie. He must not miss it.

"No, you go on, Ted. It would look as if we are terribly upset if you stayed, too. Maybe I can come up for the Sunday session with Brother and Sister Brown. I know they can't get away before Saturday morning, and when they didn't know you were coming, they invited me to go with them."

"But I haven't seen you for so long, Nellie. I came more to see you than to go to conference."

She smiled, but tears were very close. She, too, had been counting the days and the hours until they could be together. "Don't say any more," she whispered, "or I won't have courage to stay when I want so much to be with you."

She walked back into the living room and told Mary Ellen Jenkins, "I've decided not to go today. Our neighbors are coming up Saturday and have invited me to go with them. I'll feel better about not leaving the children so long with so much responsibility."

Sister Granger got up from the sofa, eyes snapping. "Well, if Louie's playing up to some Gentile, someone ought to stay and look after her. Teddy, why don't you go right now and bring her home and tell this young fellow who's trying to lead her astray to let her alone."

"Oh, we don't know that he's doing that, Grandma," Nellie protested. "He may be a very nice young man."

"But he's a Gentile, isn't he? You said so yourself."

"I don't know but what that's a good suggestion, Mother," Ted said. He had made a hasty decision. Not only did he want to find out just what the situation was with Louie and the man, but a sudden wish had come to him to see what a young man who had never been fettered by obligations like those binding him was really like. He took his hat from the peg on the kitchen wall. "Where will I find Louie, Matt?" he asked.

twenty-eight

As Ted walked toward the academy, he wondered what he would say. He didn't want Louie to think he was spying on her or that he had come to reprimand her before her companion. He hardly understood his sudden determination. He knew Nellie was worried, but he felt she was overreacting to Louie's friendship. He could not think that Louie, always so frank about everything, could be in real danger of behaving badly. Perhaps, knowing Nellie's attitude toward strangers, she had stopped talking to save her worry. And what did *he* think? What if Louie wanted to marry someone not of her faith, providing he was good and clean and ambitious and devoted to her?

He turned a corner and saw Louie and the stranger leaning against a tree. His pulses quickened. Louie had grown taller and slenderer in the months she had been away. The tilt of her dark head as she looked up at the blond young man brought back a vivid memory of the first time he had kissed Luanna. There was no doubt that Louie had the same physical attractions Luanna had, and he knew how this young man must react to them. And Louie was so young and unsophisticated. Perhaps this young man was unscrupulous. He suddenly understood Nellie's fears.

He quickened his step. Louie, glancing aside, saw him. She said something to her companion who turned to face him and, for a moment, seemed uncertain. Louie waved in greeting, then spoke again more urgently. The stranger turned quickly and walked away. Anxiety tightened about Ted's heart. A few long strides brought him to Louie's side. Scarcely looking at her, he gave her a quick embrace, his eyes on the retreating figure.

"Why did your friend hurry away? I wanted to meet him." His voice didn't sound natural. "You hurry home and get ready to go to Salt Lake with us. I want to speak to that young man."

"Oh, Papa, please don't. He's all right. You can meet him some other time. And I don't want to go to conference." She clung to his arm, but he brushed her aside and hurried on.

"Won't you wait a minute, young man?" he called.

Langdon stopped and turned around. "Sure," he said. Insolence was in his voice, curiosity in his face. He took a few steps toward Ted. "I thought you were coming to see your daughter, and I didn't want to be in the way."

Ted looked back and saw that Louie was still standing by the tree, staring after them. "I just thought I'd like to meet you if you are one of Louie's friends." Ted tried to sound casual but did not succeed very well.

"Well, you've met me. What next?"

The insolent tone angered Ted. He was convinced at once that this man was not a desirable companion for his daughter. How deep was her infatuation? How close had their association been?

"What next?" he repeated. "Well, to be as unceremonious as you, as I'm a father, I'm interested in my children's associates, and I tell you frankly I do not want my daughter to have anything more to do with you."

Langdon laughed sneeringly, "May I ask why?"

"For one thing, your insufferable insolence to me just now. That proves you are not a gentleman."

"I presume that you consider *yourself* a gentleman?" the young man said, his own face flushing with anger. "You, a philanderer, a polygamist! You have your nerve, telling me I'm not a gentleman!" He laughed mockingly. "That's good! Are you afraid I might seduce her—which I assure you would not be difficult. And why not? Didn't you seduce her mother? And two or three other women? One, at the least, I've discovered, since your own church put a ban on such rotten—"

He didn't finish the sentence. Ted heard a roaring in his ears. His fist swung with all his strength. Langdon sprawled on the ground.

Louie came running up, screaming, "Papa! Papa, stop! What are you doing?" She flung herself on her knees beside Langdon. "You've killed him! I hate you!"

For a moment, Ted had the sickening sensation that he *had* killed the man. He looked helplessly around for assistance, mechanically massaging his hand. There was no one in sight. Then as Langdon moved, she bent over him. "I love him! And no matter what you say, I'm going with him tonight. Come on, Richard. I've made up my mind. I'll go with you anywhere you say."

Ted, stunned by her words, was speechless.

Langdon, recovering from the blow, got to his feet. Brushing his clothes, he gave Louie the same sneering laugh he had given her father. "Never mind, beautiful. We won't bother to take that little trip we were planning. My wife might hear about it, and she might not be as forgiving as a Mormon wife." He dabbed at the blood oozing from his cut lip.

Louie turned white. She pressed her hands against her lips. "Your wife!" she gasped. "You said you loved me." Panic, desperation, and shame covered her face.

"Maybe I did love you a little while, at times. Ask your old man to explain it. He's experienced. And I expect to see that somebody gives him a chance to explain that last concubine of his."

Ted's fists clenched of themselves and he took a step forward. Langdon retreated, lifting his hat ceremoniously. "So glad to have met you both," he sneered, and walked away. Ted took Louie's arm and drew her in the opposite direction. She was sobbing hysterically. A man down the block standing near his fence asked Ted. "Has something happened?" He looked toward the retreating Langdon. "Is there anything we can do?"

"No, thank you," Ted answered and hurried on. The incident had happened so quickly and was so revolting that he felt ill. Mechanically he soothed Louie, holding his arm around her and whispering, "There, there, it's all over. Don't feel so bad, honey."

Before they reached home, she had quieted and turned to him. "Oh, Papa, can you forgive me? For what I've done. I told him about Minnie. I've been acting so—Did Aunt Nellie tell you? Papa, he seemed so nice, so different. Oh, I'll never forgive myself."

Ted searched her eyes, "Louie, you … you haven't let him—"

"Oh, no, no. But he was trying to coax me to go on the train with him—Oh, Papa, what if you hadn't come!"

"Thank goodness it was not worse, and it's all over with. Now you must try to forget it. Just be thankful it wasn't a more terrible experience." He gave her his handkerchief. Her own was a sodden ball. "Now see if you can't stop crying. Grandma and Bishop and Sister Jenkins are at the house. There's no need for them to know what has happened."

"Oh, no. Let's not let anybody know, not ever."

He pressed her hand reassuringly. As they neared the gate, he could see several curious faces watching at the window. "You run around to the back door and wash your face. I'll go in and have those who are going to conference get in the wagon. They're all ready and we must get going. Nellie has your things packed with hers."

Louie nodded and ran off. Ted opened the front door and called, "Are you all ready? Louie is here and will be going with us. We'd better get off if you boys have the team hitched up."

He gave Nellie a relieved smile, and she went to find Louie.

"Teddy," his mother said, "when Louie passed the window, it looked like she'd been crying. You didn't punish her too hard, did you? She's a big girl now."

"Not too hard, Mother, but please don't ask her questions or say anything about it to her—any of you. Girls her age are sensitive, you know."

Nellie came back in carrying her suitcase with Louie close behind her. She could see beneath Ted's facade to the turmoil, but Louie was smiling and chattering as she said goodbye to the children and greeted her grandmother and friends from home. As they climbed in the wagon, she whispered to Nellie, "Aunt Nellie, something terrible happened. Will you forgive me for the way I've been acting? Oh, I … I might have—"

"Don't try to tell me now, dear," Nellie whispered back. "Of course I forgive you. I can see by your eyes that you're back with us again, and I'm so glad." She gave Louie a quick kiss.

IF TED HAD EXPECTED to receive comfort from the conference, he was disappointed. No sermon commended the Saints for accepting the revelation on plural marriage and living it despite persecutions. Only in the last session did anyone mention the Manifesto. Then President Woodruff said, "I want to urge you, brothers and sisters, to obey not only the laws of the Church but also the laws of the land. We are a peace-loving people. We cannot live near to the Lord with conflict within ourselves. Such conflicts come when we are punished for disobeying the laws of the country in which we live and the government from which we desire protection."

How different, Ted thought, from the instructions he had heard previously in that very Tabernacle or from the General Authorities who had visited in his remote hometown. He recalled the agony before marrying Nellie when it seemed to him that he was drawn into plural marriage by some unseen power stronger than himself. And he brooded over the encounter with Langdon. Of course, the young Easterner was a cad who should have received more severe punishment for trying to seduce Louie. He couldn't forget that threat of causing future trouble for him. But worst of all was his humiliation as he realized—as this man's coarse words had made him realize—how his mode of life was regarded by people outside his own small world. He brooded over the insults and threats as well as over the Church's stand.

Nellie tried as always to help him see that he had done what was honorable, only what the Lord would approve. But now she could not assure him that what the Church expected of him was what the Lord wanted him to do. When she asked if the President had been speaking more for their enemies than for the Saints, a kind of deception Ted had recognized before, he pointed out that this could not be true. There was no denying that the Church was taking a stand against the doctrine it had so zealously worked to enforce. He felt betrayed. The anchor to which he had clung to maintain his integrity was shattered. He floundered between despondence, doubt, and lost idealism, wondering which loss hurt the most.

"But, Ted," Nellie begged, "please try not to feel like that. Whatever you have done, all through your life, has been what seemed honorable. You have never been thinking of yourself, always of others. Remember the sacrifice to both of us that day when we fought the battle with our own selfish feelings about sharing our lives with another? But then it seemed the right thing to do. Do you remember?"

"Do I remember? God! Could I ever forget it, that look in your face, the torture that cut through my whole being? Nellie, we became old that day. You were seventeen and I not twenty. Why didn't we rebel then? That was the time. Think what we would have escaped—all the misery, the sacrifice, the dread, if we had stood out then and demanded our own lives. We could have left the Church if necessary, as it is leaving us now. Oh, what an inextricable web we are tangled in!"

"Darling, don't let yourself feel like that. We did what seemed best. God will not let us down, even if it seems the Church has. Don't think what we have missed. Think what we have gained. You have had experiences which have made you a wonderful leader. Think of the children. What would life be like without Ted and the twins and Louie? You would sacrifice anything for any one of them. Without Luanna and Jane and Minnie, there would be only three living children instead of our wonderful fourteen. Can you feel that your life has no meaning or value when you look at them and work to make them good citizens?"

Ted sighed and was silent. As always, the children were the most telling persuasion. They gave his life meaning. He drew Nellie into his arms and kissed her. Again, she had helped him find a measure of peace after his battle with himself. He stood astounded at her limitless unselfishness, at the breadth of her understanding, and at the depth of her love for him.

A FEW WEEKS AFTER Ted returned home, Brother Cameron drove up, his face urgent and troubled. "Ted, while I was in the co-op this morning, a stranger came in asking about you. I think he's a deputy. I'm afraid another raid is beginning for you brethren who took wives after the Manifesto."

twenty-nine

When Ted learned that young Langdon had stirred up this new persecution against him, it was his anger more than anything else that made him determined to evade the law as long as possible. He didn't blame the government for enforcing the laws. It was the Church's position that troubled him. The Church authorities had taken no stand against those who continued living in polygamy after serving penitentiary terms. In fact, General Authorities had authorized some marriages contracted after that point. But now he and others were being punished by the Church for following its own teachings. It was this inconsistency, this paradox, that was hard to accept.

And now Minnie was going to have another baby. Although she continued to use Graham as her surname, Ted felt that everyone recognized the ruse. With this second pregnancy, even those who may have doubted it before were now convinced that she was Ted's wife. Taking their cue from the General Authorities, the local Church leaders became strangely aloof. Brother Christensen, who had openly lamented at the time of the Manifesto that he had not been swifter in taking more wives, was openly critical and treated Ted with a dislike he had formerly tried to conceal. The bishop no longer asked Ted's advice as he had for all the years he had been in office. At church, eyes that had been warm and friendly now looked at them askance.

By the time Nellie and the children returned from Provo, Ted was haggard. Nellie floundered before Ted's anger and despair. She knew she could no longer restore his peace of mind. Luanna was openly defiant, frequently airing her views on Ted's self-righteous critics—if possible, in their presence. It had caused a breach with Mary Ellen Jenkins, especially now that Nate was the bishop.

Then Mark received his mission call. Nellie was the first to see his letter from "Box B," the mailing address of the Church presidency. She had been helping Auntie sort the mail, as she often did when she came on daily visits to her mother. She doubted if Mark himself would be more excited than she. He had requested to serve in California, but missionaries were expected to go where they were called. If he should find his mother, what then? What would Jane be like? Eleven years living with that man must have changed her. But it was so improbable, she scolded herself. Rather, she should be asking herself how to help Mark deal with the inevitable disappointment.

She glanced up. He was hurrying down the street, knowing that the mail was in. Quickly she brought him the letter and hung over him as he ripped it open. "California!" he shouted triumphantly, then hugged Nellie exuberantly and hurried away to tell the others.

Nellie watched him go and returned to her work, chatting happily with Auntie. But a faint line of worry lay between her brows. Had she done right by urging Ted to let him go a mission when he was so young and had this secret purpose? She had never kept secrets from Ted, but she didn't know how to resolve this problem. She had given her word to Mark.

As soon as she was finished with her work, she hurried in to tell her mother the good news. Sister Hagen was almost a cripple from rheumatism. Her joints were stiff and swollen. Her hands pained even when she was not using them. Her long years of exposure to all kinds of weather, and her hard work and sleepless nights had taken their toll. She never complained, but Nellie knew that she welcomed visits as a distraction from the unceasing pain. Minnie and little Darrel were a great comfort to her, and Nellie sent one or two children down every day or evening in addition to her own visits. Auntie nursed her faithfully, but Nellie could see that it was her own visits that brought the greatest comfort.

Mark left only a week later for Salt Lake City, where he would be ordained an elder, set apart as a missionary, and briefed on the work he was to do. At the ward's farewell party, Ted, despite his dread, managed to conceal his inner feelings about both his own doubts and the critics'. Nellie felt there was something of the old regard for the family in the warm social hour that followed.

BY MIDSUMMER, NELLIE'S MOTHER was bedfast. Nellie, who had been on the farm for a few weeks, came to town to stay as long as her mother should need her. The community's shared concern and gratitude to Sister Hagen was, in fact, a strengthening bond, and the gulf that had widened during the past year closed a little.

On one of her visits to town, Luanna grumbled good-naturedly, "Ted's about as much company as an iceberg. I can't see why he has to take things so hard and feel so blue when he's done nothing but what he had to do. And Louie is so moody and irritable, I don't believe going away to school is good for her. I feel sorry for Jimmy Fergeson. He comes to see her night after night, and half the time she sits there as glum as her father. She's always been so jolly and full of fun, but now when I try to talk to her, she goes inside, shuts the door, and pulls down the shade."

Nellie wondered why Louie had not confided in her mother. It would do her good, and Luanna's "don't worry" philosophy would be good for her. Nellie said only, "Louie had a very trying experience this spring. I think if she would tell you about it, you could help her get over it. She's taking it too seriously and I don't know anyone who could help her see that so well as you."

"Well, of all things! Why hasn't she told me? What was it?" Luanna was both curious and alarmed.

"It's nothing to worry about now. I'm sure Louie would rather tell you herself. And I'm sure between you and Jimmy, she'll become her old happy self again."

Letters from Mark were excited and happy. He liked his mission president and the other missionaries. In one letter, he confessed, "Talking about the gospel is not as easy as I thought it would be, especially at street meetings where the audience is a shifting, indifferent crowd. I thought they'd be the most enjoyable part of the work. They're interesting, but they're not easy."

Nellie visualized Mark, trying to keep his mind on his text while his eyes searched the crowd, searching for his mother's face, remembered from childhood and colored with loving imagination. In all probability he would not recognize it if he saw it.

In late August, Sister Hagen's suffering ended. Nellie's prayer for almost a month had been that she could be released quickly. Every movement hurt her, and she had wasted away to nothing. Finally she asked Jane's father to come and dedicate her to the Lord rather than to administer to her for her recovery. With Brother Draper, Brother Cameron anointed her head with consecrated oil, laid their hands on her head, and prayed, reminding the Lord of her long and loving service, of her untiring effort to relieve the pain of others, of her generosity, faith, strength, and goodness. Then he dedicated her to the Lord as his beloved daughter and asked that

God's will be done. As they removed their hands from her head, Clara Hagen remained very still with her eyes closed but softly said, "Thank you. I feel better."

Nellie, noticing that her face began to lose its drawn look, breathed a silent prayer of thanksgiving. After the men left, she watched as her mother breathed slowly and easily. There seemed to be no pain. Auntie entered quietly. "She seems easy," she whispered with surprise and satisfaction.

Nellie thought of mother, Auntie, Minnie, and herself—the lives of four women, entangled by blood and marriage. What would enemies of polygamy think if they could see the devotion these four shared? Later, after Darrel was asleep, Minnie came in, blinking a little, as though the faint light hurt her.

"How is she?" she asked softly, sitting beside Auntie.

"She's been easier since the elders came," Nellie answered. "How are you feeling, Minnie?"

"Pretty good nearly all the time now."

"You mustn't worry when the time comes," Nellie said comfortingly. "Everything will be all right. Mother told me a long time ago that Sister Larsen is just as good a midwife as she ever was."

Minnie sighed. "No one will believe that."

Nellie smiled, "You'll get along fine. The second baby nearly always comes easier than the first."

"I would be glad to go through it if it were a thousand times harder."

Nellie knew that Minnie felt about motherhood as she herself did— that it was the crowning blessing of womanhood. But to Minnie, it was almost all she had. She was Ted's wife, of course, but she had had none of his companionship except for stolen hours. And so much of the physical world was shut away from her—the loveliness of dawn, the spring moonlight, the changing glory of the seasons.

Minnie grieved over Ted's persecutions in a special way. They had been brought upon him because of her. Once she told Nellie, "I should have told him that we shouldn't be married when we found out what had happened. I should have been strong and saved him from all this. But my patriarchal blessing ... I wanted babies so much."

"I know, dear. You mustn't worry. Surely things will turn out all right."

"But I should have been satisfied with Darrel. All this new trouble is so hard on all of you. The way the Church members—"

She broke off. Sister Hagen stirred. Nellie bent over the bed. Her mother muttered something, then repeated, " ... music."

"Yes," said Minnie. "Beautiful music."

Nellie caught the sound of sweet voices. "It must be the choir practicing," she said.

Auntie came quickly to the other side of the bed. "This is not the night for choir practice," she said. Her voice was low but exultant.

Nellie stared into the older woman's eyes. The music swelled around them, piercingly sweet, ringingly glorious.

Her mother stirred again and lifted her head. "Do you want a drink, Mother?" Nellie asked.

Auntie poured a glass of water from the pitcher on the dresser.

"Yes," said Clara, but she was not speaking to them. "Yes, Isaac. I'm coming." The watchers stood transfixed. The music ceased. Clara's head fell back on her pillow and turned sideways with a little gasping sigh. Nellie seized her mother's hand and groped for Minnie's with the other. Minnie gravely reached across the bed. Auntie took Minnie's hand, took in her other hand the dead hand of her sister wife, and bowed her head.

thirty

Nellie had always believed the Mormon view of death—that it was simply the passing of an immortal spirit to the next life where all sickness, unhappiness, and imperfection cease to exist. Her natural human dread of death had been assuaged by her father's peaceful death and especially by the beauty of her mother's death. She would never forget the sudden peace, light, and happiness that overspread her mother's face as she called, "Yes, Isaac, I'm coming." There was no doubt in Nellie's mind that her father had actually been in the room at that moment. And they had all heard the music—heavenly music that had wafted out during the moment the gates of heaven were ajar to let her father bring in his beloved. She smiled at her fancy. They were together now, but not as they had been when they were first married, when there had been no other wives. Minnie, Father's third wife, would be with him. Why should Nellie have that little sadness because Minnie was there? She had been with Father for a long time. Things would be the same there as here. But maybe God would make all the things that didn't seem right here perfect there.

Which of Ted's wives would go first? Where would Jane fit? If Ted went first, would he come for her? Such musings became painful, and she threw herself into her work. The children would go back to the academy in the fall. They had worked hard during the summer. Ernest, David, Jerry, even Johnny had helped with the planting, irrigating, and weeding. They were all busy now with the harvest. Ted had made several profitable transactions during recent years. He had interests in most of Southern Utah's businesses. His neighbors used to say, "If the rest of us could manage as well as Ted Chandler, this would be a prosperous community." But now they said, "Well, even if the Church doesn't approve of Chandler's last marriage, nothing interferes with his money-making."

Ted felt isolated in his community, no longer a necessary and integral part of its affairs. The strictly orthodox never questioned anything the

Church leaders did. Anyone who married after the Manifesto was disobedient. Those who had not accepted it deserved the persecutions they brought upon themselves. A few felt that a revelation could not be changed so lightly, but they remained silent and, like Ted, retreated to their own families.

ONE AFTERNOON IN LATE August, Louie came to the field where Ted and the boys were shocking up wheat. She brought a pail of lemonade and a basket of cookies that they received with whoops of joy, sitting in the shade of the shocks. After they had finished, Matt challenged the other boys to race to the other end of the field where they were to work for the rest of the day.

As they set off, Ted smiled at his daughter. "That was very nice, Louie. Did you make the cookies?"

"Yes, they're not as good as Aunt Nellie's, but I'm learning."

"I couldn't tell the difference. Tell Nellie she's a good teacher, or that she has a very apt pupil." He patted her shoulder, trying to coax a smile from her. She had been so sad all summer. Now she turned away and began to weep.

Ted put his arm around her. "What is it, Louie? Can't you tell me? You're not still grieving over Langdon, are you? Were you truly in love?"

"No, but it's my fault the deps are after you again. And the way people here treat you—oh, it's awful."

"You're wrong, Louie," he said resignedly. "Sooner or later, the persecutions would have started again. That's not your fault and much less the way people treat me. You're to blame for nothing."

"Then who is to blame? People don't speak to you. You're never asked to talk at church or even administer the sacrament. No one has come for a patriarchal blessing all summer. And you used to be bishop. It's not fair!"

Ted shifted uneasily. He had blindly hoped that the children might not notice. "Who's been talking to you, Louie?"

"No one. But I can see. Everybody can. And Jimmy ... Oh, Papa, Jimmy wants to marry me, and I wanted to marry him. But his father said it served you right, that you're getting what's coming to you. He's not worth your little finger, and I told Jimmy so and I told him not to come any more."

Ted swallowed hard. The sins of the fathers were being visited on two innocent youngsters. He pulled himself together and smiled. "So you and Jimmy have quarreled over your fathers. Don't you think that's foolish? We can take care of ourselves. Save your worries for your children. Don't you think that would be best?" Then he added, "You must like Jimmy a lot if you wanted to marry him. I think he's a fine boy, and we're neighbors. You must make up your quarrel."

Secretly he was relieved. He had wondered if her experience with a sophisticated man of the world had made her dissatisfied with the companionship of country boys.

"I did like him, I guess, before I heard that about his father. But we quarreled about other things. He says I'm stuck up since I got back from school, and it isn't true. He has no right to say that and his father has no right to talk about you, so I won't make up and I don't care if I never see him again." Her tears flowed afresh.

Comfortingly, Ted said, "Well, you'll be leaving in a few weeks and won't see him till next summer. Unless he's decided to go to the academy?"

"That's another thing," wailed Louie. "He'd like to, but his father doesn't believe in education—says it's a waste of money and spoils young people for our kind of life. So I guess Jimmy's going to be satisfied with what his father thinks is good enough. I told him dozens of boys and girls were working their way through school without any help and that he could go if he wanted to bad enough. If Jimmy had been there last year, I wouldn't have got into that horrid mess. Jimmy's smart. He argues well enough for a lawyer. But what difference does that make to me now?" She picked up the pail and turned to go.

Ted said thoughtfully, "I'm sure you like him in spite of your quarrels, and I know he thinks a great deal of you. He was lonesome while you were gone. I don't think he looked at another girl. How would it be if I had a talk with him about school? Maybe he just needs a little encouragement. You must forget what his father says about me. That shouldn't make any difference to you and Jimmy—not enough to really matter if you care for each other."

She turned back, her face happy. "Will you talk to him, Papa? And don't you really care how folks are acting toward you?"

"I'll talk with him right away. As for your other question, of course I care. It isn't pleasant to have old friends turn against you. But I care most for what it is doing to you children. Run along now and help Aunt Nellie."

Louie dropped the pail and threw her arms around her father. "Oh, Papa, you're so good! I love you, and I won't—I promise not to bring trouble to you next year."

"I know you won't, dear. I love you and want you to be happy."

As Ted walked across the field to join his boys, he was glad that the distance between him and Louie had been mended, but a pain gnawed at his heart. To be an honest man, to be held in honor among his associates—was that too much to ask? The two incentives for which he labored had been the approval of the Church and the welfare of his family. Now one of these incentives was gone. Would the time come when his family would condemn him, too? He tried not to think about it. He poured all his energies into work, trying to plan new ways to improve his financial status, that he might give his loved ones a sense of physical security, if nothing else.

MINNIE'S BABY WAS BORN the last day of August, an easier birth. Minnie wanted to name her tiny black-haired daughter Nellie, but Nellie persuaded her to give it her own name, Minnie Rose.

Ted had not been attending sacrament meetings on Sundays for some time. No one had come to him for a patriarchal blessing for months. He could no longer face the open disapproval of those who had formerly looked to him as both their spiritual and temporal leader. But since it was taken for granted by everyone in the ward that he and Minnie were married, he decided to attend church and bless and name the baby at the monthly fast meeting.

He did not leave the farm with Nellie and the children when they left to attend Sunday School at ten o'clock, making the excuse that he would finish irrigating on the upper field, then join them at two for testimony meeting. He was a little late on purpose and wondered what Bishop Jenkins would do. When Darrel had been blessed, Ted had stood in the circle with other fathers and priesthood holders. Not all fathers blessed their own children, and the bishop had made Ted's participation seem like the next logical turn for a child without a father.

But today would be a test. It would prove whether he was considered worthy to hold God's holy priesthood. The congregation was already singing the opening song as he drove up:

> *We thank thee, O God, for a prophet,*
> *To guide us in these latter days…*

Ted knew the words by heart, but now his mind twisted around the words. Did he thank God for a prophet—the man who had uttered words so opposite to those of an earlier prophet?

> *We thank thee for sending the gospel*
> *To lighten our minds with its rays...*

Had he received any lightening of his mind? No. He was groping in the dark instead of finding a serene and satisfying philosophy of life.

> *We feel it a pleasure to serve thee*
> *And love to obey thy command.*

Yes, he had felt that pleasure—to serve and even to obey. He recalled again the visit of President Young. He had experienced a genuine upsurge of spirituality. He had been happy, rejoicing in his work. What a contrast to the despondency that burdened him today. How had he come to this state? He had never purposely done anything to rob himself of the divine blessing and power the priesthood had bestowed upon him. He longed for the old peace and assurance that had gone from his life.

He slipped into the end of a vacant bench at the rear. When his other children were blessed, he had always had a place on the rostrum. Apparently, the fathers of other babies to be blessed were already sitting up there. Perhaps he should have come early. The mothers, holding babies in their long christening dresses, were sitting, as was the custom, on the front row, just below the choir seats. Bertha Larsen was there, Fran Kendall, and Nora Christensen. Ted thought that usually one of Brother Christensen's wives occupied a seat on that row. He must have almost fifty children. Of course, many had died in infancy, his wives too worn down from repeated pregnancies to give birth to healthy children. He preached constantly that a man's posterity was his glory. Nancy Parker was there, too. She looked old enough to be the child's grandmother, but she was no older than Nellie and Luanna. Minnie was there, with Nellie beside her, holding Darrel and trying to help quiet the baby.

Where was Luanna? He hadn't been in town for several days. Soon he saw her across the room, whispering to Mary Ellen Jenkins. They were looking at Nancy. There had been a rumor about Brother Parker and a girl in a hotel at Marysvale when he went to sell his wool. Surely—but Ted dismissed the thought.

He bowed his head for the opening prayer. The bishop made the announcements, then added, "Brother Parker, will you come to the stand." He had been sitting halfway down the audience with his second wife and a benchful of children. Ted waited. Would he be called next? The other fathers were all there now. He felt tense with a fearful expectancy. Then the bishop sat down. He tried to think that the bishop may not have seen him, but he was not sure.

Then the chorister began leading them in the sacrament song, "O My Father." He liked this hymn. It reminded him of the Muddy Mission when he used to watch Nellie as she sang. He sighed. How far away that time seemed. How could he and Nellie be the same people as those inexperienced, happy, dreaming sweethearts? He studied what he could see of Nellie's face from his angle. It was thin, delicate, and pale. Her hair was streaked with gray. But she still seemed beautiful. One thing that had not changed was their love. It had grown deeper and more sure.

> *When I leave this frail existence,*
> *When I lay this mortal by,*
> *Father, Mother, may I greet you*
> *In your royal courts on high?*

What was waiting after this life? The song sounded so sure. Would he want it? Would all the family ties be perpetuated as the Church taught? Where would Jimmy fit in? He sighed again.

> *Then at length when I've completed*
> *All you sent me forth to do ...*

What had God sent him forth to do? Could there be a plan, a great purpose in all the muddle that surrounded him? The sacrament prayers were pronounced. The deacons carried the bread and water among the congregation. Ted ate the little piece of bread and sipped the water mechanically. He kept his eyes on the bishop, willing him to look at him, to recognize his presence.

Why did it matter so much that he be asked to bless Minnie's baby? Anyone holding the priesthood could give the blessing. He admitted to himself that it wasn't the act of officiating that he cared about. It was the participation as a member of the community. Would he be accepted or rejected? If he could not bless his own child, then everyone in the room would know that he, once their bishop, had lost his standing in the Church.

The bishop's eyes fell on him. Ted locked gazes, holding the bishop's eyes with his own. The bishop looked away. As the deacons carried the trays back to the sacrament table, Ted felt his jaws ache with the force of his clenched muscles.

The bishop rose. "And now is the joyous time to give names and blessings to the children born among us. Will the fathers—" his eyes brushed Ted's, then he continued deliberately "—now seated on the stand please form a circle..."

Ted heard nothing else. Numbly, he saw the bishop himself pick up little Minnie Rose and carry her into the circle. He slumped back on the bench. He felt faint. He felt the pitiless eyes of God upon him, the unforgiving eyes of the congregation. As soon as he felt he could walk, he slipped away.

thirty-one

Nellie suffered with Ted. She had seen him slip into the meeting, but she could not bear to look at him after Bishop Jenkins had ignored him. No reprimand in words could have cut so deeply as that public slight.

Luanna had missed it. After church, gathered with the family around the dinner table, Luanna asked innocently, "Why didn't you bless the baby, Teddy?"

The pained flush that spread over Ted's face made Nellie almost hate Luanna. How could she have been so blind? Or was she so superficial that she could not sense the devastating undercurrent of such an incident?

"Ted was late," Nellie interposed quickly. "He stayed to finish the irrigating after we came for Sunday School. But since we're all together, perhaps we should discuss plans for the fall?"

Ted shot her a grateful glance. He was making only a pretense of eating. Again, they were trying to decide whether one of the mothers should go with the children or whether to find a suitable boarding house for Louie, Teddy, and Matt.

"Well, if what I've had hints of has any foundation," Luanna said rather irritably, "I don't think we should send the children off alone. Didn't Louie have some kind of scandalous affair with a Gentile? Being only her mother, I've never known exactly what happened."

Louie blushed painfully and stared at her plate. Nellie winced. She wished she hadn't mentioned Louie's unfortunate experience. She should have known how hard it would be for Louie to talk about it. She also knew that Luanna lightheartedly betrayed the children's confidences sometimes, because she did not take them seriously. No wonder the children were reluctant to share some things.

"Oh, there was no scandal at all," said Nellie lightly. "Just an experience any pretty girl might have, meeting all kinds of people for the first time."

"But didn't some scalawag she was running around with set the officers on your trail, Teddy, for marrying Minnie?"

"That may be so, but there's no way to know," said Ted quietly. "But it wasn't Louie's fault in any way."

"Why don't you go this year, Luanna?" Nellie asked. "You'd enjoy the lectures and concerts at the academy, and you'd meet new people."

"We don't really need anyone to look after us," said Matt. "I'm sure Ted and I can take care of ourselves, and I understand Jimmy Fergeson is going along to look after Lou."

"Well, if Jimmy's really going, one of us will have to go," Luanna said decisively. "He hasn't any sense at all about when it's time for him to go home. Wasn't it long past midnight when he left last night, Louie? And after I'd called you twice."

"Oh, it wasn't so very late, Mother," pleaded Louie, blushing again. "And he hadn't been here for ..."

"At least two nights," teased David. "They were making up after a quarrel," he snickered.

"We were planning about school, smartie," snapped Louie, "and you had no business listening." She glanced appreciatively at her father. "You encouraged him to go, didn't you, Papa?"

"Well, I don't know whether I'd want the responsibility of all of you in a strange place," said Luanna. "If nearly scandalous things can happen when Aunt Nellie was looking after you, there's no telling what would happen with me on the job."

"What if I undertook the job?" Ted sighed. They all stared at him in surprise. It came to Nellie in a flash that he desperately needed to get away. It would be the best thing in the world for him. In the larger city, he could avoid the officers more easily and would not be humiliated daily by slights from overzealous Church officers or self-righteous members.

"That's exactly what you must do, Ted," she said enthusiastically. "You must go to Provo with the children. Luanna and I can take turns being with you and staying here to look after things. I'm sure you can get Silas Hawkins to look after the farm."

After that, things seemed to fall quickly into place. Although Luanna did not like staying behind, she knew Nellie was a better manager and experienced from the previous year. "My turn will come," she said gaily, waving them off.

"I can't tell you how good it seems to get away," Ted confided to Nellie on the first evening of their trip. They were sitting on a spring seat near the wagon, a little way back from the fire where the children were cleaning up after supper. Nellie slipped her hand into his. It seemed too good to be true that they could be together and away from some of their worries.

"You'll enjoy so many things you've never had a chance to learn about before," she said.

"I'll enjoy not meeting Bishop Jenkins or Brother Christensen and having them cough and suddenly remember something in the opposite direction. If they'd come right out and tell me I'm not fit to associate with them, I could try to defend my position. But this subterfuge—pretending not to see me ..." He clenched his teeth.

Nellie tightened her fingers but could think of nothing to say. She could no longer tell him that he was doing what the Church, and therefore God, wanted him to do; if he stood condemned by the Church, did not God also condemn him? The last few weeks had been hard. He had systematically avoided contact with anyone but the family as much as possible. He had no appetite, and his sleep was broken. Always the dark brooding haunted his eyes.

Of course, he was also worried about his mother. She had felt feeble for some weeks. The night before they left, she had had a strange dizzy spell and felt a peculiar numb feeling the next morning. It was probably worry about him that had affected her own health. He wished with all his heart that he could be the only one to suffer because of their situation.

He had asked if she wanted him to stay. He was all she had. But she had urged him to go. Nellie had made her see how necessary a change was at this time. His mother had said, "No, Teddy, there's nothing you could do that someone else can't do just as well. If I don't feel better, we'll let you know, and you can come back and see me. I'm sure I'll be all right."

"I wish you were going with us," he had said. "Will you come when you feel better?"

"I can do more good here helping Minnie and the baby. I don't think I could stand to be away from little Darrel. I'm reliving the days when you were a little boy."

It was true that Sister Granger was a great help to Minnie and her children. Though she grieved over the trouble Ted's marriage to Minnie brought, she never doubted it was right. She had always been devoted to Minnie and adored the children. Between her and Auntie, Minnie had excellent care.

IN PROVO, THE CHILDREN were eager to see their old friends and get started in school. Within a few weeks, they were well settled and Nellie had the home in good running order. If it had not been for her anxiety over Ted, she would have been very happy. There was always something interesting to hear when the children came home for lunch and in the evening. She loved to hear them talk about their classes, teachers, and friends. She was proud of their extra-curricular activities.

Jimmy was working part-time as a janitor at the school; he lived with two other young men who were also working their ways through school. He was almost like one of the family. Nellie invited him often to meals and advised him about cooking and housekeeping, since he was "batching it."

Emily Claire's never-wavering ambition to be a writer and her passion for reading meant that she always had things to talk about with Nellie. Jerry loved boats and wagons. Ernest was much like Teddy, always interested in the mysteries and secrets of nature. Each contributed something unique to the family. Best of all, they loved each other dearly and were interested in each other's activities. Edna and Johnny, Jane's two youngest, were almost totally Nellie's. None of the children resembled Jane as much as Mark, though Edna looked more like her, showed artistic leanings, had Jane's quick, impulsive movements, and often wanted to be by herself. Matt and Johnny were the down-to-earth, practical type. They loved farming, animals, and regular routines.

Ted stayed home almost constantly, first helping them get settled, then helping Nellie with meal preparation and dish-washing, tasks he had never done before in all his life. He planned home tasks for the children, believing that they should all have responsibilities for character development. It seemed wonderful to Nellie to share so much of his time. In the afternoons, they would often take long walks or go shopping together. In the evenings, they went to school events—dances, games, plays, lectures, and concerts. Ted was quiet, but she hoped that he would brood less and acquire new interests. Always she tried to make the depth of her love serve as a tonic to his troubled spirit.

But, unused to even brief periods of physical inactivity, Ted soon became restless, worried about how things were going at home. He read his mother's cheerful letters suspiciously, concerned that she might be keeping something from him. He feared that Luanna might not keep in close touch with Silas Hawkins and wouldn't know if he was wasting feed or letting the farm implements sit out in the rain.

Nellie cast about for diversions. She knew she couldn't even suggest affiliation with any of the Church's auxiliary organizations. One evening when Teddy was recounting highlights of his science teacher's lecture on Michael Farraday, she suggested, "Teddy, why don't you take your father to some of your classes? He'd enjoy learning some of the things he's giving you the privilege of learning."

"Will you come, Papa?" Teddy asked eagerly. "Lots of parents visit, especially around conference time."

Ted's face had lightened at the suggestion but darkened at the word "conference." Later he told Nellie gloomily, "It's a Church school. I wouldn't feel right about taking too many advantages. And I think I'd better not be seen too much. The papers say the deps have been ordered to make another try to find us criminals." His voice was bitter.

"Well, at least the children could bring books home for you," said Nellie. "You could make up your own courses of study."

The suggestion was a godsend. Ted began spending his afternoons at the library. He had always regretted his limited education. Now he began reading methodically in the fields that interested him most, losing himself for hours with Huxley, Lyall, Darwin, Socrates, and Aristotle. He felt a strange fellowship with Socrates, who had given his life for what he thought and taught.

Then, just after October conference, came the summons home. Ted's mother had suffered the stroke they had feared earlier and died within a few hours. Ted and Nellie left the children and went home for the funeral. Ted suffered agonies of grief, and the funeral was an ordeal. It seemed that every speaker tried to stab, not comfort him. Each one told of the dead woman's faithfulness, of the trials she had endured. "The hardships of pioneer life took the strength of her youth," intoned Bishop Jenkins, "but in her later years she had a trial more difficult and soul-testing." Ted felt too crushed even to be angry. Had she really suffered so, because of him? He wished he had talked to her about his problem. He might have been able to help her understand—but how, when he didn't understand it himself? He didn't feel guilty. He had never felt guilty, because it always seemed his actions had been inevitable. He felt only crushed and embittered.

But even greater humiliation awaited him. The day after the funeral, Bishop Jenkins and his two counselors called on Ted. After a cursory sentence or two of condolence, Bishop Jenkins cleared his throat and, without looking directly at Ted, said, "Brother Chandler, we're sorry to perform this painful duty, but duty it is. Therefore I respond. We have received a communication from the General Authorities that all those who disregarded the Manifesto are to be released from their callings. There has been no decision reached as to whether they will be excommunicated, but they are not to represent the Church in any way. It is our duty to tell you that you can no longer function as a patriarch."

Nellie drew in her breath sharply, afraid Ted was going to faint. His face went white. His eyes closed. He said nothing for a long moment, then struggled to his feet. In an unnatural voice, he said, "I didn't know there were so many ways to crucify a man."

thirty-two

Nellie remained in their Provo bedroom for a long time with Mark's letter in her hand, trying to think what to do. Finally Ted came to the door. "What is it, Nellie? Has Mark heard about the bishop's action?"

She slipped the letter into her apron pocket and tried to speak normally. "No, darling." Her mouth was dry and her heart was beating so fast she felt smothered.

Ted heaved the deep, troubled sigh that was becoming habitual with him. "I thought if he has, he might feel disgraced, that he should come home. If it was only me this thing affected, I could stand the humiliation, but it's all of you."

"Oh, Ted," protested Nellie. "There's no disgrace or humiliation. We all adore you. You know that, don't you? And you haven't done anything to make you less worthy of everyone's love and respect than when you were a bishop and being praised by President Young for your wonderful work. We don't know why the Lord is letting this trial come to you, but you are just as fine and honorable as you ever were. I wish you could feel that and keep from being so hurt and crushed in spirit."

"Nellie, how can I feel any other way? I've been virtually kicked out of the church I've given my life to, and the irony is, there's no other place for me."

There was nothing she could say. She'd said the same things so many times.

They were silent for a few moments, then he asked, "Well, what did Mark write about if it wasn't about that? Why did he mark the envelope for you personally?"

She hesitated. How could she tell him? She had promised Mark. Finally she said, "Ted, come and sit down." She drew him down beside her on the bed. "Darling, I have to ask you something that may seem strange. I'll have to ask you not to mind if I don't tell you about the letter now. It involves a promise I made to Mark. There's nothing wrong with Mark and nothing for you to worry about, but he wants me to come to California. Will you give me money to go and wait for me to tell you why until I get back? It will mean more than either of us can know to Mark."

He looked at her in bewilderment, his hurt visible. "And you think your promise to Mark is more important than telling me what this is all about? Nellie, I didn't think there would ever be anything we couldn't share."

Nellie was wretched. "Oh, Ted," she cried, "I've never kept anything from you in my life. There isn't … There never will be— This is something very personal to Mark. He needs to— Oh, Ted, I'll tell you everything, even though I promised. There must never be anything that really matters between us."

He had risen, his face tense. He felt that sinister forces were crowding all around him. "Of course I wouldn't ask you to break your word," he said stiffly. "How much money will you need?"

"Oh, Ted," said Nellie breathlessly, "please don't imagine that I want to keep it from you. I can't stand to have you feel this way. I don't want to go. I'd rather do almost anything than go, but I feel I must. Please don't look at me like that. I can't bear it. I'll tell you this much. It's about Jane."

His face paled. He stared at her with a look she had never seen before, then said in a strained voice, "I had hoped that was a closed chapter in our lives, but if you choose to open it again …" He broke off, pulled his wallet out of his pocket, and laid it on the dresser. "Take what money you need. If there isn't enough there, you know where there is more."

Nellie sank back on the bed. She heard the door open and close. Her thoughts whirled blackly. She couldn't believe Ted would go out and leave her like this. She would have to send Mark a telegram … She was still crying when the children came home from school. "What's the matter?" they bombarded her with questions. "Papa's outside and he looks so strange."

Nellie struggled upright and wiped her eyes. "No, nothing's the matter." She was determined to keep the children from suffering more than necessary. "I got a letter from Mark, and he wants me to come to California. He's all right but he needs to see me. Papa said I could go."

"I wouldn't be crying if I was going to California," said Louie teasingly. "I'll take care of things while you're gone and surprise you by being the best housekeeper ever." Her voice was light but her eyes were worried.

"Why doesn't Papa go, too?" Emily Claire asked. "It would do him good."

"We don't feel we should both be gone," Nellie responded mechanically.

"When will you leave? Today?" Matt wanted to know.

"I guess so," Nellie said uncertainly. "As soon as I can."

"I'll go over to Barker's store and telephone about the trains," Teddy offered. "Papa left. Maybe that's where he went?"

"I don't think so," she managed. "Please go telephone. Oh, and Teddy, find out what time the train will get in and telegraph Mark at this address." She ripped off the bottom of the letter and handed it to him.

Louie shooed the children out. "Emily Claire, help me with supper," she ordered. "And Matt, bring Aunt Nellie's suitcase up from the basement. You can start packing now, Aunt Nellie."

Nellie smiled gratefully, but as soon as they were gone, she pulled the letter from her pocket and read it again:

> *Dear Aunt Nellie:*
>
> *I know you will help me. I have found my mother. But she is so sick and so destitute. I can't write about it. Please, Aunt Nellie, will you come to San Francisco and help me? I think she's dying. Remember you promised not to let Father know I was looking for her. All this would hurt him and he wouldn't understand why I need to do it. Please come as soon as you can. Thank you. You are so good!*
> *Love,*
> *Mark*

Nellie's resolution wavered. How could she leave Ted? Especially after keeping something from him. She felt desperate. How could she go with this feeling between them? Yet Mark's plea was so urgent. Teddy returned. There was a train at 6:20. She estimated how long it would take to get to the station. Where was Ted?

After their hasty supper, he returned with some newspapers and books. He avoided her, attempting to act as if nothing was wrong. She felt miserable, swinging every moment between feeling that she must go and feeling that she could not. She took his billfold to him as he sat reading.

"I took the fare and fifty dollars," she said, her voice trembling. "It may be more than I will need."

He took the wallet without looking at her, took out several bills and gave them to her, saying, "Take these. It will be better to have more than you will need than …" He did not finish.

"Thanks, darling," she said. "I hope everything will be all right. I'll come back as soon as I can."

He nodded without looking at her. If only he would let her read in his eyes that he trusted and loved her! Nellie turned away, a mist before her eyes.

When the taxi came, she kissed the children goodbye, gave them parting instruction, and went to Ted. He was standing by the door, looking at the mountains. She put her arms around him and drew his face down to hers. His arms were loose, his kiss without warmth. A sob escaped her. "I love you, darling," she whispered. "I'll come back as soon as I can. Please try to understand."

SHE WAS EXHAUSTED WHEN she reached San Francisco, emotionally drained by the estrangement from Ted, bewildered and confused by the strangeness of the train and the largeness of the station. Then she saw Mark coming toward her. He seemed years older, taller, and so thin that she wondered if he had been ill and not let them know. His face was deeply serious. He took her in his arms and kissed her. "Thank God you've come," he muttered, his voice husky with emotion.

He picked up her luggage and led her to a waiting taxi. As it pulled away toward the address he gave, he turned to her, the words fairly tumbling from his lips. "I was afraid you couldn't—or wouldn't—come. If you hadn't, I don't know what I should have done. It was a week ago when I first saw her. I never could have recognized her if she hadn't found me. I never would have known her. She was so white and— Oh, I can't tell you how terrible, really terrible she looked. My mother! But something about her made me keep looking at her. Of course, I didn't dream ... I never could have imagined that she would look like that.

"It was at a street meeting. I was watching her all the time, hardly knowing what I was saying. I could tell she wasn't listening—she just stared at me with a ragged piece of newspaper in her hands. I found out later it was the announcement of our meeting and listed our names.

"When Elder Scott began his sermon, I could see she was still watching me. She was starting to mumble and weave. I was sure she was drunk. She beckoned to me to come over. She was such a horrible hag, I ... Then she started yelling and a policeman grabbed her arm and dragged her away. She was fighting him and almost falling down and screaming. I couldn't understand her. The crowd began to laugh and hoot and the meeting broke up.

"Two days later, I got a letter from her. She talked about Matt and me when we were little, so I knew who she was. She begged me to come and see her. I went. I didn't tell my companion. It was horrible, the place she was in, just a hovel. I'll never forget it to my dying day—the dirt, the smell, the bottles lying around, and her lying sick in that filth. I couldn't bear to think that she was my mother, but I knew she was and I knew that what she was was not her fault."

Nellie clutched his hands in an agony of sympathy. He clenched his fists and looked away, growling, "If I can find that beast who brought her out here and left her to go to the dogs or starve, I don't know what I'll do. I didn't think such horrible things could be."

"Don't think of that now, Mark," Nellie begged. "What did you do?"

"She just looked at me, touched my hand, and told me to go—said she only wanted to see me before she died. I couldn't speak, but I sat down and held her hand. She said she always watched the papers for news about Utah and had been going to street meetings for years. When she saw my name on that announcement, she dragged herself out of bed, doped herself with whisky, and struggled to the meeting. She begged me to leave her, to let her die in that filthy hole. Oh, Aunt Nellie, I couldn't do that!"

"Of course you couldn't, Mark," Nellie answered soothingly.

"I took her to a decent rooming house and found a woman to take care of her for a few days, but I didn't know what to do. I was on a mission. The expense. She was delirious most of the time, and she would always talk about home and you and Father. I could tell how lonely she's been, maybe since she left us. I don't know when that beast Kraus deserted her. She's dying of tuberculosis. She wasn't in a condition to be sent home, even if ..."

Nellie pressed his hand. "I understand," she said, "but we would have taken her if she could have come. I'm glad you wrote to me. What would you like me to do?"

Mark looked at her, and she realized that he did not have a clear plan. The burden was too much for him. Now that she was here, the burden somehow had shifted to her.

"I asked her if I should send for someone. I thought if Granny were not too old, or maybe Edna. I didn't know what to do. Then she said, 'I'd like to see Aunt Nennie,' so I wrote to you."

"I'm glad you did and that I could come," said Nellie firmly. "Mark, it was not really her fault—what happened. It was a lot of things, things hard to explain."

"I never have thought it was her fault," said Mark, throwing himself back against the seat. "It was partly that devil who took her and partly—may you'll think I shouldn't say this—but it was partly the Church. It ruined her life, just as it's ruining Father's. What are they doing? Matt wrote me just enough that I know something's wrong. Tell me, Aunt Nellie."

To Nellie's relief, the taxi stopped at the boarding house. Jane was the most pitiful sight Nellie had ever seen. Although she was now in clean clothes and a clean bed, Nellie could imagine how her haggard, aged appearance must have shocked Mark. At first, her mind was wandering, then when Mark said, "This is Aunt Nennie," she started to cry, seized Nellie's hand and clung to it. She was confused, breaking often into tears and sometimes babbling incoherently. Nellie did not try to question her, only speaking soothingly and trying to keep her comfortable.

Nellie spoke seriously to Mark that night, counseling him to tell his mission president enough of the story, without disclosing Jane's identity, that he could make visits without feeling guilty for neglecting his missionary work. She also persuaded him to see that Ted must know the truth. With a pent-up heart, she wrote to Ted immediately:

> *My darling,*
>
> *Now I can tell you. Mark has found his mother. She is dying in impoverished circumstances. We have made her comfortable, and I will nurse her till the end, which should be very soon. You remember how desperately Mark wanted to go to California on his mission? He had the boyish fancy that perhaps he could find her, but he didn't want anyone to know. He has released me from my promise not to tell. It broke my heart to leave without telling you. Please say that you forgive me.*
> *Yours forever,*
> *Nellie*

Nellie seldom left Jane's bedside. When Jane was lucid, Nellie would talk to her about the children, telling her how they looked, what they said, and little anecdotes of the family. At such times, Jane would cling to Nellie's hand, a peaceful look in her eyes, seldom saying anything. Sometimes when she was delirious, Nellie could scarcely remain in the room, she was so revolted by the revelations of Jane's wild words about her past life. She sank visibly from day to day, and Nellie prayed that the end would come quickly.

On the day she died, she horrified Nellie by babbling about her stillborn baby. "That was the baby I killed. I wanted him to die. I didn't want him.

I prayed that he would be dead when he was born. That was the prayer God answered. But why didn't he answer my other prayers? Hundreds of prayers ... asking forgiveness ... maybe I can tell ... Why did God answer that prayer? ... I want to be buried by my baby because I killed him ..." Her voice trailed into incoherence.

She died peacefully with Mark at her side. Both were thankful that she had not gone in one of her raving fits. Because Mark had not heard his mother's wish to be buried by the baby, Nellie said nothing. It would be better, she felt, to bury Jane in California. Why raise questions for the children and attract attention?

She telegraphed Ted about the death and asked money for the burial. The money arrived promptly, but there was no message. With Mark, she arranged for a quiet funeral service in a Mormon chapel, the mission president preaching the brief sermon. His theme was the infinite goodness of Jesus Christ and his willingness to forgive. It comforted Nellie and, she hoped, Mark, but she could not tell. He sat through the service with a dark, brooding look in his eyes.

thirty-three

Nellie wired Ted that she would be home in two days. She would have gone straight to the train from the cemetery, if she could have. How she longed to see Mount Timpanogos once more, to be in Ted's arms once more, to tell him that only her love for him could have impelled her to undertake this last duty of love for Jane, but she dared not leave Mark in his lonely, melancholy state. She knew he needed to plunge back into his missionary work as a distraction, but there was so much he was not saying. His one outburst against the Church as being partially responsible worried her, but she did not have the courage to bring it up.

He left her at the rooming house to pack her things while he took care of some business at the mission home. He was making a tremendous effort to appear normal, but he looked ill. Nellie removed her hat, suddenly feeling every hour of weariness that the last five days had pressed upon her. Mechanically she began packing her own things. There was nothing of Jane's except for the trunk, hastily filled with Jane's few clothes, that Mark had brought from the hovel.

When her suitcase was ready, she steeled herself to the ordeal and opened the trunk. On top were the shabby clothes Mark had packed. Under them were great bundles of newspaper clippings, some old, some new. They all referred to Utah. Nellie thought what a pathetic story of loneliness they told. There were a few books, including Church works, and a bundle of letters. At the very bottom was a cardboard box and a small notebook. One of the letters was from Fritz Kraus, dated only a few months after the elopement. It was a cruel letter: "If I can find work, I'll send you some money, but if I can't, don't be unreasonable. Why does it matter if I don't marry you? You were never really married to that bishop anyway, so what's the difference? If you keep yelling at me about that, I'll wash my hands of you and you can go back to your bishop and your brats or make your living easy enough the way I told you."

Nellie felt faint with loathing. She could imagine Jane, deserted, humiliated, half-crazed with confusion and depression, taking this vile advice. The thought that Mark might read this letter sickened her. She burned them all and the clippings as well.

She made herself examine the notebook. It was a kind of diary with irregular entries of events and feelings. She turned the pages rapidly, grateful to see that most of them were about visits to the gardens, descriptions of nature, weather, and flowers. She would save it and perhaps see if there might be something in it for Jane's children.

The last thing in the trunk was a box. It was filled with small keepsakes, things that had belonged to the children. Among them was a tiny roll of white muslin scraps and a tiny lock of baby's hair, mementos of her last-born. So Jane *had* taken that, even after she had refused to look at the baby and had prayed for its death. Nellie wondered at Jane. She had left her very clothes behind but had stolen back in the night to take a last look at her deserted home. She had been passionately fond of the children. Nellie realized anew that they had never really known Jane, any of them. If they had, this tragedy might have been averted.

She closed the box without looking any further, seeing only the glint of Jane's plain gold wedding band. She put the box and the notebook in her suitcase, then asked the landlady if she would like the trunk. The clothing could be thrown away or used for rags.

Mark did not return that night and came the next morning only when Nellie was on the point of leaving for the station by herself. "I'm sorry I've been so long," he apologized, but he offered no explanation. The sick, desperate look still clouded his face. He looked as if he had not slept all night.

"I've settled for the room," she told him cheerfully. "Here's some money your father sent that we didn't need. He said you'd probably need some extra, and I'm sure you do. I've kept what I need to get home."

She held out the roll of bills but he did not take it. Instead, he lifted anguished eyes to hers, struggled with himself for a moment, and then said resolutely, "Aunt Nellie, I can't go on with my mission. I can't think of anything but what has happened, and I'm wondering about Father. I can't pretend to preach the gospel when I don't know whether I believe it myself or whether I despise it."

"Oh, Mark!" She took his hand. It was icy. He dropped his head. "You've been through a terrible ordeal. Won't you consider coming home with me for a while, and then see how you feel? I'm sure you can do that."

He shook his head. "You know what happens if a missionary leaves early. He's disgraced for life. Almost as disgraced as my mother ..." He broke off and began to pace the floor.

"But Mark, you're not well. Other missionaries have taken a convalescent leave."

He laughed bitterly. "It's not my body that's sick. It's my soul and my mind. No, I can't go home." He heaved a deep sigh. "I'll do this much. I'll ask my mission president if I can have a little time to pull myself together and fight it out. If I can't, I'll quit and let him report anything he wants to the Church, but I won't come home and make things harder for you by watching people point fingers. I'll get some kind of work."

"Mark, I can't bear to leave you feeling like this," Nellie said helplessly. "Would it help if I stayed for a few days while you're fighting it out? Maybe just having someone from home would help you."

"No, you mustn't say," he said impatiently. "Nobody can help me, I'm afraid, not even God." Then he took her hand penitently. "I'm sorry to be like this, Aunt Nellie. Forgive me. I'll try to do what I know you want me to do. I hate to have you worry about me. And I can never repay you for coming. I couldn't have gone through it alone."

"I wouldn't have stayed away no matter what, Mark," she said steadfastly. "You've lost one mother, but, Mark, you know you have one left."

"Oh, I know it. You've been so good. I wish for your sake and Father's that I was not like I am." She ached at the battle he would fight, so much of it inherited from Ted's doubt and Jane's rebellious spirit. She pressed the money into his hands. "You must take this, Mark. No matter what you decide to do, you will need it. You must take it so I will not feel quite so bad about leaving you."

He tried to smile. "All right." He pocketed the money and picked up her suitcase.

thirty-four

Nellie's first glimpse of Ted on the platform at the train station shattered her joy in coming home. He seemed to have aged in the last week. His shoulders were beginning to stoop. The gray on his temples was more noticeable. He gave her a perfunctory kiss and greeted her impersonally. It was unbearable—this cold restraint between them. Was it only because she had kept Mark's confidence from him? But she had written him all about it. She was baffled and unhappy. She would have insisted on talking about the feeling between them, but there seemed to be no time in the bustle of baggage and taxi. She would not admit, even to herself, that she was afraid. Confronting him might make terribly apparent something that she did not want to know.

At home, the children swarmed over and around her with questions about Mark and the ocean and San Francisco, full of news of their own doings. Louie was dancing on the outskirts of the mob impatiently, then dragged Nellie into the kitchen to spill out her news breathlessly. She and Jimmy wanted to be married at Christmas in the temple, then start keeping house as they continued school.

"Papa thinks it will be all right," Louie said, "But he wanted us to wait until you got back before we decided for sure. We'll study all the harder, I know. And it will be a lot better for Jimmy. About the only decent meals he has are the ones he eats here. When fellows cook for themselves, they waste a lot and make a mess, don't you think so, Aunt Nellie? We'll be awfully economical. His folks don't send him much and he only gets about thirty dollars a month for his janitorial work, but Papa says he'll keep on paying my tuition and we could have some of the supplies we bring from home. And oh, Aunt Nellie, couldn't we live in that back bedroom where the little boys sleep? They could have their bed in the den, couldn't they? That bedroom has an outside door so we wouldn't have to bother the family too much, and we could fix it up so cozy. Don't you think we could do that, Aunt Nellie?"

Nellie, overwhelmed, burst out laughing and then kissed Louie's flushed and anxious face. When she thought of her worry about Louie last spring, this plan seemed wonderful, and Ted's approval meant a good deal. It was good to know he had been thinking of things other than her absence. "I'm sure we can work it out, dear," she said. "What does your mother say?"

Louie danced around the kitchen, barely able to control herself. "I haven't told her yet, but I'm going to write, now that you're home. I know she'll think it's all right. She liked Jimmy even before I did."

Ted had gone straight to the living room when they reached home and read until supper-time. Louie and Emily Claire had prepared a festive meal, at which Jimmy was a guest, so the conversation rose vivaciously despite Ted's silence. Even afterwards, when the children were studying, someone was always remembering another item of news to tell. Nellie felt worried. There was more color in Ted's face than usual, but it seemed unnatural. Was he ill? How could he be absorbed in a book when he must want to know about Mark, Jane, herself? He must know how hungry she was for his love and reassurance. Ted went to the bedroom while she was putting cereal to soak for breakfast, and when she joined him, he was already in bed, feigning sleep. She felt deeply hurt that he was keeping up this coolness and indifference. It was not like him. He must be suffering so deeply that perhaps there was no room to perceive the unhappiness of others. Her love overflowed, crowding out resentment.

She slipped in bed beside him and put her arms around him. "Darling," she whispered, "it's so good to be back. Let's never be separated again. These last days away from you seemed endless."

A deep, troubled sigh escaped Ted. Then almost fiercely he drew her to him. She thrilled with happiness. Lost in his arms, she felt the certainty of his passionate love. That was all in the whole world that mattered. But presently he began to talk, his voice strange, unnatural: "Nellie, maybe you think I don't know what you have been through, but I could read between the lines. It must have been ghastly for you and Mark. How can you care for me when I've dragged you through something like that? Dozens of times, all through our married life, you've suffered as no one ought to suffer for this damnable principle of polygamy."

His words were so full of intensity that she drew away from him, startled. "Darling, what are you saying?"

"Saying? The truth! At last the truth. The truth I should have seen more than twenty years ago. That horrible time when they made me think I must marry a second wife. They told us it was a divine revelation. It was no more divine—"

She interrupted, "Don't, please, Ted. You don't know what you're saying."

"For the first time I *do* know what I'm saying," he exclaimed. "I've always taken the word of those men who say they're inspired. Inspired by the devil! They say it's the will of God for us to take wives and more wives. They make people like you believe. People like your mother. You've got more goodness in your little finger than they do in their whole bodies. They threaten us with danger of eternal punishment if we don't do what they say, then tell the world it's wrong to do what they told us to do. We kill our conscience and self-respect to do what they say is God's will. We suffer humiliation, give up our citizenship. Then they tell us we sinned when we obeyed before. The very church we thought we were serving humiliates us, kills our integrity. We are cast out. We're lost." He groaned in agony.

Nellie tried to soothe him. She had never seen him so wrought up, so bitter. But he would not listen.

"I've been looking into these revelations, Nellie," he cried, wrenching himself up in bed. "The Book of Mormon itself says we should have only one wife. Joseph Smith and Brigham Young both said they had only one when they had more. Did God tell them to lie? Did God give them one revelation one time and another a different time? God is supposed to be eternally the same. Why would he tell a prophet to wreck the lives of us dupes who followed him? Nellie, I've wrecked the lives of my whole family. Jane was the most honest of us all in trying to get away before it was too late. We're lost. I'm lost!"

He was trembling as he almost shouted these words. Nellie was weeping hysterically in fear and shock. What could she do? She must get help. Ted sank back on his pillow and began to sob. Panic-stricken, she slipped out of bed and knelt beside it. "Father in Heaven," she began.

Ted seized her clasped hands roughly. "Don't be a fool," he commanded, his voice thick and unnatural. "God won't hear you. Maybe there isn't a god. I've prayed and prayed. He doesn't hear my prayers. He won't hear yours."

His hands were hot. He was burning with fever. Why hadn't she realized before how sick he was? His grip was hurting her. She was afraid of him and for him. She must get a doctor.

Suddenly the door opened. Teddy and Matt stood there, faces white and frightened.

"We heard—"

"What's the matter? Is something wrong?"

Ted looked at them wildly, his eyes burning. "Is anything wrong?" He laughed gratingly. "I'll tell you what's wrong. God is dead. We're all dead and in hell!"

The boys stood stunned. Nellie tried to get to her feet but he held her. "Do you hear? That God you were talking to can't hear. He never could hear. There is no God!" He laughed again, a horrible, grating laugh. "I killed him. He wouldn't answer my prayers and I killed him. I killed him because he let us humans wander around like lost animals and wouldn't answer our prayers. Now he's dead!" He sank back on the pillows, trembling so violently that he shook the bed. He began to sob again.

Nellie rose, suddenly calm, holding Ted's burning hands firmly. The other children had crowded into the hall behind the boys. "Matt, go for Dr. Richards as quick as you can. Teddy, bring me a cold towel. Children, your father is sick, very sick. You must be very quiet. Please go into the living room with Louie and Emily Claire and pray for him."

The children scattered. Teddy brought the cold towel. She put it on Ted's forehead. "Now heat some water and fix a hot-water bottle for his feet," she whispered. "Then look to see if the doctor is coming." It seemed an age since Matt left. She bent over Ted, breathing words of love into his unresponsive ears or pleading silently to God to save him from such tortures.

At last Dr. Richards came, a kindly, middle-aged physician whom Nellie had called last year when Ernest was ill. She wanted every kind of help it was possible to get. She felt she couldn't endure to see Ted lying there like that.

Dr. Richards examined him, listening carefully as Nellie described his strange behavior. At last he straightened. "Has he had a shock, or a long mental strain?"

"Yes, both," she told him but volunteered no details.

"The fever is not too serious, although it will leave him weak. He has had a nervous collapse, and it will probably take a long time to recover. I'll give him a sedative that will help him sleep for several hours. Keep him as warm and quiet as possible. He may still be delirious when he wakes if the fever hasn't broken. Humor and soothe him as you would a child. Patience and love are the best medicine for cases like this."

"He shall have both," Nellie promised. "He—he will get well, won't he?"

The doctor hesitated. "We'll hope so, and we'll do our best. But such sicknesses are more uncertain than most kinds of illnesses. I'll come again tomorrow."

Nellie, already worn out with nursing Jane, disregarded her own fatigue. At Louie's insistence, she sent for Luanna, but Ted did not know her. He gave little direct sign that he knew any of them, but they noticed that he became restless when Nellie was out of the room. If she was beside him, speaking gently, smoothing his brow, or holding his hand, he would usually lie quietly, as if asleep. But even then, he would sometimes rouse with sudden strength and cry out a wild accusation against the Church or the law, wailing in despair and anger. Then he could not hear Nellie, and with the aid of the boys, she would administer the sedatives. He showed little interest in food, although Nellie coaxed him to eat.

Luanna and Nellie had never been more united or more effective in working together. Both of them faced the fact that Ted might not recover, and both of them also faced the fact that this might be for the best. Luanna quickly imposed order on the household and infused it with her own cheerful spirit. Both she and Nellie insisted that Louie and Jimmy should go ahead with their marriage plans. The one insuperable problem was managing the farm and the ranch. With neither of them on the site, would Silas carry on competently? Certainly someone had to be there in time for spring work.

Nellie wrote to Mark, telling him of Ted's illness and asking if he would like to come home. He wrote that he would stay in the mission field for the time being. "I'm still in a miserable muddle," he confessed. "I tried to talk to President Martin right after it happened, but something seemed to lock up and I couldn't talk. He's been away. Maybe I'll try to talk to him again when he gets back. I'm just going around in a blind circle." Sometimes he despised the Church for what it had done to his mother and father; sometimes he recognized its perfect philosophy as the foundation for a healthy and admirable life. He was struggling to do missionary work. "What am I going to do with my life?" he scrawled wretchedly.

Nellie wrote back what comfort she could, counseling patience. She was glad that Ted could not know how much Mark's spiritual conflict was like his own. He would have only blamed himself.

Louie and Jimmy were married a few days before Christmas. Luanna and Nellie were both sorry that there were so few of the exciting preparations any girl would enjoy. They bought her some new clothes and fitted up the back bedroom, but there were no gatherings of friends. No one from Jimmy's family attended. Luanna went with them to the temple, then the whole party returned to Provo. Nellie had suggested that Louie and Jimmy remain in Salt Lake City for a few days as a bit of a honeymoon, but they refused.

Jimmy had a chance to work during the holidays, Louie wanted to fix up their little home, and both of them were resolved to study hard during the holidays so they would not fall behind in their classes.

Luanna, who had left the younger children with Auntie and Minnie, returned to Orderville with several young people who were returning for the holidays. "If there was anything I could do here, I'd stay," she said resolutely. "But there isn't. Louie and Emily Claire can take over much of the housekeeping while you're nursing Ted, Jimmy's here, and someone has to be sure that the farm is prepared for spring or we'll all be in a pickle." Neither of them expressed their financial worries.

"There's so little anyone can do," said Nellie honestly. "It would be a relief to milk cows and spade up the garden."

"At least he wants you," Luanna said. "He knows you. He doesn't even recognize me."

Nellie knew this was true. She felt sorry for Luanna, yet glad he knew and needed her. She put her arms around Luanna and they wept together.

thirty-five

As winter yielded to spring and the trees budded in March, Ted began to improve. He ate a little more. The episodes of raving came less frequently. He seemed to sleep, rather than lie in a stupor, but he still did not seem to recognize the children, and he never spoke lucidly. The doctor was hopeful, however, that in another few months, he would be himself again.

Nellie was able to spend more time with the children, understanding only then how bravely they had struggled with their own terrors. She did not realize how exhausted she was. It amused her that she could fall asleep folding the laundry or stirring the soup. The new worry that consumed her was Mark's break with the Church.

In late January, he wrote a long letter saying that he had not been able to find any heart for completing the last year of his mission, so he had gone to his mission president, told him he was disheartened by his mother's death and father's illness, worried about his brothers and sisters, and struggling with his faith. Although braced for a negative reaction, he was shocked when President Martin announced, "You must have done something wrong, or you would not have lost the spirit of the gospel to the point that you would leave your mission early. Confess your sin!" The man's reaction convinced Mark that he had made the right decision. He wrote:

> I felt sorry for Brother Martin, for I knew he is sincere and he
> has my welfare at heart. I respect and love him, but I have
> no sin to confess. God knows I have struggled to keep my
> faith. I long for the peace I used to think a mission would
> give me. I could not tell him more about Mother than he
> already knew. It would be a desecration of her memory, but
> that convinced him that I was holding something back.
> I won't give you all the details that followed. They would
> only grieve you.

He expressed sorrow for the disappointment his action would bring to the family and his great concern about Ted. He expressed appreciation for the Church and its standards. "They will keep me a clean, honest man, if not a religious one," he wrote. He expressed particular appreciation for the values of family love, loyalty, and unity. "I hope that even though I am cutting myself off from them by cutting myself off from the Church that you will still keep a place for me in your hearts." He planned to find work and, if possible, go to art school where he could receive some training in sculpture.

Nellie wrote back at once, assuring him that their love for him remained unchanged, but she could not bring herself to tell the rest of the family about his decision. She hated the deception, but she could not help feeling that Mark just needed a little more time to get over the shock of finding his mother and then seeing her die. He had not written to the other children for months, and she was almost certain that he would not mention it if he did write. But what would she tell Ted? And how would he respond?

At least Ted seemed out of danger from the laws. In January, when he had been so desperately ill, a U.S. marshal had arrived with a warrant for his arrest. Fortunately, the younger children were in the kitchen and the older children were at a dance. Nellie had been calm as she confronted the marshal and explained that Ted was too ill to see anyone.

The man smiled skeptically. "I've got to see for myself."

Quietly she led him to the bedroom. In the faint lamplight, Ted looked cadaverous, breathing stertorously, emaciated and waxen pale.

The deputy drew back and retreated to the hall. "Well, he looks sick all right, but we never can tell. You say he's been this way for months?"

"Yes, since November. It's a nervous collapse."

"Well, it would be my guess he won't be breaking any more laws," the deputy said musingly. He glanced sympathetically at Nellie. "You getting help for him? Doctors?"

Nellie nodded.

He glanced back at the door. "If it will help you any, I won't be bothering him while he's like this."

"Thank you," she whispered.

Their bishopric had come only once. After the membership records of the children and Nellie had been transferred to their Provo ward, the bishop, who knew them from the previous year, had read them in to receive the sustaining vote of the other members. In response to queries, Louie explained that Nellie was home with her father, who was ill. The bishop had come to call, mildly puzzled that no membership form had been included for a father but concerned about Ted's illness. "Would you like us to administer to him?" he asked.

Nellie desperately wanted to say yes. It would have been a great comfort to her, and she had faith it would do Ted good, but what if it triggered one of his wild outbursts? "He's resting," she apologized. "We have to keep him as quiet as possible."

"Well, let us know if there's anything we can do," the bishop said heartily. He had not come back. Nellie had thought about calling them. She knew that the elders' ministration to her mother the night of her death had opened the gate between mortality and immortality through which her father had come to take her mother home. Could there not be a similar miracle for Ted?

ONE MORNING IN APRIL Ted opened his eyes and looked at her with complete recognition. At first, she was afraid to believe it. She sat beside the bed, her heart bounding so fast that it almost choked her. He shifted and reached out his hand. Seizing it, she bent over him.

"Nellie, where am I? Why am I in bed?"

It was so good to hear him speak naturally that tears streamed down her cheeks. "You've been dreadfully sick, darling, but you're getting better." She struggled to speak normally. "You must be careful for a long time. The doctor wants you to rest and not talk."

"Why?"

"He said if you overdo it you'll have a relapse. You've had a nervous collapse. But you'll be a little stronger every day. Here, have a drink. Then when you wake, you'll be stronger and can eat."

She kissed him gently, hoping he would not notice the trembling of her lips and hands. He looked into her face trustingly, gave her one of his old sweet smiles, then closed his eyes.

Gradually, he grew stronger. Nellie coaxed him to eat and fed him pieces of news as carefully chosen as the puddings and broths she prepared. She told him of Louie's marriage, of Teddy's engagement to Betty Kimball and his hope to go to an eastern university the next year, of Luanna's visit and of how diligently Silas was tending the farm. She read some of Luanna's, Auntie's, and Minnie's letters and showed him photographs of Minnie's babies, taken by a traveling photographer, read some of Emily Claire's poems and stories, and showed him some of Edna's lovely illustrations. He was particularly interested in Luanna's accounts of the children. Luanna would be coming in three weeks, when he was stronger. Little Kay, the baby, was already learning to ride a pony. David was anxious to come to school next year. Martha and Jeannie were anticipating the trip to Marysvale and the railway terminal when the family returned.

Then one morning, Ted asked, "How is Mark? You haven't read any of his letters."

She had practiced her answer but it still came falteringly. "He took his mother's death very hard and felt he couldn't go on with his mission, dear. I wanted him to come home, of course, but he felt it would be easier on the family if he wasn't where people could gossip. He's working for a newspaper company now. I sent him money for an art course, but he said the hard work was good for him and it was good for him to be on his own."

To her relief, Ted simply listened passively, then sighed deeply. "The sins of the father." He closed his eyes and lay still. She watched anxiously, hoping he had fallen asleep, but as she watched, tears slowly pushed through his closed eyelids.

PART 4

Home

Provo, Utah, and Orderville, Utah

In which:

- Ted suffers

- The family settles more permanently in Provo

- The children move forward with education, marriage, and work

- Ted and Mark reach a new understanding

- Ted passes away

- Nellie guides the family and is celebrated

thirty-six

Luanna came to Provo for a few days, then hurried back to the farm, but she made Ted laugh while she visited. In late May, as the end of the school year drew near, Nellie began making preparations for the family's return to the farm for the summer. Ted sat up part of the time and took short walks. He was strangely quiet and would sit for hours by the east window, looking absently at the mountains, or reading. Sometimes he would drop the book and close his eyes. Nellie watched to see if he was napping, but after a few minutes the old haunted look would come back. He would open his eyes and, with an effort of will, pick up his book.

He had never mentioned his mental and spiritual perplexities, and Nellie had never mentioned his wild ravings on the night of his collapse, but she was sure he was still tormented by them, perhaps in a new form. She was glad the books gave him something that would break the dark train of his thoughts, and she worked hard to coax him into a smile. Still, it seemed as if part of him was locked away from her, even from himself.

The day school closed, the children came home chattering excitedly about their partings from friends, plans for the trip home, and the joy of being with other family members and friends. Ted had sat silently, watching. Despite her multitude of tasks, Nellie was aware of his every mood. His face was flushed. A worried look clouded his eyes.

Finally, Nellie brought her work basket and came to sit beside him. "Are you tired, darling?" she asked. "You haven't lain down all day."

"No, not that kind of tired," he answered. Then, with sudden resolution, he announced, "Nellie, I can't go back."

She tried to show no surprise and answered immediately, "Well, why should you?" He gave her a look of such relief that she knew he had been struggling with this decision. "While you're so weak, you should be here where the doctor can see you occasionally. We can keep this house over the summer. Louie and Jimmy will be here with you. I've been worried about you taking that long trip home, but I didn't like to say anything."

"I don't think I can ever go back," he said, then continued quickly, "I've been thinking we should buy this house. It's been for sale all year. The children will be in school a long time. We could maybe sell Luanna's home or some other property."

Nellie had a queer sensation. "You mean, have Luanna come up here to live permanently?"

"Well, no, but one or the other of you. The boys can run the farm in the summers, and we can leave it with someone like Silas in the winter. I don't suppose I'll ever be much good at farming again."

"Oh, Ted," she protested, "you're getting stronger every day. I can see a difference each morning. But I think having a permanent home here is wise. I could stay on the farm. You and Luanna have been separated for such a long time."

He caught her hand. "You don't understand. It isn't that I'm wanting Luanna. I just don't want to go back to what I went through and what may still be waiting. I'm surprised I've been left in peace here." She kept her face still to betray nothing of the news she had shielded from him. "They'll probably find me again, but the children could go home without either of us. Perhaps Teddy and Matt could sell some property and make a down payment on a place here. Do you think they could take such a responsibility?"

"Yes, I do," she said promptly, "and it would be good experience for them. Matt especially loves to farm and is full of ideas from his courses. And Ernest will be a big help, before too many years. They love the soil and will make it pay."

"I don't know about cattle and sheep," Ted mused. "And Teddy doesn't seem very interested."

"No," Nellie agreed. "He's so wrapped up in science and Betty and going to school in the East that life in Orderville is far from what he needs. He wants to be a chemist. One of his professors has recommended him for some kind of scholarship—"

"We'll have to try and make it possible whether he gets it or not." Ted spoke with so much more interest than he had shown for a long time that Nellie was thrilled.

"He and Betty will probably marry before he goes on," said Nellie. "At commencement last year and this, the apostles who spoke warned the young men to marry Mormon girls before they went away to big cities and exposed themselves to the evils of the world."

"They warn them, do they?" Ted roused himself. "I'd like him to have a chance to see some other kind of life than ours. I'm not worried about the temptations of the world. What worries me is the humiliations he'll have to suffer for our kind of life—because of me."

Nellie thought she could see symptoms of the old frightening wildness coming into his face. "Oh, you won't need to worry about that," she said soothingly. "And Teddy will make friends anywhere and a name for himself. No one will care—"

"What his parents were?" Ted interrupted savagely. "I wish I could be sure of that. When I think—"

"Please, Ted, don't ..."

"Begin that old brooding that sent me crazy? Sometimes I think it's a pity I got partially over it." His voice was bitter.

"Don't, darling. Please don't talk like that," Nellie pleaded. "You know your sickness was caused by many things. If you'll take recovery slowly, you'll soon be as well as ever. That's why you should stay here. I can go home with the children and let Luanna come to be with you for a while. She needs a change, and it would do you good to have her with you. Maybe I could help the boys with the sales. My brother Brig has a good business head. He'll help us, I know." She was trying desperately to change his train of thought.

"I don't need a change of company, Nellie. You know I couldn't do without you very long. But we must keep things going financially so the children can have their chance. That's my only remaining satisfaction—the hope that I can give them a chance to make good in the world in spite of me. I mean to make up a little for what they will have to suffer because of me."

"Ted, darling, you know that every one of our children are proud of you. They adore you. They'll always be devoted to you. No matter what others may think or say, they know you are the most wonderful father in the world."

"I wish I could believe that," he said morosely.

Nellie was called from the room, and he picked up his book again.

THE DECISION WAS MADE that Nellie would go home with the children, leaving Emily Claire to take care of Ted until Luanna should come. Luanna was delighted with the decision. She had worked uncomplainingly, endured loneliness and uncertainty, and forced herself to pay attention to the details that were drudgery to her, all for the family's sake. Nellie's heart overflowed with gratitude to her, even as she dreaded the summer—without Ted but filled with worries about him and the farm's burdens. She would be caring for all the children. Only little Kay was accompanying Luanna.

The summer was hard for her, and she longed for Ted's strength. But the knowledge that he most needed what she was doing helped her as she, Teddy, and Matt, with the aid of her brother Brig, sold a tract of land and enough sheep to make a down payment on the Provo home. The rest would be made in installments, much like rent. She spent Sundays with Auntie, Minnie, and her children. To see Minnie's happiness with her little son and daughter was a recompense for much the family had gone through because of them. Another great consolation was a letter from Ted saying that the sale had been so successful that Teddy could definitely count on going east to school that fall.

The children worked hard during the summer. The older ones had the incentive of returning to school and the younger ones the promise of a visit with their father and sightseeing in Salt Lake City when they went up to Provo with their family. "They need your management and guidance, and I need you, too," Ted wrote. His plan was to rent a small house or apartment elsewhere in Provo for Luanna, to avoid attracting undue attention.

At the end of summer, Luanna wrote that she would like to remain in Provo for a while longer, if Nellie didn't mind, but she didn't know how she could manage with all the children who hoped to come. Nellie replied, through her disappointment, that she would stay in Orderville, if that seemed best.

However, Ted wrote that she must come and bring all the children. She and Luanna could both be in Provo, at least for the winter. Louie was pregnant, they had given up their plans for school, and Jimmy was willing to take care of the farm, with Silas's help. They could live in the farmhouse. Part of Luanna's home would be rented to a schoolteacher, but they could use the rest when they were in town. Nellie was delighted with this plan and equally delighted to see that Ted was regaining his old interests and lost vitality. She prayed constantly that he would never again lose his grip on life, but the doctor had warned her it was a possibility if he had to endure extreme pressure or a great shock.

GRATEFULLY, NELLIE RETURNED TO Provo, thankful to see Ted much stronger and more relaxed. His time with Luanna had done him good. Nellie, despite her loneliness for Ted, had not grudged the time alone. Instead, she plunged in with Luanna, preparing her new home, getting the children's clothing ready for school, and making preparations for Teddy's wedding to Betty Kimball. Nellie was grateful that Brother and Sister Kimball did not ask prying questions about Mark. Professor Kimball had only said sadly, "I understand Mark had a great shock on his mission that made it too difficult for him to continue. It often happens that way. The very sensitivity that made him such a powerful missionary also makes him feel other things much more keenly and puts him in danger in a way that another person wouldn't feel. Please give him our love when you write."

After the wedding, Teddy and Betty took the train for Madison, Wisconsin, where Teddy had received a scholarship that would pay their tuition and part of their living expenses.

At the train station, Teddy hugged his father warmly, and said, "Father, I can't thank you enough for this chance you're giving. I promise to do my best to make you proud of me."

"I'll always be proud of you, son," Ted replied with feeling. "I only hope you will not have too many occasions when you cannot be proud of me." He spoke the words with difficulty, but Teddy laughed.

"I don't know what you mean. I'm proud of being Mormon, too. It doesn't matter to me what other people believe. I know we've got the truth, and that's all that matters. I'm sorry for all you've had to suffer for our way of life."

Ted sighed. He hoped Teddy would not have a painful awakening. He was glad most of the children had escaped inheriting his doubting spirit. Perhaps Teddy's frankness and forthrightness would protect him from the embarrassment and humiliation he was almost sure to encounter.

In the busy weeks that followed, Ted read a great deal and spent periods of silence looking into space. He seldom talked, even to Nellie, of his old, tormenting conflicts. But she felt sure they were still with him.

MINNIE AND HER CHILDREN came up for Christmas. Auntie accompanied them as far as Springville. On Christmas Eve, all the family gathered at Nellie's home. Light from the fire twinkled on the metal clips holding colored candles on the branches, polished apples, popcorn and cranberry chains, and colored paper ornaments. All afternoon the children had been wrapping presents they had made or purchased from their special Christmas allowances and placing them under the tree. The presence of bright little Darrel and baby Rose was a treat for the other children, who petted and played with them.

The pantry shelves were stocked with the bread, pies, and cookies Nellie and Luanna had been baking for the past three days. A panful of chewy popcorn balls sat on the sideboard, and a platter of honey candy cooled near an open window. The scent of roasting chicken, mincemeat, and plum pudding drifted through the house.

Ted had been watching the sunset on the snow-covered mountains until dark closed in. Then he moved to the fireplace, sitting quietly in the busy circle of happy children. Luanna and Nellie were preparing supper, hurrying back and forth. Emily Claire and Edna were setting the dining room table, lengthened to its full size. Martha and David were attaching leftover decorations to the window curtains. The older boys were outside, finishing up the chores. Minnie sat in a low rocker opposite Ted, her hands busily knitting. Her face was soft and contented. Ted felt the old familiar pang. She was barely a wife, yet motherhood satisfied her.

A peace he seldom experienced filled his heart. He thought of the first Christmas after Louie was born, and now Louie would soon make him a grandfather. Time had slipped by so unobtrusively yet so quickly. Life was so different from what he had imagined it would be. What could he have left out and still had this? The thought of Jane still brought special pain, but Matt was a son to fill any father's heart with pride. His feelings for Mark were more complicated—pity and grief that he had bequeathed such doubts to him, but admiration for his independence and artistic gifts. All of the children were worth much more than he had suffered. How could he feel so and yet have such hatred for the principle that had made their existence possible? He sighed. Life was full of paradoxes and perplexities, but moments like this nourished the spirit.

Three children were missing from the family circle. Teddy and Betty were together and happy. So were Louie and Jimmy. Christmas letters and presents had arrived from them. But Mark? No word had come. It was not the neglect that hurt but the thought of his isolation and loneliness. Perhaps he was feeling guilty and low in spirits.

Ted could feel depression settling around him and shook it off with an effort. He must not cast gloom on this happy occasion. The voices of Nellie and Luanna floated from the other room. Emily Claire called to David and Ernest to put the chairs around the supper table, backs to the table, waiting for the circle who would soon kneel there. He wished he could keep the happiness of that moment, the feeling that it was worth the doubt, the humiliation, and the injustice of past years. His contentment was almost like a tangible blessing, and he wanted to hold it.

Nellie popped into the dining room. "Supper is ready!" she called. Her cheeks were flushed, a little streak of flour powdered one side of her nose, and tendrils of graying hair curled around her temples. Her happiness shone in her eyes. She was beautiful. How he blessed her for her sweetness, goodness, and devotion. Ted started toward her, but she tipped her head toward Minnie, and he silently obeyed her.

"Where's Matt?" Nellie asked, surveying the group.

"Upstairs writing to his girl, I think," Jerry volunteered.

"Which one?" Edna questioned. "He has so many."

"Ernest, will you tell him we're waiting?" asked Nellie.

"Maybe Matt's going to have as many wives as Papa," Martha observed. The children laughed. Ted cringed. Matt came bounding downstairs and took his place. The family knelt.

Nellie's eyes scanned the happy group, then sought out Ted's. Her heart rejoiced to see contentment in his countenance. *If only he would offer the prayer tonight*, she thought. He had not prayed aloud with the children since his recovery. If he could find it in his heart to call upon God audibly, she was sure some of the load would lift from his spirit.

He looked at Matt, then at Nellie. She sent him a silent plea. He cleared his throat. Just then, a step sounded on the porch. Then someone stamped snow from his feet. The door opened and a tall young man stepped into the room.

There was a quick scrambling toward the door and a mingling of glad cries. "Mark! It's Mark!"

thirty-seven

The Chandler family enjoyed the week after Christmas—a carefree, loving time—almost like the old days when the children were small. Then one morning, Mark announced he would have to catch the evening train to return to his job in California.

He had not mentioned his break with the Church during the week, but that afternoon, he came into the living room where Ted sat with his book by the window. He sat down uneasily. For a moment, neither spoke.

Then Ted said, "Son, I can't tell you how much it has meant to us all to have you home."

Mark toyed with the crocheted fringe on a plant stand cover next to him, then he looked directly at Ted. "I'm glad I came, Father. I've worried a lot about your illness. I wondered if I had caused it. I think that made me want to come back when I … I didn't know whether I had a right to … to—to try and explain."

Ted put a hand on Mark's knee. His eyes rested affectionately on Mark's troubled face. He spoke feelingly, "I'm sorry you ever thought you had anything to do with my sickness. You had nothing to do with it, and you don't need to explain, Mark. I'm not censuring you for your decision about the Church. I never have. If anyone is to be blamed, it's me. You inherited a tendency to question and doubt from me. You can't help wondering about matters we as Church members are not supposed to question. From your mother you inherited other gifts and talents. One was the courage to act as you felt you must. I don't suppose I'm making myself clear, but I believe you had to do what you did, and I'm not blaming you."

Ted's voice was low and compassionate. Mark pressed his father's hand appreciatively. He felt a great weight lift. He had never dared talk with Ted about Jane before, sure that Ted must despise her. Now he felt a new kind of love for Ted.

Ted continued to talk slowly, looking alternately at Mark and out the window at the white mountains. "Yes, you inherit from your mother courage to act when conditions seem intolerable. Some of us lack such courage. We go on, even when we feel that we are being destroyed by mental and spiritual conflicts beyond our power to resolve. No, Mark, it was not what you did that brought on my illness. It was the long battle within myself." He hesitated for a long moment, groping for words but failing to find them.

"You have talent, Mark," he finally said, changing the subject. "We have known it since you were a baby. That's also a gift from your mother. I hope it will bring you more happiness than she knew."

Mark was touched by his father's insight and tenderness. "Thanks, Father," he said unsteadily. "I'm more grateful than you can know. I want to do something worthwhile with my life. Although I've lost my faith, I promise never to do anything to disgrace your name more than I already have done. I hope someday you can be proud of me."

Ted sat up straight and gripped Mark's arm. "Mark, you have never done anything to disgrace our name. You must get such a thought out of your mind. I've always been proud of you. I know what you went through. If you feel that you must go back to California, I insist that you let us help you with your education, just as we're helping Teddy and the others. That's all I have left to live for ... helping you children make the most of your possibilities."

"But you spent so much on my mission, and Matt's expenses, and to have no return ..."

"If those experiences helped you find yourself, there are good returns. I know you want to study art. To get anywhere with such a subject, you must study intensively, not in little snatches. I want to send you a check each month for your living expenses, so you can devote full time to your study. You must let us do that for you."

"I don't feel that you should," Mark muttered, "but it would help me to get into it in earnest." He brightened. "I can't tell you how glad I am that I came home. You don't know how I've wanted to come—how much you all mean to me."

Matt called down from upstairs. "Mark, will you have time to go visit Florence Barnes with me before your train leaves? I promised her visiting cousin that I'd bring my handsome brother around."

"No, Matt, I can't go," Mark called back. "I'd rather spend the time visiting Aunt Nellie." He turned to Ted, "Father, do you know where Aunt Nellie is? I think I hear her in the kitchen." He stood up and started for the door, then turned back. "No one can know how wonderful she's been to me. I couldn't have gone through it if she hadn't helped me. She's wonderful."

Ted repeated the last words to himself. How he regretted making it hard for Nellie to go to Mark when he needed her so badly. He was grateful for his talk with Mark. It brought a consoling peace, a feeling of gladness that life's dark shadows could be shot through with sunlight, warm and comforting.

AFTER THE HOLIDAYS, THE rest of winter passed uneventfully. Teddy and Betty decided to remain in the East and go to summer school. The scholarship had been a great help. Betty wrote often about sightseeing trips, concerts, and lectures which would have been impossible luxuries without the scholarship.

In late spring, however, Teddy wrote that Betty was going to have a baby. They had decided that he would discontinue school and get a job to prepare for this extra expense. Ted wrote immediately that Teddy must stay in school. He had already arranged to sell another piece of land and to help Jimmy and Louie financially so they could come back to Provo the next year and Jimmy could continue with his studies. He closed his letter with a passionate plea to Teddy to continue. His greatest satisfaction was helping his children.

This purpose, Nellie felt, had become almost an obsession with Ted. He seemed to feel that he must bend every effort of his life to make up to the children for what they might suffer because of him.

When school was out, Nellie took most of the children to the farm, while Luanna stayed in Provo with Ted. Matt was very interested in trying out new theories on soil conservation and cattle feeding. He planned to transfer to the state agricultural college the next year, where he could get greater help for some experiments he wanted to try out. Ernest was much like Matt and loved to work with him. However, he would remain at the academy for a few years with Emily Claire, Edna, and David.

Mark wrote frequently. He was doing well and had been invited to enter a sculpture in a fall exhibit.

SOON NELLIE WAS PREPARING for the return to school. This time, Louie, Jimmy, and baby Theodore Mark, whom everyone called T.M., would accompany them. The children adored this baby and continually volunteered to tend him.

David was the most religious of the children. He particularly liked his theology classes. To him, the gospel was God's perfect plan for people during life on Earth and the life to come. Everything about it was sacred. He almost worshipped the General Authorities who held the keys to the plan of salvation. He, too, anticipated serving a mission, but his sole purpose was to lead as many people as possible into the path of salvation. His favorite books were the standard works of the Church, and he begrudged the time he had to spend studying his other courses.

Occasionally, David would question Ted about his church inactivity. Ted's illness and long convalescence satisfied most of the children, but not David. "You've been a bishop, Father," he would protest.

One Sunday after the morning session of stake quarterly conference, he reported the sermons of two visiting apostles who had urged all Church members to keep actively engaged in the Lord's work. "It's the only way to keep our testimonies strong and carry the message to others not so blessed." He looked searchingly at Ted. "You haven't even taken the sacrament for so long, Father," he said. "You'd be well enough to go to meeting this afternoon, wouldn't you? We could take a cab."

He got up from the lunch table. "Let me call a cab right now. If he came at 1:30, we'd be there in fifteen minutes and you could rest a few minutes before conference began."

Nellie watched Ted's face anxiously. She, like David, received so much spiritual satisfaction from church services that she wished Ted could have the blessings she and the others were receiving. Surely there was no danger from the law, not at this point. She desperately hoped he would consent.

Ted was silent for a moment, then said emphatically. "Don't call a cab. I don't feel like going to conference."

"But you are well enough," David persisted. "Of course you are. It will do you good. Why won't you come?"

Ted flushed deeply. "I can't go to church," he said in a strange, thick voice. Nellie rose to her feet, panic-stricken. He flashed her a look that froze her in her tracks. "Don't you children know why I can't go to church?" He pushed back from the table, his face distorted and flushed. He struggled to compose himself and gripped the back of his chair with shaking hands.

Nellie hurried to him, cold with fear. "Your father is not well," she said soothingly to the children. "You all know that. Ted, come and lie down." She tried to draw him toward the bedroom, but he threw off her arm.

"I'm well enough physically to go to church," he said, his voice loud and thick. "But you children need to know sooner or later."

"Please, darling," Nellie pleaded. "Don't upset the children. Come into the other room."

"No," shouted Ted, staring at the frightened children. "I should have told them long ago, instead of letting them go on respecting me, loving me. The reason I can't go to church is because the Church thinks I'm not fit to associate with its sanctified members, not fit to work in its organizations. They took away my offices. They have probably taken my name off their records. I've been cut off from the Church—damned! Damned!"

"But why? Why?" David demanded. His face was white. "I can't—I can't believe—"

Ted laughed harshly, his tone wild and embittered. "Why? Because I obeyed its teachings and begot you. That's why—"

Nellie put her hand over his mouth. She couldn't bear to have the children hear what he was about to say. Ted crumpled into his chair, leaned forward onto his crossed arms, and began to sob.

"Call the doctor, quick!" Nellie commanded, kneeling beside him. For a moment, no one moved.

David stared unbelievingly. "Did the Church do that to him? Is what he said the truth?"

Matt came swiftly to Nellie's side. "We've got to get him into bed," he said, slipping his strong arm around Ted's convulsed body and lifting him. "David, go now!"

The doctor gave Ted a sedative and he soon lay, slack and inert. When Nellie begged him for reassurance, the doctor looked at her gravely with deep sympathy and said quietly, "I'm afraid it won't be long. And perhaps it will be better. There will certainly be recurrences—more often, more violent, more heartbreaking."

Matt had wired for Luanna, and she was due on the morning train. Emily Claire put the youngest children to bed, but the older children moved about the house all night, dozing uneasily in the living room, or asking Nellie what they could do. Nellie, absorbed in caring for Ted, felt her heart wrung with pity for the horror she saw in their eyes. Why had God permitted such a terrible thing? Would any of them forget that awful scene, the transformation of their father into someone they had never seen before? The only thing he wanted was their respect.

Nellie insisted that the children go to school. They left reluctantly, Matt arranging to come back and meet Luanna's train. When Luanna arrived with her children, Nellie clung to her for a brief moment and saw her own fear reflected in Luanna's eyes. She had never prized Luanna's resilience more.

Briskly, Luanna unpacked and set Nellie making lunch while she sat with Ted. Afterward, Nellie slept exhaustedly, then spelled off Luanna. By the time the children arrived home from school, the house felt almost normal. Supper was subdued, but not desperate, and Nellie let the children come in and kiss Ted goodnight. He had not roused all day, and his breathing was becoming heavy and rasping.

Luanna took the first watch. At midnight, Nellie woke suddenly, fully alert, and came down to take her turn. Hour after hour, she watched and prayed, asking that he could go in peace and wondering, even as she prayed, how she could live if Ted died.

Dawn was breaking with faint, rosy tints on the slopes of Mount Timpanogos. Ted stirred and sighed heavily. Unconsciously, Nellie spoke, mingling prayer with reassurances to Ted. "Dear God, … Ted, can you hear me? Heavenly Father, in thy merciful goodness, do not let him suffer. You know what his life has been, how hard he wanted to do right. He is so good, but if he can't get well … Oh, Ted, Ted, you'll be all right, darling. Please take him in peace, in the name of thy son, Jesus Christ, amen."

Ted's unconscious mind caught the last words. "Christ!" he muttered. "Crucified … on the cross … My cross …"

Then he clutched wildly at her hands. "Nellie, Nellie, don't leave me … in the dark … Nellie, where are you …"

"I'm here, darling," Nellie said soothingly, though tears were running down her face. "I will never leave you." She gripped his hands and bent over him. "I will always be by your side."

A shudder ran through his body. He gasped. Then it was over. Nellie felt darkness rise up around her, then Luanna's hands were easing her into a chair, and she heard Matt's voice speaking to the other children. Pushing back the swoon into which she was sinking, she heard herself say, "Let us all kneel and thank God that he was ours and that he did not have to suffer long."

thirty-eight

Time went swiftly after Ted's death. Sometimes, it seemed to Nellie that it had happened only yesterday. Every detail of those last two terrible days and nights were fresh in her mind. So was the crushing weight of responsibility of trying to carry on without him. Everyone helped, but everyone looked to her for the final decisions. And underneath it all was the aching void of her own loss. She longed for his physical nearness, the touch of his hand, the sound of his voice, the comfort of his arms around her. It seemed that Ted's death took her soul with him so that she was only an empty shell of her former self, so long had her thoughts and feelings merged into her love for him.

It was odd, but she always remembered the night of his death as cold and dark with a dismal rain falling, yet she knew the moon had been shining silver outside, and dawn was turning the sky rosy when he died. But the whole world seemed darker, as if the sun had been eclipsed since his death. Was the whole physical world transformed by her sorrow?

She would not give way to her grief. That would have been unworthy of their love. She bestirred her numb faculties to think of the children's futures, helping them become the kind of men and women Ted had wanted them to become. The funeral had gone well. Nellie was grateful that people had been civil and kind, and that they had not been close enough to anyone for curiosity to have a foothold.

Jane's father, Brother Cameron, though aged by years and grief, spoke at the funeral, at Nellie's request. His sincere tribute to Ted and emphasis on his devotion to the Church in his youth, his outstanding service to the United Order, and his unwavering sense of duty to his family were very impressive. The bishop uncomfortably praised Nellie's devotion to the children's schooling and care of Ted during his long illness, without mentioning Luanna. He commented on the children's faithful attendance and participation, singling out David for special praise. But he scarcely mentioned Ted, nor did he preach the magnificent Mormon beliefs of the Lord's forgiveness and love, and the assurance of a happy reunion after death and of eternal joy. Nellie had been longing for this comfort and felt chilled by the omission. Still, her faith in the justice of her Heavenly Father was so profound that she did not doubt she would join Ted after her own death or that they would all be united on the morning of the first resurrection. She felt sure that God understood Ted's essential goodness and would not punish him for his doubts and failure to conform.

WHILE TEDDY WAS HOME, Nellie and Luanna went over Ted's books with the older boys. He had written extensive notes after his early illness. Devastatingly, they revealed his feeling that he might not be with them long. But encouragingly, they showed that he had thought carefully ahead. The assets Ted had accumulated exceeded fifty thousand dollars, excluding the homes. He had written down many ideas and suggestions about mapping their financial future—land that should be purchased or traded, investment possibilities, and suggestions for each child. These notes were encouraging and helpful. They took the place of a will, and Nellie was sure he had wanted them to work out any problems as a family.

"We all know how it would grieve your father if friction should come into the family over property," Nellie said. "Now we must decide the best way to handle what he left us." She looked from Luanna and Minnie to the children.

"Aunt Nellie," Teddy began self-consciously, "according to law, as Father's legal wife, you're entitled to one-third of his property, and —"

Nellie gasped and stared at him, deeply hurt. "Teddy, you know as well as I do that we are all equal wives and full brothers and sisters. You know how your father felt about that."

"Of course, I know," Teddy apologized quickly. "I'm sorry."

"It would be easy to divide the total assets by the number of people in the family," Nellie continued, "but we must consider what is best for the whole family. Your needs as individuals are different. Some of you children will need more than others to prepare you for your life's work."

"And aren't some more deserving?" David asked, darting a glance at Mark.

"Why, David Chandler!" exclaimed Luanna, shocked. "Apologize this minute!"

Nellie said calmly, "Not in your father's eyes, David, nor in God's. God knows much more about us than we know about each other or ourselves. I'm sure your father considers you equally deserving of anything he could give you."

"But David is right," Mark said determinedly, his manner tense. "I have already received much more than I expected or deserve."

"Please, Mark, don't pay any attention to David," begged Luanna. "He's always said things he shouldn't and doesn't really mean."

"I was only—" David began sullenly.

Teddy interrupted swiftly. "Since Father always gave us what we needed, why don't we just have Aunt Nellie do the same? We all know you'd be just as fair as Father was, and as wise."

Before Nellie could protest, there was a chorus of agreement, everyone speaking at once. Even David was nodding. But she felt inexperienced, incapable. And surely the children's feelings would change, and what would she do then?

"Oh, I couldn't. I don't know enough about—" she began to protest.

Minnie, who had been silent until then, said firmly, "Of course you could do it, Nellie."

Luanna added, "You'll have to, Nellie. Who could, if you can't?"

Nellie hesitated. More than anything else, Ted wanted family unity. And who else had the authority? Luanna? Matt? Teddy? She realized that she was the only one. And what would Ted want her to do? She clenched her hands in her lap and looked slowly around the table. Finally, she said, "If you all want me to, I'll do the best I can." She felt she was speaking to Ted.

Before anyone else spoke, Nellie added, "I'll have to have help. I'll need a committee. If you don't mind, I'll ask Teddy and David to be the other members. Does that suit the rest of you?"

Luanna, still provoked at David, asked, "Why David? I think Matt should be on the committee. Then there would but one from each family, except Minnie's. And of course, Darrel is too young."

"Oh, Luanna," said Nellie. "How can you say *each* family? You know we're *one* family. Ted kept us that way. For his sake, as well as our own, let us always keep it *one* family. I want David on the committee, but we could have Matt, too." Nellie's seriousness impressed them all.

The other decisions seemed simple. Teddy would return to school and finish as quickly as possible. Matt and Ernest, assisted by Louie and Jimmy, took over the farm. Nellie would retain the Provo home as a base for school-bound children, while Luanna would return to Orderville.

Nellie crammed each day with work and service to the children, grateful for the blanket of exhaustion that swept over her each night. She disciplined her grief to quiet moments when she could be alone.

Luanna would sometimes exclaim, "Nellie, I can't understand you. How can you hum those old tunes that Teddy used to sing? They break my heart." She brooded over what she might have done to make Ted's life easier. "When I think how I acted before Teddy was born, I could cry my eyes out," she would say. "I was horrid plenty of times, and extravagant and careless. There were times I was jealous of you, Nellie. Oh, don't you wish we could live our lives over again?"

"Certainly there are moments I wish I could relive," Nellie answered steadily. "I doubt if anyone in the world who ever lost a loved one doesn't think such things. But we mustn't dwell on such thoughts. No good can come of such regrets. Instead, we must find something useful to crowd out our regrets."

She and Luanna both worried about David. He grieved because he felt he had precipitated the attack by pressing his father to attend conference. He worried because Nellie and Luanna had insisted Ted be buried in his temple clothes. Weren't they afraid of God's punishment? He suffered over Mark's apostasy, and felt that he must live irreproachably to atone for his father and brother. The next year, he served a mission. He planned to get a degree and teach in the academy's religious education department.

Mark won a coveted scholarship at a famous art institute in Boston and went there to continue his studies. In a few months, he wrote to Nellie, asking if Edna might not join him in Boston and begin studying art. Like Mark, she had inherited her mother's talent for sketching. Nellie was very troubled. She understood why Mark had broken with the Church, had felt nothing but sympathy for him, but had never lost hope that someday he would return to the Church. She always remembered him in her prayers. But what would happen to a girl reared as Edna had been, suddenly sent into a worldly environment?

On the other hand, did she have a right to refuse her chance? She was talented. How could Nellie condemn her to a life wasted on trifles, as Jane's life had been? Would her going to Mark perchance be a means of restoring his faith? What would Ted have done? How she missed him when such problems arose.

But the answer was clear to her. Ted would let her go. He always contended that each individual had the right to live life fully, as unhampered as possible by circumstances. His own life had been so circumscribed by poverty, isolation, and ecclesiastical pressures that he had never known real freedom. But Nellie still brooded. The gospel had always meant more to her than it had to Ted. She felt responsible for Edna's soul, as well as her talent. Though she seemed well-grounded in her faith, she was very young. She had Jane's impulsiveness and might be easily swept into actions she would later regret.

As she turned the options over, praying for guidance, she received a second letter from Mark. In it he acknowledged that she was undoubtedly hesitant to let Edna leave the influence of home and the Church. With obvious pain, Mark wrote:

> *I won't blame you if you decide against my proposal, but I want you to know that I would give my life to keep her from going through what I did. I do appreciate what home and church ties mean to any young person. And I promise that if Edna comes, I will do everything I can to help her remember and honor those ties.*
>
> *If she comes, she can live with a Mormon family. Their daughter is studying at my art institute, and a son is studying music. They are wonderful people and live by their religious teachings. I would encourage my little sister to live as they do and to keep her contacts with the Church. And of course, Aunt Nellie, she will always be held in the strait way by her love for you.*

It was the assurance Nellie was seeking. Edna was delighted with the opportunity, but she wavered at the thought of being on her own. "I want to go, Aunt Nellie, but I don't know whether I should. I have to have somebody help me make decisions or I ... well, you know. I act so crazy sometimes it scares me."

"Don't be afraid to ask Mark for help, or the Bernhard family," Nellie counseled. "And you'll always have me to write to. I hope you'll have so many questions that you'll write very often, for I'm going to miss you more than you can know."

"And I'll miss all of you so much I ..."

"You'll miss us, of course, but you'll be seeing new things, having new experiences every day. But here at home, we'll be wondering what you're doing, seeing your empty place at the table, listening for your laugh—"

"And looking for the clothes you forgot to hang up and the things you forget to put away," Emily Claire finished, and they all laughed.

Edna was glad there was a branch of the Church in Boston and resolved to work in the auxiliary organizations just as she did at home. "And I've made up my mind to try to do some missionary work as well as to study art. Aunt Nellie," she dropped her eyes shyly, "I dreamed that I got Mark to come back into the Church. Wouldn't that be wonderful?"

"The most wonderful thing I can think of," Nellie told her.

As they were packing Edna's trunk, Nellie brought a small box from her own closet. "Edna," she said, "here is something I have kept for you for a long time. Some day you and Mark can open it together. It contains a few keepsakes that belonged to your mother and a sort of diary. I'm sure it will make you want to make your dreams come true. She loved you children, Edna, and she loved the Church, too."

Edna touched the box slowly, then tucked it into a corner of her trunk. "She seems almost like someone in a story to me. You're the only mother I've ever known."

FOR A TIME, LETTERS from Edna came two or three times a week, then slowed until they were less frequent than Mark's. Nellie came to the sad realization that Edna had forgotten her dream of bringing Mark into the Church. She seldom mentioned the Bernhard family but instead talked about her friends at the art institute. Then came the letter about a Polish artist. She was in love with him. They were going to be married. She hoped the family would understand.

Then came a silence of months. Mark continued to write a few times each year, telling little about himself, but always expressing love for the family and gratitude for his relationship with them. He had become a successful sculptor and asked Nellie to stop sending him checks.

Little Johnny, Jane's youngest, was crippled when some homemade firecrackers for the Fourth of July exploded, permanently laming his hand and arm. The long series of surgeries that saved amputation reduced the family's resources so that Nellie had to curtail other expenses.

Teddy and Betty lost their second baby just as he finished his post-graduate study. Nellie insisted that Luanna stay with them until they were relocated in a nearby city where Teddy had been given a position as chief chemist in a textile plant. His course had been expensive and he needed financial help for a time after finding this job.

Luanna enjoyed traveling, meeting new people, making friends, and sightseeing with Teddy and Betty. Her natural friendliness and good humor attracted people wherever she went; on the way home, she met a fellow traveler on the train who showed great interest in her. Before they reached Omaha, his destination, he painted a glowing picture of a new business which was sure to be a great financial success. Sympathetic about her son's heavy expenses, he offered as a special favor to sell her fifty shares of stock for only seventy-five dollars down, since that was all she had with her. She could send him the balance of $375 when she reached home. Dazzled with the promise of double the investment in a year, she gave him the money and signed the papers. The paper she had signed turned out to be legally binding, even though the investment later proved to be a complete loss. The man disappeared.

Matt married Elaine Brooks, a girl he met at the academy. A Salt Lake City girl, she couldn't adjust to living on a farm in southern Utah. Though Matt loved the farm, he finally gave it up and started working for Elaine's father. Nellie felt sorry for him. It was ironic that he who had always been so popular with the girls had not found complete happiness in his marriage, for he always secretly missed the farm. Nellie insisted that he retain his right to part of the farm, hoping that Elaine would have a change of heart and find contentment wherever her husband's interests lay.

Emily Claire married Tom Dangerfield, a young student in the cattle business with his father and brothers in Arizona. After their marriage, they came to Utah only once or twice a year. When Emily Claire's first baby was born, Nellie went to be with her while Luanna stayed with the children in Provo. When Nellie first held her baby granddaughter, she remembered the joy of Emily Claire's birth and felt that Ted was near her. She could almost see the smile in his loving eyes. She often felt Ted's nearness and believed that his spirit was actually near on those occasions—that he often helped her know what to do when she was perplexed and worried.

Emily Claire named the baby for Nellie, and it was a source of joy for Nellie to make things for her and dream about the years ahead when perhaps she, too, would attend Brigham Young Academy.

Minnie and Auntie still lived together. Auntie was in her eighties but, with Minnie's help, kept up the home and made a happy life for Darrel and Rose until they were old enough to come to Provo.

Ernest married Bishop Jenkins' daughter Sally, took charge of the farm after Matt left, and seemed totally happy. Nellie spent part of each summer with them, rejoicing in their contentment and enjoying the memories.

Some of Nellie's friends sympathized because Ernest had not chosen some more intellectual line of work, but Nellie was as proud of his skills, strength, and maturity as if he had chosen to be an artist like Mark, a scientist like Teddy, or a teacher like David. She only wished all of the children could find as much satisfaction in life as Ernest and Sally.

Nellie knew that no situation could be perfect, but she prayed unceasingly for Mark and Edna, from whom they seldom heard, was sad that Matt and Elaine were not better adjusted, and wished that David, still overzealous, were not so concerned about the transgressions of others that he could not be happy himself. She grieved over Johnny's injury but even more for the self-consciousness he felt and his remorse over his carelessness. He had become an introvert, even bitter. And there was Minnie. How could they provide for Minnie and Johnny as they grew older?

Six of the fifteen—Martha, Jeannie, Kay, Jerry, Darrel, and Minnie Rose—were still in school, all healthy, happy, and normal. If they could just complete their educations, she was sure they could make good lives for themselves. She couldn't think that they would become so selfish as to neglect the welfare of the less fortunate, but she wanted to make sure of what was right and best for them all.

A SHORT TIME BEFORE Nellie's sixtieth birthday, she received a letter inviting her to spend her birthday on the farm. It had been Minnie's idea, and Nellie arrived to find a family reunion in progress. Tents in the orchard provided sleeping quarters for those coming from a distance. Daughters, daughters-in-law, and granddaughters were helping in the kitchen. Tables were being set up on the lawn behind the house. Louie and Jimmy and their children were arriving from North Dakota, where Jimmy was in the Forest Service. Luanna was arranging a program, and Auntie was writing a sketch of Nellie's life for the children to read.

On her birthday morning, Nellie lay dozing in the upstairs bedroom, the sounds of preparations for breakfast weaving through her memories and dreams. This old farmhouse had been home to so many, and so many experiences had taken place within its walls. There had been the frightening time when the deputies first came, yet how thoroughly they had been tamed by the family's hospitality. How many meals had been served on the big table downstairs? How many children had gone to sleep with the warm summer breeze blowing through the window? She would hardly have been surprised to hear Ted's voice, waking the boys, or whispering that he loved her.

Then she heard feet on the stairs, and Emily Claire was calling, "Mother! Oh, Mother!"

The embraces, laughing, and talking that followed were sweet. Then Emily Claire was saying, "Hurry, or they'll all be here before you're ready."

"All?" Nellie asked, bewildered.

"Yes, everyone's coming!" Emily Claire exclaimed. "Everyone except Mark and Edna, I guess. I remember quarreling with Edna because she said you were her mother as much as mine. And you settled it by saying that birthing children was such a small part of being a mother."

They hurried downstairs where Matt and his family had just arrived. As soon as Nellie extricated herself from their embraces, Luanna swept in from the town with another group.

"Isn't this grand, Nellie?" exclaimed Luanna. "None of us will ever forget it."

Luanna's fresh beauty still sparkled with the vivacity and charm of youth. Why had Luanna never remarried? She had certainly had offers. Nellie herself had never considered another man after Ted, but it was different for Luanna. Or so she had always thought. Now she wondered with a little twinge if Luanna's love for Ted was as deep and lasting and single as her own, if the bond between them was as sweet and unforgettable as hers and Ted's.

Nellie broke away to kiss Minnie, who was knitting a baby sweater in the sunshine by the window.

"It's so good to have the children back, but even more wonderful to have you, Nellie. We miss you so much," said Minnie. "How can we thank you for all—"

"Why should you even think of thanking me? What would I do without the children?" protested Nellie. "I dread to think about the time when they will all be through coming to school."

"Don't worry, Aunt Nellie," laughed Louie. "The grandchildren will overlap them. You can count on T.M. in just a few years."

Nellie went forward to meet Auntie, who had become painfully frail since their last meeting, but there was nothing frail about her mind or spirit.

David arrived in his new car from Beaver, where he was teaching at Murdock Academy. He had married a girl he had converted on his mission to the Southern States, and they had three children. David was almost too austere to fit in with his own family, but Mignonne, with her southern accent and friendly charm, had captivated them all.

Teddy and Betty had stopped in Nephi to visit some of Betty's relatives, so they did not arrive until mid-morning. They had not been home for three years, so this was a joyous homecoming for them.

As the visiting continued, questions, exclamations, and laugher all mingled together. Nellie studied each face with loving solicitude. She wished she could help Elaine. She didn't look happy, even though Matt had given up the life he loved for her. Elaine watched Matt, puzzled, as he delightedly pumped Ernest for every detail connected with the farm. Then she volunteered to go help Ernest and Mignonne with the children's program.

"I don't suppose Mark and Edna will be here?" Teddy asked Sally. Nellie held her breath for the answer.

"We're afraid not," Sally answered sadly. "Ernest put in a special note but we didn't get an answer."

Nellie hadn't really expected anything different, but she still felt disappointed. They seldom wrote. Although their letters were warm and appreciative, they lived in sophisticated circles, their names known and respected. Their world was strange to most of their brothers' and sisters'. Nellie had thought several times that she would write to them about Johnny's handicap, thinking they might know of some medical treatment. But since they had grown so far away from the Church, she feared that if Johnny should go to them to be treated, he might become indifferent, too.

They were all happily visiting in little groups, some inside the house, some on the porches and lawns, when Sally announced that dinner was ready. Noisily they gathered around the long table, the children at one end, where the hired help would look after them, and the adults at the other where they could continue their conversations. Just as everyone hushed for the blessing on the food, one of the children called, "Someone's coming! There's a big car stopping at the gate!"

Matt and Ernest left the table and walked down the driveway. Some of the others moved so they could see the car. Automobiles were still rare. Two men, a woman, and two children got out.

"It's them! I do believe it's them!" Luanna whispered excitedly to Nellie. "Isn't that Mark?"

"Yes, it is. See how he stands—just like Ted."

Matt and Ernest greeted the newcomers warmly and hurried them toward the party. Around Nellie, whispers surged. These apostate members of the family had been away so long. How would they fit in? And Edna's husband—famous, worldly, always a Gentile. What would he think of them?

But Nellie was not worried. She hurried eagerly to meet them, overcome by Mark's affection as he clasped both her outstretched hands and bent to kiss her.

"It was so wonderful for you to come," she said unsteadily.

"Nothing could have kept us away," he said warmly. "It's a disgrace that it's been so long." He hugged her warmly, then passed her to Edna behind him and turned to the others. Mark had lost his younger reserve and brooding mood. His outgoing ease and cordiality were a reward in themselves.

Edna held Nellie close and kissed her over and over. "Oh, Aunt Nellie, I've missed you more than you can know, even if I've been so terrible not to write more. I can't forgive myself for neglecting you. I love you so much. It's like heaven to see you again."

She presented her husband, Ivan, tall and distinguished in appearance, with such charm and easy manners that Nellie liked him at once. She felt that perhaps Edna's marriage to an outsider was not the tragedy it had always seemed. There was always the hope that she and Mark would come back into the Church, and what if they could bring this fine gentleman with them? The thoughts swirled rapidly through Nellie's head as he held her hands and smiled down, "So this is Aunt Nellie! I've waited too long to meet you, but I have known you as long as I've known your girl."

Immediately Nellie knew she could talk to them about Johnny. They would not try to lure him away.

Edna's children, a lovely girl and bright-faced boy, were somewhat bewildered by so many hugs, kisses, and exclamations. Their fine clothes and formal manners set them apart from their country cousins, but they were so friendly and interested in this new experience that everyone wanted to make them feel at home.

Finally Sally reminded everyone of the cooling food and pressed the newcomers into hastily added places. Ernest said genially, "We were just about to have the blessing on the food when we were so happily interrupted. Teddy, you're the oldest among us. Will you take over?"

Teddy looked around the group. David straightened self-consciously, aware of his reputation for the most devout. Teddy's glance rested on Nellie. "Aunt Nellie, this is your day. Whom would you like to have say the blessing?"

Nellie lifted her eyes to her waiting loved ones. Without hesitation, she said, "I think we would all like to give our own special thanks today. Let us bow our heads for a moment of silent prayer."

AFTER THE DINNER CAME a program of music, skits, stories of bygone days, and tributes to Nellie. Auntie's biography of her, read by Luanna, brought laughter and tears. Emily Claire's original poem expressed the love and appreciation they felt for this woman who was a beloved mother to them all.

Nellie felt as if she were dreaming. How could she be the person about whom all these wonderful things were being said? When they asked for her response, she felt too full of emotion to speak. Struggling for composure, she replied. "I hope you know how happy I am and how proud and thankful I am for the love you are showing me today, for the love you have always given me. I feel as if I have been to my own funeral. I'll just ask you not to bury me for a little while."

They laughed and the program turned into spontaneous reminiscing. Many who had taken no part with the arranged program now paid tribute to Nellie or told anecdotes. Elaine surprised them all by saying, "I want to apologize to you all as a family. I have never felt really part of you before. I know it's been my own fault. I wanted to be near my own folks, not Matt's, and I hated this farm. But today I see things differently. When I see what one woman with a sense of family loyalty and years of unselfish devotion has done, well, I'd like to try to do my part to become really a member of this wonderful family. This will surprise Matt, but I want to tell him and the rest of you that I'd like to move back here and live near the rest of you, for I know I could love it now as he always has, if you'll take me in."

The hearty applause assured Elaine of a true welcome.

Later in the afternoon while the children were playing games, Edna's husband came to Nellie as she rocked gently on the front porch.

"Aunt Nellie, while the others were paying their tributes to you, I wanted to bear my testimony, as I believe you call it. This has been one of the most wonderful experiences of my life. I must tell you that I fell in love with Edna in spite of myself and in spite of a deep prejudice against the Mormon people. I'm sure it must have grieved you to have her leave your Church. I want you to know that it was my fault, not hers. I may never understand your gospel and philosophy, but through Mark and Edna, I have come to admire the courage and ideals of your people. As we drove through your beautiful state, I marveled at the accomplishments of your pioneers. I honor and respect a people who have the zeal and courage and idealism of yours. I can better understand how it was possible when I know a woman such as you. Mark and Edna have told me what a marvelous mother you have been to them. I wouldn't have missed coming to your birthday party for a great deal."

Nellie, touched, responded, "Nor can I tell you how glad I am to meet you. I won't worry about Edna any more. Of course it grieved me to have her leave the Church, and I've always hoped and prayed that she'd come back. But it eases my heart to know that she is married to a good man." She twinkled up at him then, "But I'll still hope and pray."

He smiled and patted her hand. She tugged him down to the step beside her and told him about Johnny. "See," she said. "He's standing by the fence, watching the others. His handicap is crippling his spirit, something that is much worse than his crippled arm. Can something be done to help him?"

Ivan watched the boy thoughtfully and said, "Certainly corrective surgery will make his hand and arm much more useful, and there are therapies that can help him accept himself. Will you let us take him home with us? I promise that we will not interfere with his religion, and if Edna wants to affiliate with your church in Boston again, I certainly shall interpose no obstacle."

Nellie's feelings prevented her from speaking as she squeezed his hand gratefully. What a fine man he was! How she wished Ted could have known him. Every moment of that beautiful day, she wished that Ted were with them. Surely he was with them in spirit! How proud he must be of this group of fine, clean men and women with their own children, most of them carrying part of Ted himself. Surely this was his reward for all he had suffered.

Later in the evening, Mark brought a wrapped box to her. Nellie had been enjoying the scores of cards and letters from friends and the many beautiful gifts she had received during the day.

"Aunt Nellie," Mark inquired, "do you still have your little china flower girl on your dresser?"

"Of course," said Nellie. "It symbolized all the beauty we lacked in the hard pioneer years. It has fed my soul's hunger for beauty during many bleak days."

"I've tried to make a mate for it," Mark said, handing her the small box and hovering over her as she unwrapped it. "This girl is older but just as beautiful. I tried to give her your face."

Nellie held up an exquisite piece of sculpture and gasped with joy. "Oh, Mark, how beautiful! And you made it for me!"

Mark's arms were around her, his voice muffled against her hair. "She has fruit in her basket now, not flowers. I hope it expresses a little of my love and thanks for you."

LATE THAT NIGHT, AFTER Nellie was ready for bed, she sat holding Mark's gift tenderly, looking at the little basket of exquisite fruits. Had she brought some of the flower-like dreams of her youth to fruition? She hoped so. She placed it beside her flower girl and climbed into bed, tired but too happy to sleep. She thought of meeting Ted in the swing in the poplar grove, how he had comforted her over her father's new marriage, and how she had tried to make him see that it was right, even though it was breaking her heart. She recalled the real heartbreak, when she knew she must accept plural marriage in her own life, the strange wedding night spent alone on the window seat of a rooming house, and the sadness of the days when she thought motherhood would be denied her.

Moonlight sifted through the window curtains, gleaming as it had on the night of Ted's death, making patches of brightness and shadows on her white bedspread. *Like life,* she thought dreamily. It was made up of lights and shadows. It was the shadows that helped make the pattern more interesting, more beautiful.

Some of the older grandchildren were singing on the lawn below her window. It was beautiful. She drowsily recalled the heavenly music she had heard the night her mother died, when she was sure her father had come. Would Ted come for her? She felt sure he would. At that moment, he seemed very near. Would there be music when the gates opened for him to come? She wondered … And hoped that there would be … And that it would not be too long.

Shadows and Sunshine

By Elsie Chamberlain Carroll

Life's panorama shows shadows and sunshine:
Days filled with pleasure alone;
Days filled with heartbreak and anguish,
When it seems that the sun never shone.

We would choose, if we could, only gladness;
Pure gold, never mixed with alloys.
But pleasures are heightened when sorrow
Has fallowed our souls; then our joys

Are made sweeter by contrast,
Deeper the tones of life's song.
Shadows in life and alloys in gold
Help to make both of them strong.

Photographs

First Wife offers a fictional description of Elsie's real, lived experiences as a daughter in a polygamous family. She wasn't for or against plural marriage; it was simply part of her story, her life—and it was a rich, fulfilling one at that. She saw, as she concluded in her novel, both the sunshine and the shadows in plural marriage. Her grandson Jon remembers her sharing some of the sunnier moments; for example, the children (often Elsie) would be assigned to gather bouquets of wildflowers to have at the dinner table—there was always beauty in that special gathering. During a time when Elsie was living away from many of her brothers and sisters, she would go up to the third floor of the home and cry of loneliness because she missed having her *whole* family around. Thomas Chamberlain and his wives learned to make plural marriage work for them.

In *First Wife,* the character Nellie is based on Elsie Chamberlain Carroll's mother, Elinor. Ted was based on her father, Thomas, and Luanna was based on Thomas's second wife, Laura. For more details, see the Introduction to this book written by Helen Carroll Lloyd, Elsie's daughter.

The first twelve photos are from Jonathan and Beverly Chamberlain's *Happy is the Man: A Social Biography of Thomas Chamberlain* (Brigham Young University Printing Services, 2010). They graciously provided a CD-ROM with over 200 photos of the Chamberlain family. The final photo is courtesy of Jon Lloyd.

Elinor Hoyt Chamberlain, first wife of Thomas Chamberlain, Jr.

Thomas Chamberlain, Jr., (1854–1918) circa 1889

Photos courtesy of Jonathan and Beverly Chamberlain, *Happy is the Man: A Social Biography of Thomas Chamberlain* (Provo, UT: Brigham Young University Printing Services, 2010).

Elinor Hoyt Chamberlain and children; *Back:* Elsie Chamberlain (b. 1882),
Elinor Hoyt Chamberlain, Israel Hoyt Chamberlain (b. 1884);
Front: Amanda Chamberlain (b. 1888),
Eustace Josiah Chamberlain (b. 1886), Ella Chamberlain (b. 1891)

Thomas Chamberlain and five of six wives
Left to right: Laura Sumner Fackrell, Chastie Ellen Covington,
Ann Elizabeth Carling, Elinor Angeline Hoyt (First Wife),
Ellen Alvira Carling; Mary Elizabeth Woolley (wife 6) is missing

Photos courtesy of Chamberlain, *Happy is the Man,* 2010.

Thomas Chamberlain, Jr., and some of his sons, 1912

Thomas Chamberlain, Jr., and some of his daughters, 1912;
Elsie Carroll is eighth from the left

Photos courtesy of Chamberlain, *Happy is the Man*, 2010.

Elsie Chamberlain Carroll

Thomas Chamberlain, Jr., with wives and
most of his children and grandchildren

Photos courtesy of Chamberlain, *Happy is the Man*, 2010.

Chamberlain family dinner in Orderville, Utah

Thomas Chamberlain, Jr., and other polygamists in Utah Territorial
Prison, 1888; Thomas is standing, fifth from the left

Photos courtesy of Chamberlain, *Happy is the Man*, 2010.

Utah Penitentiary April 7th 1888
Dear Family
I hope these few lines will find
you all enjoying good health. I am
well, feel first rate. I had three visits
last Thursday. Uncle Reslie called his
son Charlie & me out. then Sister Fackrell
called Bro. Covington & I. Then in the after
noon we had a visit from Amon and
Birt Allen they are up attending Conferance I am expecting a visit from Bros.
Woolley, Begmiller & Mariger. Also from
uncle Winsdor Farr & Wife some time during Conferance. There is lots of visiting going on during this Conferance time.
I recieved a letter Thursday from Henry &
Edna written on the 24 of last month
that is the last letter I have had from him
I had a letter from my Mother a few—

Letter from Thomas Chamberlain, Jr., to family while incarcerated
in Utah Territorial Prison for polygamy, 1888

Chamberlain family reunion after the death of Thomas

Photos courtesy of Chamberlain, *Happy is the Man*, 2010.

Elsie with her husband and their two children;
from left: Elsie Chamberlain Carroll, Charles Carroll,
Helen Carroll Lloyd, and Charles Hardy Carroll

Photo courtesy of Jon Lloyd.

Editor's Note

by Kendra Williamson

Elsie Chamberlain passed away fifty-five years before 2022, the year I started editing the manuscript that would finally be published as *First Wife*. She had left the manuscript to her daughter, Helen, who retyped it and made some editorial changes, as discussed in the Introduction. Much later, Helen's grandson Weston worked on converting the typewritten manuscript into a digital format. Despite the care taken by Elsie, Helen, editors, and transcribers, I occasionally encountered minor discrepancies in characters and plots, as well as confusing or distracting wording. Without having the author to consult, I have tried to address these minor issues to create a uniform, consistent story, while maintaining the integrity of Elsie's and Helen's manuscripts. As did Helen in her version of Elsie's manuscript, I have standardized punctuation and capitalization and other finer points.

In addition to editing the *First Wife* manuscript, I have worked with Elsie's grandson, Jon Lloyd, and great grandson, Weston Lloyd, to divide the manuscript into four parts with overviews. We have also provided supplemental materials, including a list of characters, a glossary, and photographs of the people who inspired the story.

Finally, a word about polygamy, or plural marriage, and The Church of Jesus Christ of Latter-day Saints, which some may call the LDS Church or the Mormon Church. Many members of this church today bristle at the mention of polygamy; for some it's like a bad memory that is confusing, hard to come to terms with, and better forgotten. However, plural marriage had a real place in the Church and among the ancestors of many of its modern members; it wasn't a system of oppression, though Elsie does indicate that some abused it in that way, but it was a way of life. The Church today acknowledges the former practice and briefly explains its historical roots in the Gospel Topics Essay titled "Plural Marriage in The Church of Jesus Christ of Latter-day Saints" on <u>ChurchofJesusChrist. org</u>. This article clarifies the Church's official stance: that the typical standard of marriage is between one man and one woman, but that at times in biblical and more recent history, God has instituted the practice of plural marriage to be practiced by some individuals. Beginning in the first decade of the 1900s, and continuing today, members who enter into plural marriage face excommunication from the Church. Readers looking for more in-depth, scholarly insights into plural marriage in the Church may appreciate reading Kathryn Daynes's book, *More Wives Than One.*

In addition to the uncomfortable premise of polygamy, this novel represents historic Latter-day Saint beliefs and practices that may be jarring to modern readers. These include negative perspectives of outsiders ("Gentiles," as labeled in *First Wife*), belief in the infallibility of Church leaders, the expectation of unquestioning faith, and a focus on the "gospel" as a social structure rather than the teachings of Jesus. Readers would do well to remember that this novel is a single historical perspective rather than a representative sample.

First Wife is best read as a fictional story that creates a window into real events and how they affected people on a very personal level. This book is a treasure—a gift of compassionate insight into a time that many people struggle to understand or access. Having grown up in a polygamous household, author Elsie Chamberlain Carroll witnessed this lifestyle firsthand: she provides glimpses into the practice of day-to-day life within a plural marriage, its merits and challenges, and how the Church's break with the practice created significant and complicated hardship for some of its members, yet she shows all of this without speaking out for or against the practice.

Not all of the historical details represented in this novel may be accurate, but we have left them as edited by Helen Carroll Lloyd (see Introduction). Some efforts have been made to correct dates, yet a few inaccuracies may remain. The views presented in this book do not represent an official or complete statement of history, doctrine, policy, or practice of The Church of Jesus Christ of Latter-day Saints.

Glossary*

- **Apostle:** One of fifteen Latter-day Saint church leaders chosen to serve as special witnesses of Jesus Christ, as were the apostles who served with Jesus Christ during His earthly ministry. These apostles include the prophet, his two counselors, and the Quorum of the Twelve Apostles.

- **Bishop:** The lay leader of a Latter-day Saint congregation. His role is similar to that of a pastor or rabbi, but is done without pay and while simultaneously carrying out one's career and family life. He has two counselors to assist him.

- **Book of Mormon:** A record of some of the Israelite inhabitants of the ancient Americas and a witness of Jesus Christ's interactions with this population. It is believed by Latter-day Saints to be scripture and is read alongside the Bible. The Book of Mormon is the origin of the nickname "Mormon" (see "Mormon" below).

- **Celestial Marriage:** Marriage of a worthy Latter-day Saint man and woman performed in a ceremony that seals them together "for time and all eternity." Until the Manifesto (1890), the term meant plural marriage (polygamy).

- **Edmunds Act (Edmunds Anti-Polygamy Act of 1882):** An act that defined polygamous living as "unlawful cohabitation," making it a misdemeanor punishable by a fine of $300 and imprisonment up to six months. Any Church member who appeared to practice plural marriage could be prosecuted. Under this law, men and women in plural marriages lost voting rights and opportunities to serve on juries or in political office.

- **Edmunds-Tucker Act:** An 1887 amendment to the Edmunds Act that gave the courts greater power to prosecute people in plural marriages; among other things, the government was given authority to confiscate certain Church properties and further reduce voting rights.

* Many of these entrees are modified from Bruce R. McConkie, *Mormon Doctrine* (Salt Lake City: Bookcraft, 1958).

- **Endowment House:** A building in Salt Lake City used in 1855 – 1889 as a temporary temple while the Salt Lake Temple was under construction. In the Endowment House (and temples), worthy members of the Church could make promises (covenants) with God, including the sealing covenant, or marriage covenant.

- **Gentile:** A term sometimes used to refer to individuals who were outside the covenant, or not members of The Church of Jesus Christ of Latter-day Saints (also understood to include non-Jews). Like Israel of old, Mormons referred to themselves as a "covenant people." In thinking of themselves as Israel, they began to refer to non-Mormons as "Gentiles," not in derision but as a symbol of their own special status.

- **God (Father in Heaven):** Latter-day Saints believe that God the Father is the literal father of our spirits, and therefore, we are His children. They also believe God is an exalted man with a body of flesh and bone.

- **Latter-day Saint:** A member of The Church of Jesus Christ of Latter-day Saints, often used interchangeably with "Mormon." The term can also be used as an adjective, in which case it may be abbreviated "LDS." The Church officially prefers "Latter-day Saint" over "Mormon."

- **Manifesto:** A declaration signed by the fourth Church President, Wilford Woodruff, in 1890, officially promising the abolition of the practice of polygamy. This was in response to allegations that Mormon leaders were still teaching and encouraging the practice of plural marriage even though it was illegal. Woodruff claimed these charges were false and that the leaders were not "teaching polygamy or plural marriage, nor permitting any person to enter into its practice."

- **Mormon:** As a noun, Mormon is a common nickname for members of The Church of Jesus Christ of Latter-day Saints; however, it came to be used more broadly to refer to break-off sects that were no longer officially affiliated with the Church. As an adjective, it may refer to the Church or its members. Officially, the Church dislikes the use of the term and prefers "Latter-day Saint." The label "Mormon" originates with the Book of Mormon, in which Mormon is an ancient prophet who compiled and preserved records that were later translated and viewed as scripture.

- **Mother in Heaven:** Latter-day Saints believe that people born on this earth have their premortal origins with a literal Mother in Heaven as well as a Father in Heaven.

- **Muddy Mission:** The town of St. Thomas was founded by Mormon settlers sent by Brigham Young in 1865. With a population of about 500 at its peak, it became an established town of cotton farms. The Mormons abandoned St. Thomas in February 1871, after a land survey shifted the state line of Nevada one degree longitude to the east, placing all of the Mormon settlements known as the Muddy Mission in Nevada instead of

Arizona or Utah. The state of Nevada then attempted to collect taxes for previous years payable only in gold from the residents. The Muddy River Mission members chose to leave without paying in 1871 and instead moved to Utah, where many of them founded new towns in Long Valley (present day Glendale, Orderville, and Mount Carmel).

- **Patriarchal Blessing:** Conditional, personal prophetic utterance given to a Latter-day Saint either by a relative or by an ordained patriarch appointed by The Church of Jesus Christ of Latter-day Saints.

- **Polygamy/Plural Marriage:** Marriage between one man and more than one woman. Early Mormons considered plural marriage to be a doctrine of the restored gospel; from the 1830s until 1890, worthy male members of the Church with sufficient means were encouraged to have multiple wives in order to receive greater blessings in eternity. Plural marriage was practiced by 10-15% of Mormons during this time. The practice was later abandoned by the Church, which disassociated itself from break-off sects that continued to practice polygamy.

- **"The Raid":** a period of Utah history following the passage of the Edmunds-Tucker Act, during which the federal government made vigorous efforts to find and imprison polygamists.

- **Stake:** Regional grouping of three or more wards (congregations).

- **Temple:** A sacred building, considered the house of the Lord, in which Latter-day Saints perform sacred ceremonies and ordinances of the gospel for themselves and, by proxy, for the dead.

- **Testimony:** A personal expression of one's convictions or beliefs about the gospel of Jesus Christ.

- **Tithing:** The donation of one tenth of one's income to the Church.

- **United Order:** A social and economic order in which Church members, in an act of consecration, deeded their property to a bishop, who allotted stewardships and resources according to need. This communal way of living is believed to be of divine origin and was intended to achieve income equality, eliminate poverty, and increase group self-sufficiency. It is not currently practiced by Latter-day Saints.

- **Ward:** Local Latter-day Saint congregations made up of members from a particular geographic location, usually consisting of between 200 – 500 members. Three or more wards make up a stake. In this book, the Orderville experiment on the United Order is often referred simply as "the Order."

- **Zion:** The "pure in heart." In the early days of the Church, members were counseled to build up Zion by living in faith communities, so Zion was also an elevated term used to refer to Mormon communities.

Acknowledgements

by Jon and Weston Lloyd

The miracle of this book, beyond its writing by Elsie Chamberlain Carroll, is having the courage to start the arduous task of preparing it for publication. We are grateful for the many individuals who have played various roles in enabling and sustaining that courage.

First and foremost, we acknowledge our ancestor and the author of this story, **Elsie Chamberlain Carroll** (1882-1967), who, with equal amounts of esteem for her heritage and courage to write her story accurately, didn't publish the story during her lifetime for fear of offending members of her family. We also gratefully acknowledge Elsie's mentor and advisor at Columbia University, **Dorothy Scarborough** (1878-1935). She was an English professor and American writer who wrote about women's life in the Southwest. She encouraged Elsie to write her "Mormon novel" and critiqued her early chapters.

We are grateful to the many family members who have been invested in remembering Elsie's life and story. **Helen Carroll Lloyd**, who is Elsie's daughter, Jon's mother, and author of the Introduction to *First Wife*, co-edited the manuscript and then offered it to the next generation to publish it. We took the bait. Weston's parents, **Bill and Bonnie Lloyd**, are our family genealogists who collected photos, letters, and other artifacts of the Chamberlain's and maintained close ties with the Chamberlain family. Jon's late wife **Jackie Lloyd** and their daughter **Hilary Farr Lloyd** are proud of their Chamberlain heritage and were relentless in nagging Jon to keep working on getting *First Wife* published. Jon's younger sister, **Elsie Lynette Lloyd Brooks**, became more like an older sister when she witnessed Jon's efforts and offered sage advice and encouragement.

Carol Ann Lloyd-Stanger, Elsie's great granddaughter and a Shakespeare scholar, made some of the first edits to the manuscript and assisted more recently in preparing it for publication. **Brian C. Hales** is a thoughtful scholar, anesthesiologist, relative, and friend who has published seven books on polygamy and recognized the value of Elsie's first-hand experiences. As Bonnie Lloyd's cousin, Brian shares an early, familial connection to *First Wife*, and he offered his help and expertise in the arduous publishing process. Special thanks goes to Weston's sisters and Elsie's great granddaughters, **Ivey Mitchell** and **Merrilee Gottfredson**, for their encouragement and support, as well as for their superior proofreading skills.

We thank the many professionals who have helped *First Wife* get to this point. First is **Lavina Fielding Anderson**, a scholar, writer, editor, and feminist whose work focuses on Mormonism. She worked with Helen on the initial editing of the manuscript in the 1990s. **Kathryn M. Daynes** is associate professor emerita of history at Brigham Young University and a historian of Latter-day Saint polygamy. She expressed great interest in Elsie's story and encouraged us to seek an audience beyond our family. She provided detailed guidance on making the manuscript historically accurate and writing proposals for publication.

Editor **Kendra Williamson** provided the final edits and organizational tools within the manuscript, and she carefully wrote and edited the supplemental materials. A surgeon of words, she came to know Elsie through her writing. In addition to countless rounds of editorial and design feedback, she guided us through the logistics of self-publishing. We are so appreciative of our designer, **Melissa Neely**, who, quickly and with good judgement, brought this manuscript to life. Her skills and patience are deeply appreciated. Thank you both.

Finally, we acknowledge the many other individuals who have reviewed, encouraged, and expressed interest in Elsie's story. These include **Tania Lyon**, a friend of Jon's and also a hospital administrator and adjunct professor, who insisted that we "get that manuscript of your grandmother's published" and connected us with people who could help. **Terrell Harris Dougan** is a friend from Jon's high school days, a former *Deseret News* columnist, and blogger for *Huffington Post*. She is also a published author who shares family history of polygamy, and she encouraged us and offered helpful suggestions for publication. **Valerie Merrell**, a friend and organizational genius, corrected and cleaned up the initial digital copy of the manuscript and graciously connected us with our final editor and designer.

Magda Loeber is a healthcare researcher and writer whose interest in the manuscript motivated and sustained our efforts to publish *First Wife.* She particularly suggested that we add photos and other illustrations. **James Hiram Morris** is professor emeritus of computer science at Carnegie Mellon University and former Dean of Carnegie Mellon School of Computer Science who reviewed the manuscript and provided valuable advice and support. **Marilyn Anderson Sumner** is a dear friend of Jon's, a retired school teacher, and a stickler for grammatically and syntactically correct writing. She assisted greatly in helping us refine and proofread applications to publishers. **Evan Stoddard** is a long-time church friend of Jon's, former director of Pittsburgh Department of Economic Development, and former associate dean at Duquesne University. Many thanks to Evan for sharing his experience with self-publishing several books and offering advice on our role in the process. **Ron Schuler** is a Pittsburgh attorney who likewise shared advice and helpful tips on publishing. He has published two books, *Angeleños: L.A.'s Golden Age* and *The Steel Bar: Pittsburgh Lawyers and the Making of America,* with more in the works.

We are grateful to the late **Jonathan and Beverly Chamberlain** for their social biography of Thomas Chamberlain, *Happy is the Man.* Their book is thoroughly researched, rich in detail, and generously illustrated. They included a CD-ROM with hundreds of photographs, from which we've selected thirteen to illustrate *First Wife.*

We express our deep gratitude for all the individuals who have shown an interest in Elsie's story. Your interests, questions, and skills have brought us this piece of history.

About the Author

Elsie Chamberlain Carroll (1882 - 1967) was a talented author, poet, and educator. She received her B.A. and M.A. degrees from Brigham Young University (BYU) before performing graduate work at the University of Minnesota, Stanford University, and Columbia University. She began her remarkable career in education as an elementary and high school teacher, and she finished her career as a college professor at BYU, where she taught in the English Department for nearly twenty-five years. At BYU she is memorialized with an essay contest in her name; she is also the namesake of Carroll Hall, one of the former Heritage Hall dorms.

Elsie Chamberlain Carroll

Elsie received numerous literary awards and published various poems and short stories, many of which appeared in periodicals for The Church of Jesus Christ of Latter-day Saints. She also published a children's book, *Pioneer Bobby* (1947), and a book of poetry entitled *Sunshine and Shadows* (1966). Additionally, she co-compiled and co-edited *History of Kane County* (1960). A more complete list of Elsie's published works can be found online: https://mormonarts.lib.byu.edu/people/elsie-c-carroll/.

Elsie married Charles Hardy Carroll, her childhood sweetheart from Orderville, in 1907. They had two children. Elsie retired from her professorship at BYU in 1950 and moved to Salt Lake City, where she continued to teach through BYU correspondence courses. She lived in Utah most of her life but loved adventure and traveled extensively. Elsie was known for making the best chocolate chip cookies in the neighborhood.

Mother's Thimble

By Elsie Chamberlain Carroll

One of the keepsakes in my treasure chest
Is a little gold thimble. It lies with the rest
Of precious possessions I've kept through the years,
Made sacred by memories and hallowed by tears.

When I look at that thimble, I see a small hand,
So soft with caresses, yet strong to command
When evil assailed. Its touch was a balm
For physical ills; for spirits a calm.
Always at work on tasks to be done
From the first tints of dawn past the setting of sun;
How often I've seen on that busy hand
This thimble which matched a thin wedding band.
Millions of stitches it helped to push through
All kinds of fabrics — both old and new:
Stitches on baby-clothes, dainty, straight seams;
On patches of denim and coarse, heavy jeans;

Stitches for trousseaus and bridal array;
For scores of things to be given away;
Stitches for quilts and for rugs for our home,
Where love and contentment with simple things shone.
As I think of the past, I whisper a prayer
Of humble thanksgiving that I had a share
In weaving, through years, that fine tapestry
That makes up the story of our family;
And I see as the symbol of what makes it strong

This little gold thimble I've treasured so long.